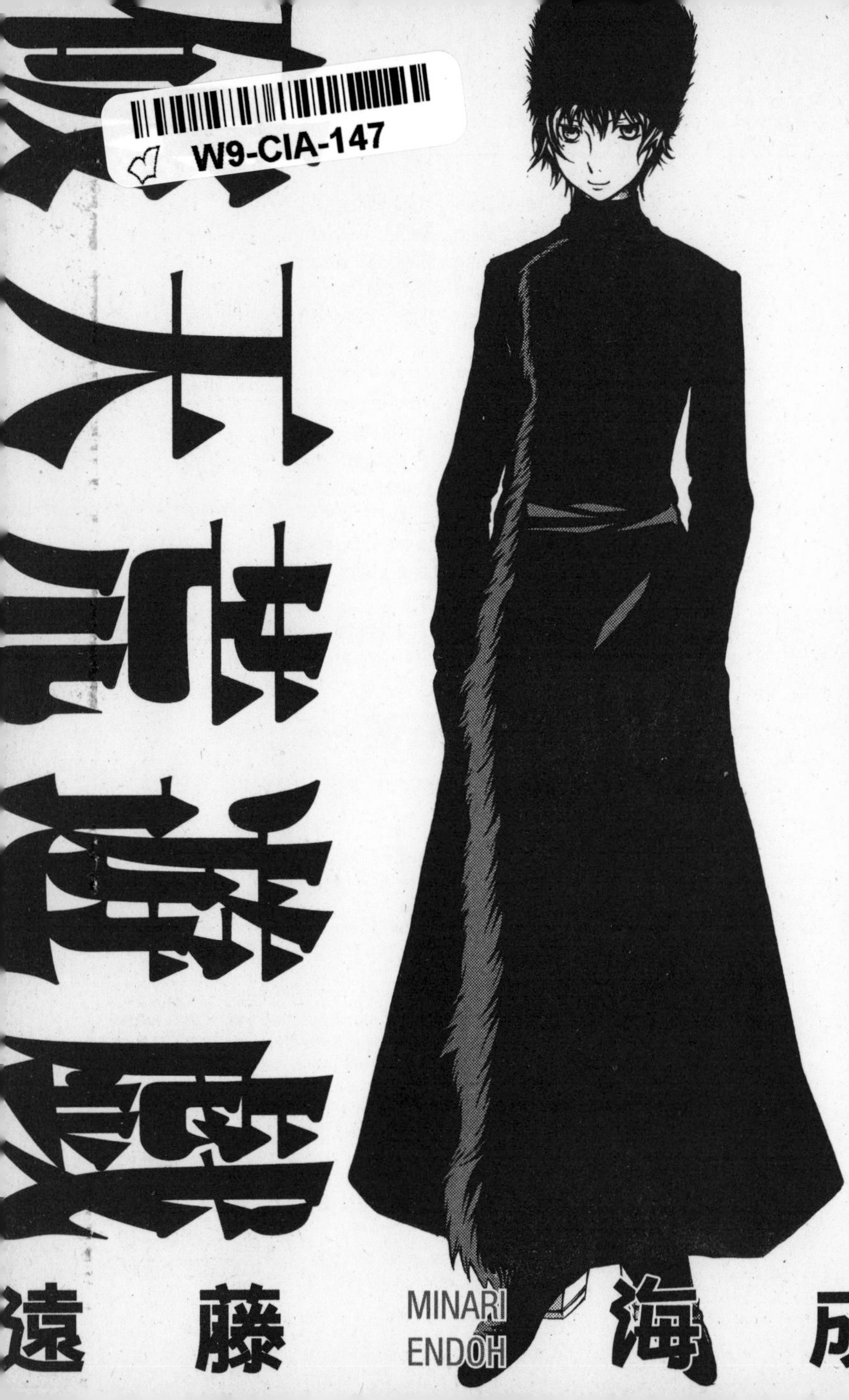

遠藤 海成
MINARI ENDOH

Dazzle Volume 10
Created by Minari Endoh

Translation - Yuko Fukami
English Adaptation - Karen S. Ahlstrom
Retouch and Lettering - Star Print Brokers
Production Artist - Michael Paolilli
Graphic Designer - Jose Macasocol, Jr.

Editor - Alexis Kirsch
Pre-Production Supervisor - Vicente Rivera, Jr.
Pre-Production Specialist - Lucas Rivera
Managing Editor - Vy Nguyen
Senior Designer - Louis Csontos
Senior Designer - James Lee
Senior Editor - Bryce P. Coleman
Senior Editor - Jenna Winterberg
Associate Publisher - Marco F. Pavia
President and C.O.O. - John Parker
C.E.O. and Chief Creative Officer - Stu Levy

A  Manga

TOKYOPOP Inc.
5900 Wilshire Blvd. Suite 2000
Los Angeles, CA 90036

E-mail: info@TOKYOPOP.com
Come visit us online at www.TOKYOPOP.com

ISBN: 978-1-4278-1304-6

First TOKYOPOP printing: January 2009
10 9 8 7 6 5 4 3 2 1
Printed in the USA

DAZZLE™

Vol. 10

Minari Endoh

HAMBURG // LONDON // LOS ANGELES // TOKYO

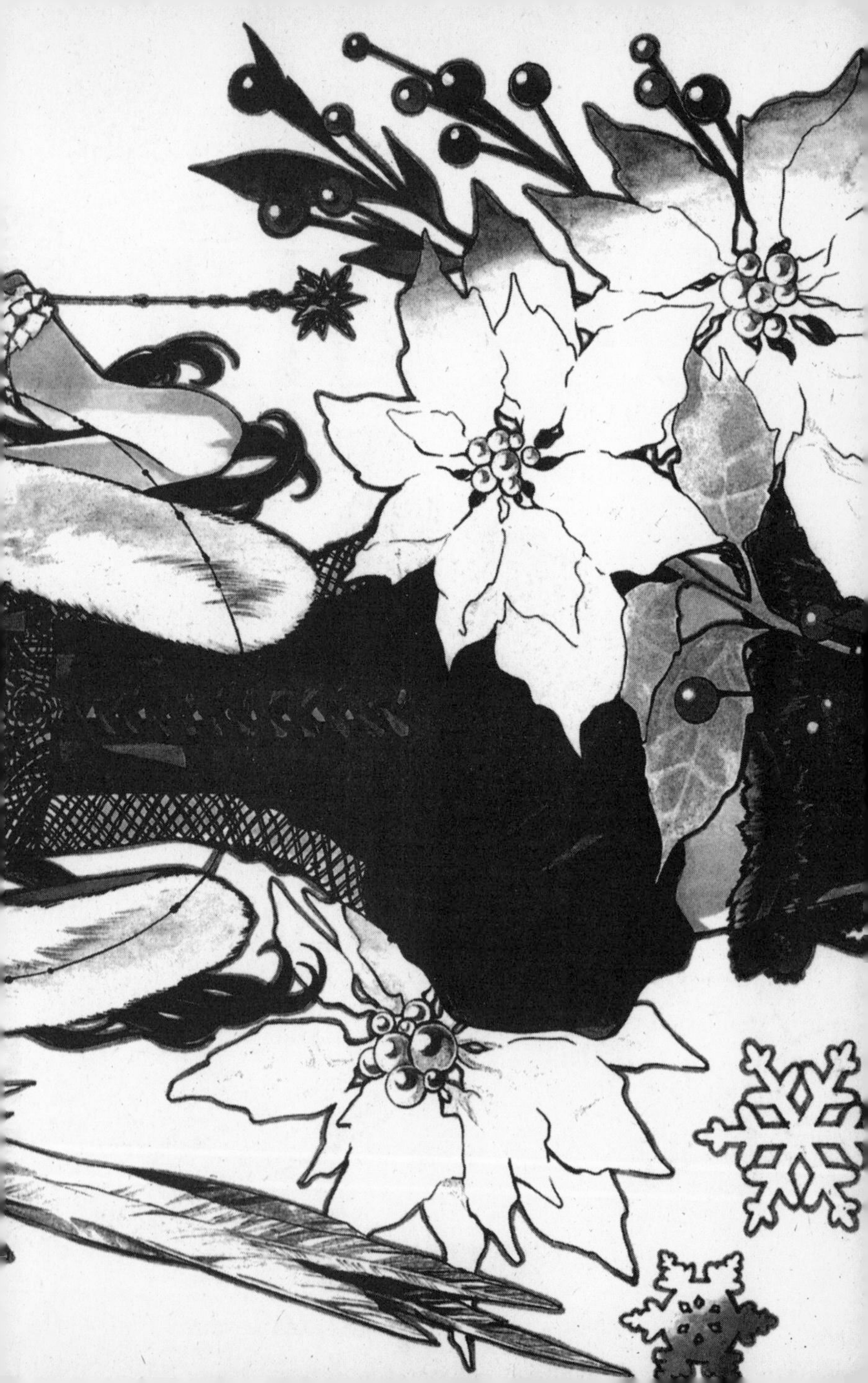

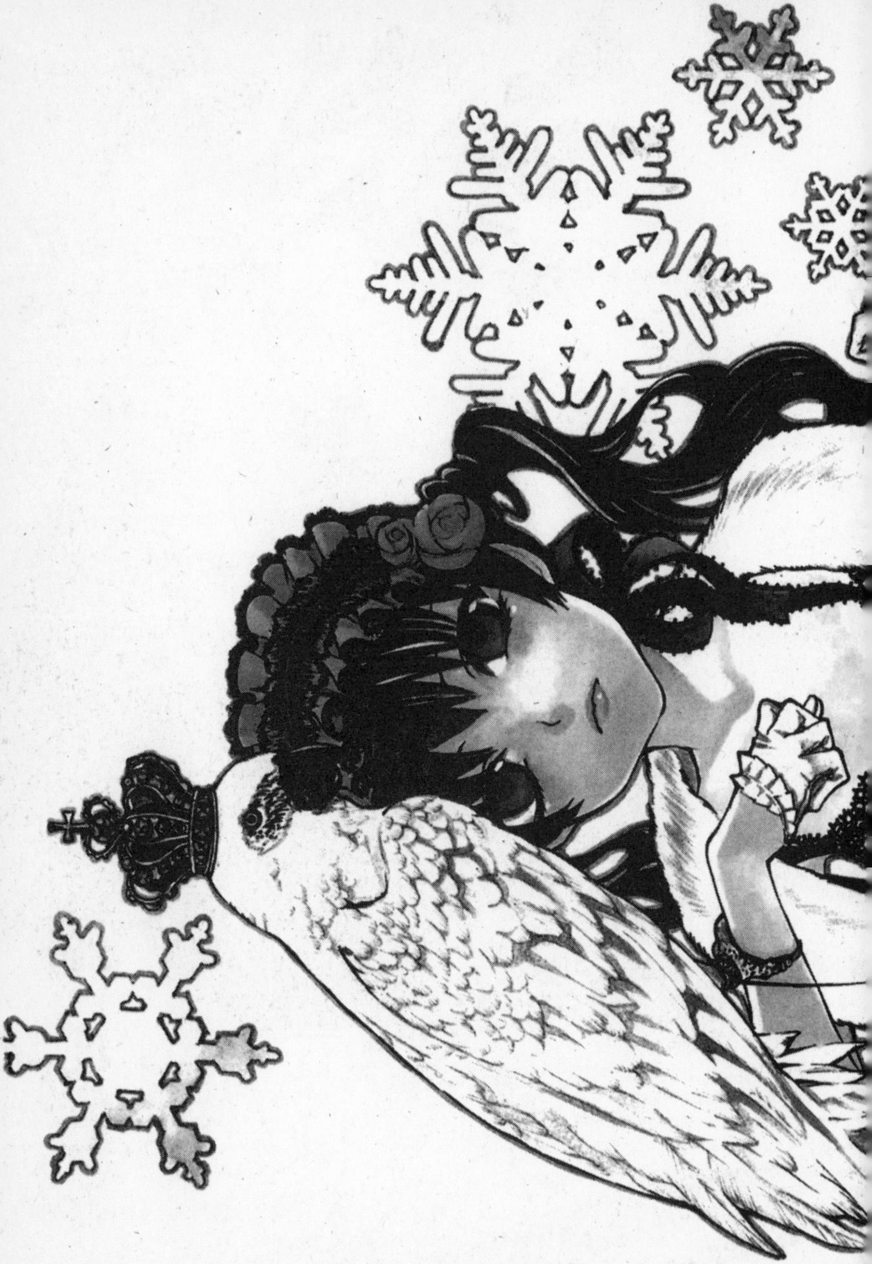

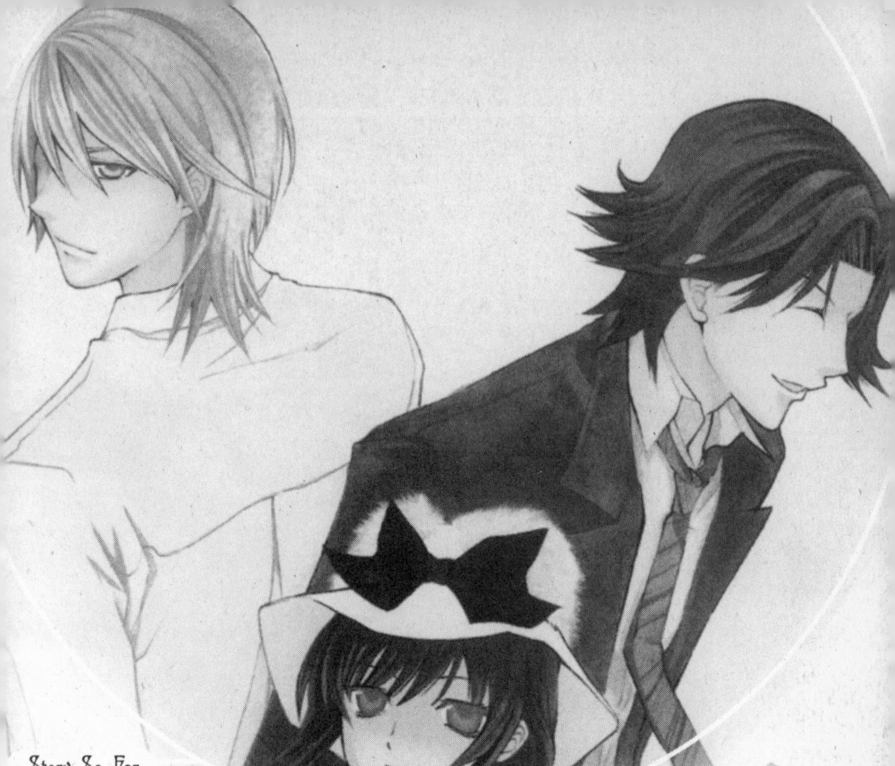

Story So Far

Rahzel's adoptive father Serateed sent her on a training journey to hone her magical abilities, but now that he's discovered his younger brother Kiara has entangled Rahzel in a sinister plot of unknown ends, Serateed has brought her back home. He's reluctantly also taken in the two traveling companions with whom Rahzel has formed a special bond; his playboy youngest brother Baroqueheat and the albino magic user Alzeid, the clone of Serateed's oldest friend, a scientist named Second.

Alzeid has been searching for the woman who killed his "father" ten years ago, but his description of her matches the woman who Second shockingly murdered years before Alzeid was born Natsume, the woman who Serateed and his siblings adored by turns as a sister, as a mother, or as the lover they could never have. Natsume's death at the hands of her lover Second destroyed her family, and each sibling dealt with it in their own way, Kiara's way being the most dangerous of all.
Alzeid was not the only clone who Second made. His first try was Alzeid's older brother, a "failed" clone also called Alzeid who had no powers and who never aged. But now that clone does Kiara's bidding, his powers somehow unlocked in a simpleminded psychopathy that strikes fear in all who have seen his horrific attacks, including Rahzel who he calls "big sister" for some reason. When Alzeid fought his brother for the first time, he realized he was sorely outmatched.

Also in Rahzel's town are visitors from the town of Prometheus which Natsume and Second founded including the capricious Shogetsu, the clone girls Befyladita and Salasaneia, and the scissor-wielding Fay Lisette. They too showed Alzeid his woeful lack of fighting skill, and even Rahzel herself learned so much in her months on the road that she was able to defeat Alzeid in a duel. As Alzeid wallows in self-pity, and Serateed worries about what plans Kiara might have for his daughter, Rahzel now faces a perennial challenge the start of a new school year...

Contents

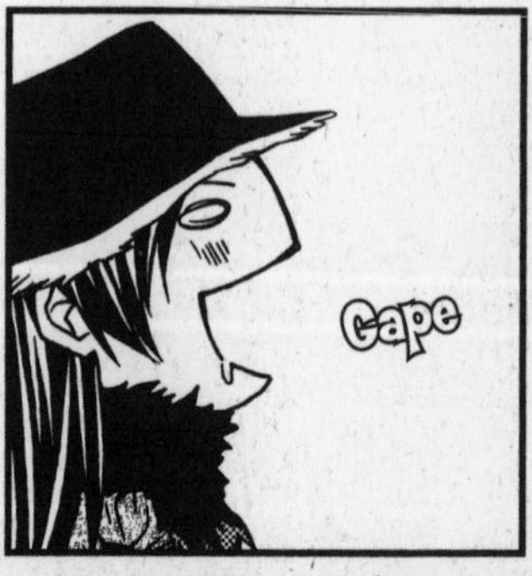
Gape

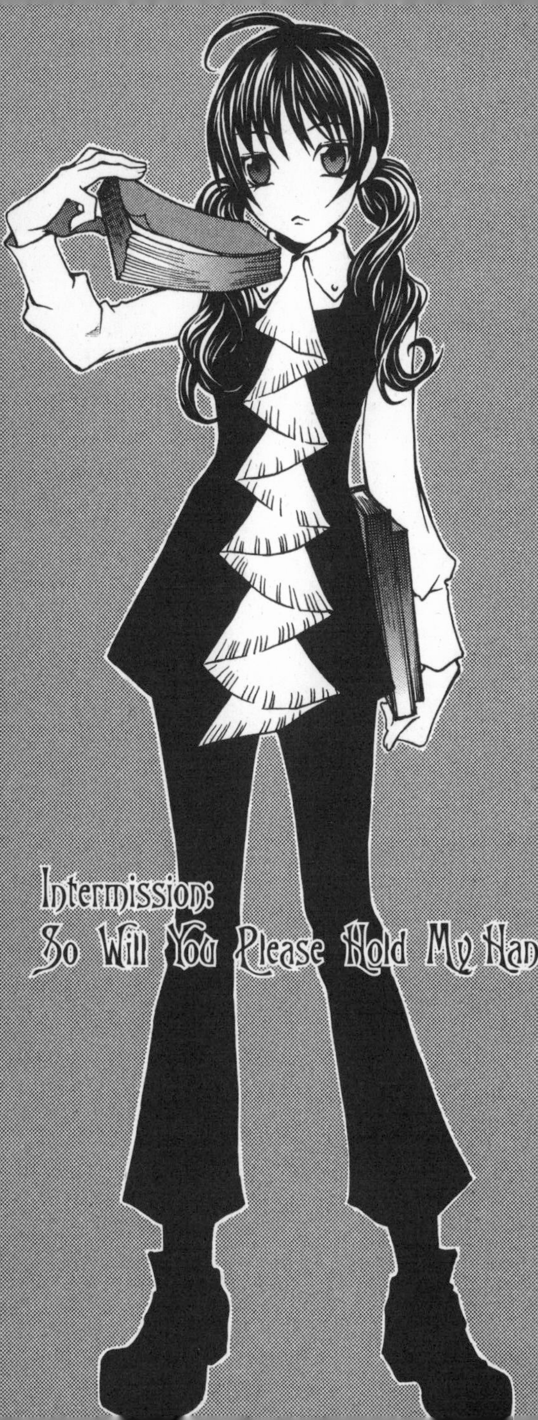

Intermission: So Will You Please Hold My Hand Tonight?

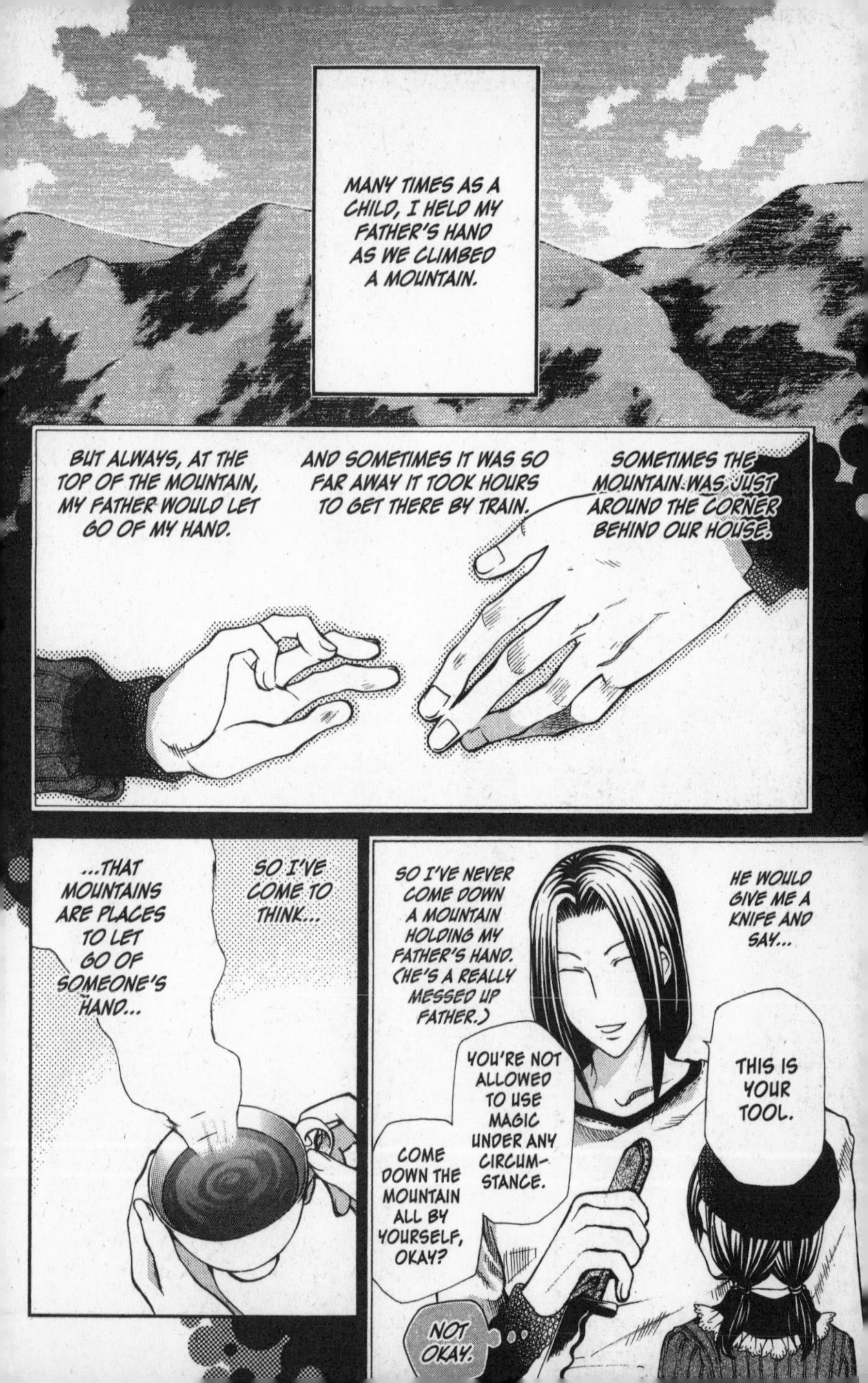

MANY TIMES AS A CHILD, I HELD MY FATHER'S HAND AS WE CLIMBED A MOUNTAIN.
SOMETIMES THE MOUNTAIN WAS JUST AROUND THE CORNER BEHIND OUR HOUSE.
AND SOMETIMES IT WAS SO FAR AWAY IT TOOK HOURS TO GET THERE BY TRAIN.
BUT ALWAYS, AT THE TOP OF THE MOUNTAIN, MY FATHER WOULD LET GO OF MY HAND.
HE WOULD GIVE ME A KNIFE AND SAY...
THIS IS YOUR TOOL.
YOU'RE NOT ALLOWED TO USE MAGIC UNDER ANY CIRCUM-STANCE.
COME DOWN THE MOUNTAIN ALL BY YOURSELF, OKAY?
SO I'VE NEVER COME DOWN A MOUNTAIN HOLDING MY FATHER'S HAND. (HE'S A REALLY MESSED UP FATHER.)
NOT OKAY.
SO I'VE COME TO THINK...
...THAT MOUNTAINS ARE PLACES TO LET GO OF SOMEONE'S HAND...

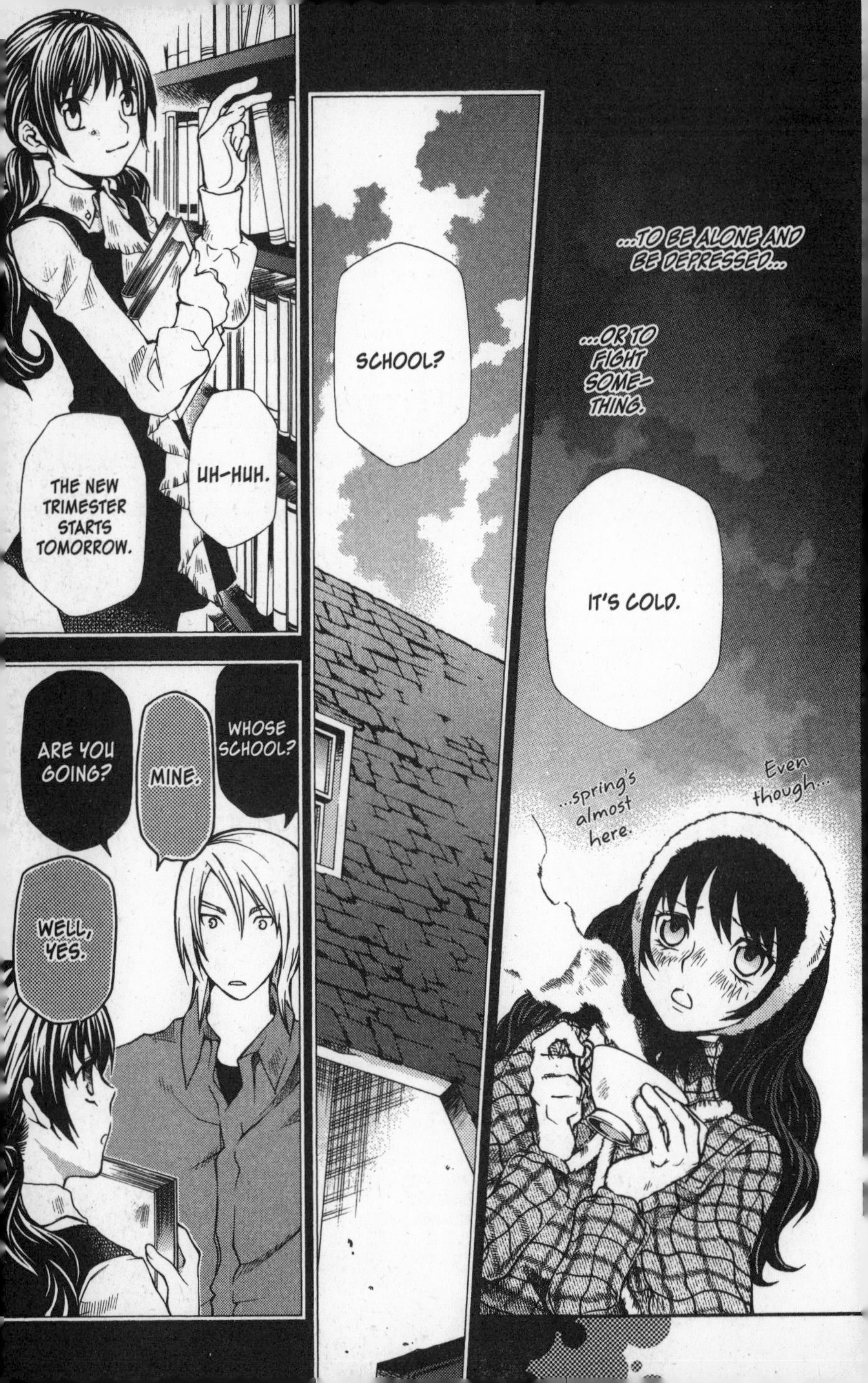
...TO BE ALONE AND BE DEPRESSED...
...OR TO FIGHT SOME-THING.
IT'S COLD.
Even though...
...spring's almost here.
SCHOOL?
UH-HUH.
THE NEW TRIMESTER STARTS TOMORROW.
WHOSE SCHOOL?
MINE.
ARE YOU GOING?
WELL, YES.

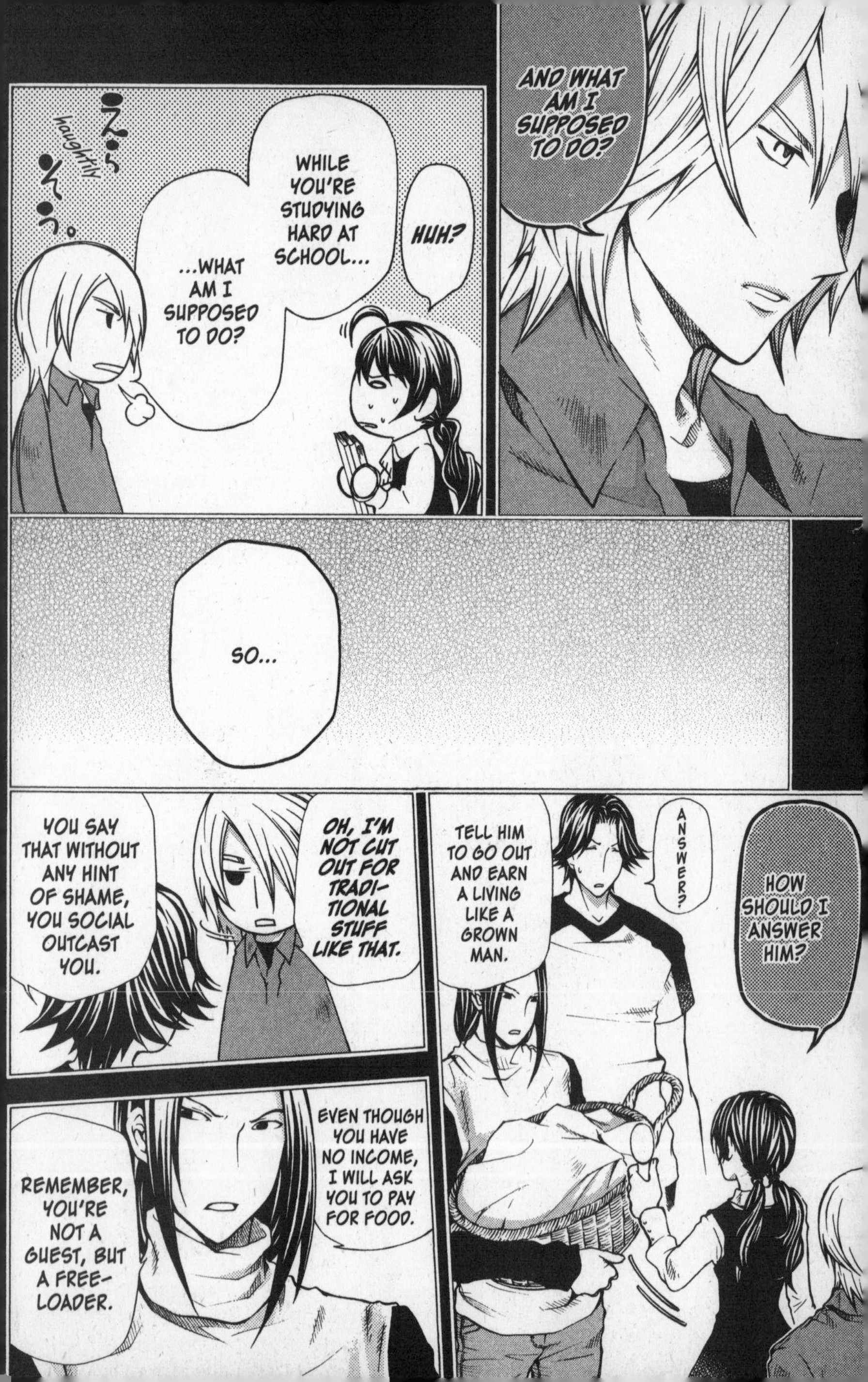
AND WHAT AM I SUPPOSED TO DO?
HUH?
WHILE YOU'RE STUDYING HARD AT SCHOOL...
...WHAT AM I SUPPOSED TO DO?
haughtily
SO...
HOW SHOULD I ANSWER HIM?
ANSWER?
TELL HIM TO GO OUT AND EARN A LIVING LIKE A GROWN MAN.
OH, I'M NOT CUT OUT FOR TRADI-TIONAL STUFF LIKE THAT.
YOU SAY THAT WITHOUT ANY HINT OF SHAME, YOU SOCIAL OUTCAST YOU.
EVEN THOUGH YOU HAVE NO INCOME, I WILL ASK YOU TO PAY FOR FOOD.
REMEMBER, YOU'RE NOT A GUEST, BUT A FREE-LOADER.

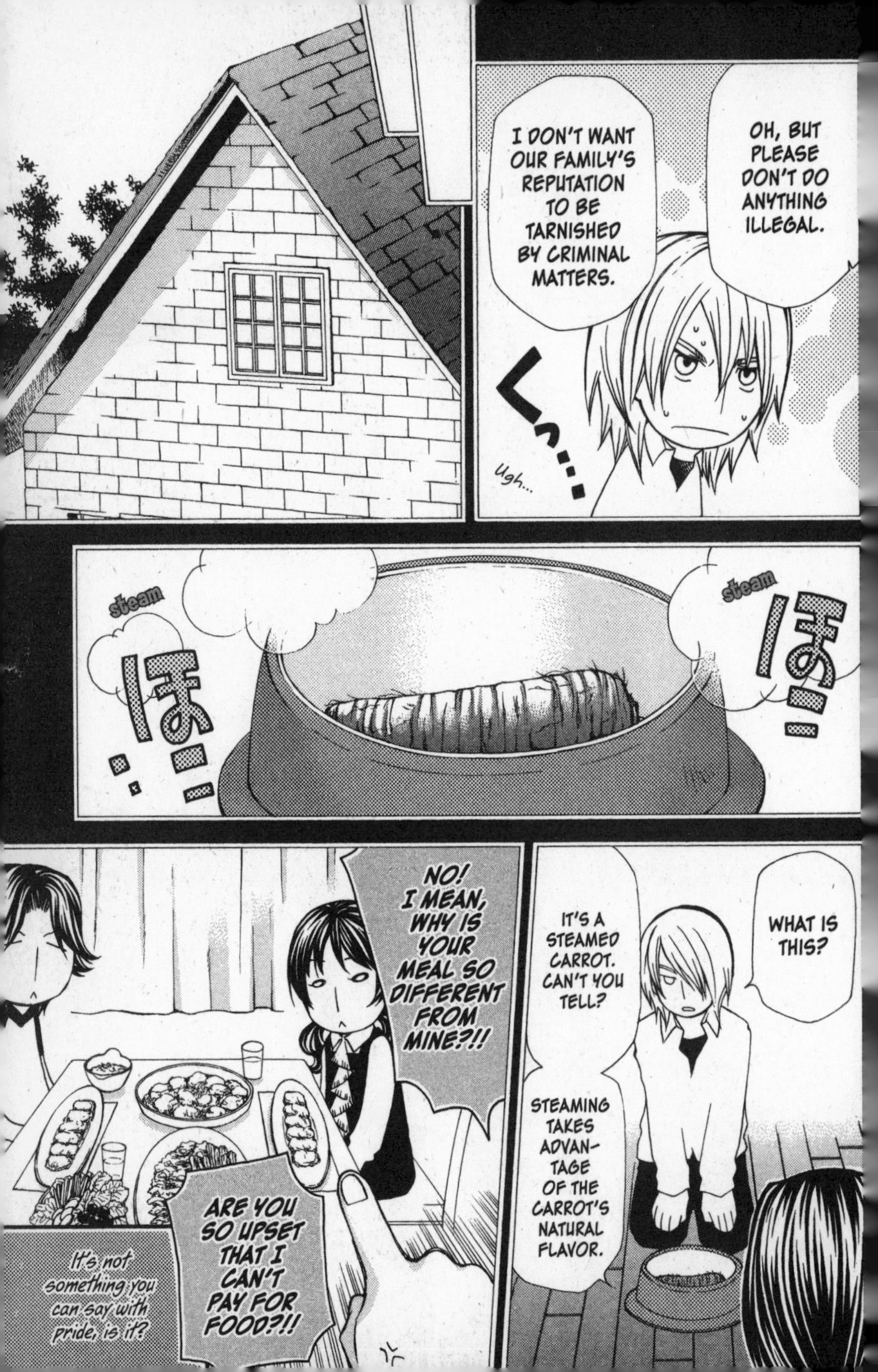
OH, BUT PLEASE DON'T DO ANYTHING ILLEGAL.
I DON'T WANT OUR FAMILY'S REPUTATION TO BE TARNISHED BY CRIMINAL MATTERS.
Ugh...
steam
steam
WHAT IS THIS?
IT'S A STEAMED CARROT. CAN'T YOU TELL?
STEAMING TAKES ADVAN-TAGE OF THE CARROT'S NATURAL FLAVOR.
NO! I MEAN, WHY IS YOUR MEAL SO DIFFERENT FROM MINE?!!
ARE YOU SO UPSET THAT I CAN'T PAY FOR FOOD?!!
It's not something you can say with pride, is it?

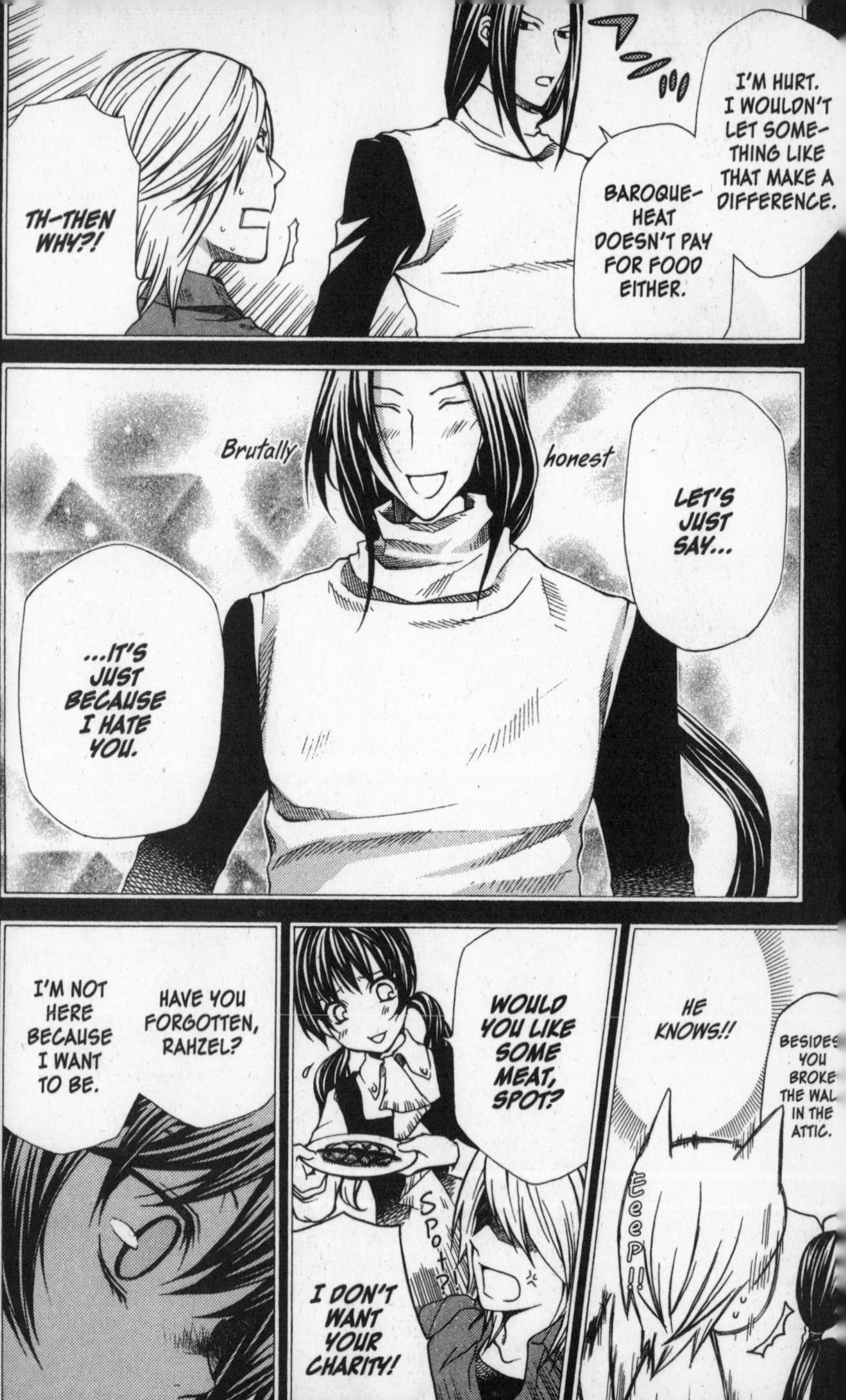
I'M HURT. I WOULDN'T LET SOME-THING LIKE THAT MAKE A DIFFERENCE.
BAROQUE-HEAT DOESN'T PAY FOR FOOD EITHER.
TH-THEN WHY?!
LET'S JUST SAY...
Brutally honest
...IT'S JUST BECAUSE I HATE YOU.
BESIDES YOU BROKE THE WAL IN THE ATTIC.
HE KNOWS!!
Eeep!!
WOULD YOU LIKE SOME MEAT, SPOT?
Spot?
I DON'T WANT YOUR CHARITY!
HAVE YOU FORGOTTEN, RAHZEL?
I'M NOT HERE BECAUSE I WANT TO BE.

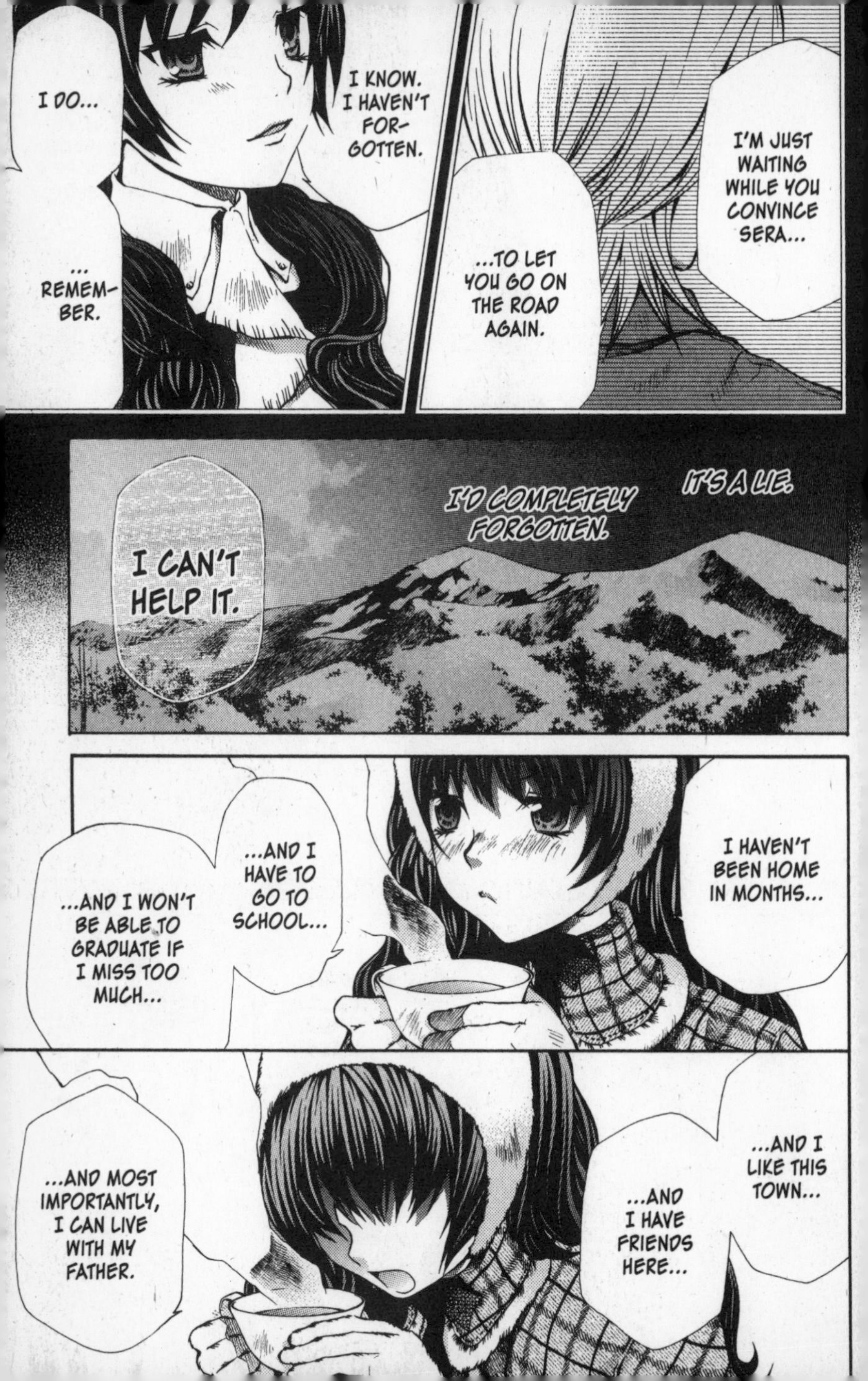
I'M JUST WAITING WHILE YOU CONVINCE SERA...
...TO LET YOU GO ON THE ROAD AGAIN.
I KNOW. I HAVEN'T FOR-GOTTEN.
I DO...
...REMEMBER.
IT'S A LIE.
I'D COMPLETELY FORGOTTEN.
I CAN'T HELP IT.
I HAVEN'T BEEN HOME IN MONTHS...
...AND I HAVE TO GO TO SCHOOL...
...AND I WON'T BE ABLE TO GRADUATE IF I MISS TOO MUCH...
...AND I LIKE THIS TOWN...
...AND I HAVE FRIENDS HERE...
...AND MOST IMPORTANTLY, I CAN LIVE WITH MY FATHER.

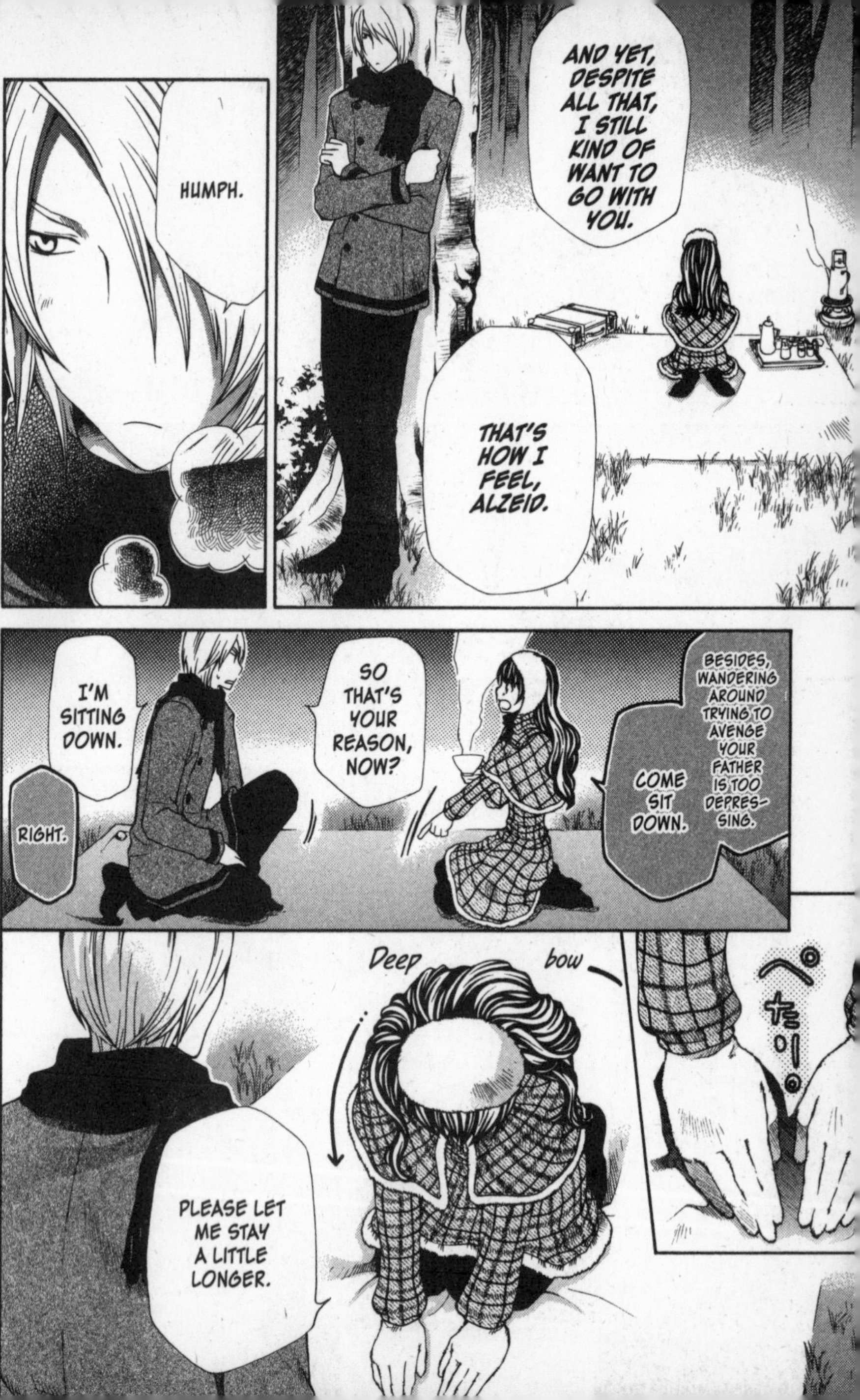
AND YET, DESPITE ALL THAT, I STILL KIND OF WANT TO GO WITH YOU.
THAT'S HOW I FEEL, ALZEID.
HUMPH.
BESIDES, WANDERING AROUND TRYING TO AVENGE YOUR FATHER IS TOO DEPRES-SING.
COME SIT DOWN.
SO THAT'S YOUR REASON, NOW?
I'M SITTING DOWN.
RIGHT.
Deep bow
PLEASE LET ME STAY A LITTLE LONGER.

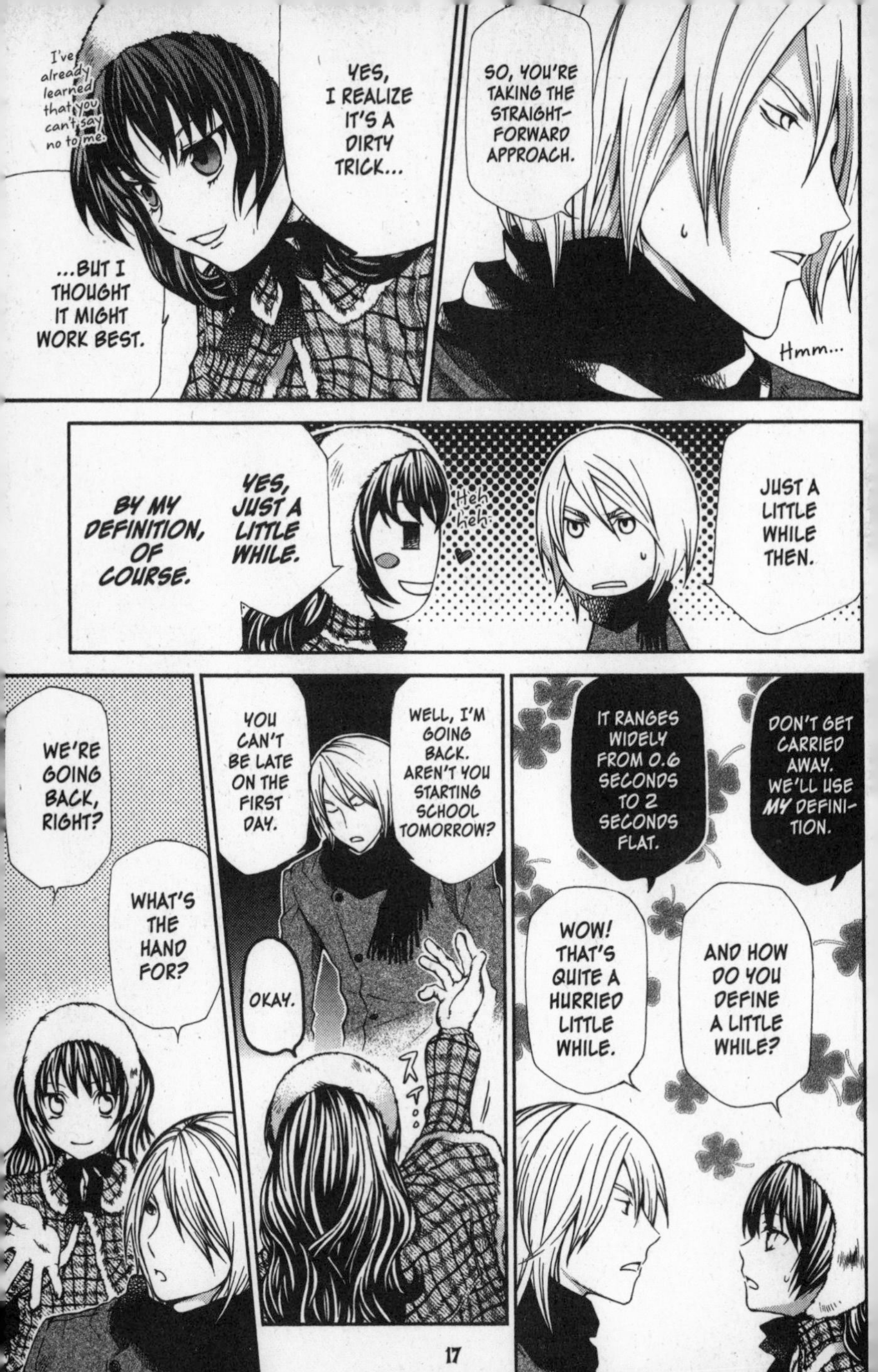
SO, YOU'RE TAKING THE STRAIGHT-FORWARD APPROACH.
Hmm...
YES, I REALIZE IT'S A DIRTY TRICK...
I've already learned that you can't say no to me.
...BUT I THOUGHT IT MIGHT WORK BEST.
JUST A LITTLE WHILE THEN.
Heh heh
YES, JUST A LITTLE WHILE.
BY MY DEFINITION, OF COURSE.
DON'T GET CARRIED AWAY. WE'LL USE MY DEFINITION.
IT RANGES WIDELY FROM 0.6 SECONDS TO 2 SECONDS FLAT.
AND HOW DO YOU DEFINE A LITTLE WHILE?
WOW! THAT'S QUITE A HURRIED LITTLE WHILE.
WELL, I'M GOING BACK. AREN'T YOU STARTING SCHOOL TOMORROW?
YOU CAN'T BE LATE ON THE FIRST DAY.
OKAY.
WE'RE GOING BACK, RIGHT?
WHAT'S THE HAND FOR?

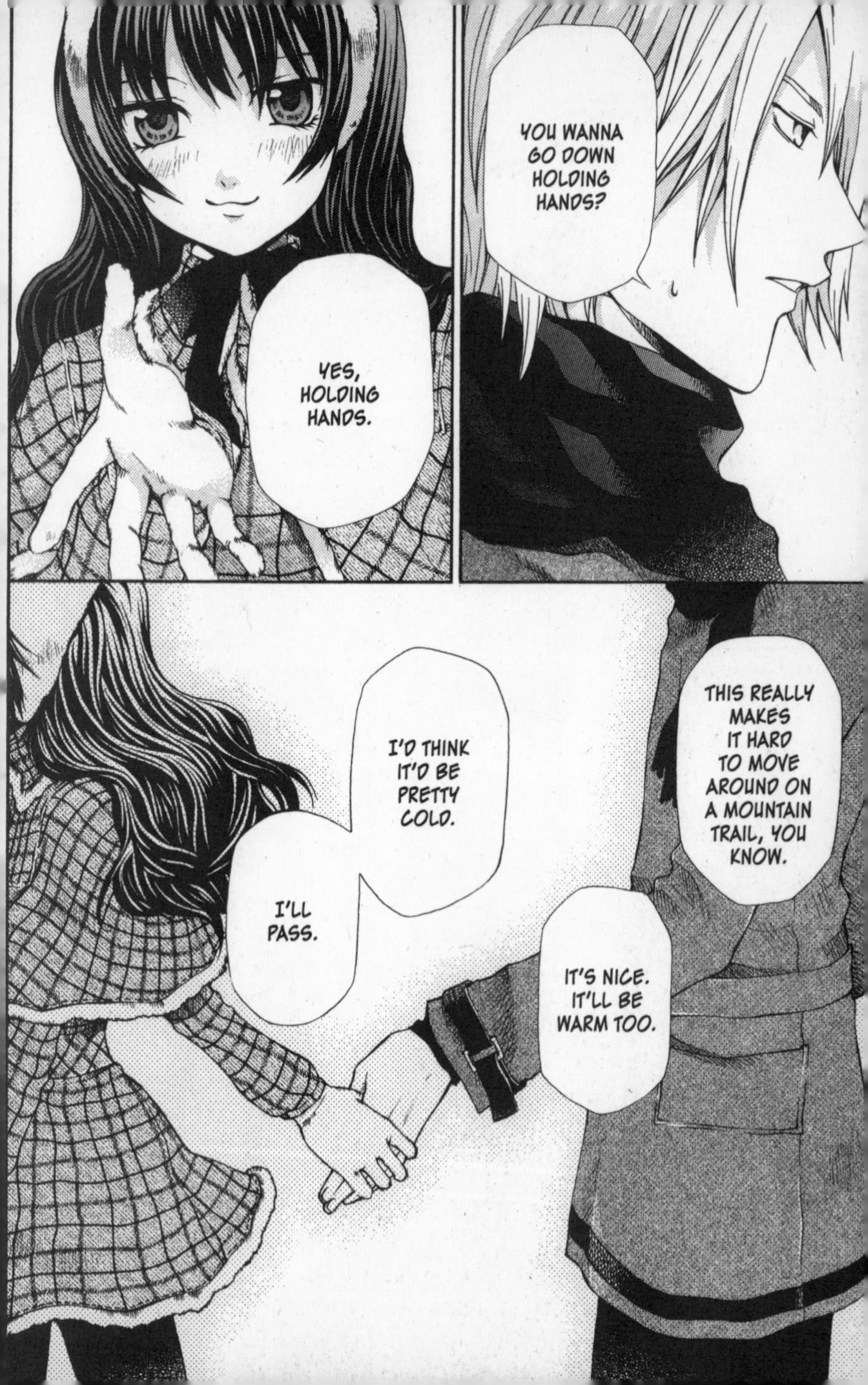
YOU WANNA GO DOWN HOLDING HANDS?
YES, HOLDING HANDS.
THIS REALLY MAKES IT HARD TO MOVE AROUND ON A MOUNTAIN TRAIL, YOU KNOW.
IT'S NICE. IT'LL BE WARM TOO.
I'D THINK IT'D BE PRETTY COLD.
I'LL PASS.

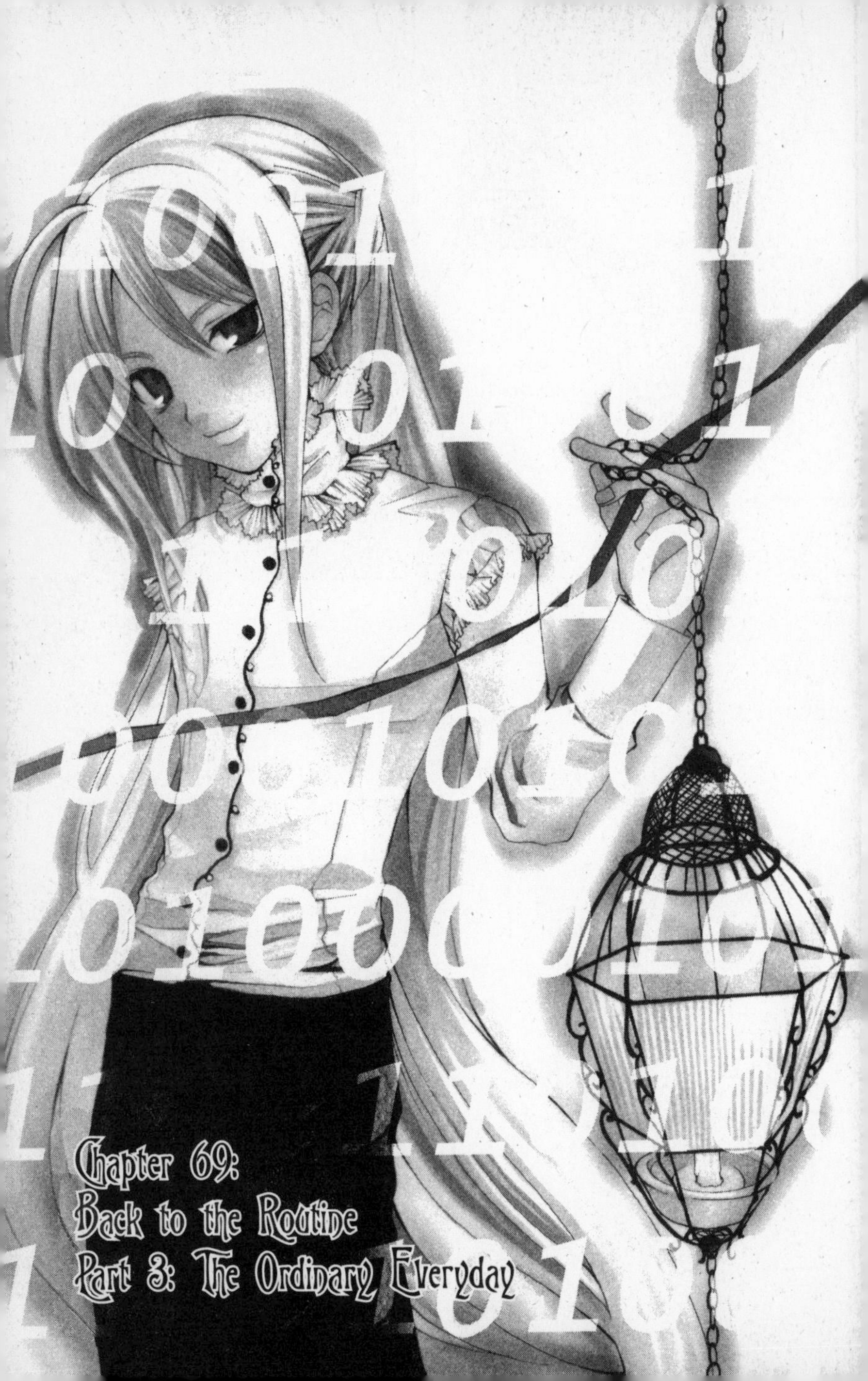
Chapter 69:
Back to the Routine
Part 3: The Ordinary Everyday

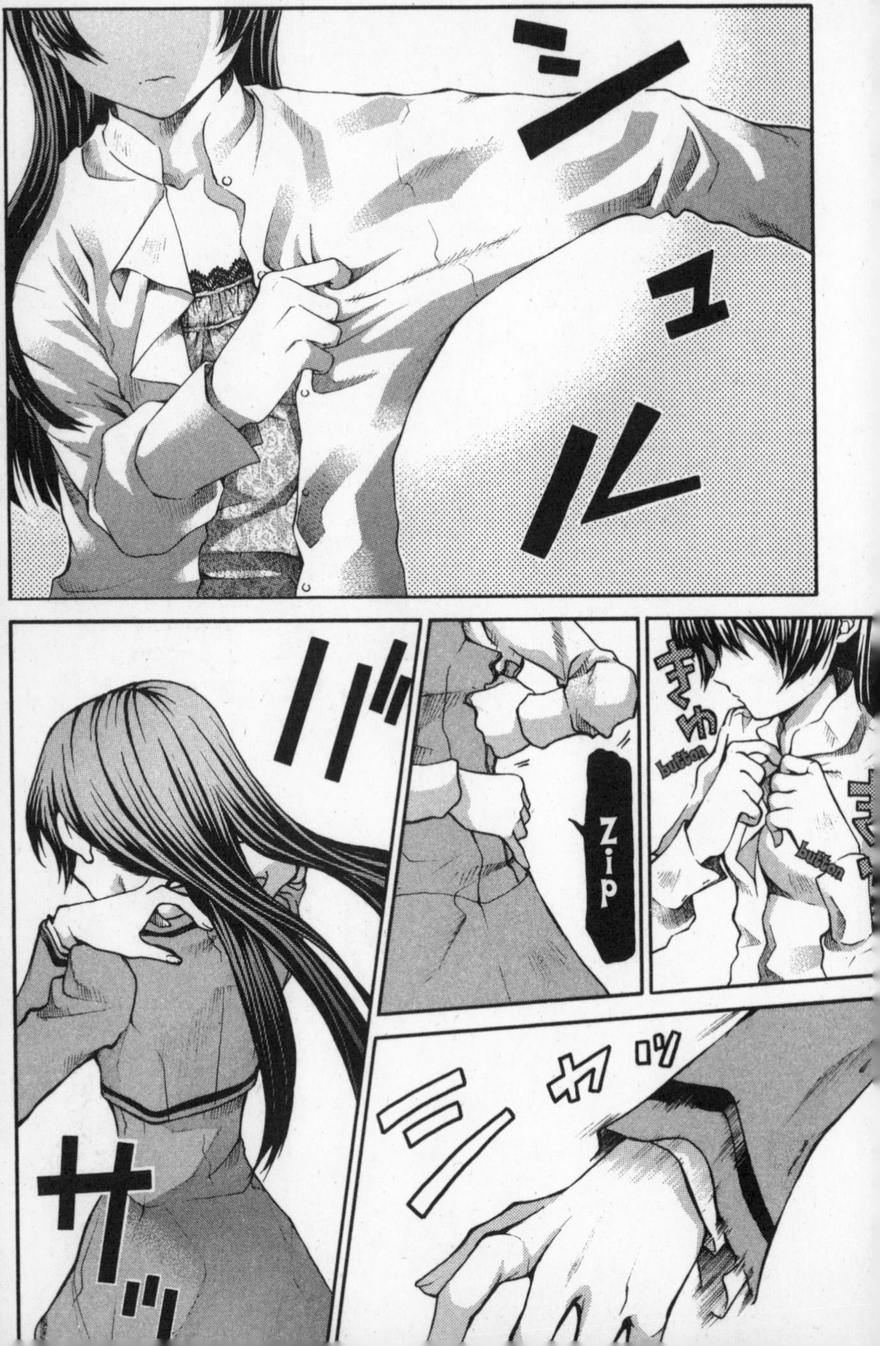
シュル
きゅ
button
button
Zip
シャッ
バ
サッ

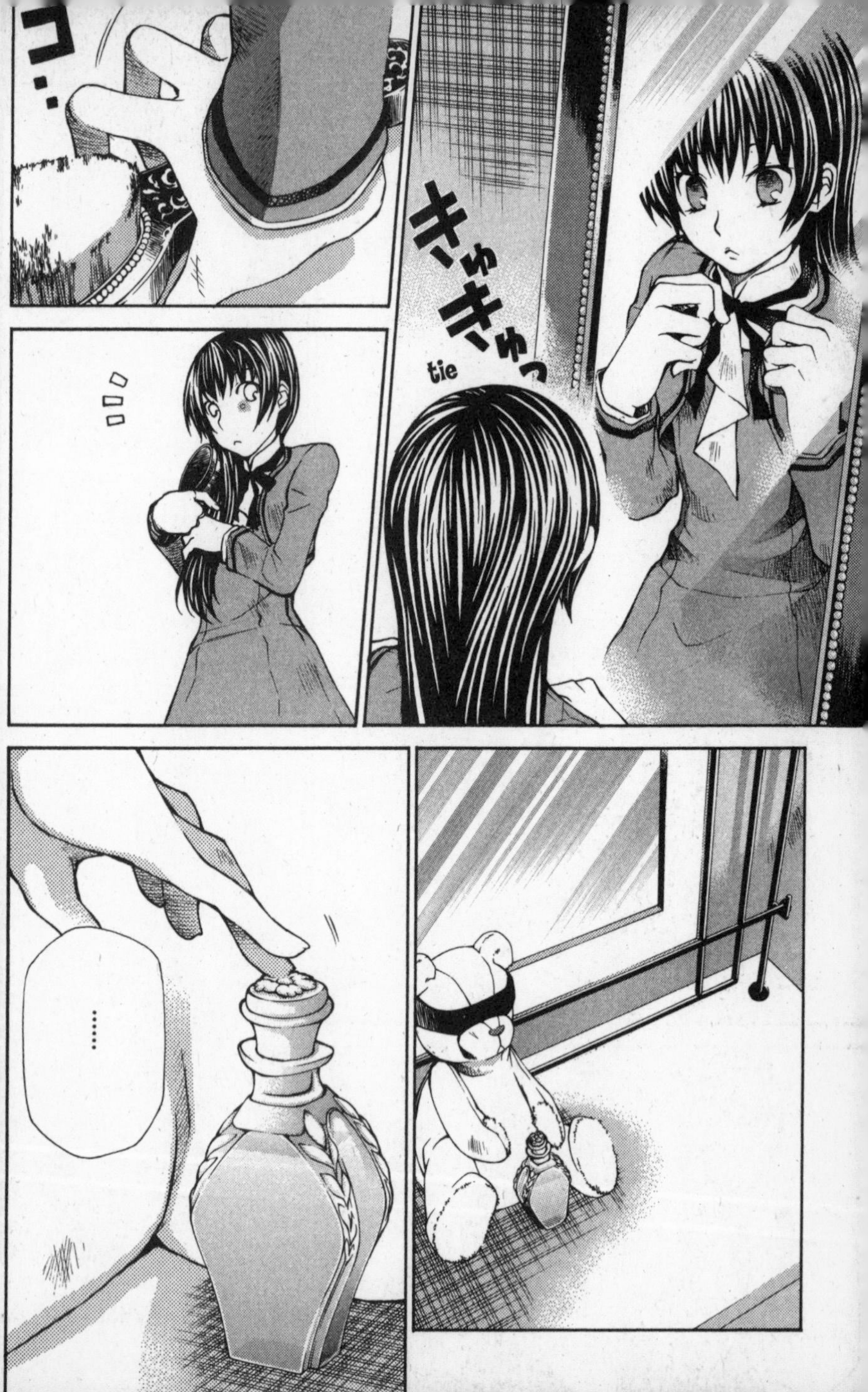
きゅきゅっ
tie
コ…
……

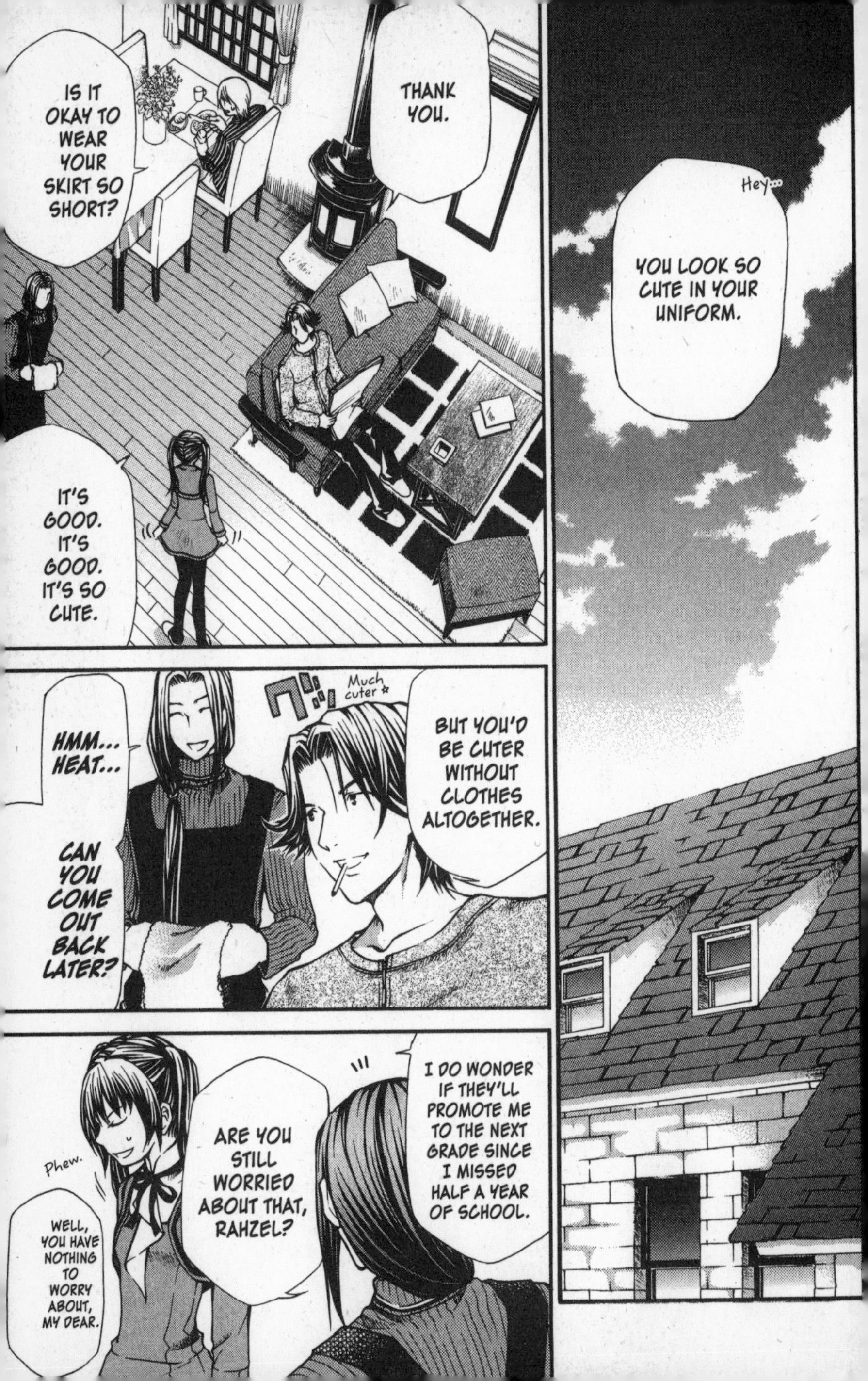
Hey...
YOU LOOK SO CUTE IN YOUR UNIFORM.
THANK YOU.
IS IT OKAY TO WEAR YOUR SKIRT SO SHORT?
IT'S GOOD. IT'S GOOD. IT'S SO CUTE.
Much cuter ☆
BUT YOU'D BE CUTER WITHOUT CLOTHES ALTOGETHER.
HMM... HEAT...
CAN YOU COME OUT BACK LATER?
I DO WONDER IF THEY'LL PROMOTE ME TO THE NEXT GRADE SINCE I MISSED HALF A YEAR OF SCHOOL.
ARE YOU STILL WORRIED ABOUT THAT, RAHZEL?
Phew.
WELL, YOU HAVE NOTHING TO WORRY ABOUT, MY DEAR.

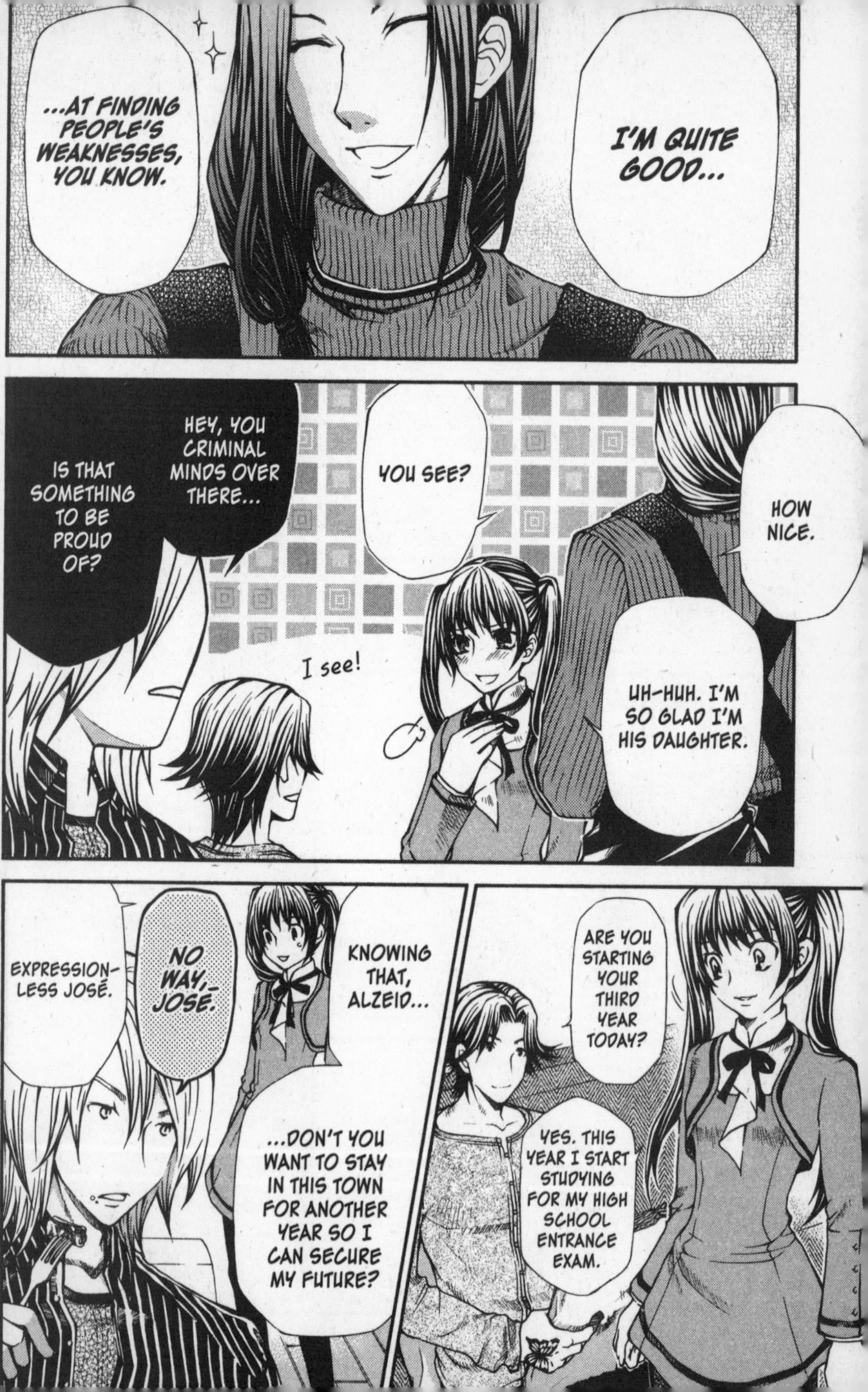
I'M QUITE GOOD...
...AT FINDING PEOPLE'S WEAKNESSES, YOU KNOW.
HOW NICE.
UH-HUH. I'M SO GLAD I'M HIS DAUGHTER.
YOU SEE?
I see!
HEY, YOU CRIMINAL MINDS OVER THERE...
IS THAT SOMETHING TO BE PROUD OF?
ARE YOU STARTING YOUR THIRD YEAR TODAY?
YES. THIS YEAR I START STUDYING FOR MY HIGH SCHOOL ENTRANCE EXAM.
KNOWING THAT, ALZEID...
...DON'T YOU WANT TO STAY IN THIS TOWN FOR ANOTHER YEAR SO I CAN SECURE MY FUTURE?
NO WAY, JOSÉ.
EXPRESSION-LESS JOSÉ.

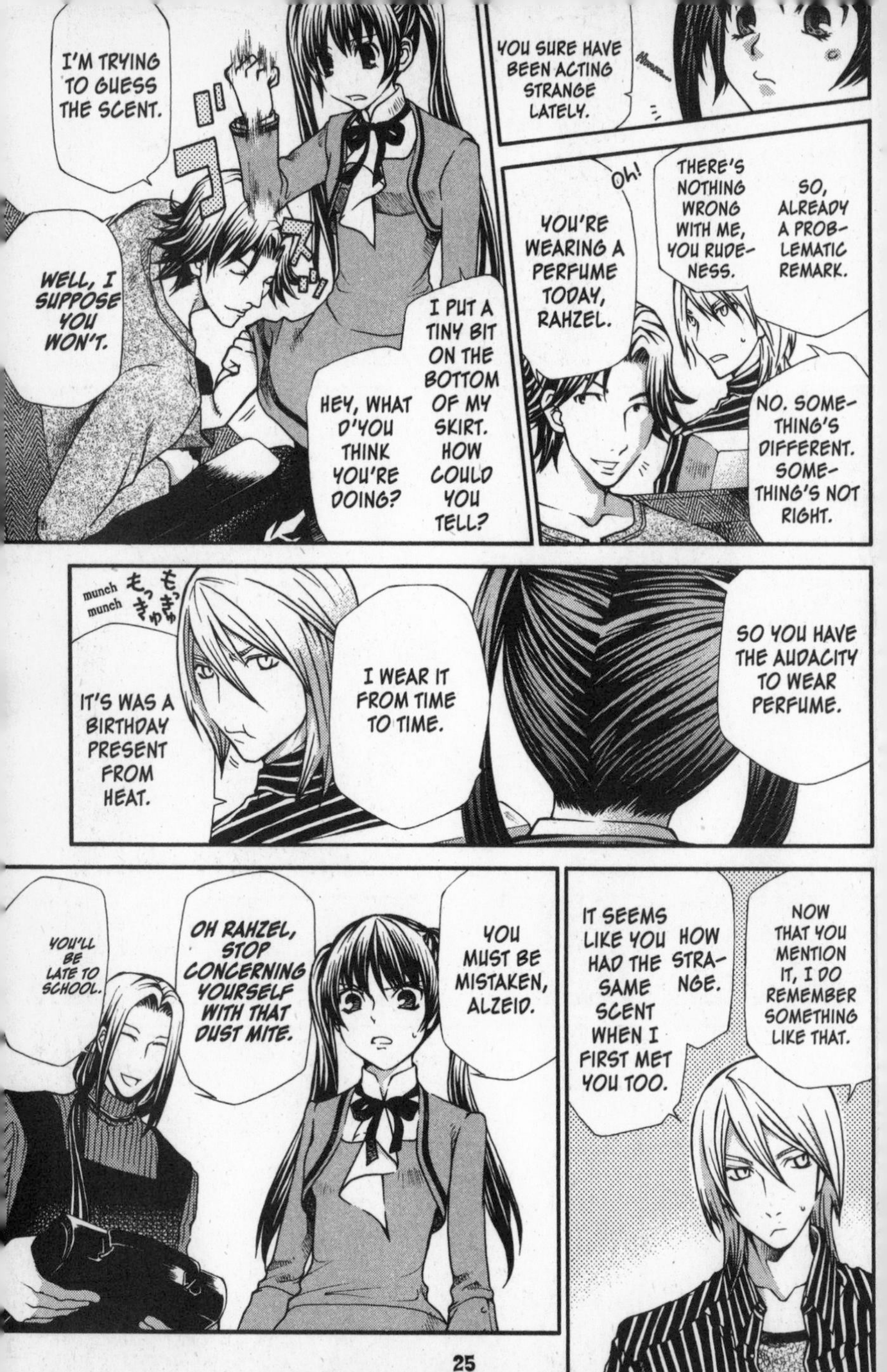
Hmmm...
YOU SURE HAVE BEEN ACTING STRANGE LATELY.
SO, ALREADY A PROBLEMATIC REMARK.
THERE'S NOTHING WRONG WITH ME, YOU RUDENESS.
Oh!
YOU'RE WEARING A PERFUME TODAY, RAHZEL.
NO. SOMETHING'S DIFFERENT. SOMETHING'S NOT RIGHT.
I PUT A TINY BIT ON THE BOTTOM OF MY SKIRT. HOW COULD YOU TELL?
HEY, WHAT D'YOU THINK YOU'RE DOING?
I'M TRYING TO GUESS THE SCENT.
WELL, I SUPPOSE YOU WON'T.
SO YOU HAVE THE AUDACITY TO WEAR PERFUME.
I WEAR IT FROM TIME TO TIME.
munch munch もっきゅもっきゅ
IT'S WAS A BIRTHDAY PRESENT FROM HEAT.
NOW THAT YOU MENTION IT, I DO REMEMBER SOMETHING LIKE THAT.
HOW STRANGE.
IT SEEMS LIKE YOU HAD THE SAME SCENT WHEN I FIRST MET YOU TOO.
YOU MUST BE MISTAKEN, ALZEID.
OH RAHZEL, STOP CONCERNING YOURSELF WITH THAT DUST MITE.
YOU'LL BE LATE TO SCHOOL.

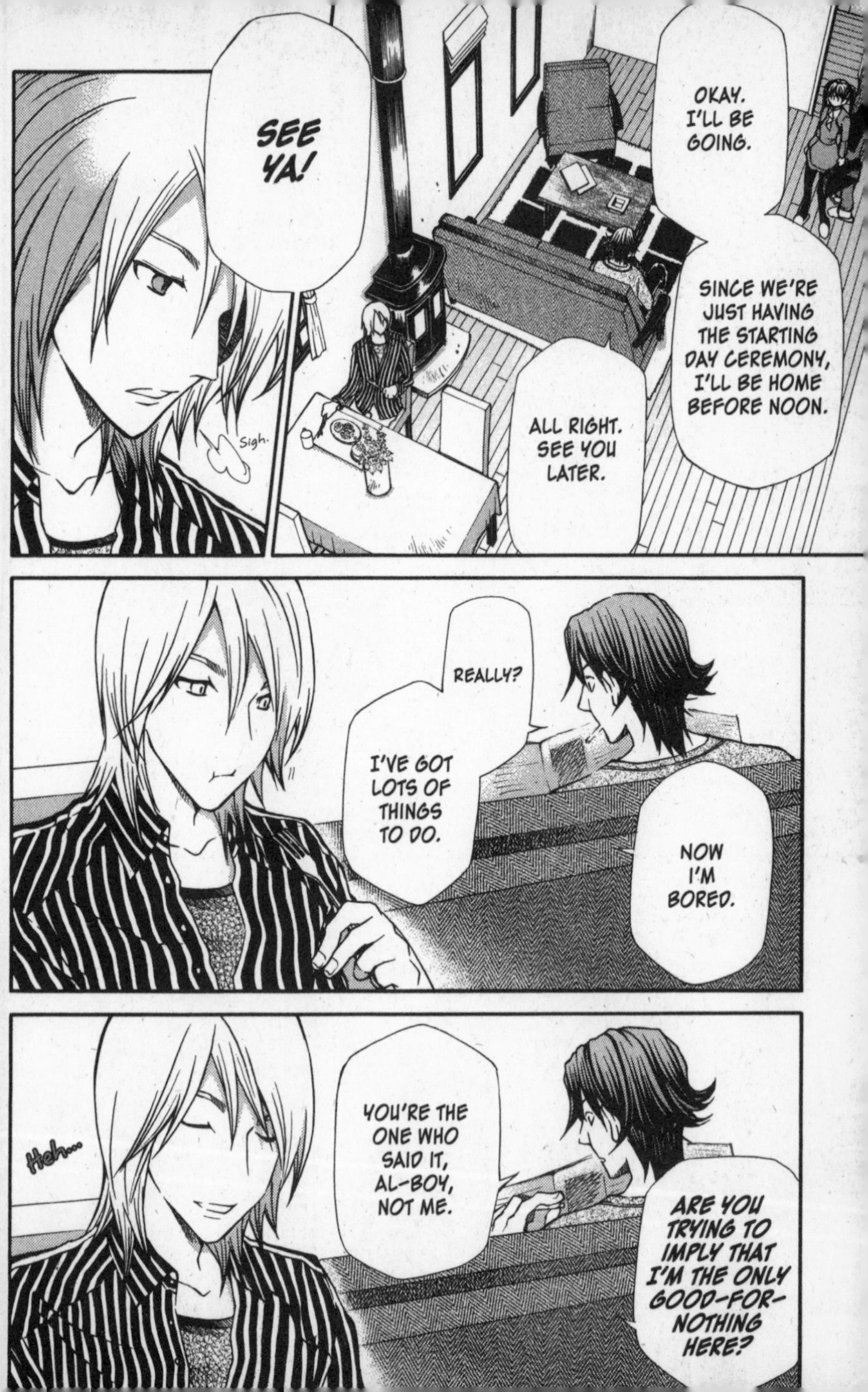
OKAY. I'LL BE GOING.
SINCE WE'RE JUST HAVING THE STARTING DAY CEREMONY, I'LL BE HOME BEFORE NOON.
ALL RIGHT. SEE YOU LATER.
SEE YA!
Sigh.
NOW I'M BORED.
REALLY?
I'VE GOT LOTS OF THINGS TO DO.
ARE YOU TRYING TO IMPLY THAT I'M THE ONLY GOOD-FOR-NOTHING HERE?
YOU'RE THE ONE WHO SAID IT, AL-BOY, NOT ME.
Heh...

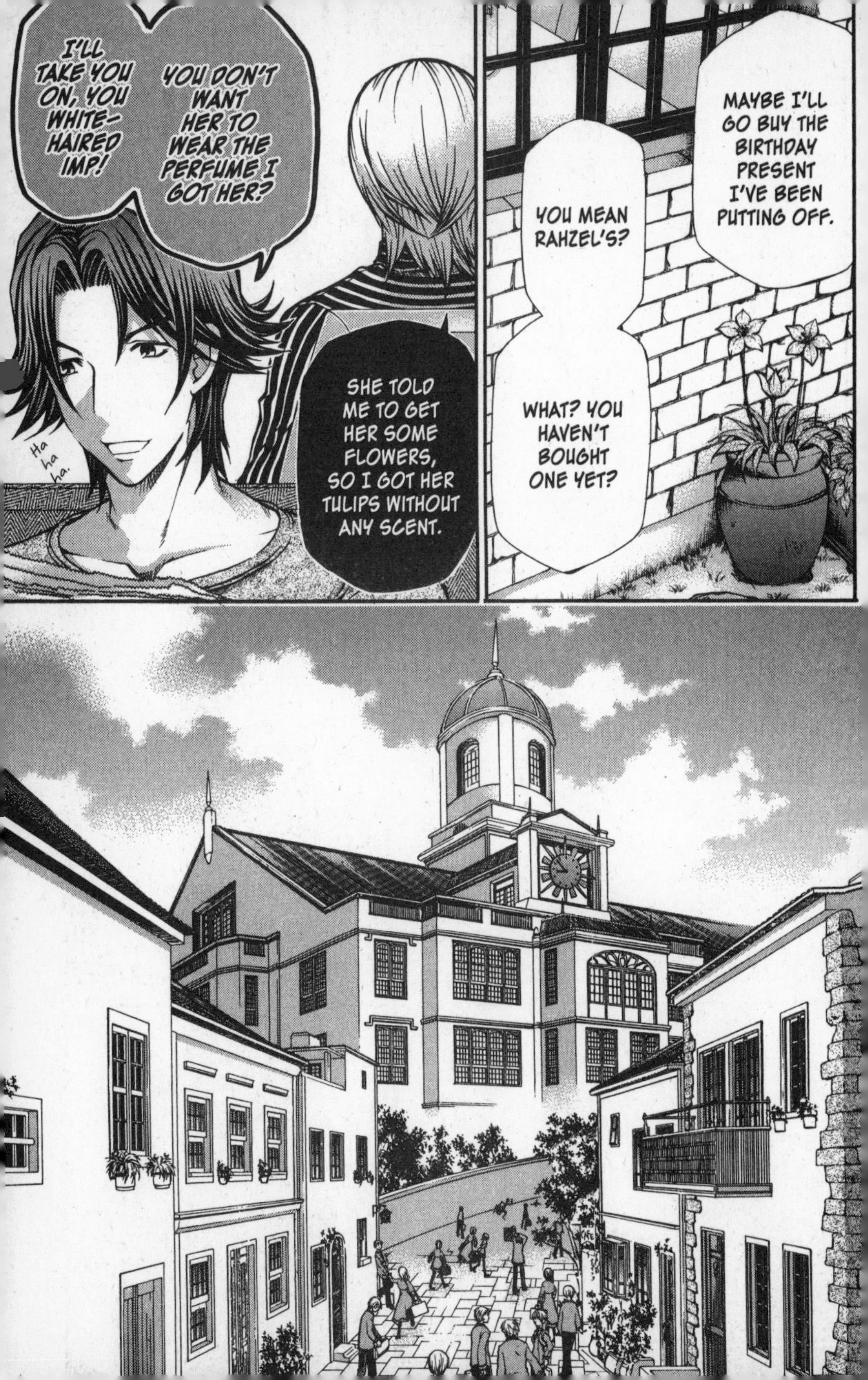
MAYBE I'LL GO BUY THE BIRTHDAY PRESENT I'VE BEEN PUTTING OFF.
YOU MEAN RAHZEL'S?
WHAT? YOU HAVEN'T BOUGHT ONE YET?
YOU DON'T WANT HER TO WEAR THE PERFUME I GOT HER?
I'LL TAKE YOU ON, YOU WHITE-HAIRED IMP!
SHE TOLD ME TO GET HER SOME FLOWERS, SO I GOT HER TULIPS WITHOUT ANY SCENT.
Ha ha ha.

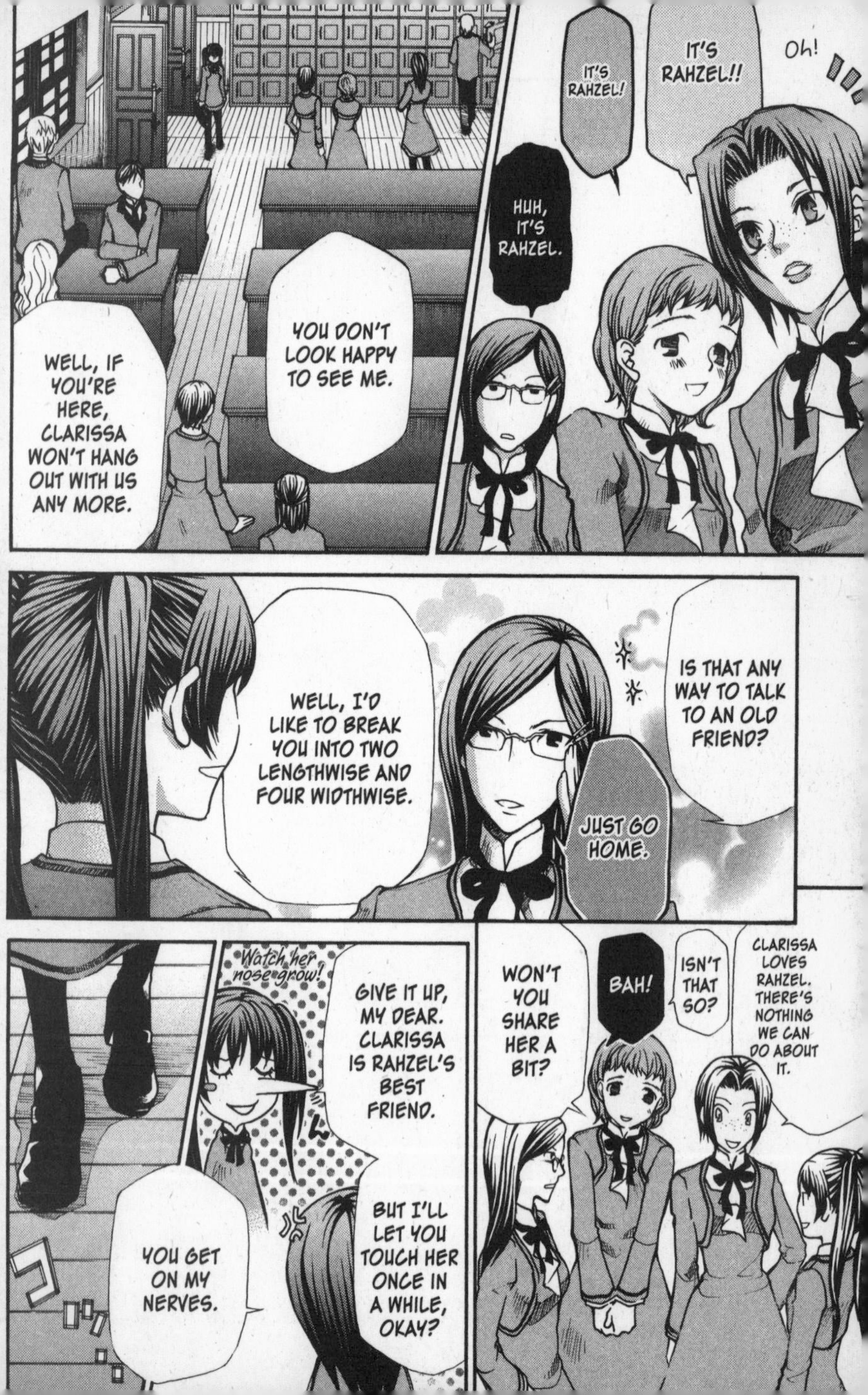
Oh!
IT'S RAHZEL!!
IT'S RAHZEL!
HUH, IT'S RAHZEL.
YOU DON'T LOOK HAPPY TO SEE ME.
WELL, IF YOU'RE HERE, CLARISSA WON'T HANG OUT WITH US ANY MORE.
IS THAT ANY WAY TO TALK TO AN OLD FRIEND?
JUST GO HOME.
WELL, I'D LIKE TO BREAK YOU INTO TWO LENGTHWISE AND FOUR WIDTHWISE.
CLARISSA LOVES RAHZEL. THERE'S NOTHING WE CAN DO ABOUT IT.
ISN'T THAT SO?
BAH!
WON'T YOU SHARE HER A BIT?
Watch her nose grow!
GIVE IT UP, MY DEAR. CLARISSA IS RAHZEL'S BEST FRIEND.
BUT I'LL LET YOU TOUCH HER ONCE IN A WHILE, OKAY?
YOU GET ON MY NERVES.

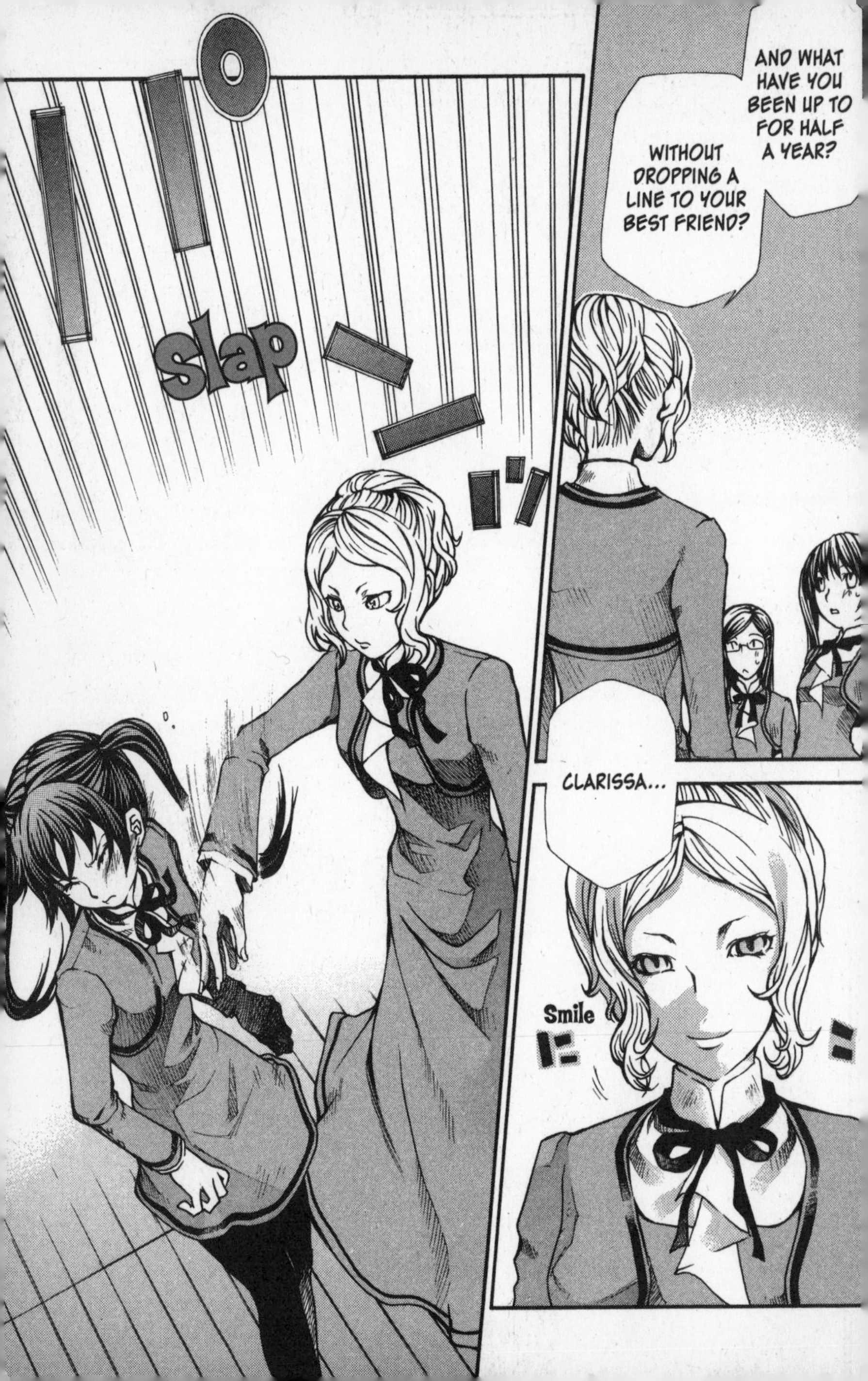
AND WHAT HAVE YOU BEEN UP TO FOR HALF A YEAR?
WITHOUT DROPPING A LINE TO YOUR BEST FRIEND?
CLARISSA...
Smile
slap

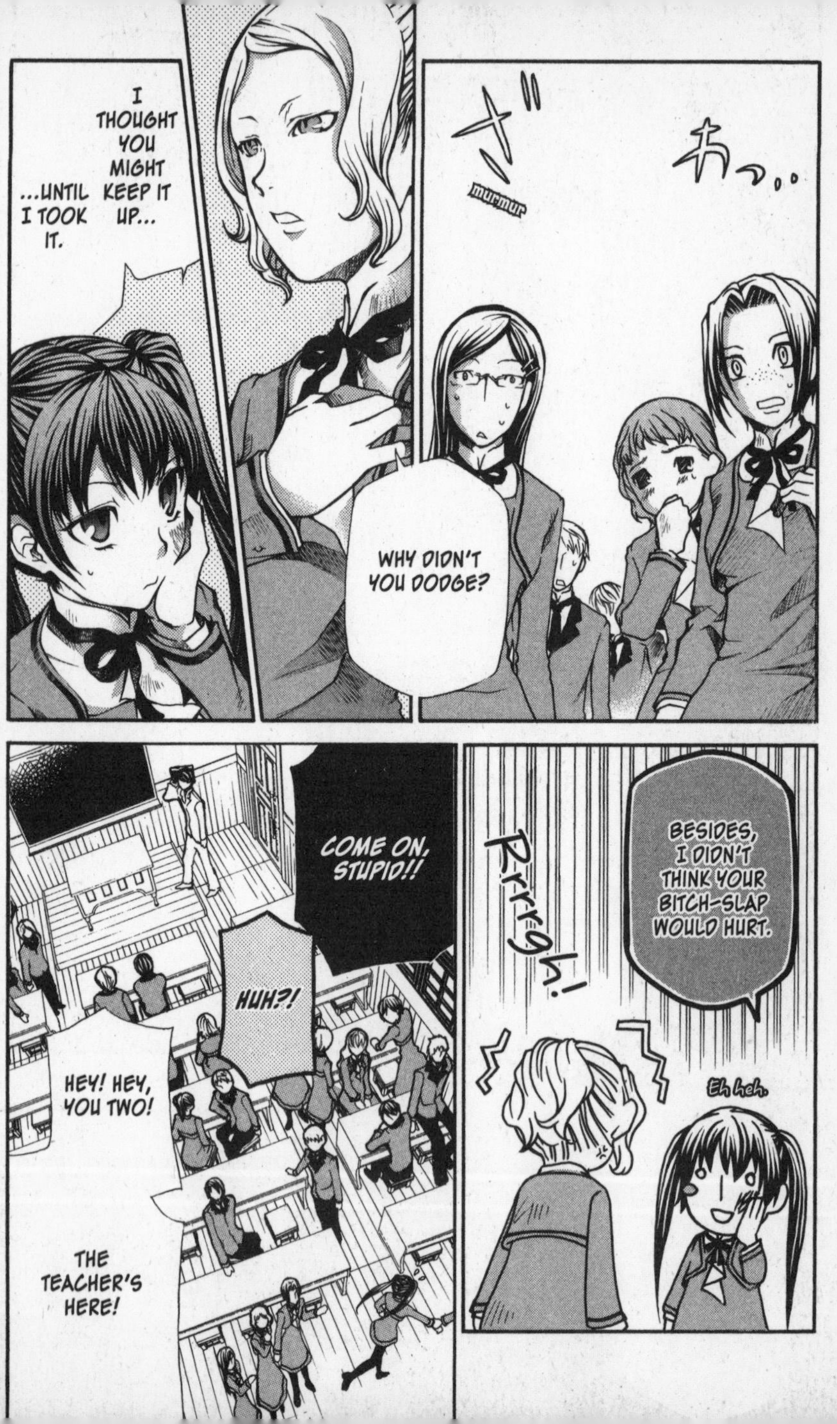
ざ
murmur
わっ..
WHY DIDN'T YOU DODGE?
I THOUGHT YOU MIGHT KEEP IT UP...
...UNTIL I TOOK IT.
BESIDES, I DIDN'T THINK YOUR BITCH-SLAP WOULD HURT.
Rrrrgh!
Eh heh.
COME ON, STUPID!!
HUH?!
HEY! HEY, YOU TWO!
THE TEACHER'S HERE!

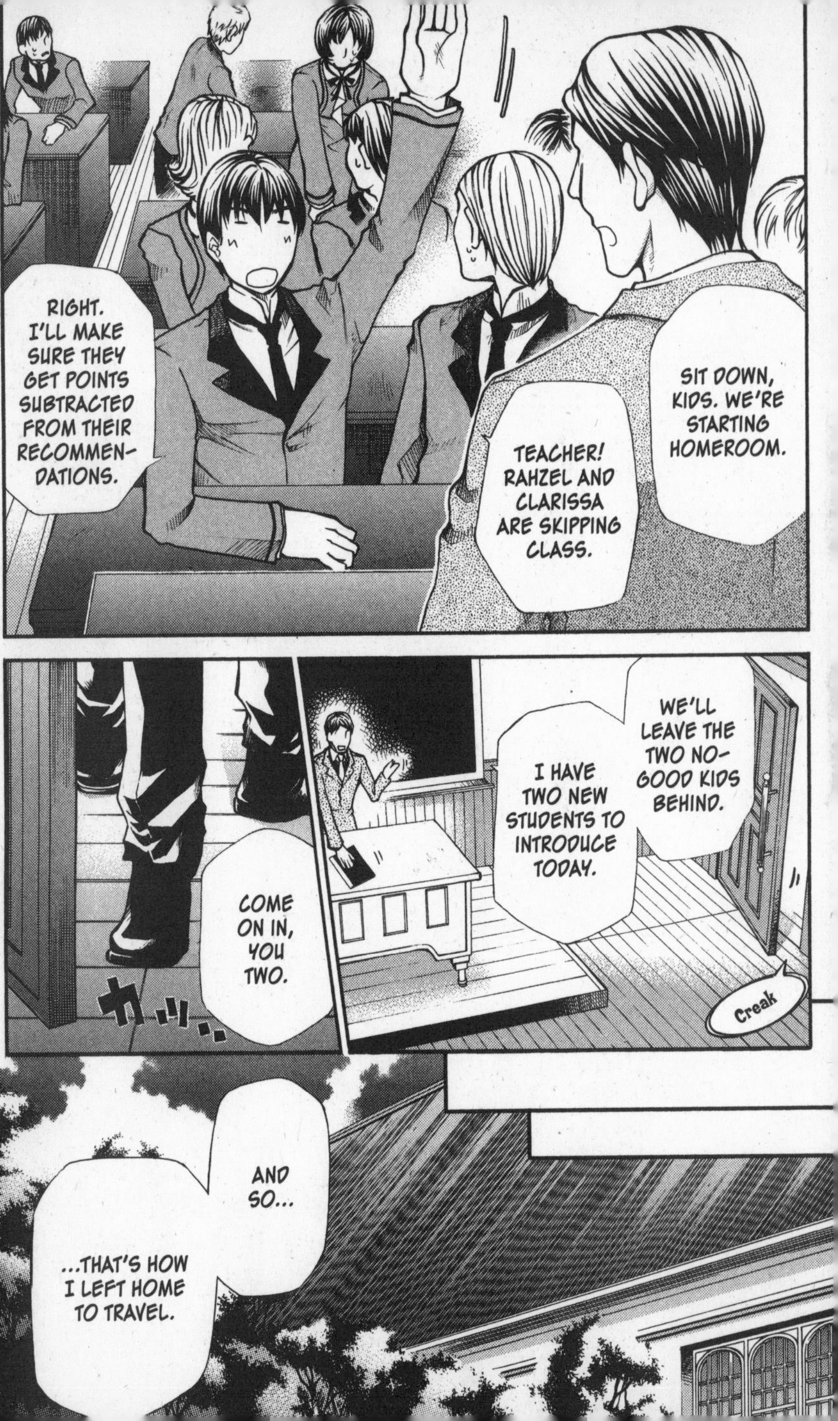
SIT DOWN, KIDS. WE'RE STARTING HOMEROOM.
TEACHER! RAHZEL AND CLARISSA ARE SKIPPING CLASS.
RIGHT. I'LL MAKE SURE THEY GET POINTS SUBTRACTED FROM THEIR RECOMMEN-DATIONS.
WE'LL LEAVE THE TWO NO-GOOD KIDS BEHIND.
I HAVE TWO NEW STUDENTS TO INTRODUCE TODAY.
Creak
COME ON IN, YOU TWO.
AND SO...
...THAT'S HOW I LEFT HOME TO TRAVEL.

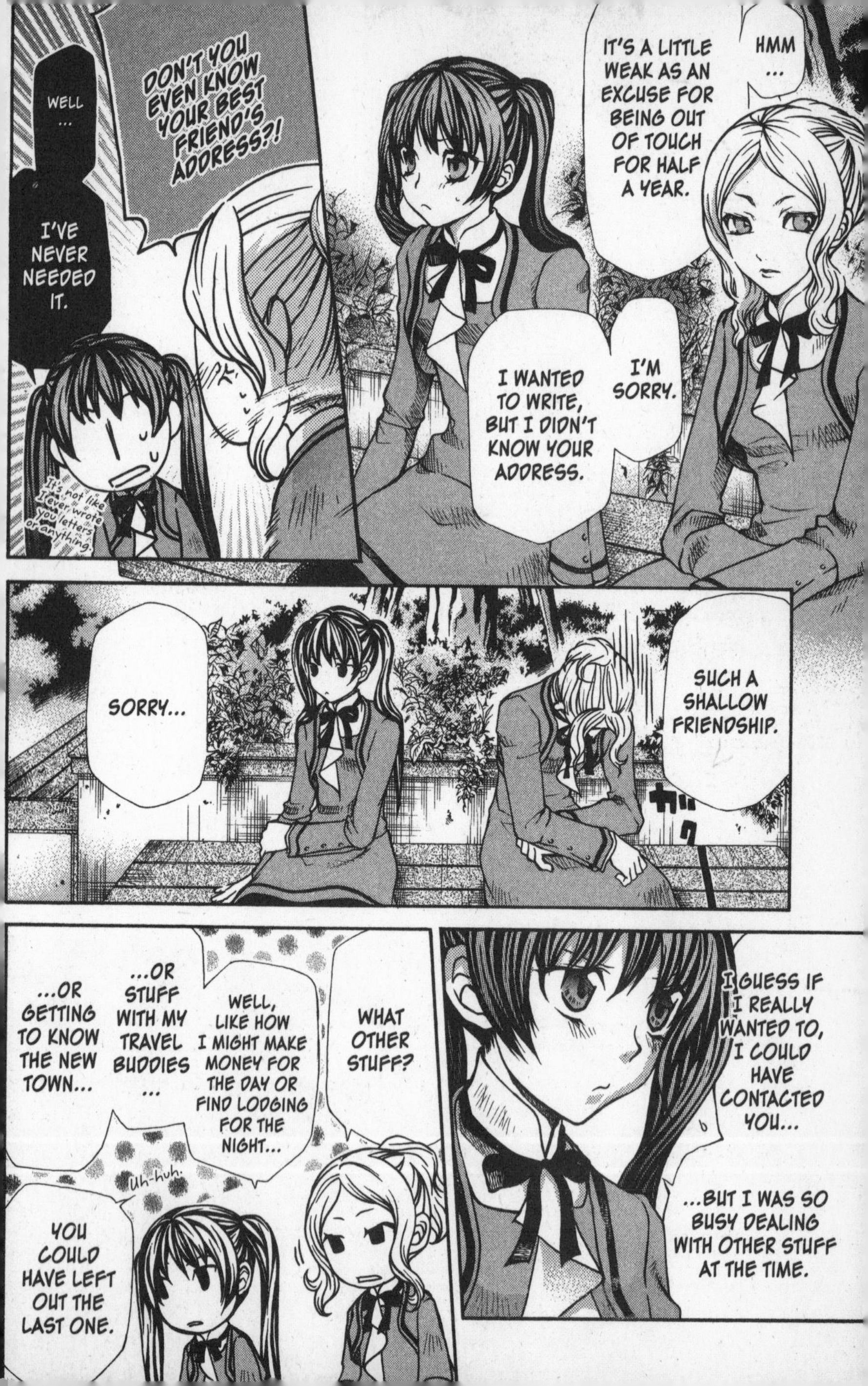
HMM ...
IT'S A LITTLE WEAK AS AN EXCUSE FOR BEING OUT OF TOUCH FOR HALF A YEAR.
I'M SORRY.
I WANTED TO WRITE, BUT I DIDN'T KNOW YOUR ADDRESS.
DON'T YOU EVEN KNOW YOUR BEST FRIEND'S ADDRESS?!
WELL ...
I'VE NEVER NEEDED IT.
It's not like I ever wrote you letters or anything.
SUCH A SHALLOW FRIENDSHIP.
SORRY...
I GUESS IF I REALLY WANTED TO, I COULD HAVE CONTACTED YOU...
...BUT I WAS SO BUSY DEALING WITH OTHER STUFF AT THE TIME.
WHAT OTHER STUFF?
WELL, LIKE HOW I MIGHT MAKE MONEY FOR THE DAY OR FIND LODGING FOR THE NIGHT...
...OR STUFF WITH MY TRAVEL BUDDIES ...
...OR GETTING TO KNOW THE NEW TOWN...
uh-huh.
YOU COULD HAVE LEFT OUT THE LAST ONE.

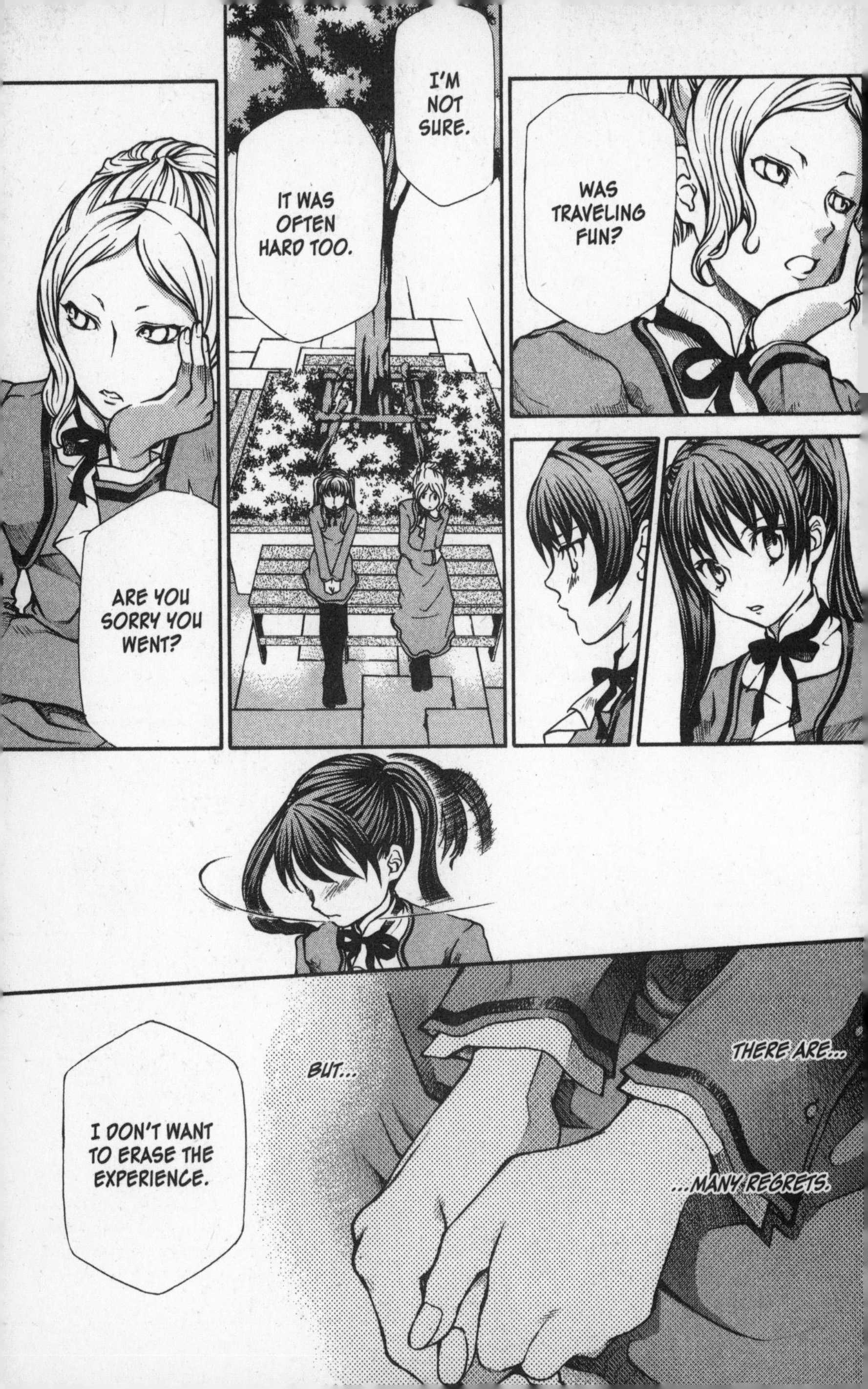
WAS TRAVELING FUN?
I'M NOT SURE.
IT WAS OFTEN HARD TOO.
ARE YOU SORRY YOU WENT?
THERE ARE...
...MANY REGRETS.
BUT...
I DON'T WANT TO ERASE THE EXPERIENCE.

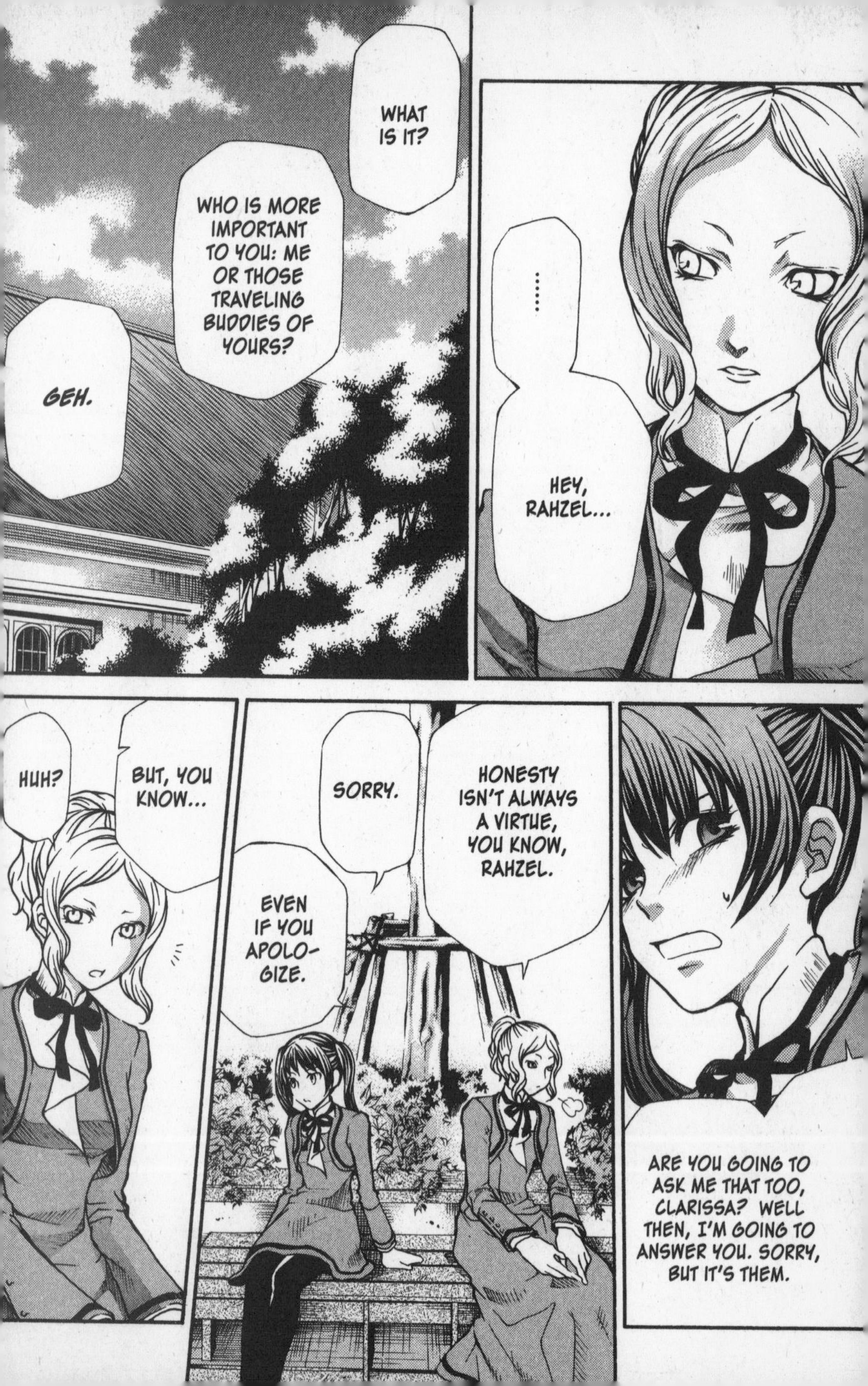
......
HEY, RAHZEL...
WHAT IS IT?
WHO IS MORE IMPORTANT TO YOU: ME OR THOSE TRAVELING BUDDIES OF YOURS?
GEH.
ARE YOU GOING TO ASK ME THAT TOO, CLARISSA? WELL THEN, I'M GOING TO ANSWER YOU. SORRY, BUT IT'S THEM.
HONESTY ISN'T ALWAYS A VIRTUE, YOU KNOW, RAHZEL.
SORRY.
EVEN IF YOU APOLOGIZE.
BUT, YOU KNOW...
HUH?

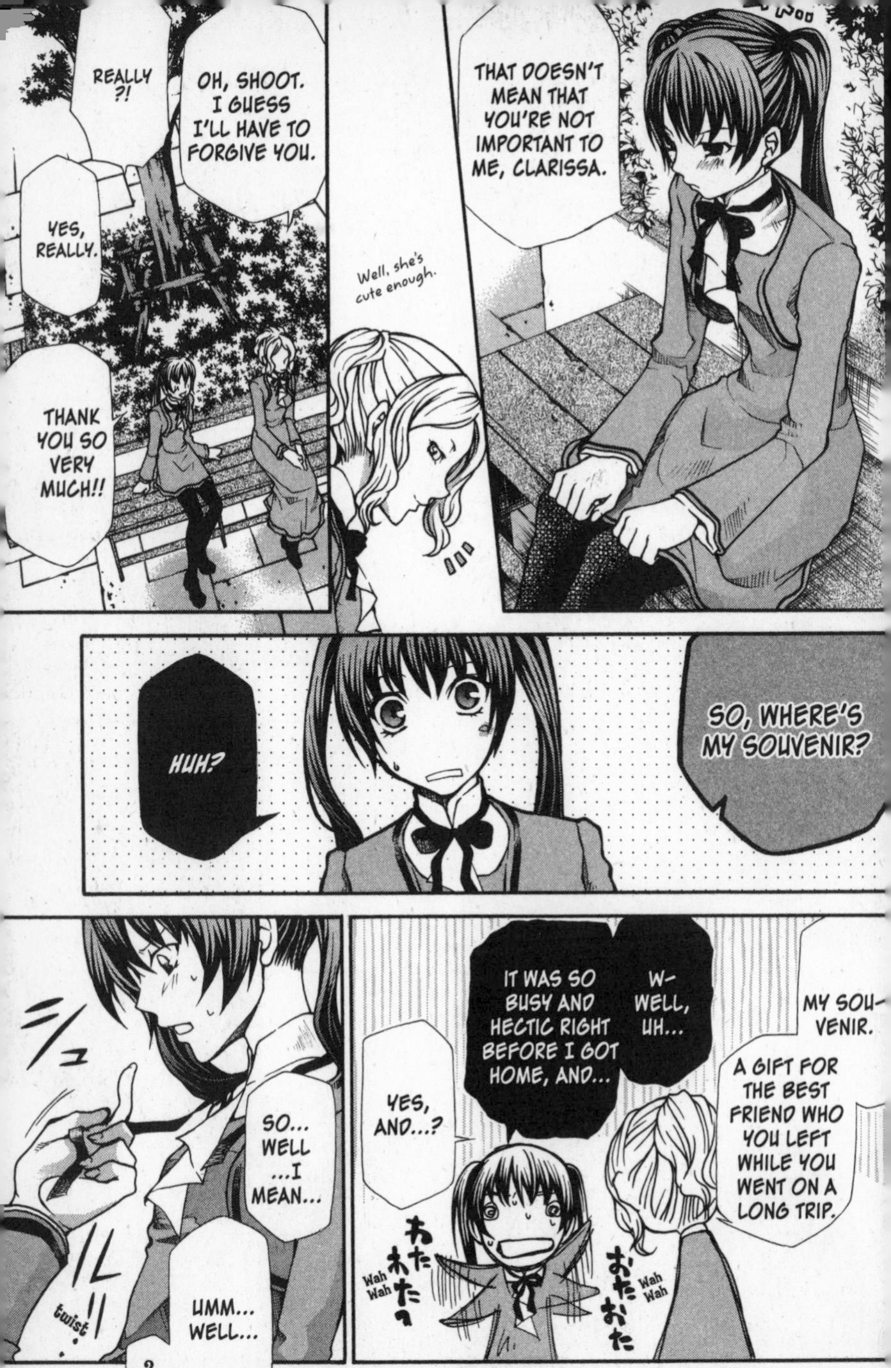
THAT DOESN'T MEAN THAT YOU'RE NOT IMPORTANT TO ME, CLARISSA.
Well, she's cute enough.
OH, SHOOT. I GUESS I'LL HAVE TO FORGIVE YOU.
REALLY ?!
YES, REALLY.
THANK YOU SO VERY MUCH!!
SO, WHERE'S MY SOUVENIR?
HUH?
MY SOU-VENIR.
A GIFT FOR THE BEST FRIEND WHO YOU LEFT WHILE YOU WENT ON A LONG TRIP.
W-WELL, UH...
IT WAS SO BUSY AND HECTIC RIGHT BEFORE I GOT HOME, AND...
YES, AND...?
おたおた
Wah Wah
Wah Wah
SO... WELL ...I MEAN...
UMM... WELL...
?
twist!

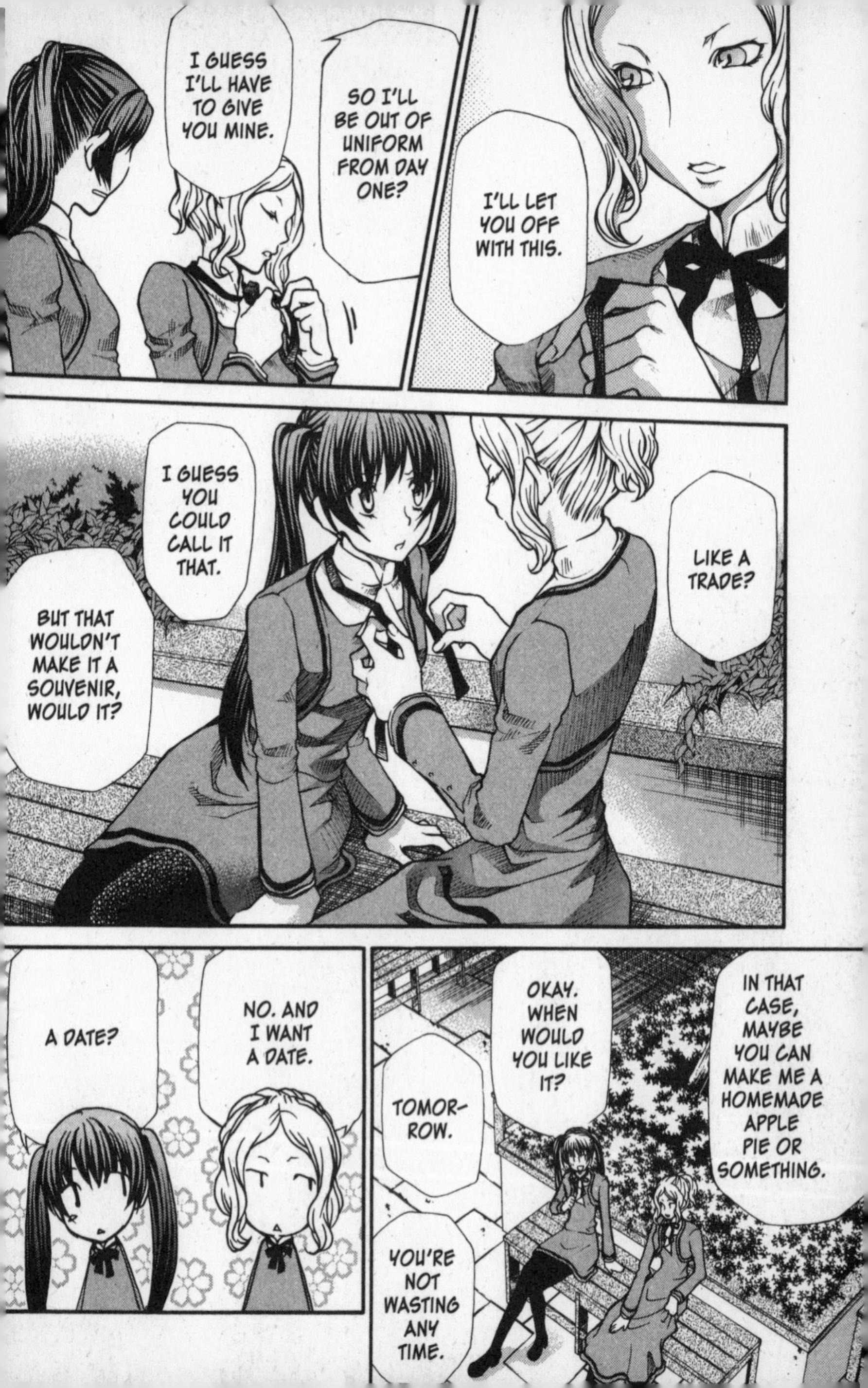
I'LL LET YOU OFF WITH THIS.
SO I'LL BE OUT OF UNIFORM FROM DAY ONE?
I GUESS I'LL HAVE TO GIVE YOU MINE.
LIKE A TRADE?
I GUESS YOU COULD CALL IT THAT.
BUT THAT WOULDN'T MAKE IT A SOUVENIR, WOULD IT?
IN THAT CASE, MAYBE YOU CAN MAKE ME A HOMEMADE APPLE PIE OR SOMETHING.
OKAY. WHEN WOULD YOU LIKE IT?
TOMOR-ROW.
YOU'RE NOT WASTING ANY TIME.
NO. AND I WANT A DATE.
A DATE?

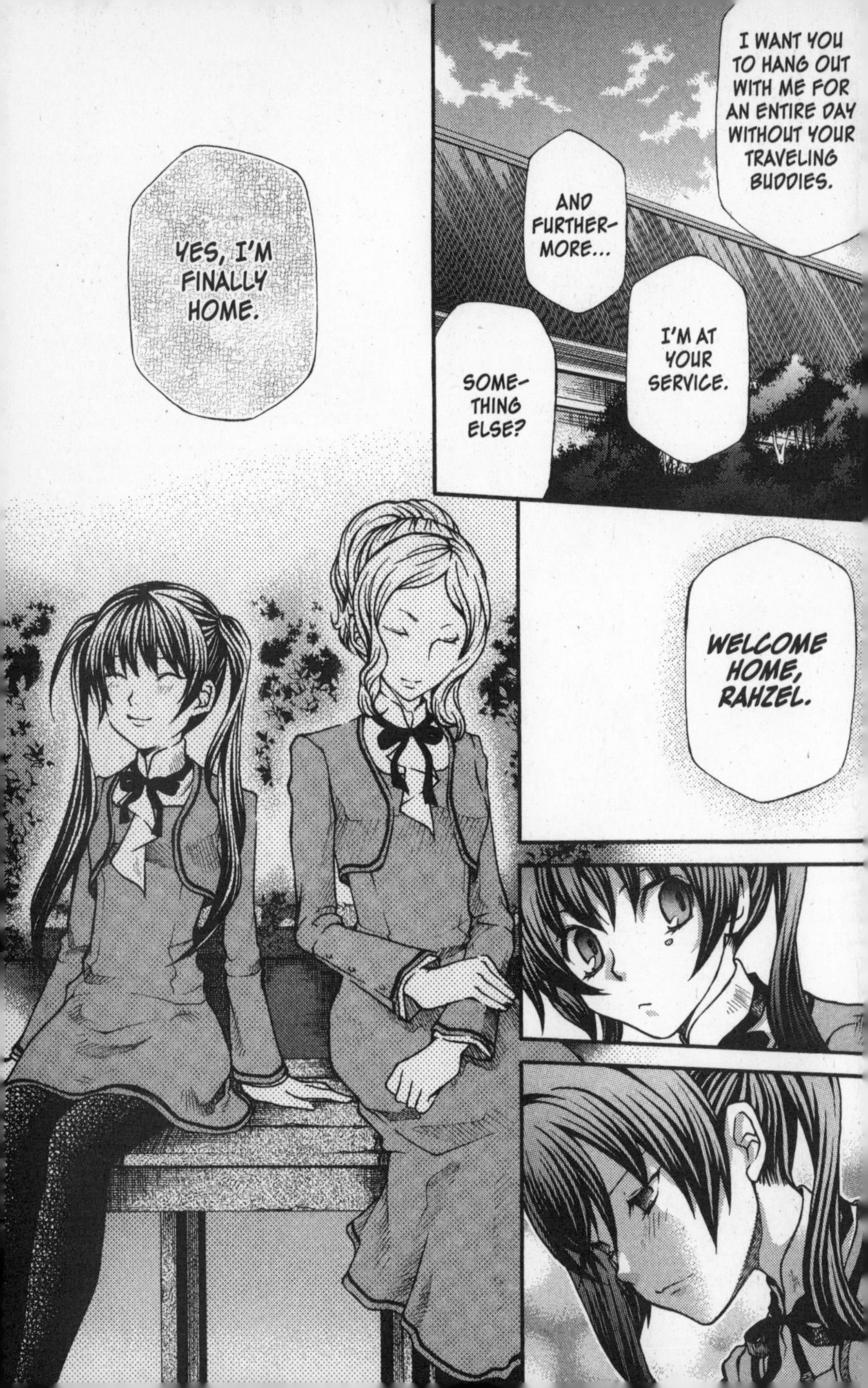
I WANT YOU TO HANG OUT WITH ME FOR AN ENTIRE DAY WITHOUT YOUR TRAVELING BUDDIES.
AND FURTHER-MORE...
I'M AT YOUR SERVICE.
SOME-THING ELSE?
WELCOME HOME, RAHZEL.
YES, I'M FINALLY HOME.

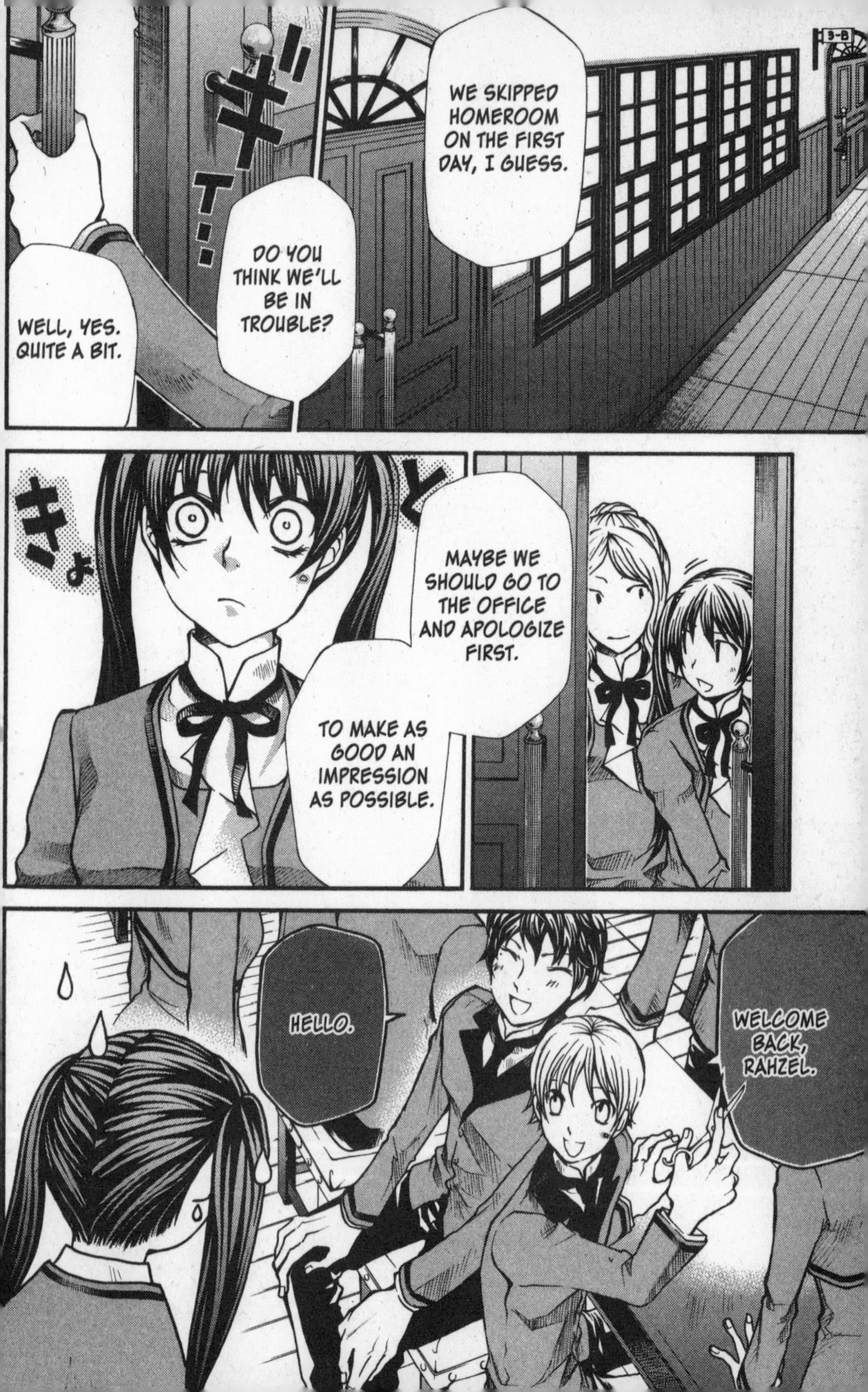
3-B
WE SKIPPED HOMEROOM ON THE FIRST DAY, I GUESS.
DO YOU THINK WE'LL BE IN TROUBLE?
WELL, YES. QUITE A BIT.
MAYBE WE SHOULD GO TO THE OFFICE AND APOLOGIZE FIRST.
きょと
TO MAKE AS GOOD AN IMPRESSION AS POSSIBLE.
WELCOME BACK, RAHZEL.
HELLO.

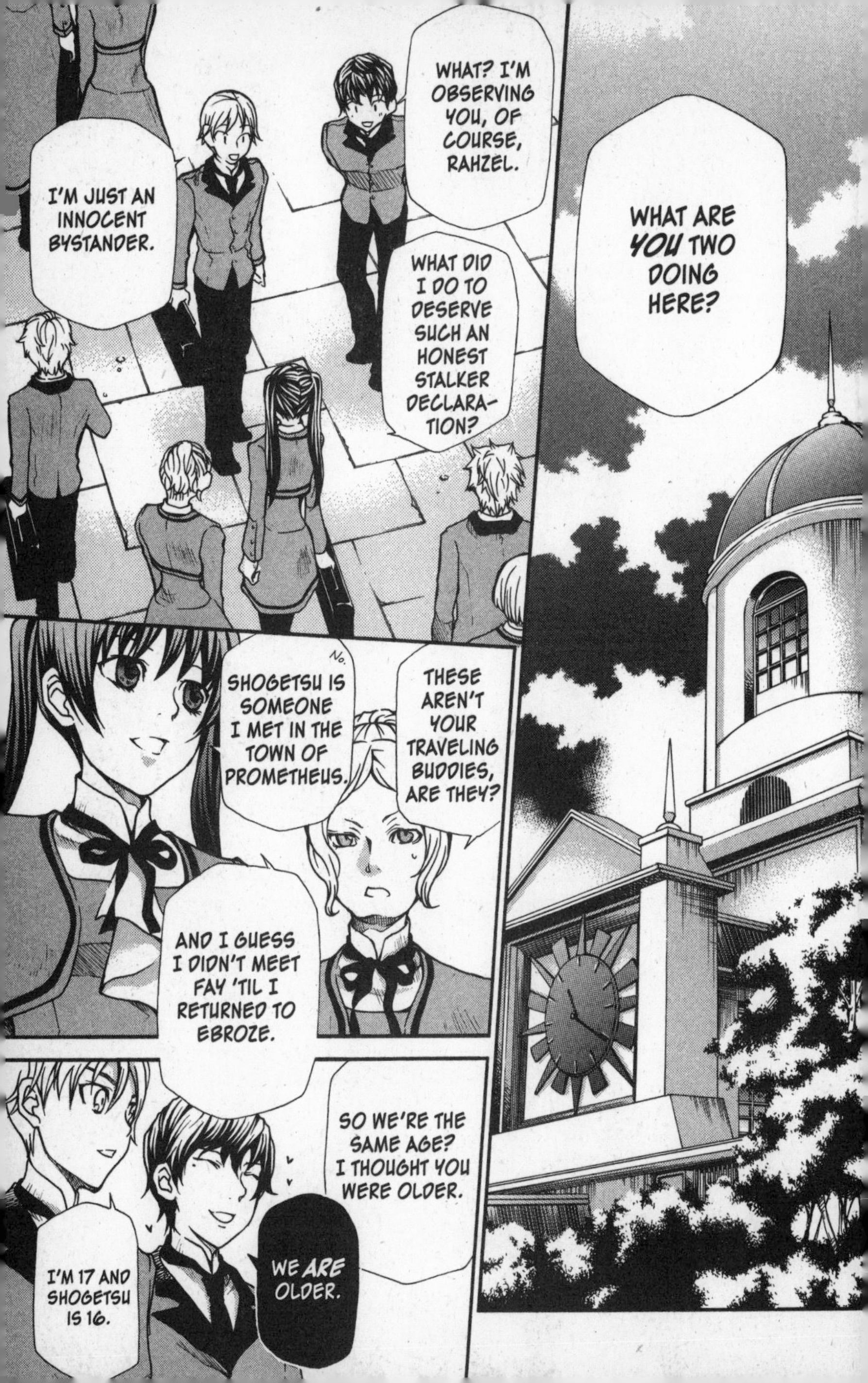
WHAT ARE *YOU* TWO DOING HERE?
WHAT? I'M OBSERVING YOU, OF COURSE, RAHZEL.
I'M JUST AN INNOCENT BYSTANDER.
WHAT DID I DO TO DESERVE SUCH AN HONEST STALKER DECLARATION?
THESE AREN'T YOUR TRAVELING BUDDIES, ARE THEY?
No.
SHOGETSU IS SOMEONE I MET IN THE TOWN OF PROMETHEUS.
AND I GUESS I DIDN'T MEET FAY 'TIL I RETURNED TO EBROZE.
SO WE'RE THE SAME AGE? I THOUGHT YOU WERE OLDER.
WE *ARE* OLDER.
I'M 17 AND SHOGETSU IS 16.

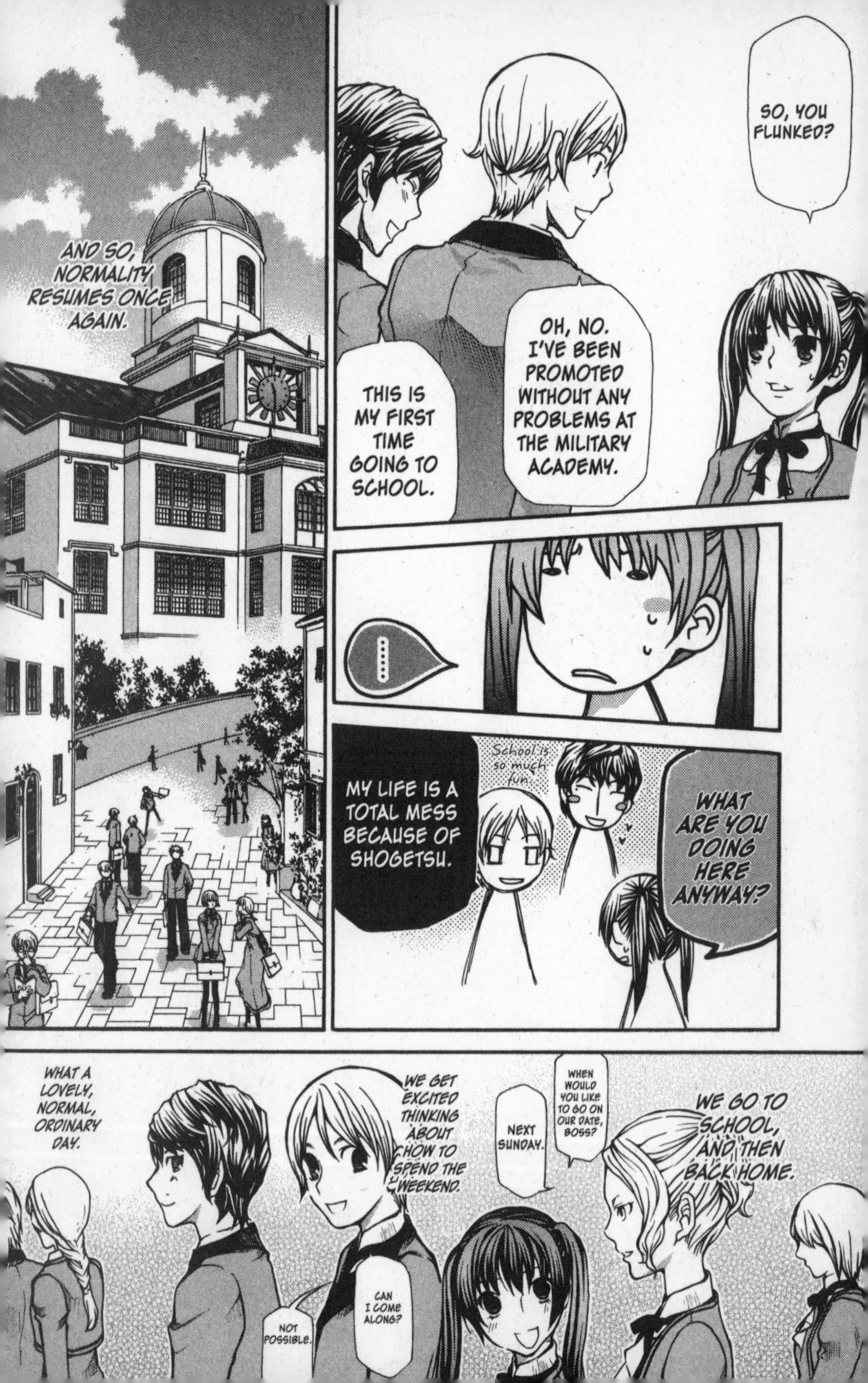
SO, YOU FLUNKED?
OH, NO. I'VE BEEN PROMOTED WITHOUT ANY PROBLEMS AT THE MILITARY ACADEMY.
THIS IS MY FIRST TIME GOING TO SCHOOL.
......
WHAT ARE YOU DOING HERE ANYWAY?
School is so much fun.
MY LIFE IS A TOTAL MESS BECAUSE OF SHOGETSU.
AND SO, NORMALITY RESUMES ONCE AGAIN.
WE GO TO SCHOOL, AND THEN BACK HOME.
WHEN WOULD YOU LIKE TO GO ON OUR DATE, BOSS?
NEXT SUNDAY.
WE GET EXCITED THINKING ABOUT HOW TO SPEND THE WEEKEND.
WHAT A LOVELY, NORMAL, ORDINARY DAY.
CAN I COME ALONG?
NOT POSSIBLE.

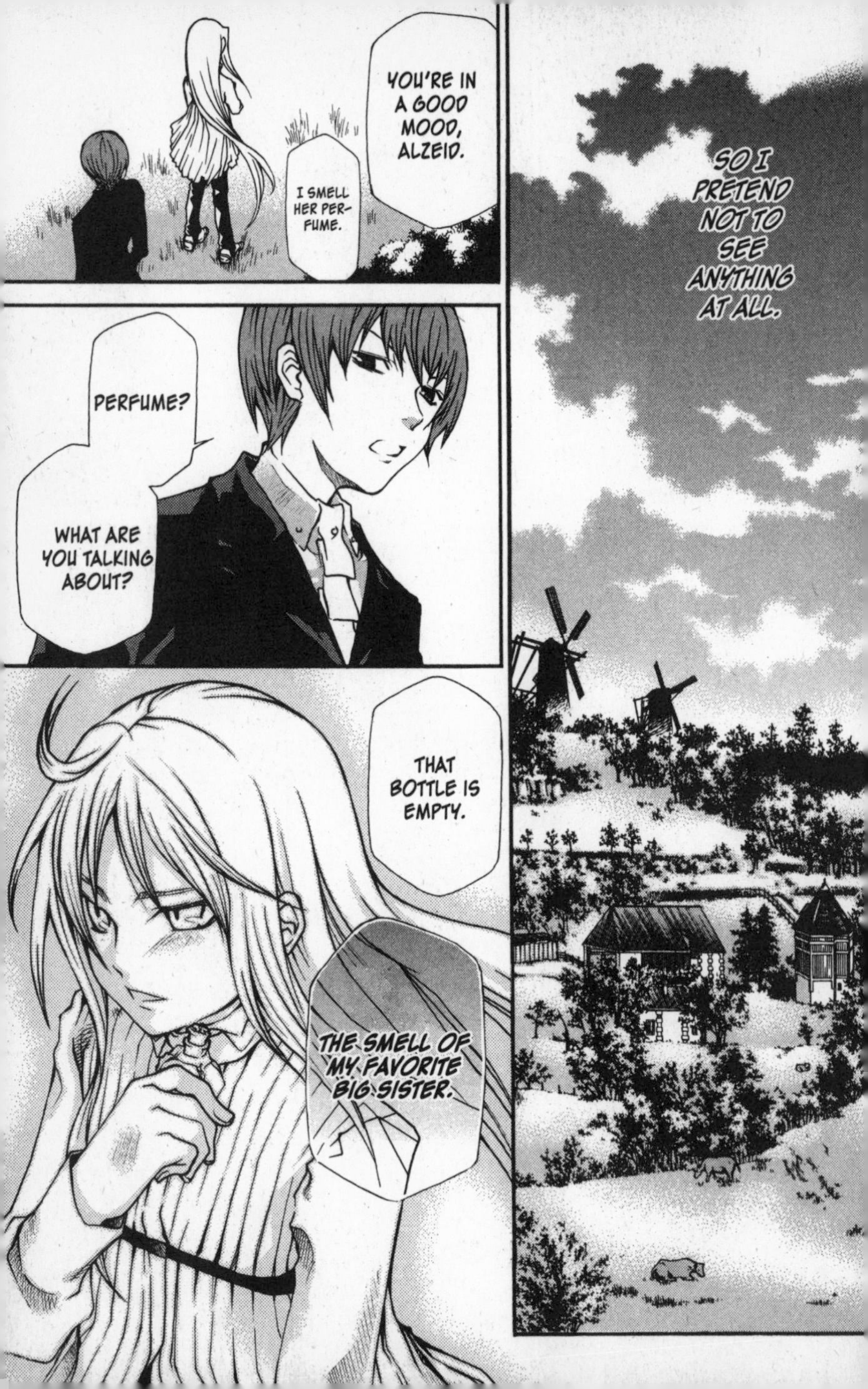
SO I PRETEND NOT TO SEE ANYTHING AT ALL.
YOU'RE IN A GOOD MOOD, ALZEID.
I SMELL HER PERFUME.
PERFUME?
WHAT ARE YOU TALKING ABOUT?
THAT BOTTLE IS EMPTY.
THE SMELL OF MY FAVORITE BIG SISTER.

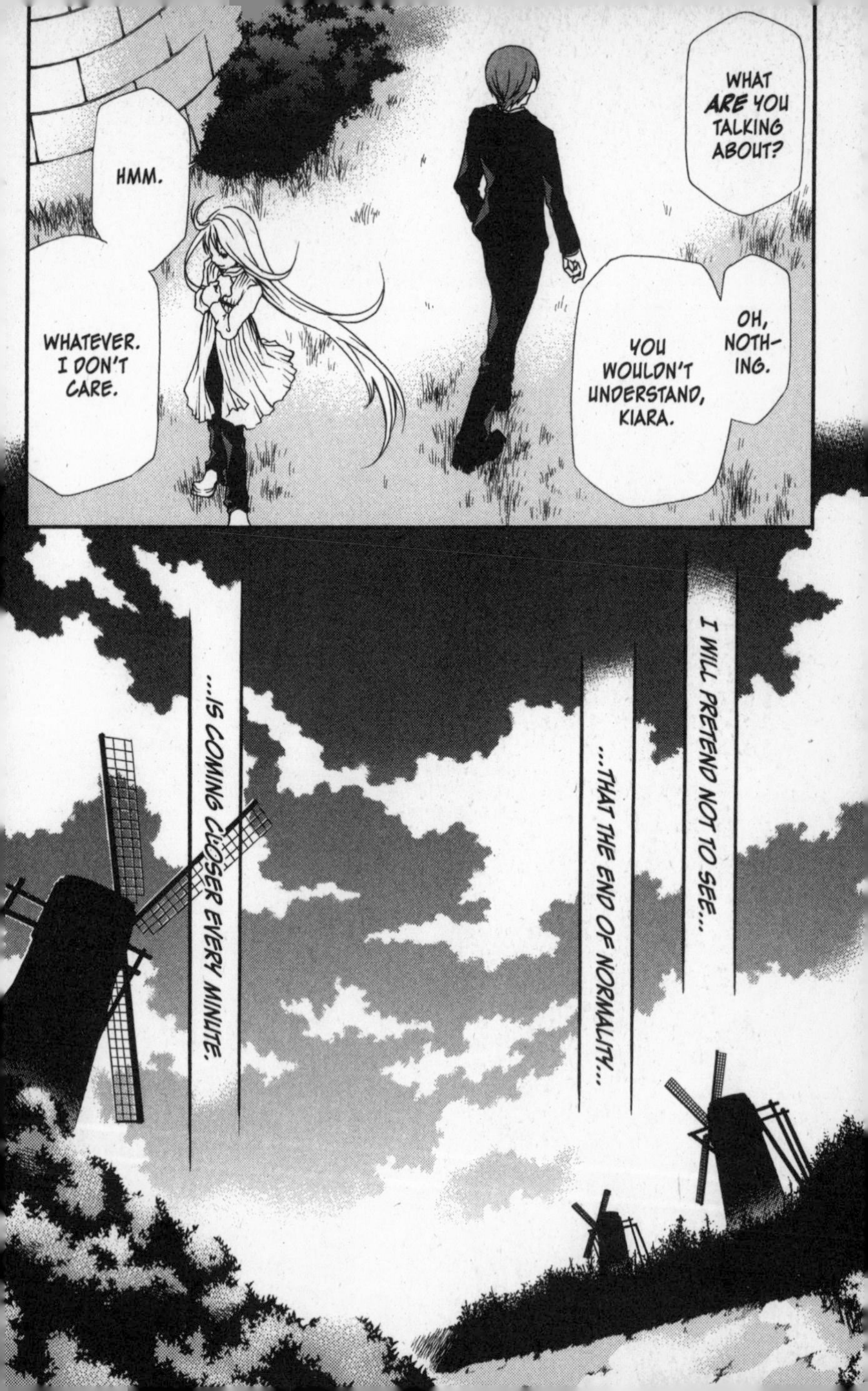
WHAT ARE YOU TALKING ABOUT?
OH, NOTH-ING.
YOU WOULDN'T UNDERSTAND, KIARA.
HMM.
WHATEVER. I DON'T CARE.
I WILL PRETEND NOT TO SEE...
...THAT THE END OF NORMALITY...
...IS COMING CLOSER EVERY MINUTE.

Chapter 70: Back to the Routine Part 4: The Destroyer Cometh

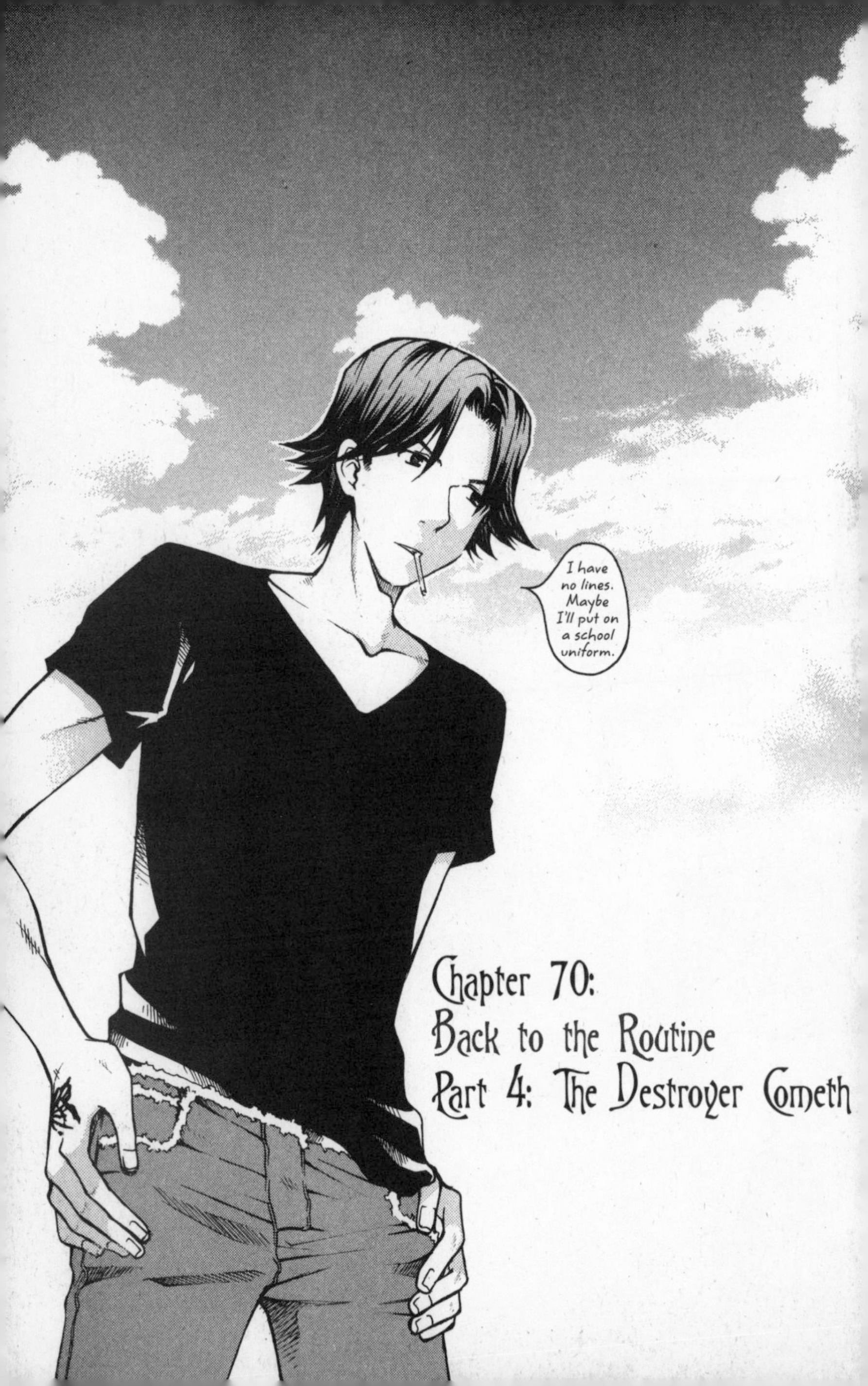
I have no lines. Maybe I'll put on a school uniform.

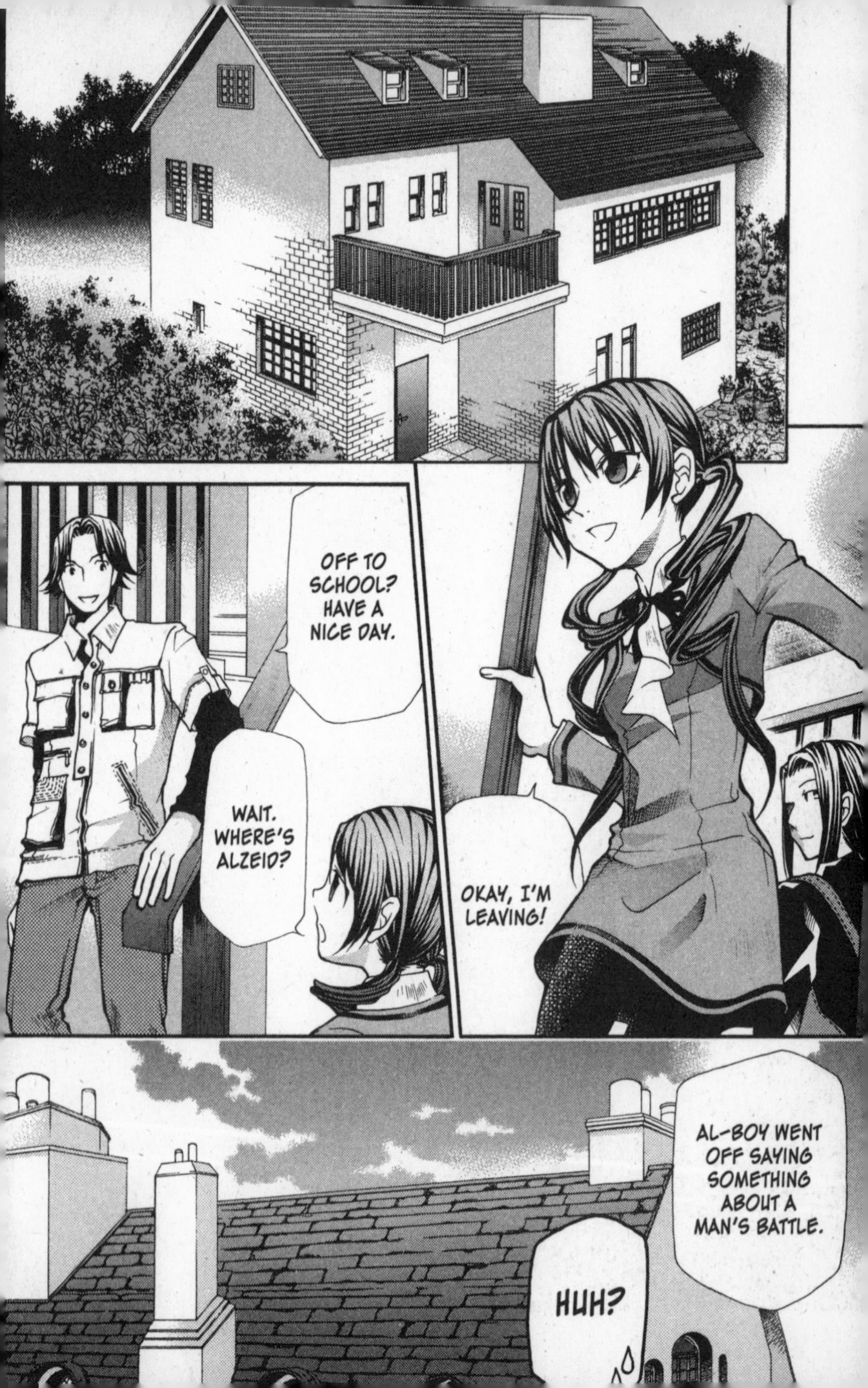
OKAY, I'M LEAVING!
OFF TO SCHOOL? HAVE A NICE DAY.
WAIT. WHERE'S ALZEID?
AL-BOY WENT OFF SAYING SOMETHING ABOUT A MAN'S BATTLE.
HUH?

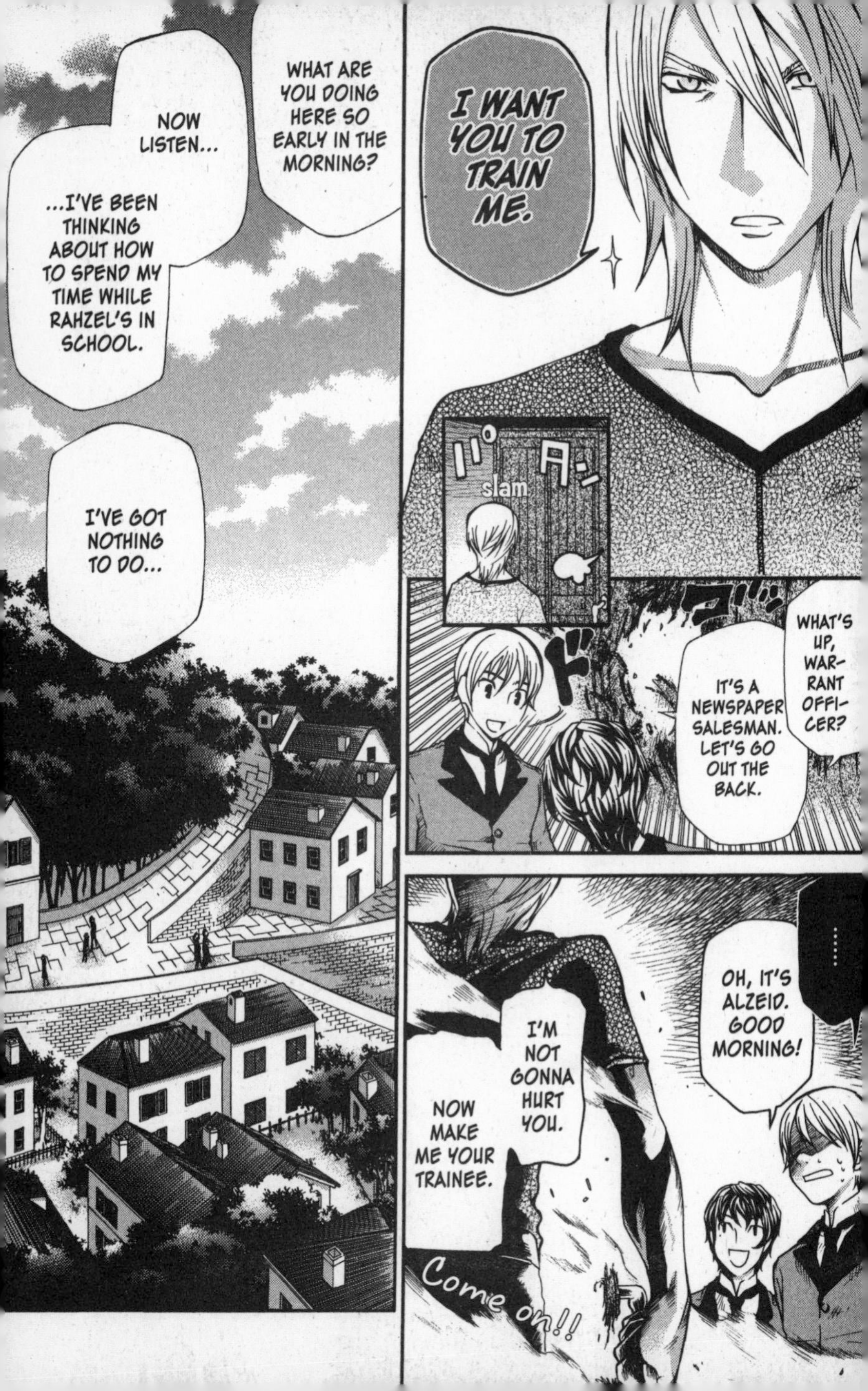
I WANT YOU TO TRAIN ME.
slam
WHAT'S UP, WAR-RANT OFFI-CER?
IT'S A NEWSPAPER SALESMAN. LET'S GO OUT THE BACK.
……
OH, IT'S ALZEID. GOOD MORNING!
I'M NOT GONNA HURT YOU.
NOW MAKE ME YOUR TRAINEE.
Come on!!
WHAT ARE YOU DOING HERE SO EARLY IN THE MORNING?
NOW LISTEN...
...I'VE BEEN THINKING ABOUT HOW TO SPEND MY TIME WHILE RAHZEL'S IN SCHOOL.
I'VE GOT NOTHING TO DO...

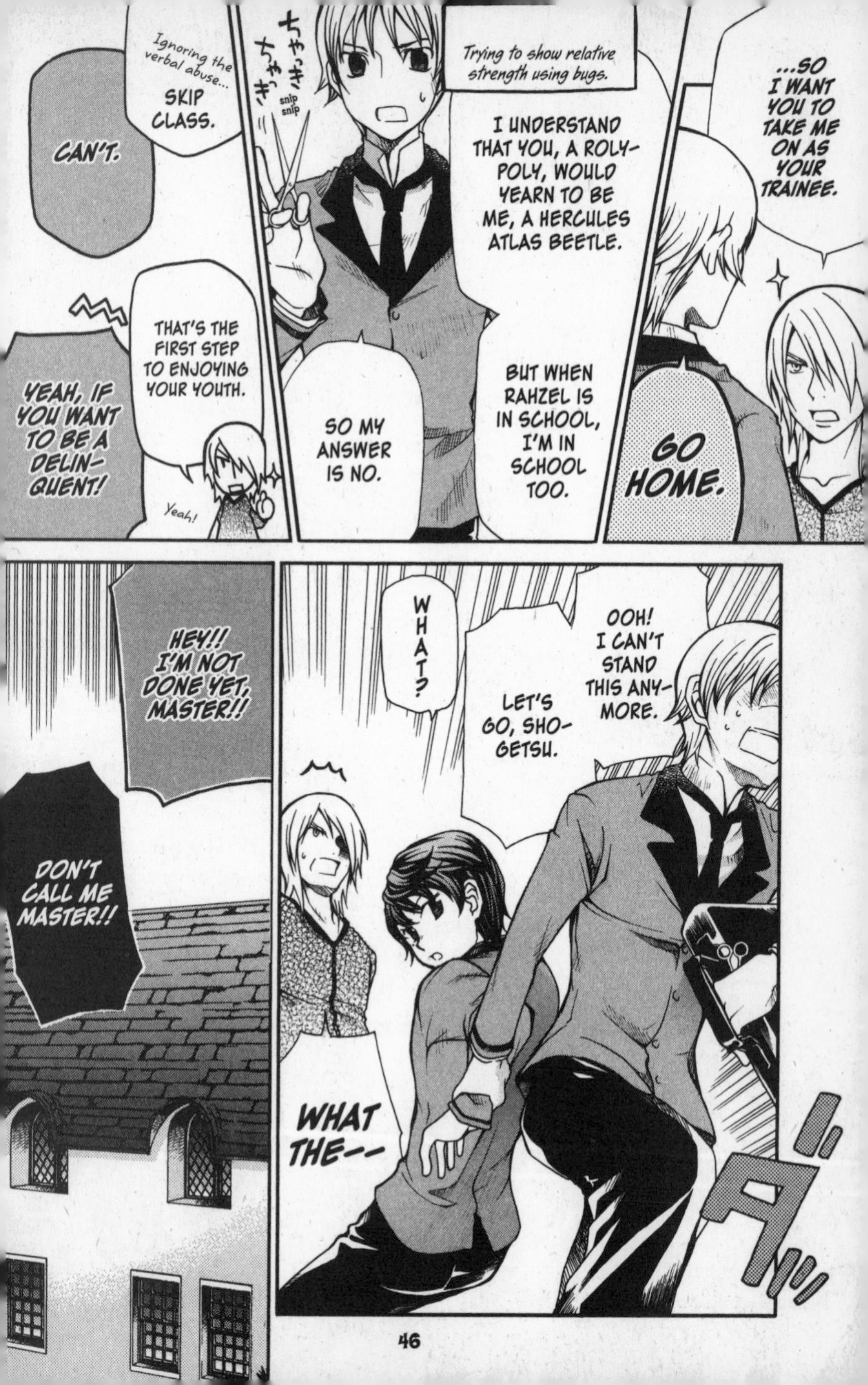
...SO I WANT YOU TO TAKE ME ON AS YOUR TRAINEE.
GO HOME.
Trying to show relative strength using bugs.
I UNDERSTAND THAT YOU, A ROLY-POLY, WOULD YEARN TO BE ME, A HERCULES ATLAS BEETLE.
BUT WHEN RAHZEL IS IN SCHOOL, I'M IN SCHOOL TOO.
ちゃっきちゃっき
snip snip
SO MY ANSWER IS NO.
Ignoring the verbal abuse...
SKIP CLASS.
CAN'T.
THAT'S THE FIRST STEP TO ENJOYING YOUR YOUTH.
YEAH, IF YOU WANT TO BE A DELIN-QUENT!
Yeah!
OOH! I CAN'T STAND THIS ANY-MORE.
LET'S GO, SHO-GETSU.
WHAT?
WHAT THE--
HEY!! I'M NOT DONE YET, MASTER!!
DON'T CALL ME MASTER!!

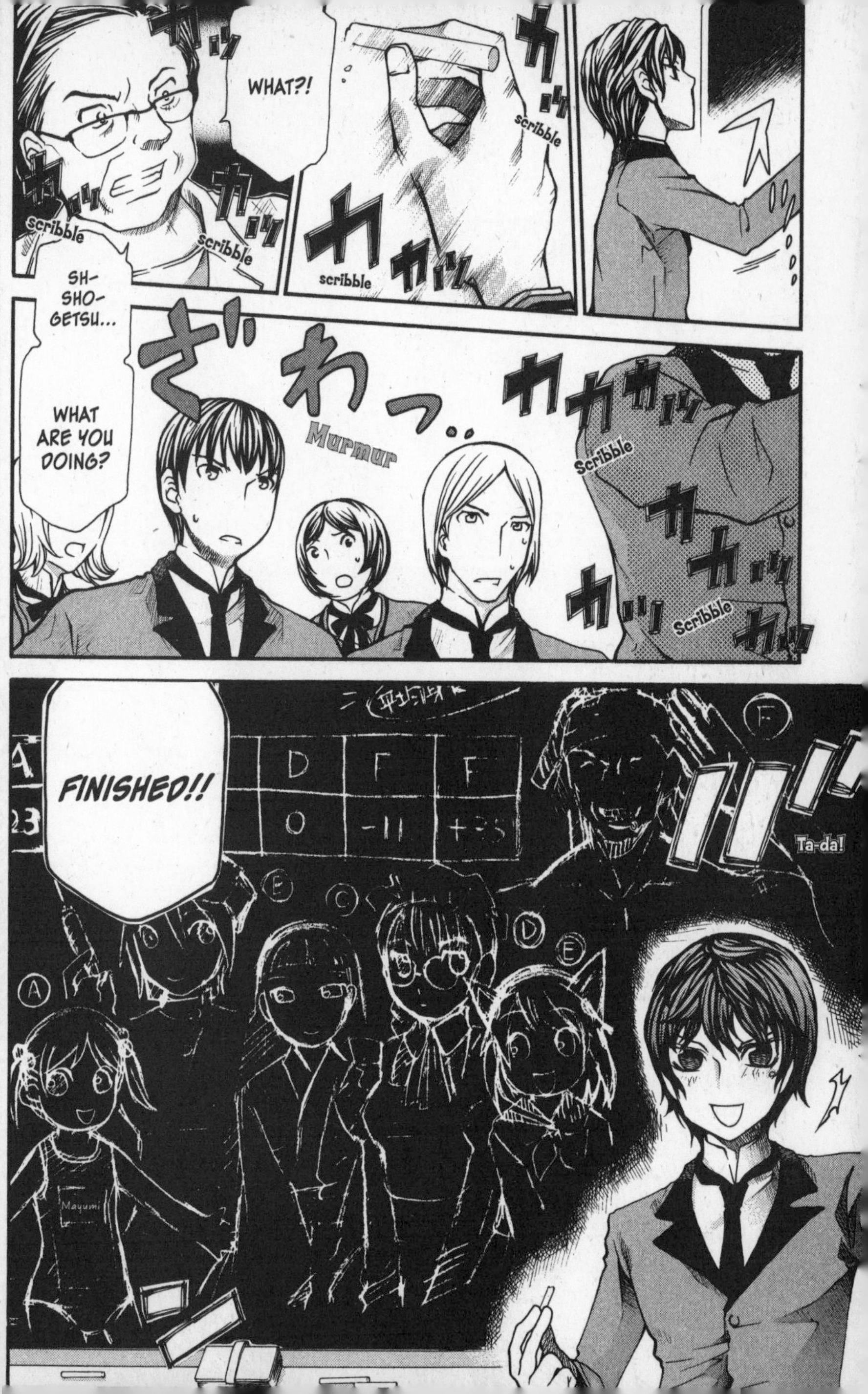
scribble
WHAT?!
scribble
scribble
scribble
Scribble
Scribble
Murmur
SH-SHO-GETSU...
WHAT ARE YOU DOING?
Ta-da!
FINISHED!!
Mayumi

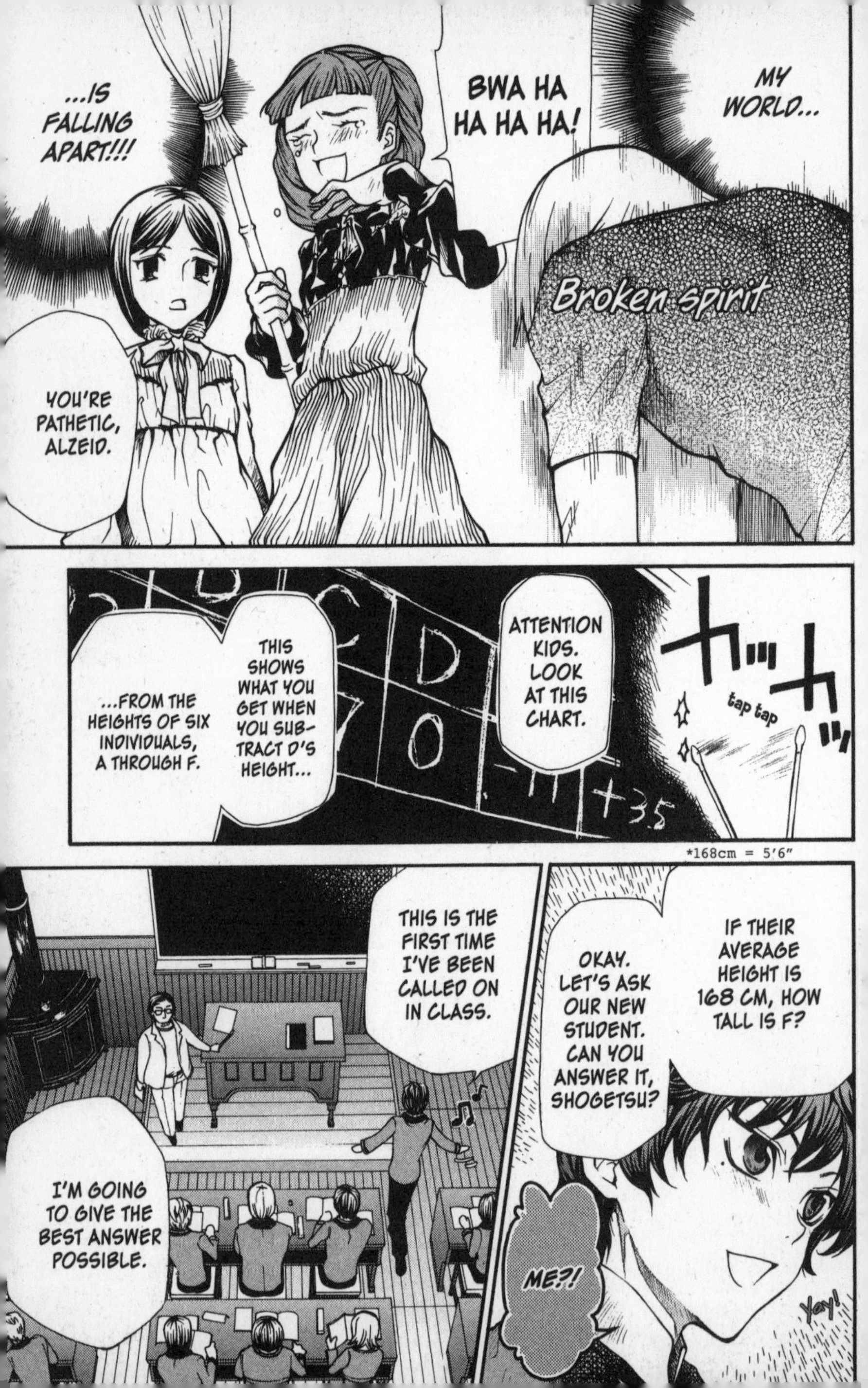
MY WORLD...
BWA HA HA HA HA!
...IS FALLING APART!!!
Broken spirit
YOU'RE PATHETIC, ALZEID.
tap tap
ATTENTION KIDS. LOOK AT THIS CHART.
THIS SHOWS WHAT YOU GET WHEN YOU SUBTRACT D'S HEIGHT...
...FROM THE HEIGHTS OF SIX INDIVIDUALS, A THROUGH F.
IF THEIR AVERAGE HEIGHT IS 168 CM, HOW TALL IS F?
OKAY. LET'S ASK OUR NEW STUDENT. CAN YOU ANSWER IT, SHOGETSU?
Yay!
ME?!
THIS IS THE FIRST TIME I'VE BEEN CALLED ON IN CLASS.
I'M GOING TO GIVE THE BEST ANSWER POSSIBLE.

*168cm = 5'6"

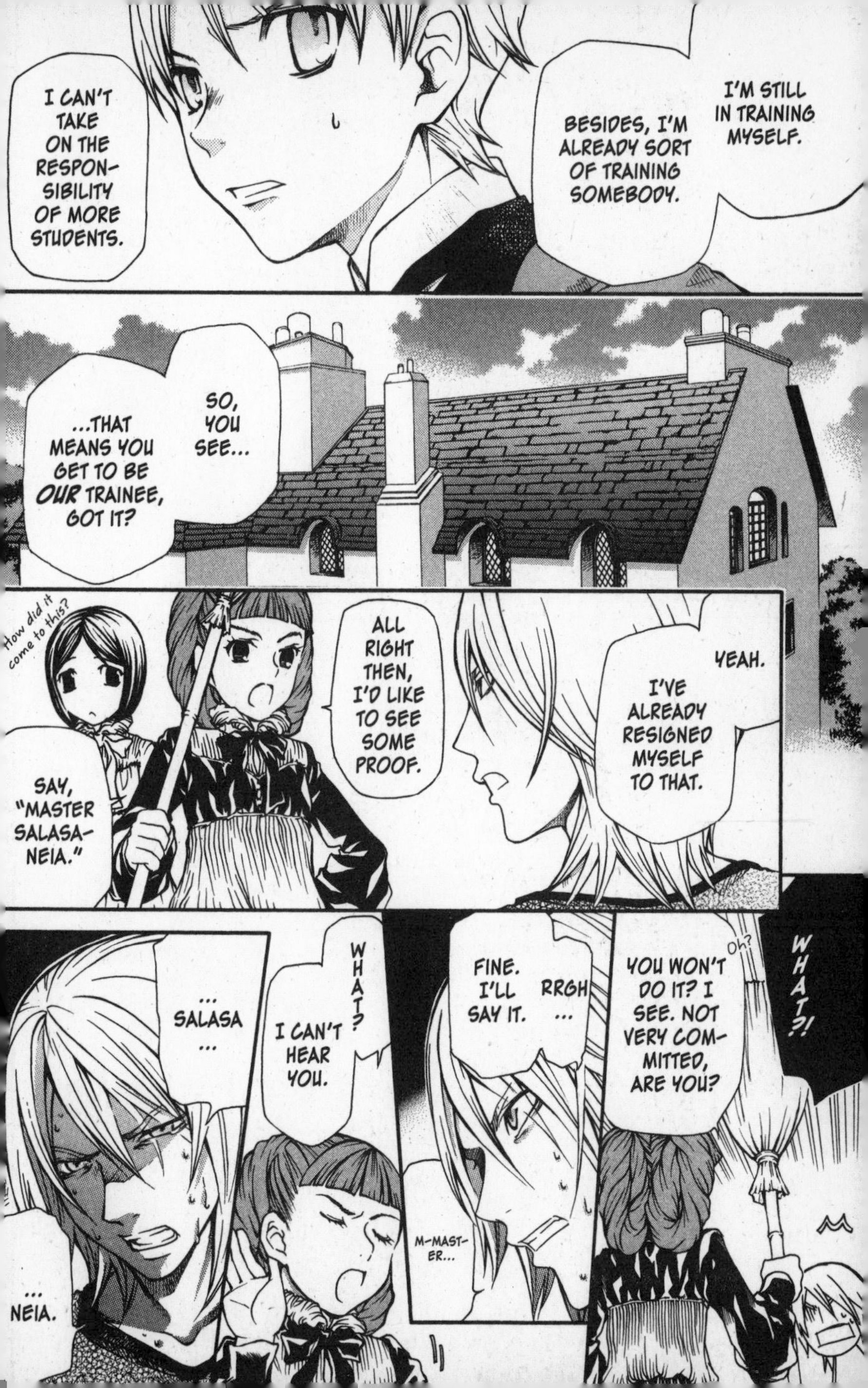
I'M STILL IN TRAINING MYSELF.
BESIDES, I'M ALREADY SORT OF TRAINING SOMEBODY.
I CAN'T TAKE ON THE RESPON-SIBILITY OF MORE STUDENTS.
SO, YOU SEE...
...THAT MEANS YOU GET TO BE OUR TRAINEE, GOT IT?
YEAH.
I'VE ALREADY RESIGNED MYSELF TO THAT.
ALL RIGHT THEN, I'D LIKE TO SEE SOME PROOF.
SAY, "MASTER SALASA-NEIA."
How did it come to this?
WHAT?!
Oh?
YOU WON'T DO IT? I SEE. NOT VERY COM-MITTED, ARE YOU?
RRGH...
FINE. I'LL SAY IT.
M-MAST-ER...
WHAT?
I CAN'T HEAR YOU.
...SALASA...
...NEIA.

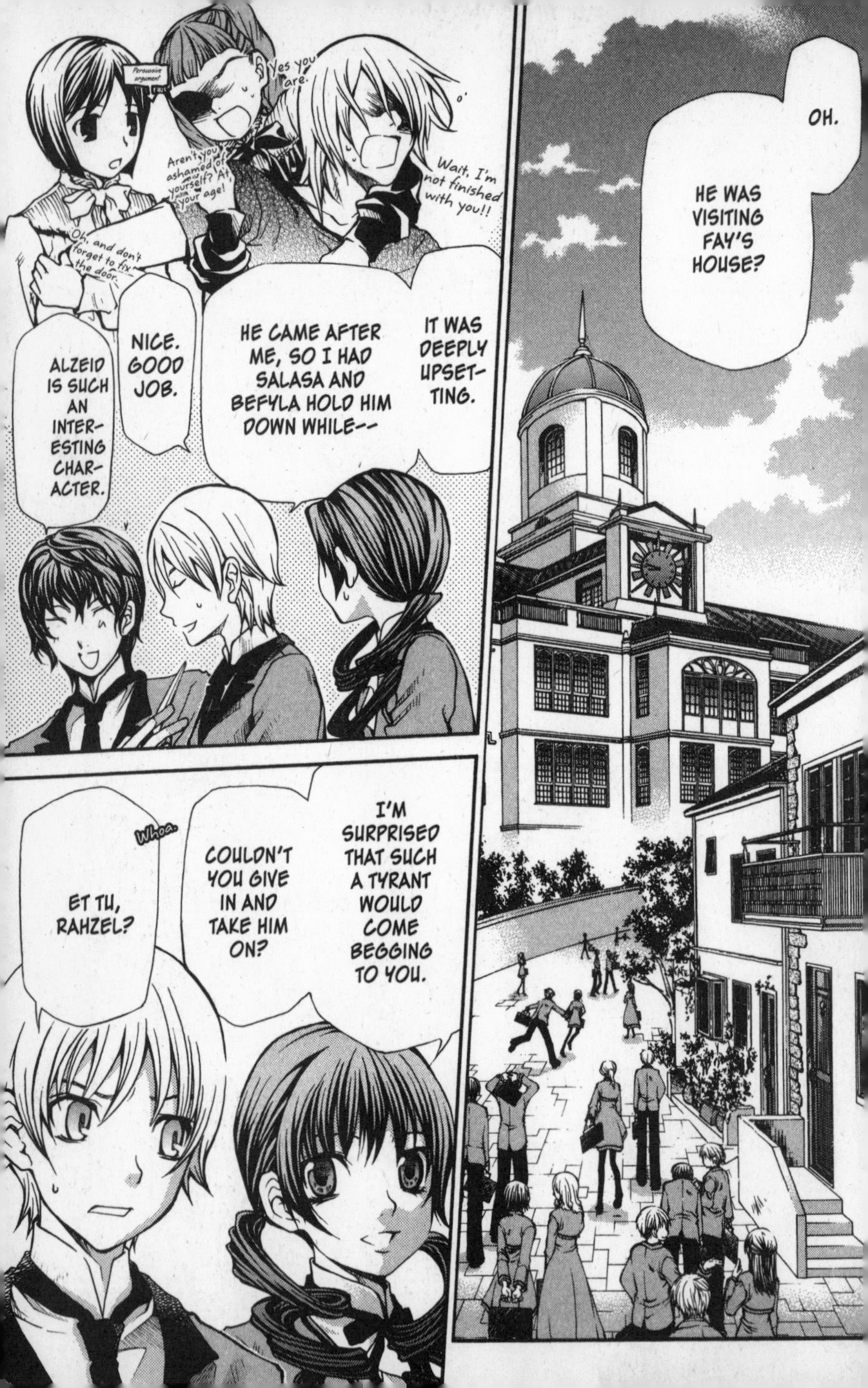
OH.
HE WAS VISITING FAY'S HOUSE?
Wait, I'm not finished with you!!
Yes you are.
Persuasive argument
Aren't you ashamed of yourself? At your age!
Oh, and don't forget to fix the door.
IT WAS DEEPLY UPSET-TING.
HE CAME AFTER ME, SO I HAD SALASA AND BEFYLA HOLD HIM DOWN WHILE--
NICE. GOOD JOB.
ALZEID IS SUCH AN INTER-ESTING CHAR-ACTER.
I'M SURPRISED THAT SUCH A TYRANT WOULD COME BEGGING TO YOU.
COULDN'T YOU GIVE IN AND TAKE HIM ON?
Whoa.
ET TU, RAHZEL?

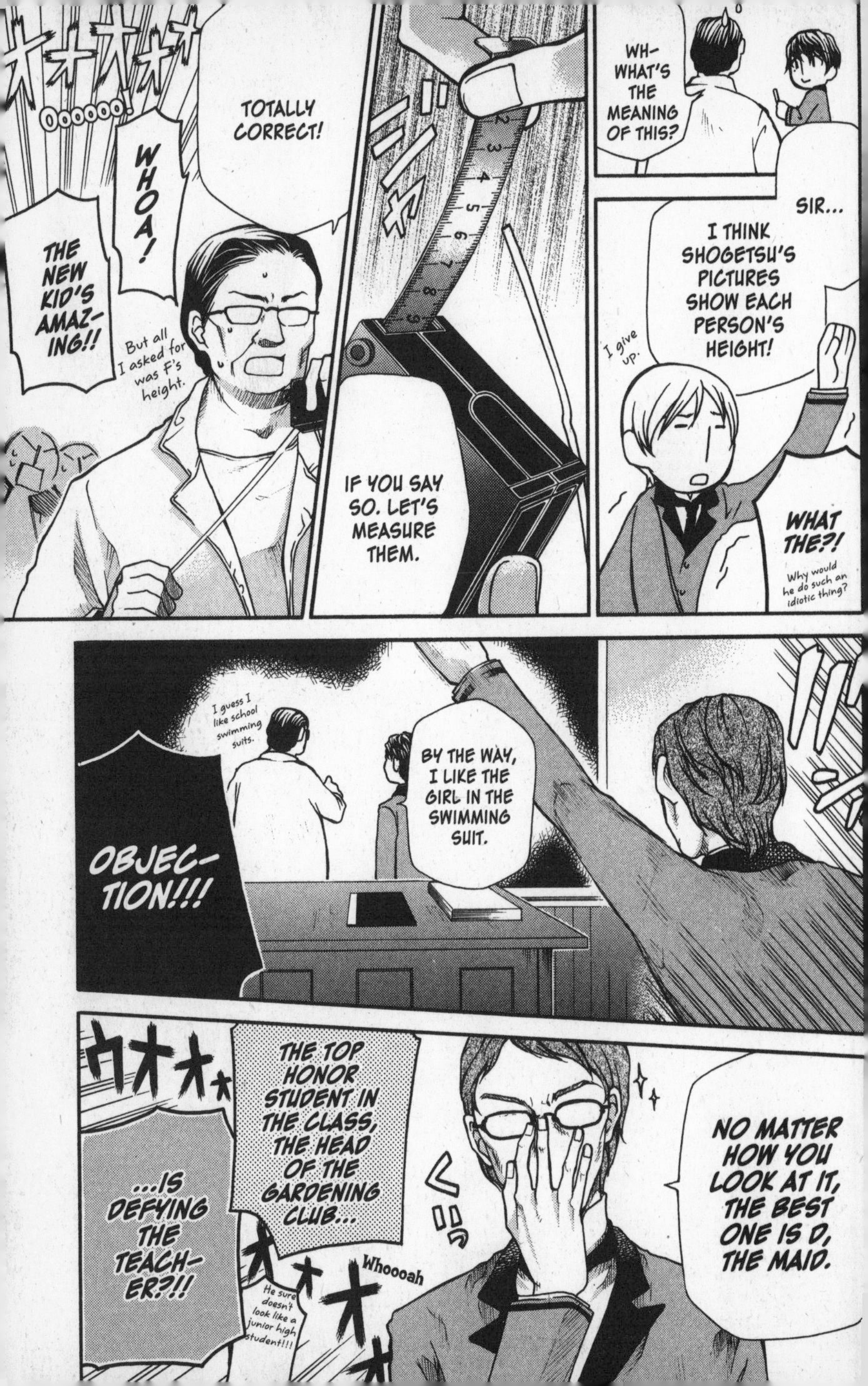
WH-WHAT'S THE MEANING OF THIS?
SIR...
I THINK SHOGETSU'S PICTURES SHOW EACH PERSON'S HEIGHT!
I give up.
WHAT THE?!
Why would he do such an idiotic thing?
IF YOU SAY SO. LET'S MEASURE THEM.
TOTALLY CORRECT!
WHOA!
THE NEW KID'S AMAZING!!
But all I asked for was F's height.
Oooooo!
BY THE WAY, I LIKE THE GIRL IN THE SWIMMING SUIT.
I guess I like school swimming suits.
OBJECTION!!!
NO MATTER HOW YOU LOOK AT IT, THE BEST ONE IS D, THE MAID.
THE TOP HONOR STUDENT IN THE CLASS, THE HEAD OF THE GARDENING CLUB...
...IS DEFYING THE TEACHER?!!
Whoooah
He sure doesn't look like a junior high student!!!

OF COURSE, I'M PARTIAL TOWARD THE GENTLEMAN, F.

HIS BEAUTY IS ALMOST CRIMINAL...

ALL RIGHT. I'M GOING TO PASS AROUND SOME PAPER, AND EVERYONE WILL VOTE.

MAKE SURE YOU VOTE FOR ONE PERSON FROM A TO E.

NO FAIR!! WHAT ABOUT F?!! CAN'T YOU VOTE FOR F, TEACHER?!!

OVERRULED!!

SCHOOL IS SUCH A FUN PLACE, WARRANT OFFICER.

YOU THINK SO? I'M GLAD.

HOW WOULD YOU LIKE TO PUT YOUR NECK INSIDE THIS ROPE?

Boo hoo

E... may-be...

IF YOU HANG OUT THE WINDOW, IT MIGHT BE EVEN MORE FUN.

ding dong

キーン

コン

カン

SINCE I MET YOU, MY LIFE HAS BECOME A TOTAL MESS!

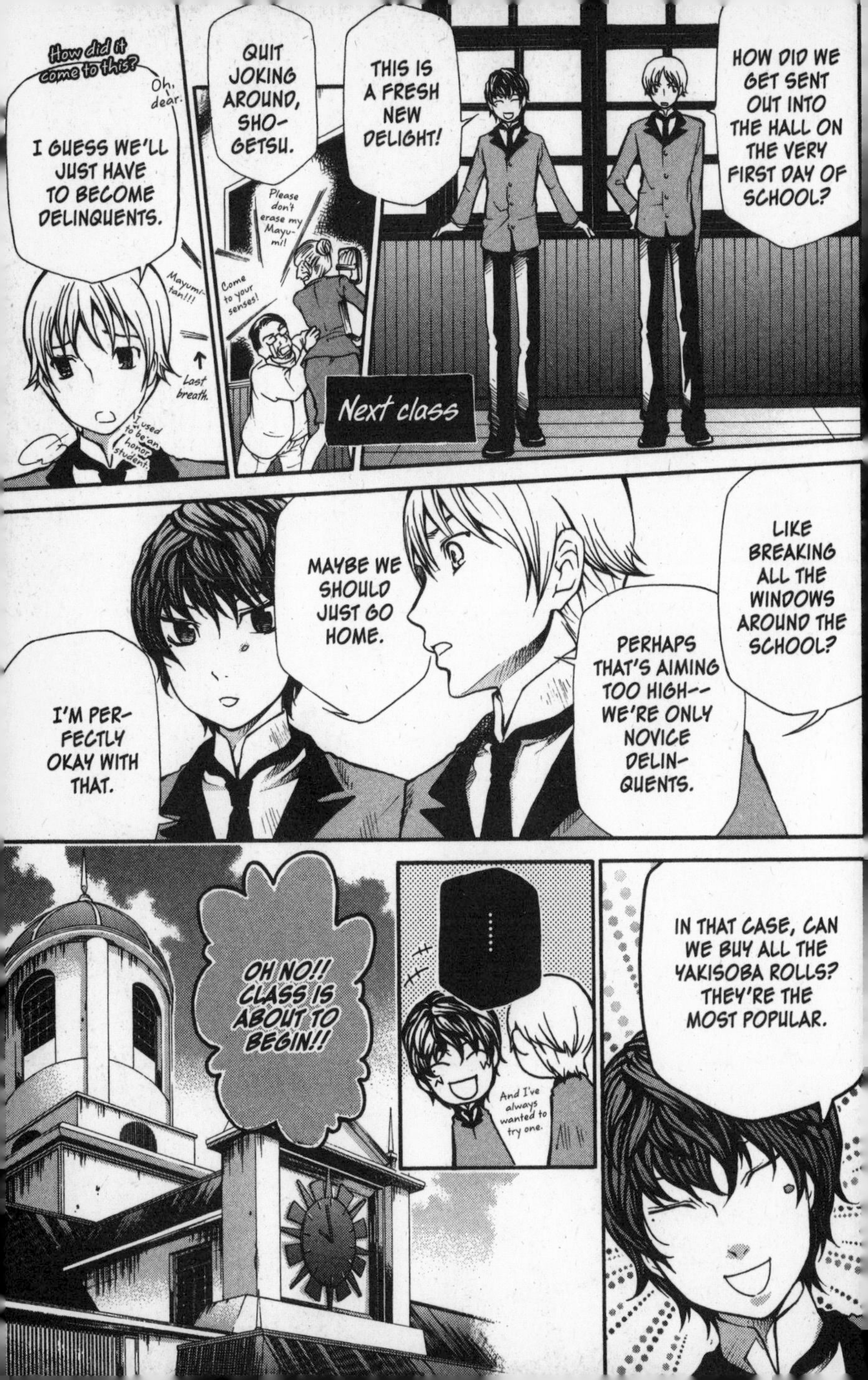
HOW DID WE GET SENT OUT INTO THE HALL ON THE VERY FIRST DAY OF SCHOOL?
THIS IS A FRESH NEW DELIGHT!
QUIT JOKING AROUND, SHO-GETSU.
Next class
Please don't erase my Mayumi!
Come to your senses!
Mayumi-tan!!!
Last breath.
How did it come to this?
Oh, dear.
I GUESS WE'LL JUST HAVE TO BECOME DELINQUENTS.
I used to be an honor student.
LIKE BREAKING ALL THE WINDOWS AROUND THE SCHOOL?
PERHAPS THAT'S AIMING TOO HIGH--WE'RE ONLY NOVICE DELIN-QUENTS.
MAYBE WE SHOULD JUST GO HOME.
I'M PER-FECTLY OKAY WITH THAT.
IN THAT CASE, CAN WE BUY ALL THE YAKISOBA ROLLS? THEY'RE THE MOST POPULAR.
......
And I've always wanted to try one.
OH NO!! CLASS IS ABOUT TO BEGIN!!

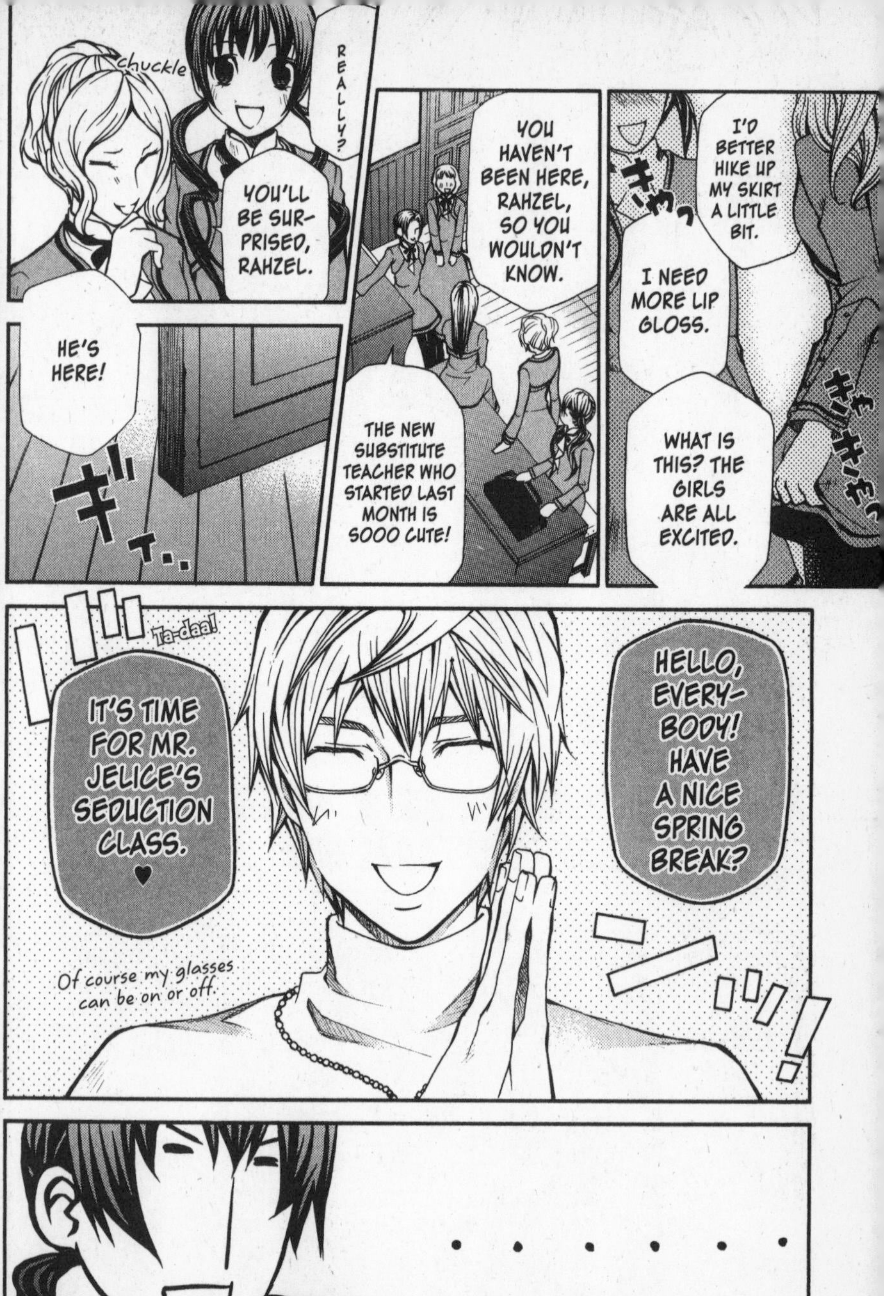

I'D BETTER HIKE UP MY SKIRT A LITTLE BIT.
I NEED MORE LIP GLOSS.
WHAT IS THIS? THE GIRLS ARE ALL EXCITED.
YOU HAVEN'T BEEN HERE, RAHZEL, SO YOU WOULDN'T KNOW.
THE NEW SUBSTITUTE TEACHER WHO STARTED LAST MONTH IS SOOO CUTE!
REALLY?
chuckle
YOU'LL BE SURPRISED, RAHZEL.
HE'S HERE!
HELLO, EVERYBODY! HAVE A NICE SPRING BREAK?
Ta-daa!
IT'S TIME FOR MR. JELICE'S SEDUCTION CLASS. ♥
Of course my glasses can be on or off.
. . . . . .

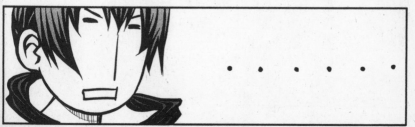

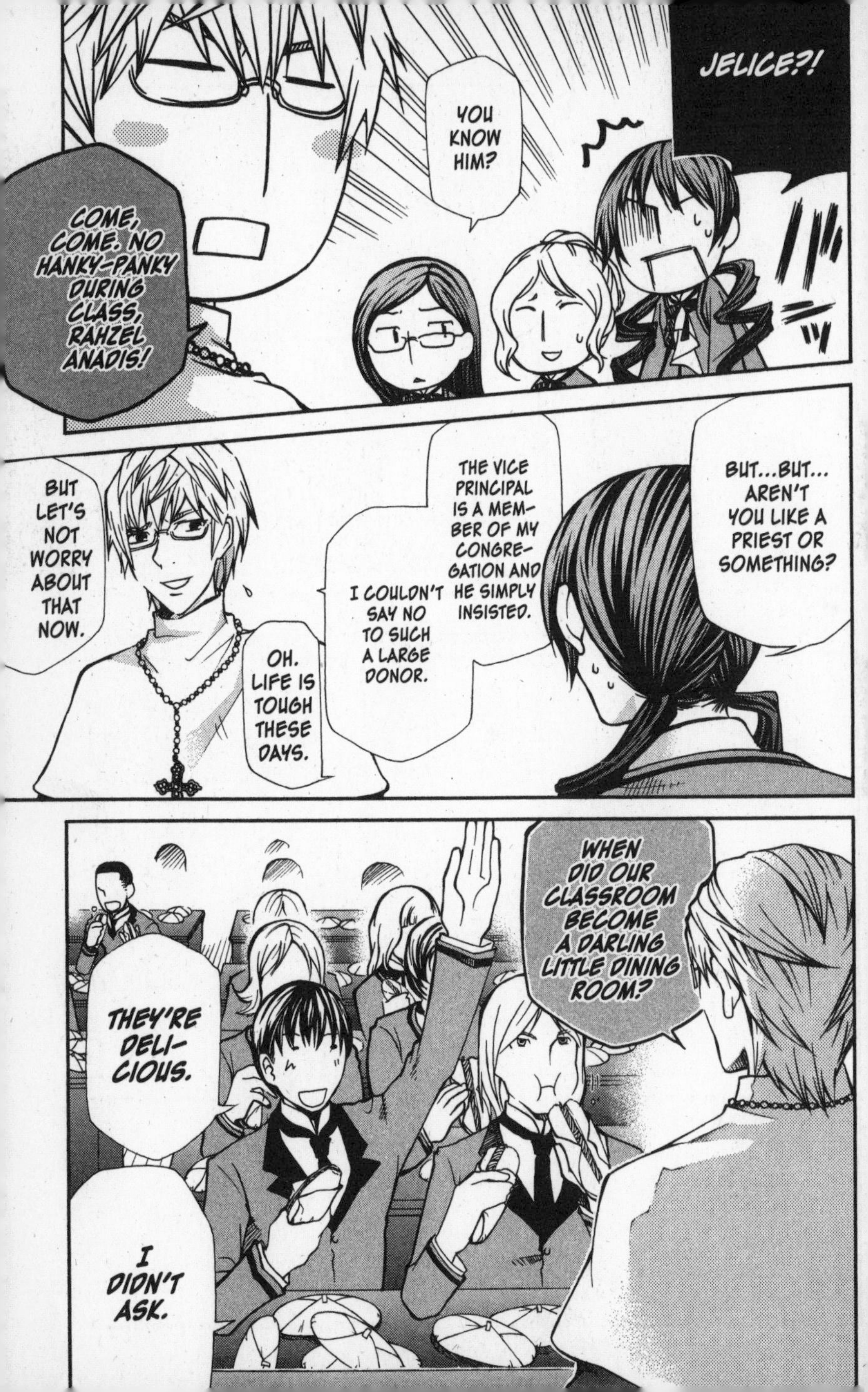
JELICE?!
YOU KNOW HIM?
COME, COME. NO HANKY-PANKY DURING CLASS, RAHZEL ANADIS!
BUT...BUT... AREN'T YOU LIKE A PRIEST OR SOMETHING?
THE VICE PRINCIPAL IS A MEMBER OF MY CONGREGATION AND HE SIMPLY INSISTED.
I COULDN'T SAY NO TO SUCH A LARGE DONOR.
OH. LIFE IS TOUGH THESE DAYS.
BUT LET'S NOT WORRY ABOUT THAT NOW.
WHEN DID OUR CLASSROOM BECOME A DARLING LITTLE DINING ROOM?
THEY'RE DELICIOUS.
I DIDN'T ASK.

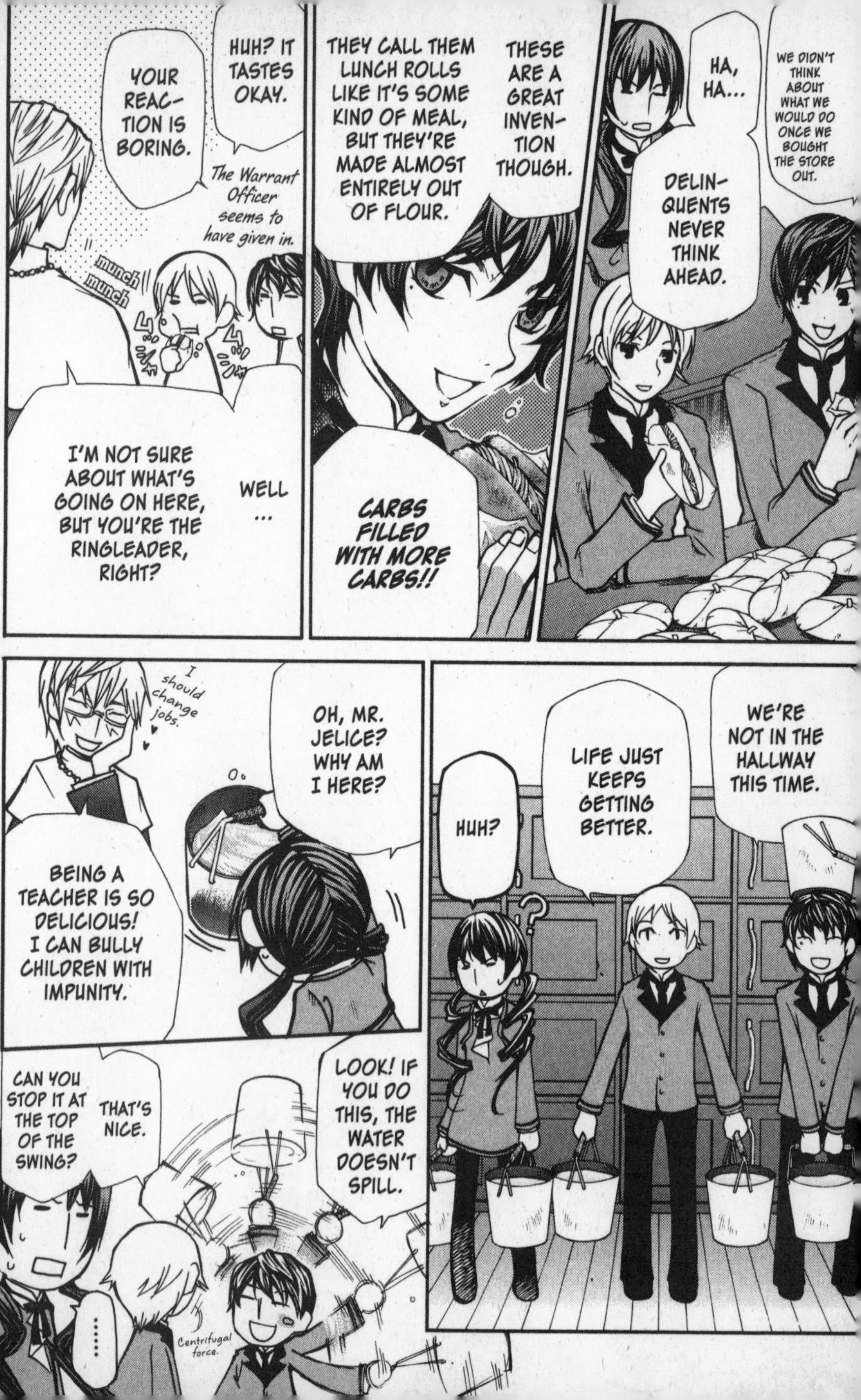
WE DIDN'T THINK ABOUT WHAT WE WOULD DO ONCE WE BOUGHT THE STORE OUT.
HA, HA...
DELIN-QUENTS NEVER THINK AHEAD.
THESE ARE A GREAT INVEN-TION THOUGH.
THEY CALL THEM LUNCH ROLLS LIKE IT'S SOME KIND OF MEAL, BUT THEY'RE MADE ALMOST ENTIRELY OUT OF FLOUR.
CARBS FILLED WITH MORE CARBS!!
HUH? IT TASTES OKAY.
YOUR REAC-TION IS BORING.
The Warrant Officer seems to have given in.
munch munch
WELL ...
I'M NOT SURE ABOUT WHAT'S GOING ON HERE, BUT YOU'RE THE RINGLEADER, RIGHT?
WE'RE NOT IN THE HALLWAY THIS TIME.
LIFE JUST KEEPS GETTING BETTER.
HUH?
OH, MR. JELICE? WHY AM I HERE?
I should change jobs.
BEING A TEACHER IS SO DELICIOUS! I CAN BULLY CHILDREN WITH IMPUNITY.
LOOK! IF YOU DO THIS, THE WATER DOESN'T SPILL.
THAT'S NICE.
CAN YOU STOP IT AT THE TOP OF THE SWING?
......
Centrifugal force.

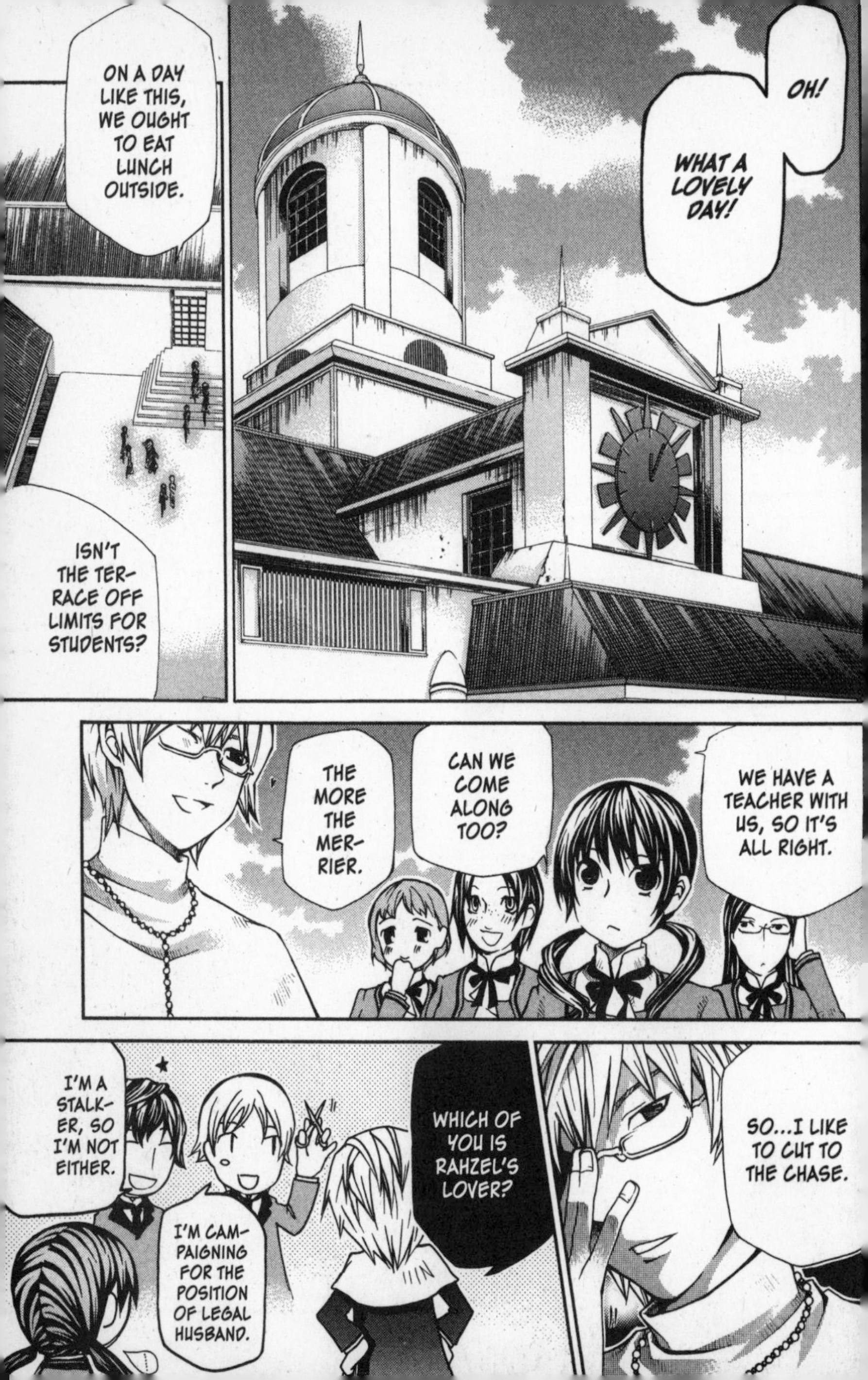
OH!
WHAT A LOVELY DAY!
ON A DAY LIKE THIS, WE OUGHT TO EAT LUNCH OUTSIDE.
ISN'T THE TER-RACE OFF LIMITS FOR STUDENTS?
WE HAVE A TEACHER WITH US, SO IT'S ALL RIGHT.
CAN WE COME ALONG TOO?
THE MORE THE MER-RIER.
SO...I LIKE TO CUT TO THE CHASE.
WHICH OF YOU IS RAHZEL'S LOVER?
I'M CAM-PAIGNING FOR THE POSITION OF LEGAL HUSBAND.
I'M A STALK-ER, SO I'M NOT EITHER.

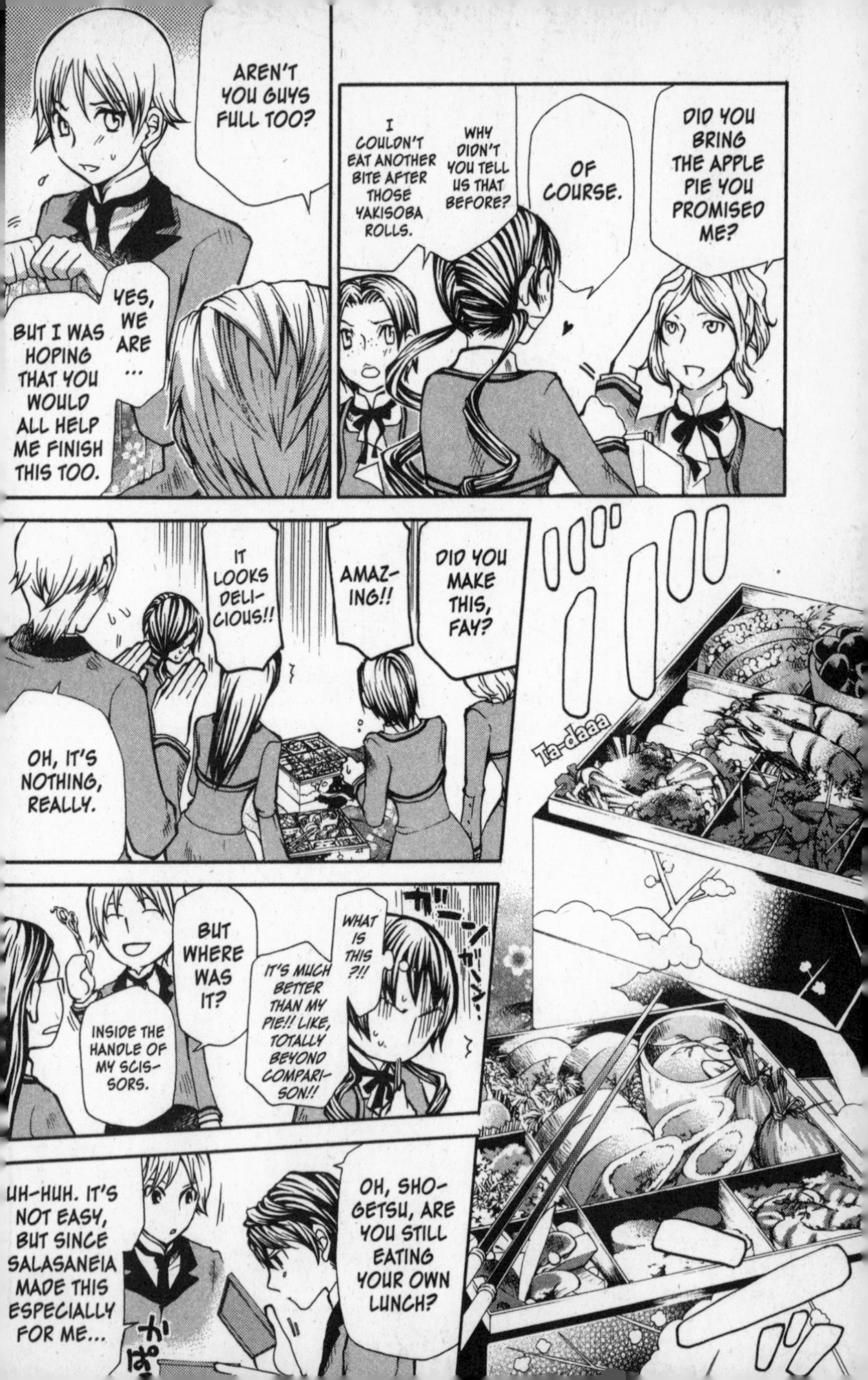
DID YOU BRING THE APPLE PIE YOU PROMISED ME?
OF COURSE.
WHY DIDN'T YOU TELL US THAT BEFORE?
I COULDN'T EAT ANOTHER BITE AFTER THOSE YAKISOBA ROLLS.
AREN'T YOU GUYS FULL TOO?
YES, WE ARE ...
BUT I WAS HOPING THAT YOU WOULD ALL HELP ME FINISH THIS TOO.
Ta-daaa
DID YOU MAKE THIS, FAY?
AMAZING!!
IT LOOKS DELICIOUS!!
OH, IT'S NOTHING, REALLY.
WHAT IS THIS?!!
IT'S MUCH BETTER THAN MY PIE!! LIKE, TOTALLY BEYOND COMPARISON!!
BUT WHERE WAS IT?
INSIDE THE HANDLE OF MY SCISSORS.
OH, SHOGETSU, ARE YOU STILL EATING YOUR OWN LUNCH?
UH-HUH. IT'S NOT EASY, BUT SINCE SALASANEIA MADE THIS ESPECIALLY FOR ME...

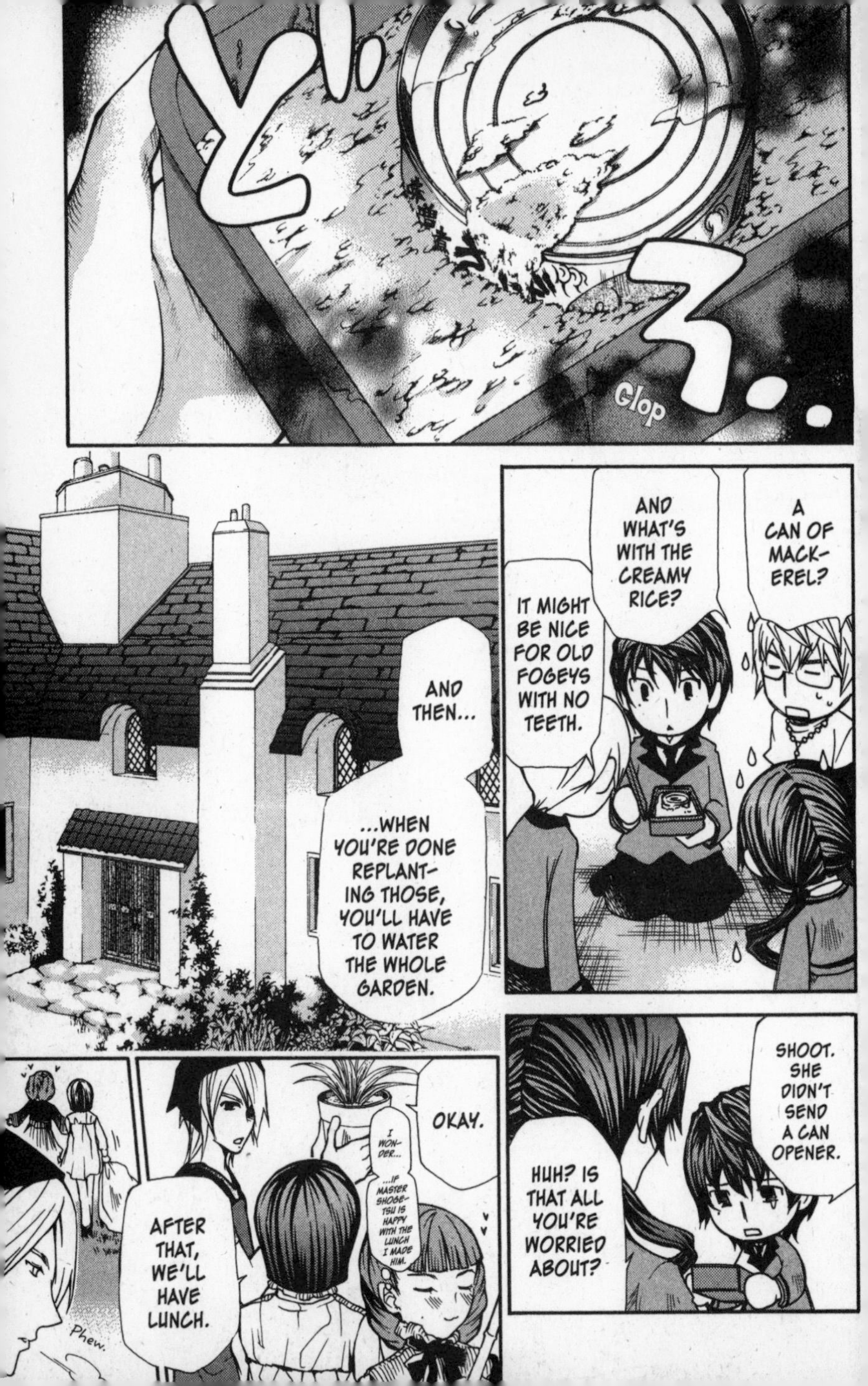
Glop
A CAN OF MACK-ERREL?
AND WHAT'S WITH THE CREAMY RICE?
IT MIGHT BE NICE FOR OLD FOGEYS WITH NO TEETH.
AND THEN...
...WHEN YOU'RE DONE REPLANT-ING THOSE, YOU'LL HAVE TO WATER THE WHOLE GARDEN.
SHOOT. SHE DIDN'T SEND A CAN OPENER.
HUH? IS THAT ALL YOU'RE WORRIED ABOUT?
OKAY.
I WONDER...
...IF MASTER SHOGE-TSU IS HAPPY WITH THE LUNCH I MADE HIM.
AFTER THAT, WE'LL HAVE LUNCH.
Phew.

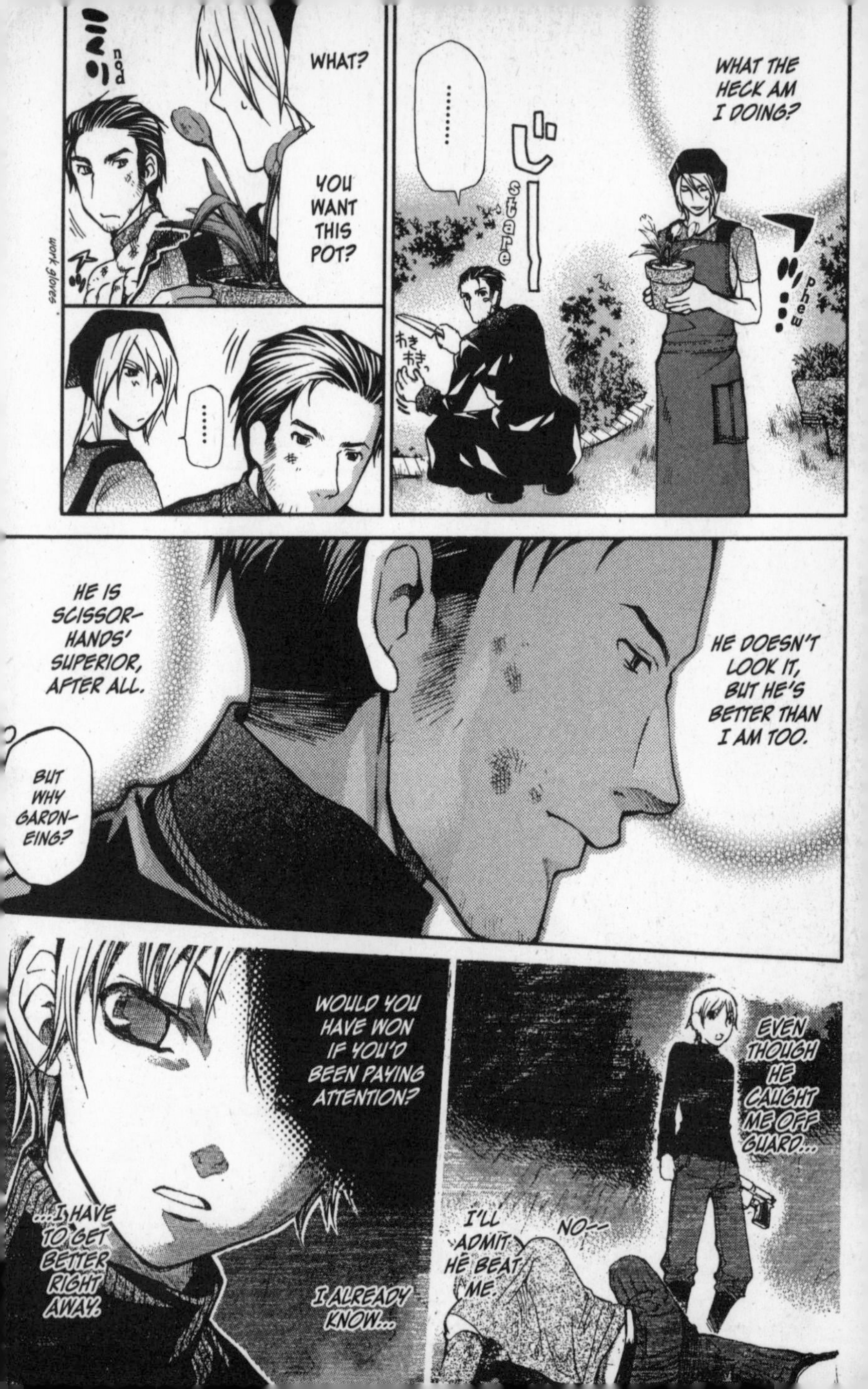
WHAT THE HECK AM I DOING?
phew
stare
......
わきわきっ
WHAT?
YOU WANT THIS POT?
nod
work gloves
......
HE DOESN'T LOOK IT, BUT HE'S BETTER THAN I AM TOO.
HE IS SCISSOR-HANDS' SUPERIOR, AFTER ALL.
BUT WHY GARDN-EING?
EVEN THOUGH HE CAUGHT ME OFF GUARD...
NO--
I'LL ADMIT HE BEAT ME.
WOULD YOU HAVE WON IF YOU'D BEEN PAYING ATTENTION?
I ALREADY KNOW...
...I HAVE TO GET BETTER RIGHT AWAY.

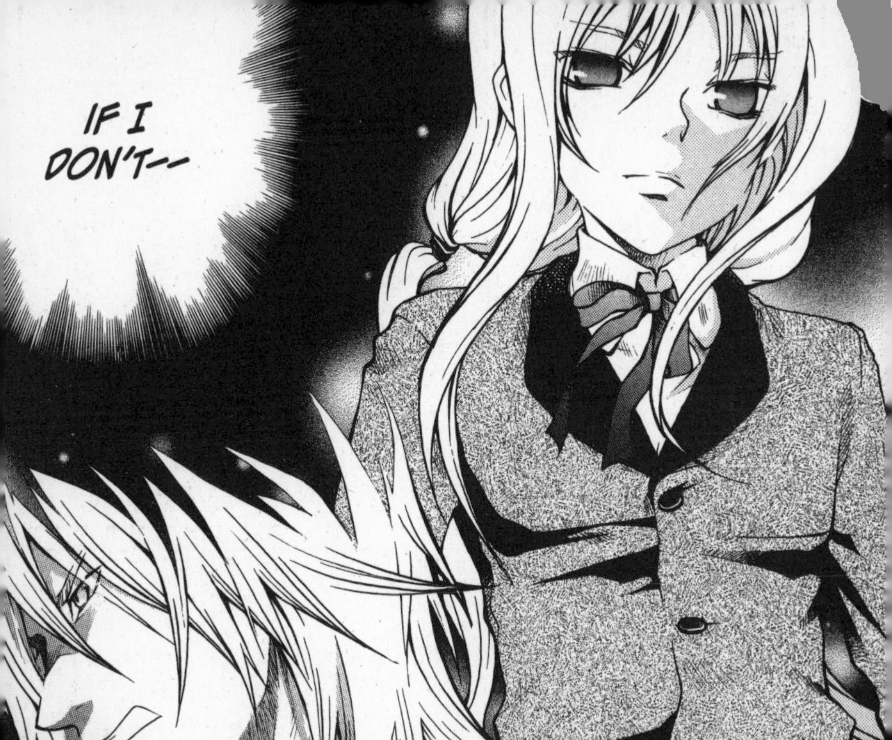
IF I DON'T--

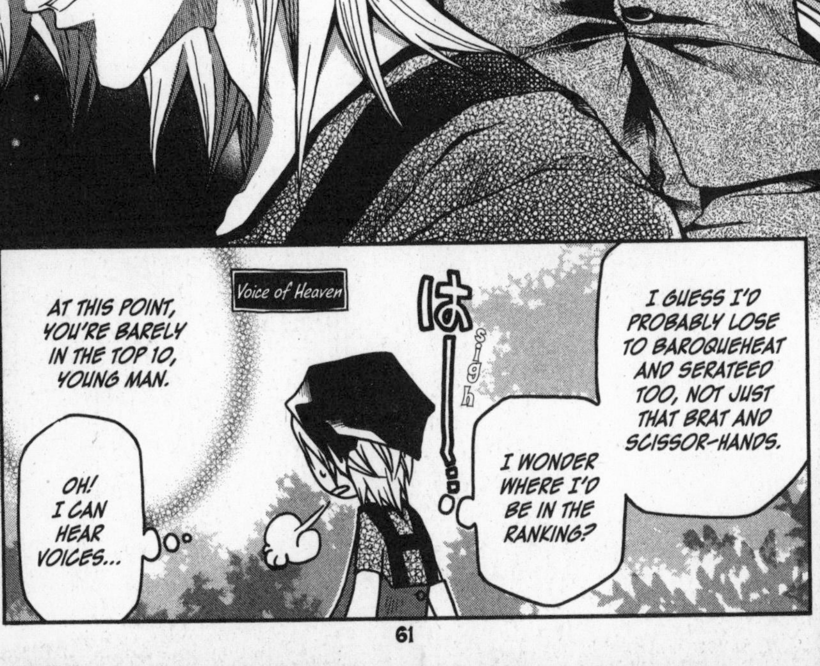
I GUESS I'D PROBABLY LOSE TO BAROQUEHEAT AND SERATEED TOO, NOT JUST THAT BRAT AND SCISSOR-HANDS.
I WONDER WHERE I'D BE IN THE RANKING?
sigh
Voice of Heaven
AT THIS POINT, YOU'RE BARELY IN THE TOP 10, YOUNG MAN.
OH! I CAN HEAR VOICES...

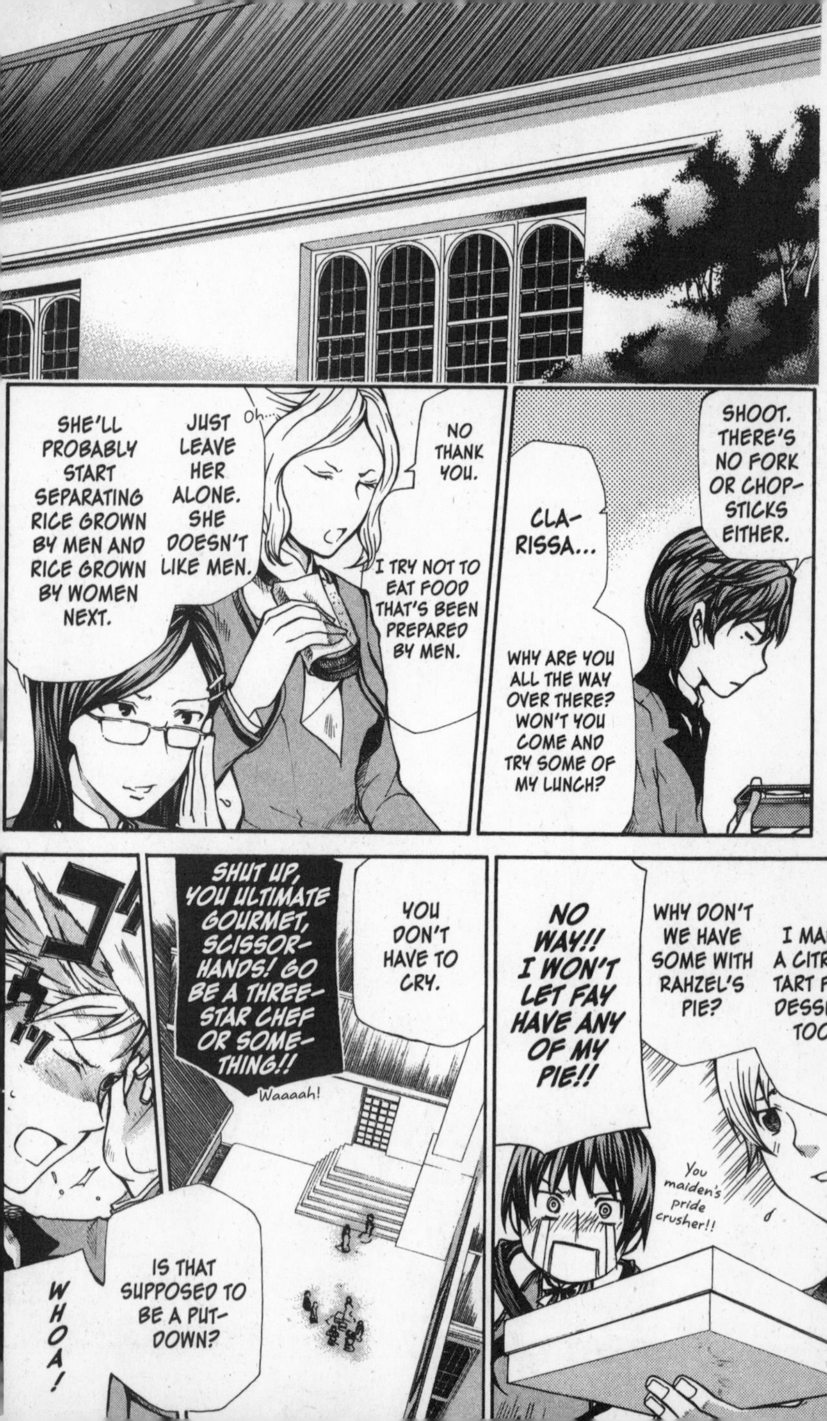
SHOOT. THERE'S NO FORK OR CHOPSTICKS EITHER.
CLARISSA...
WHY ARE YOU ALL THE WAY OVER THERE? WON'T YOU COME AND TRY SOME OF MY LUNCH?
NO THANK YOU.
I TRY NOT TO EAT FOOD THAT'S BEEN PREPARED BY MEN.
Oh...
JUST LEAVE HER ALONE. SHE DOESN'T LIKE MEN.
SHE'LL PROBABLY START SEPARATING RICE GROWN BY MEN AND RICE GROWN BY WOMEN NEXT.
I MADE A CITRON TART FOR DESSERT TOO.
WHY DON'T WE HAVE SOME WITH RAHZEL'S PIE?
NO WAY!! I WON'T LET FAY HAVE ANY OF MY PIE!!
You maiden's pride crusher!!
YOU DON'T HAVE TO CRY.
SHUT UP, YOU ULTIMATE GOURMET, SCISSORHANDS! GO BE A THREE-STAR CHEF OR SOMETHING!!
Waaaah!
IS THAT SUPPOSED TO BE A PUT-DOWN?
WHOA!

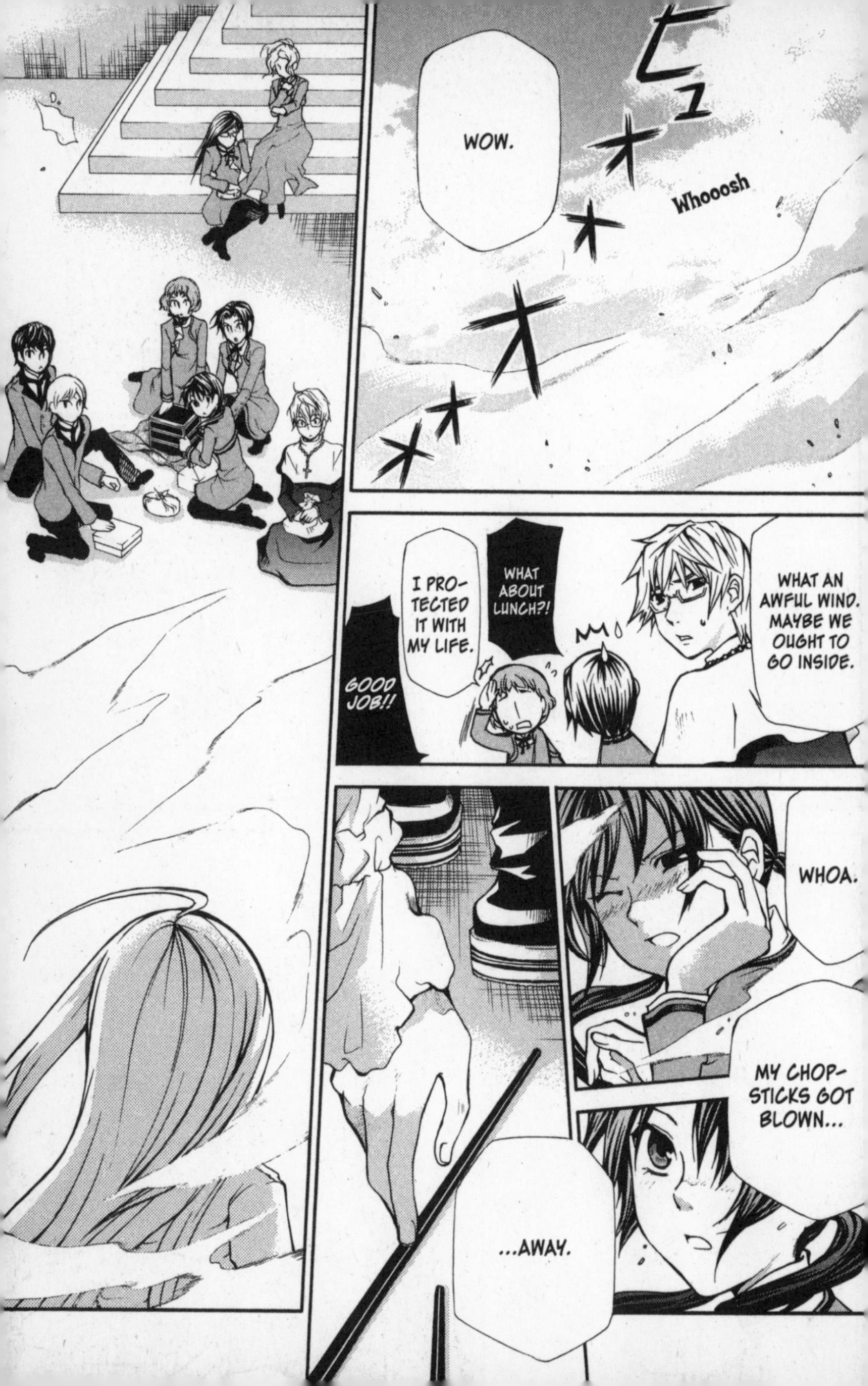
Whooosh
WOW.
WHAT AN AWFUL WIND. MAYBE WE OUGHT TO GO INSIDE.
WHAT ABOUT LUNCH?!
I PRO-TECTED IT WITH MY LIFE.
GOOD JOB!!
WHOA.
MY CHOP-STICKS GOT BLOWN...
...AWAY.

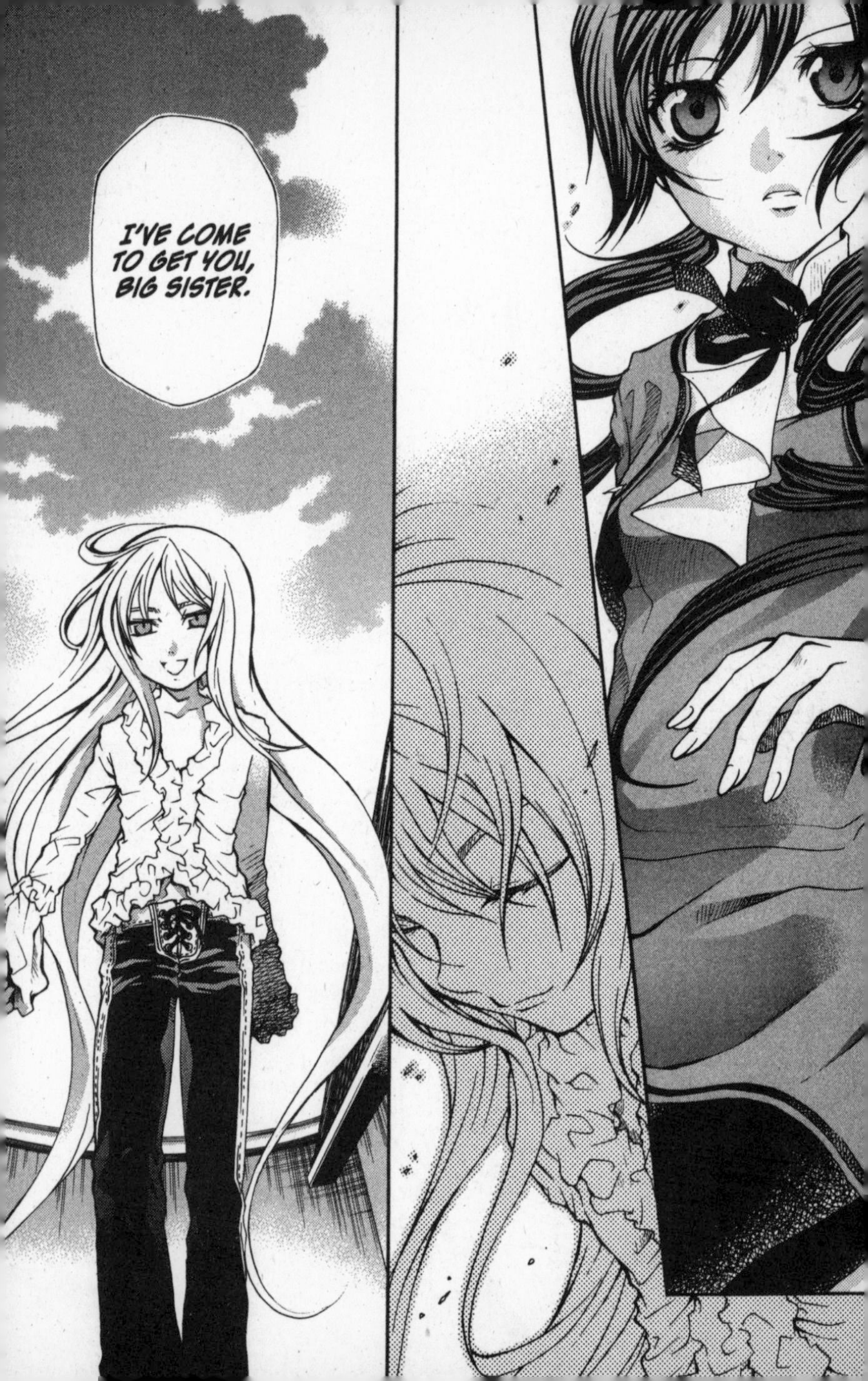
I'VE COME TO GET YOU, BIG SISTER.

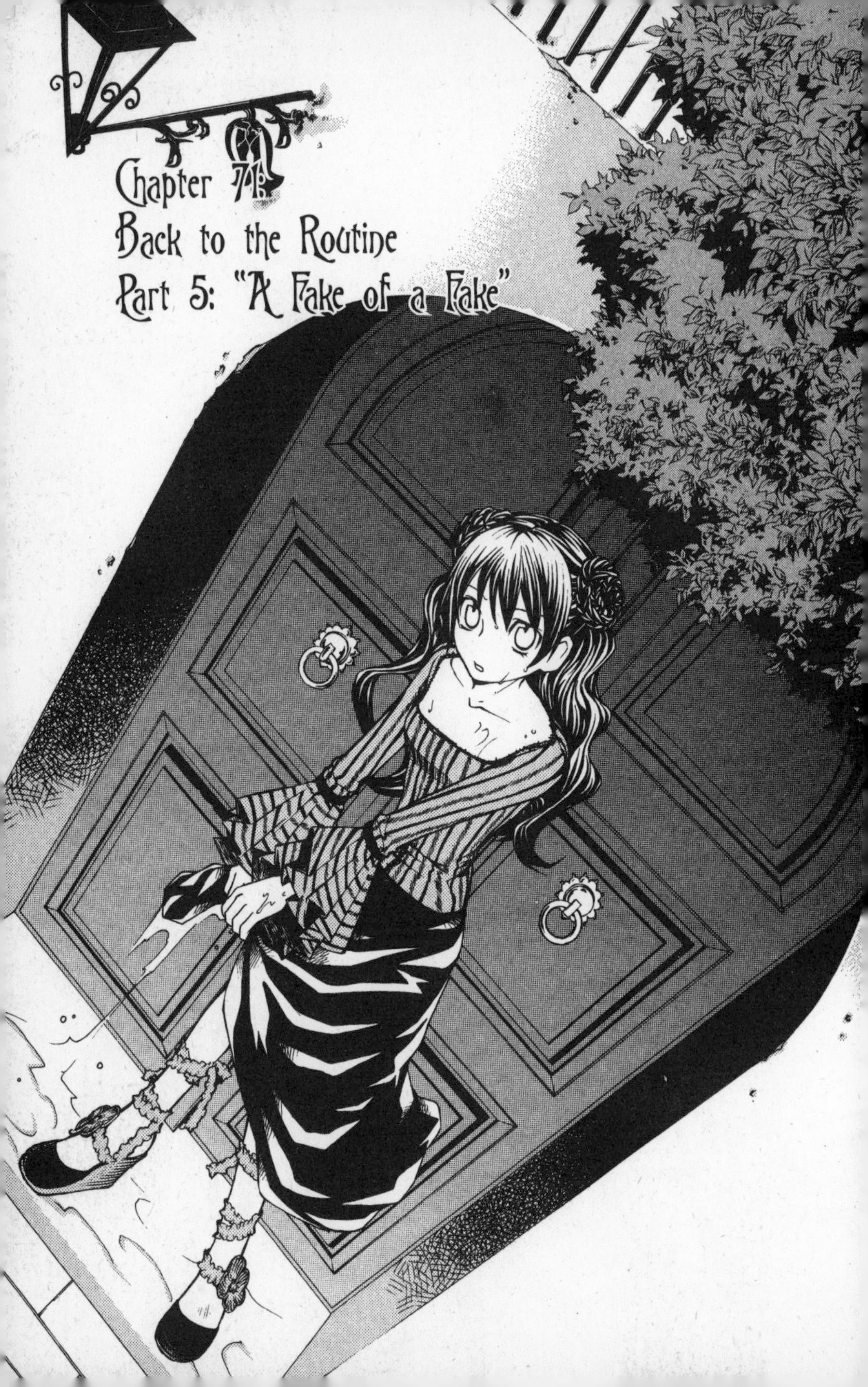
Chapter 71:
Back to the Routine
Part 5: "A Fake of a Fake"

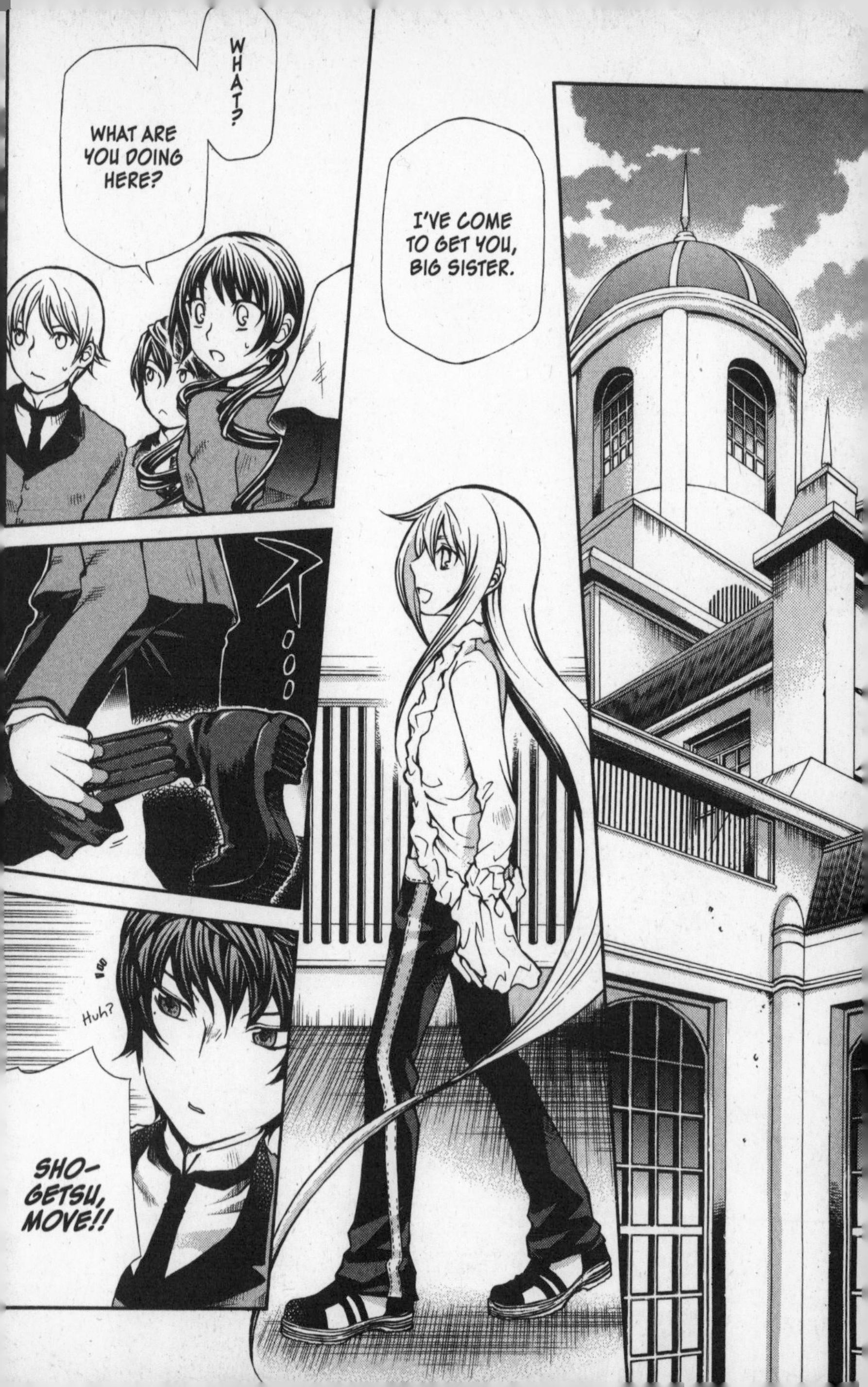
I'VE COME TO GET YOU, BIG SISTER.
WHAT?
WHAT ARE YOU DOING HERE?
Huh?
SHO-GETSU, MOVE!!

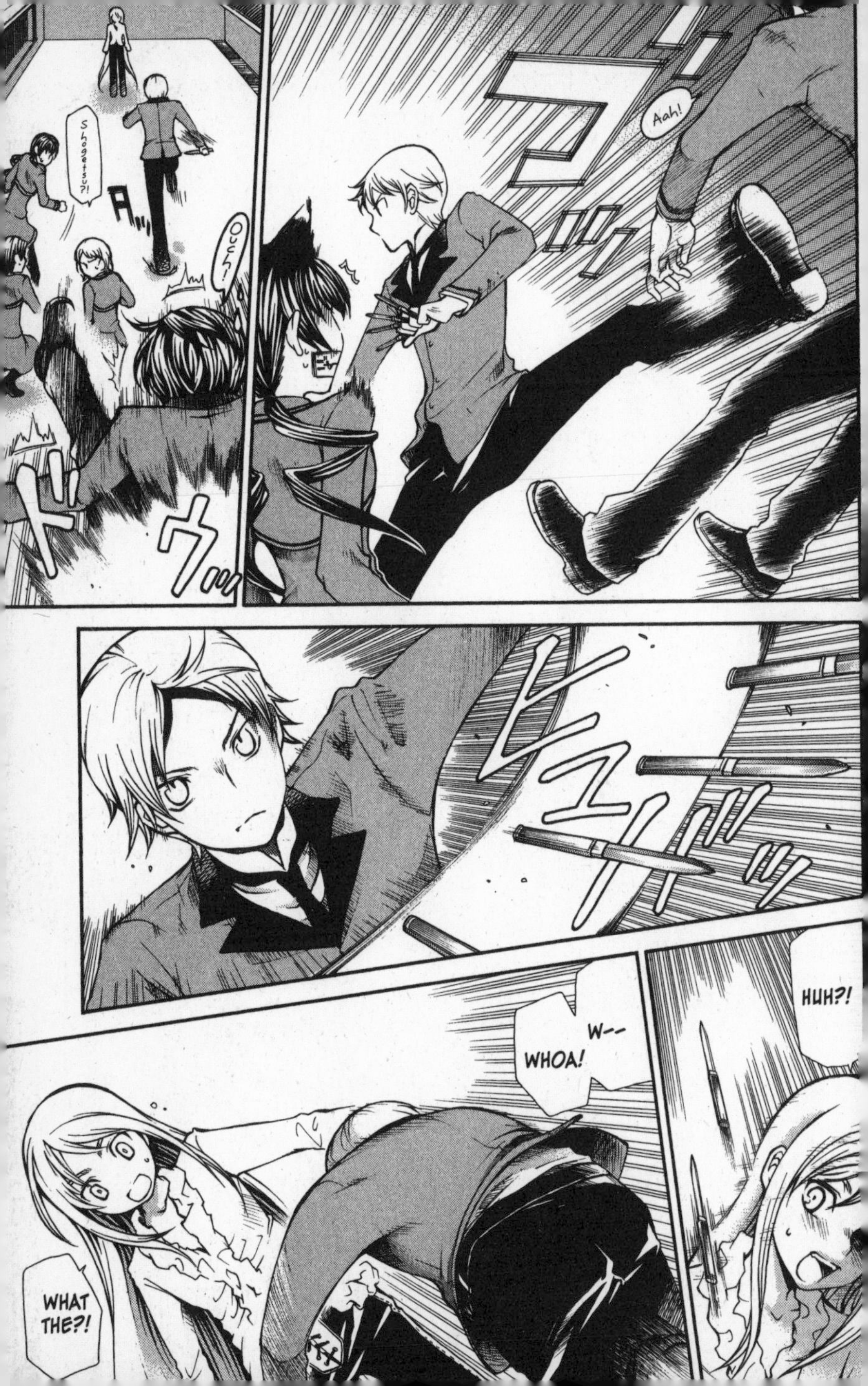
Aah!
Ouch!
Shogetsu?!
HUH?!
W-- WHOA!
WHAT THE?!

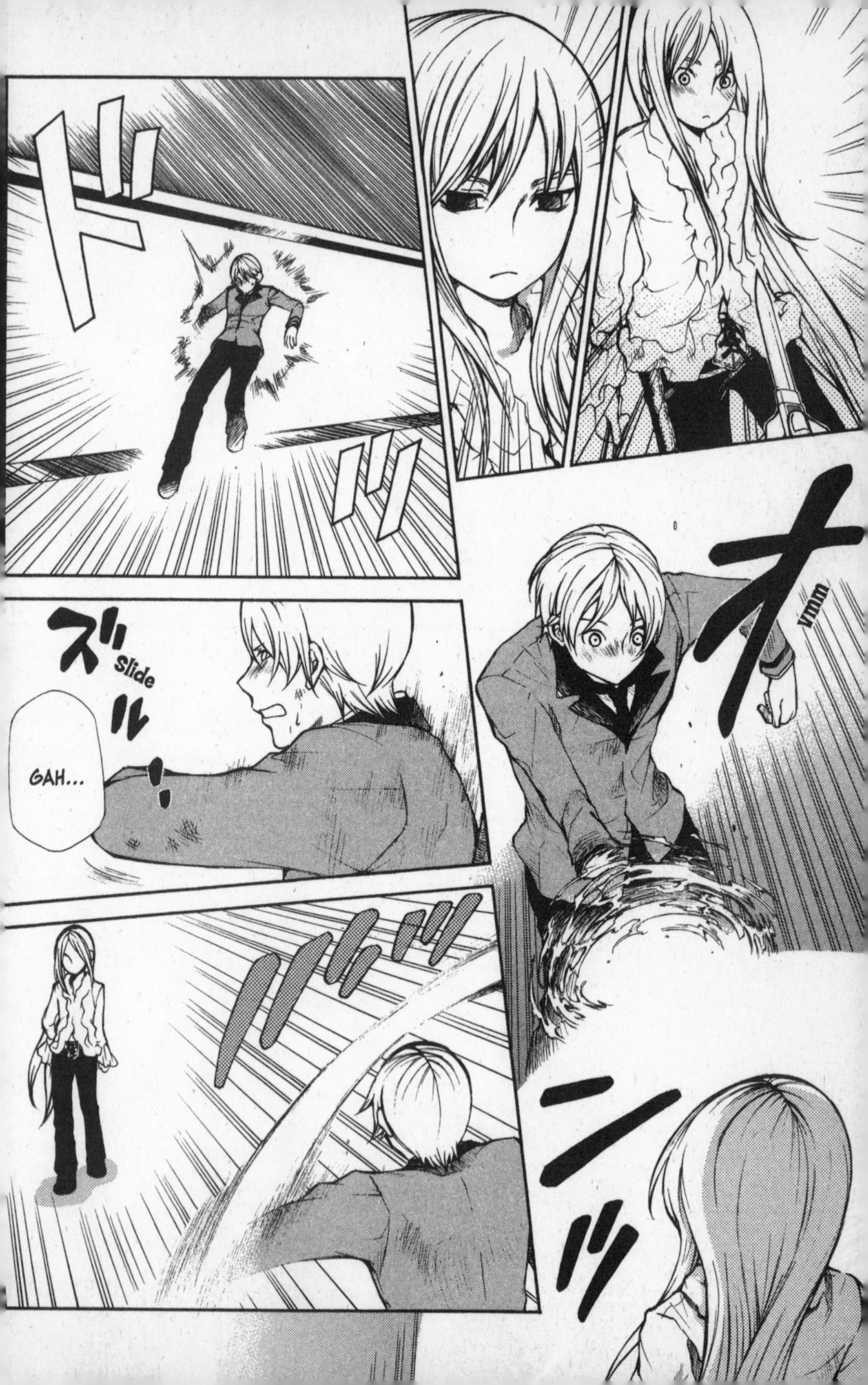
vmm
Slide
GAH...

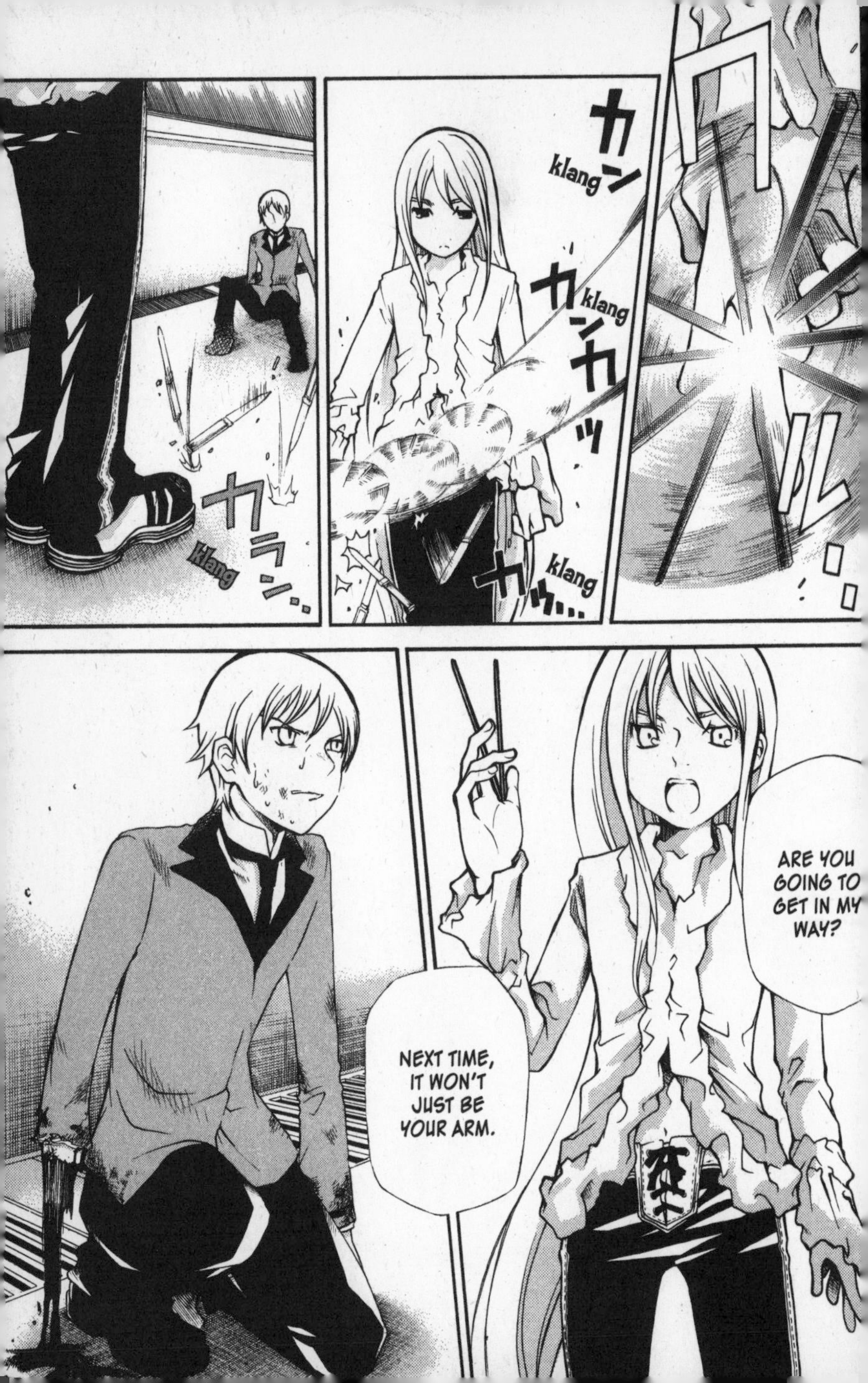

クル...
カン
klang
カンカッ
klang
klang
カッ...
カラン...
klang
ARE YOU GOING TO GET IN MY WAY?
NEXT TIME, IT WON'T JUST BE YOUR ARM.

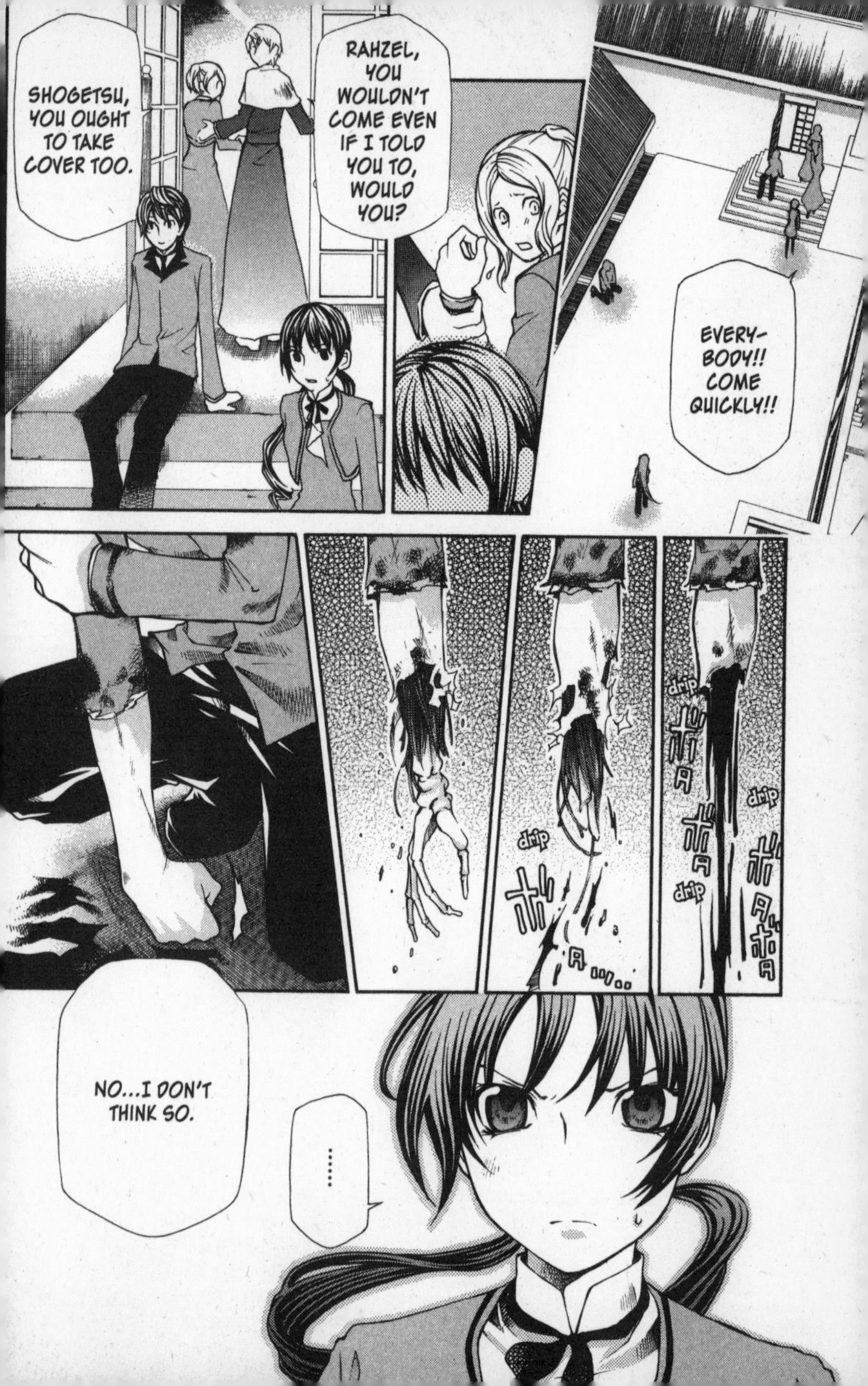

EVERY-BODY!! COME QUICKLY!!
RAHZEL, YOU WOULDN'T COME EVEN IF I TOLD YOU TO, WOULD YOU?
SHOGETSU, YOU OUGHT TO TAKE COVER TOO.
drip
drip
drip
drip
......
NO...I DON'T THINK SO.

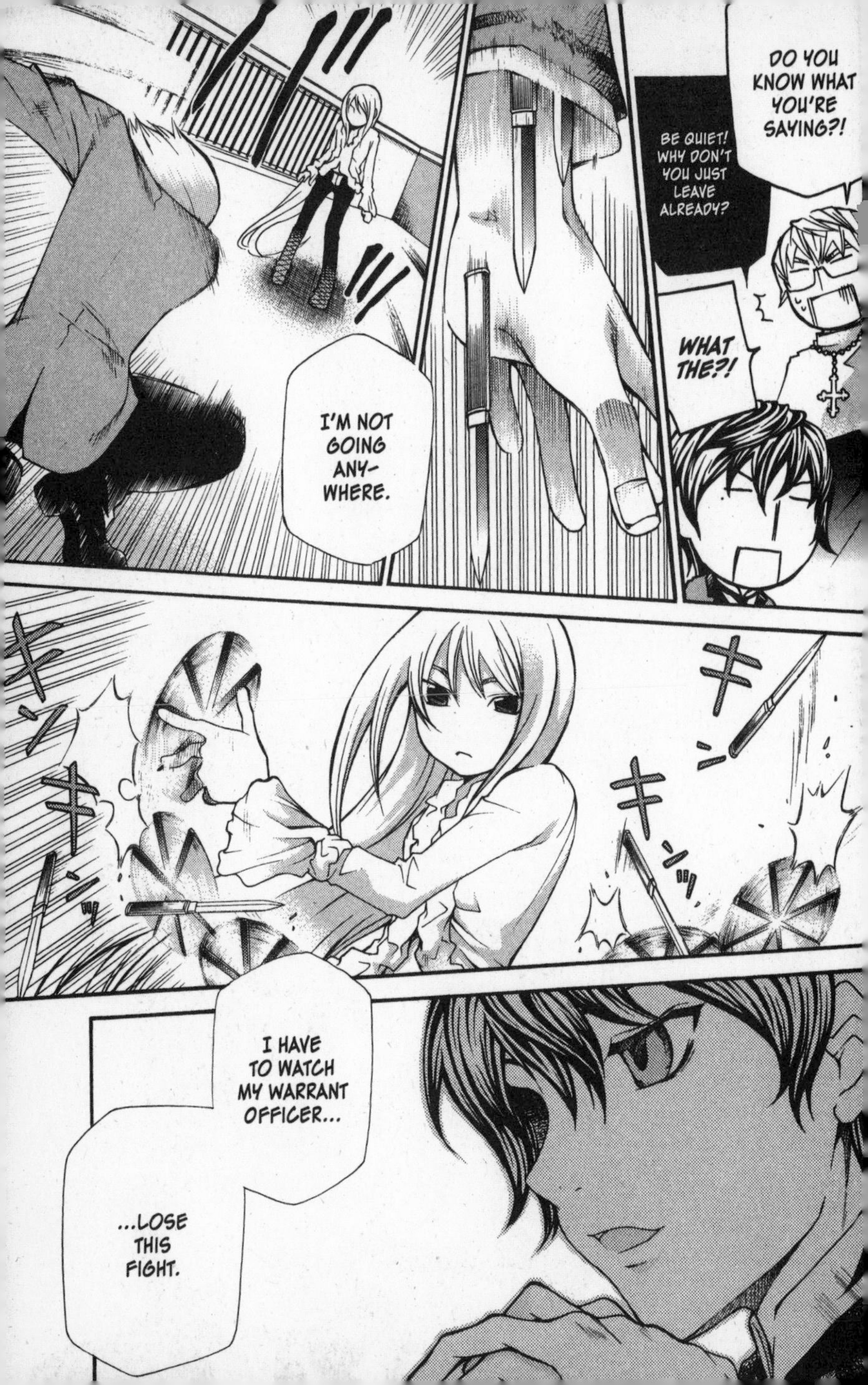
DO YOU KNOW WHAT YOU'RE SAYING?!
BE QUIET! WHY DON'T YOU JUST LEAVE ALREADY?
WHAT THE?!
I'M NOT GOING ANY-WHERE.
I HAVE TO WATCH MY WARRANT OFFICER...
...LOSE THIS FIGHT.

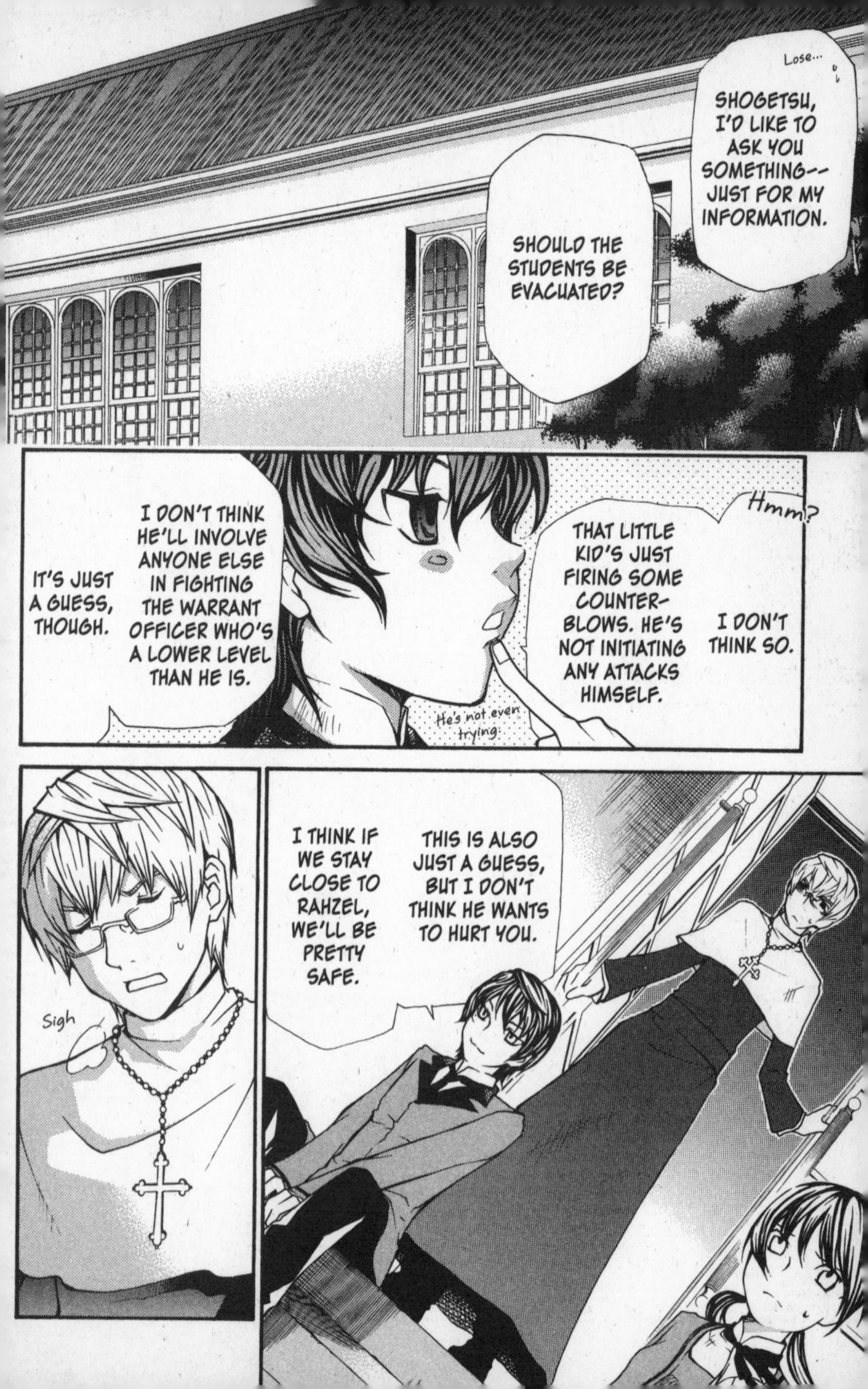
Lose...
SHOGETSU, I'D LIKE TO ASK YOU SOMETHING-- JUST FOR MY INFORMATION.
SHOULD THE STUDENTS BE EVACUATED?
Hmm?
I DON'T THINK SO.
THAT LITTLE KID'S JUST FIRING SOME COUNTER-BLOWS. HE'S NOT INITIATING ANY ATTACKS HIMSELF.
He's not even trying.
I DON'T THINK HE'LL INVOLVE ANYONE ELSE IN FIGHTING THE WARRANT OFFICER WHO'S A LOWER LEVEL THAN HE IS.
IT'S JUST A GUESS, THOUGH.
THIS IS ALSO JUST A GUESS, BUT I DON'T THINK HE WANTS TO HURT YOU.
I THINK IF WE STAY CLOSE TO RAHZEL, WE'LL BE PRETTY SAFE.
Sigh

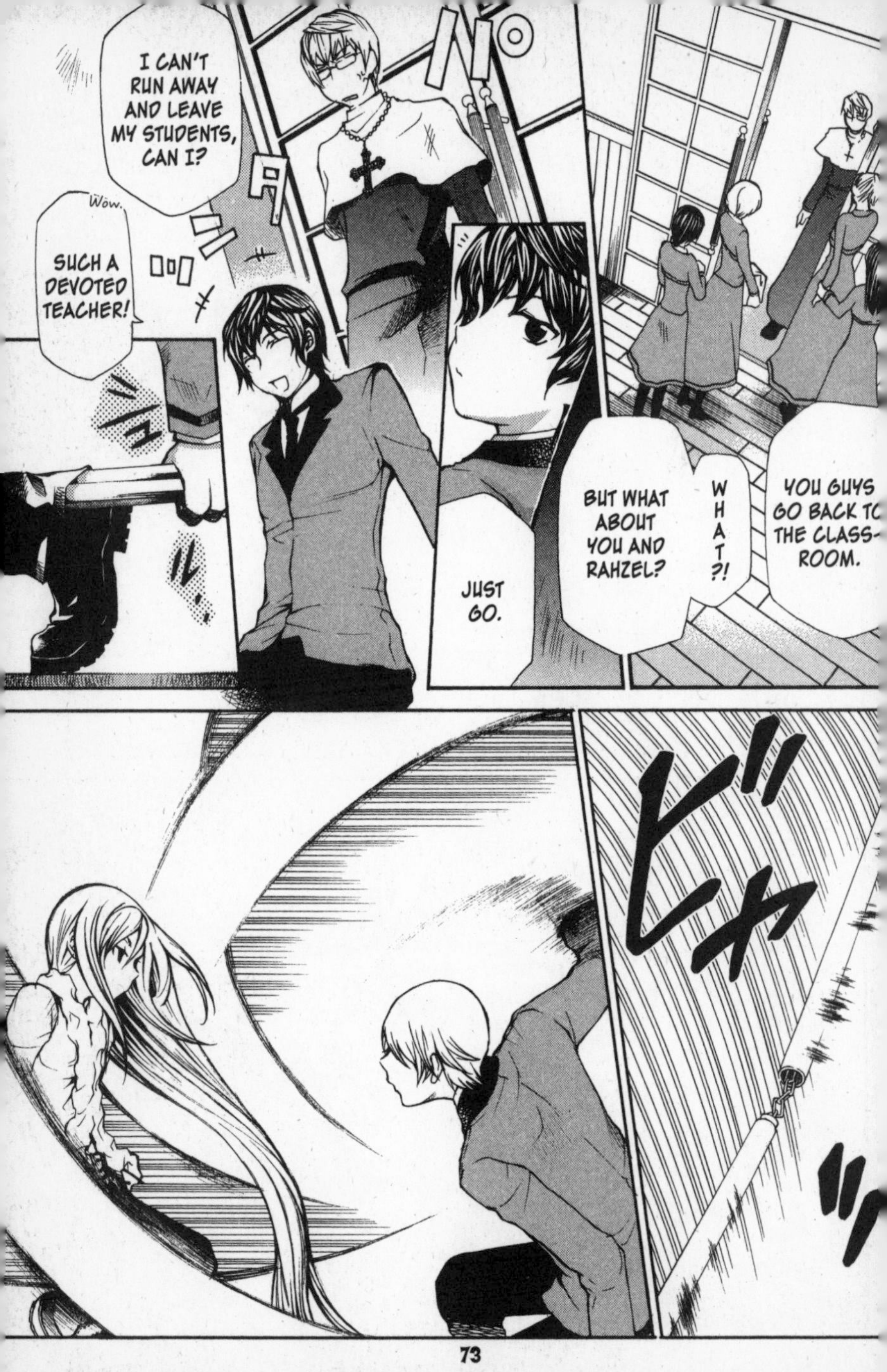
YOU GUYS GO BACK TO THE CLASS-ROOM.
WHAT?!
BUT WHAT ABOUT YOU AND RAHZEL?
JUST GO.
I CAN'T RUN AWAY AND LEAVE MY STUDENTS, CAN I?
Wow.
SUCH A DEVOTED TEACHER!

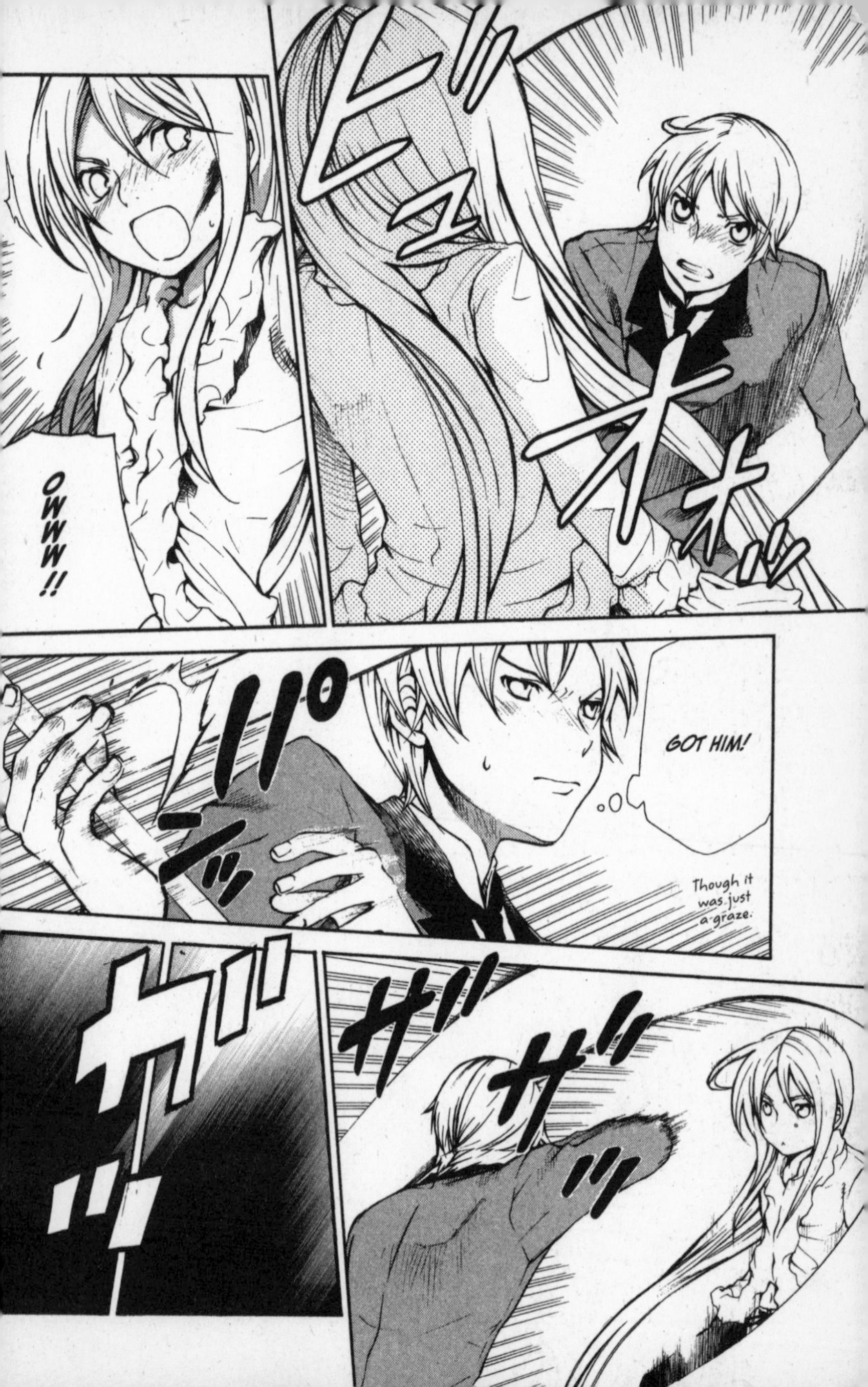
OWWW!!
GOT HIM!
Though it was just a graze.

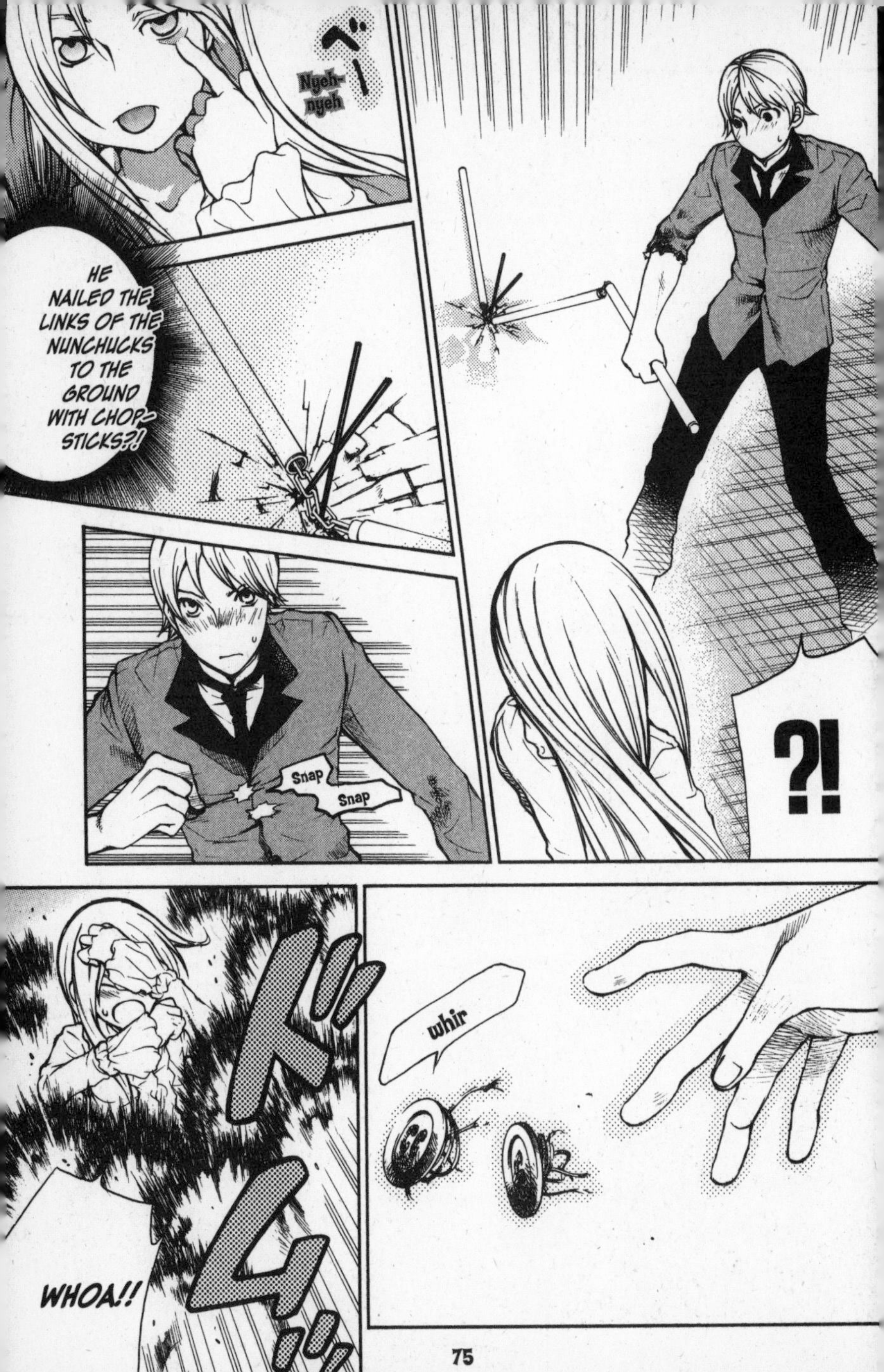
?!
べー
Nyeh-nyeh
HE NAILED THE LINKS OF THE NUNCHUCKS TO THE GROUND WITH CHOP-STICKS?!
Snap
Snap
whir
ドム
WHOA!!

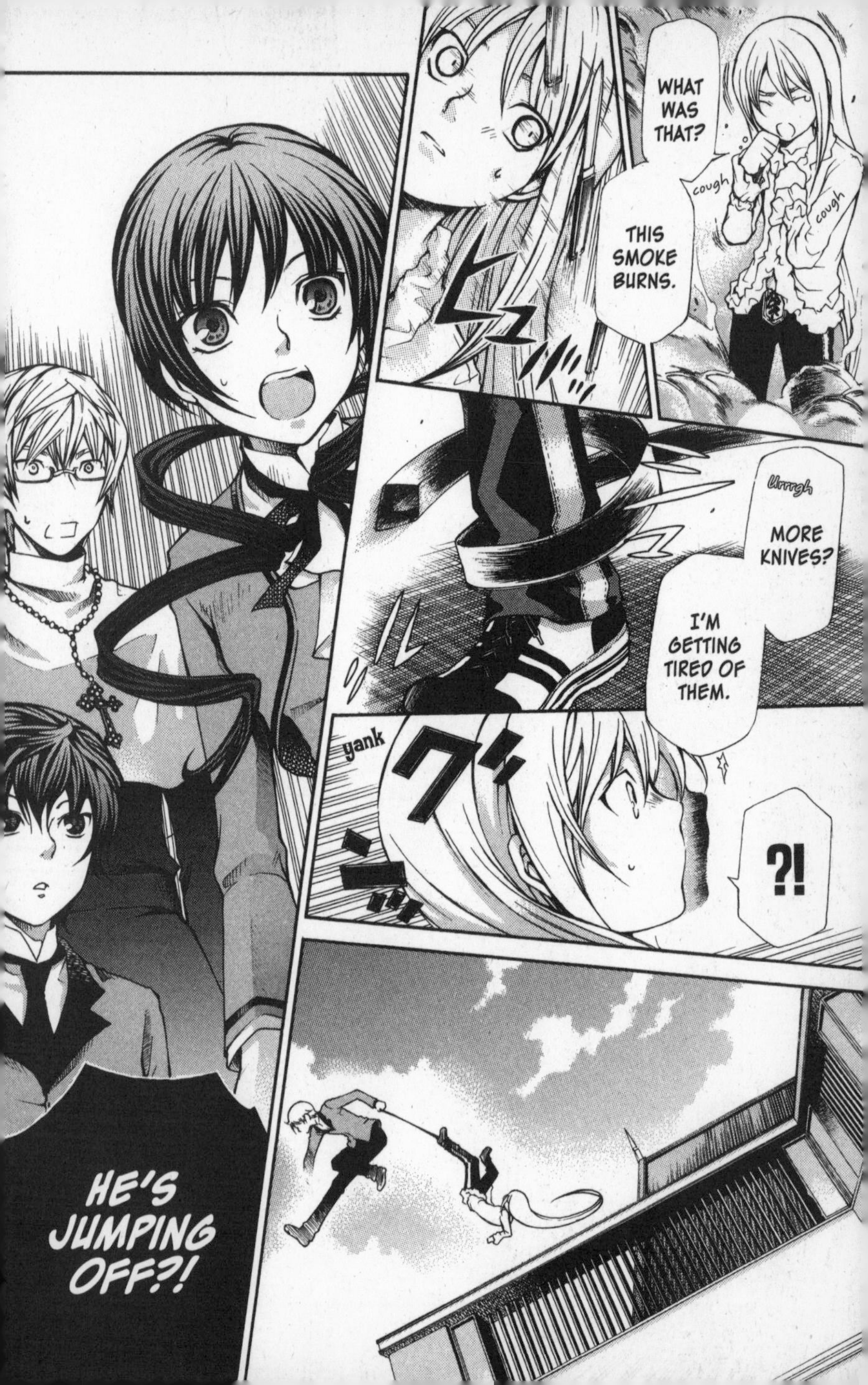
WHAT WAS THAT?
THIS SMOKE BURNS.
cough
cough
Urrrgh
MORE KNIVES?
I'M GETTING TIRED OF THEM.
yank
?!
HE'S JUMPING OFF?!

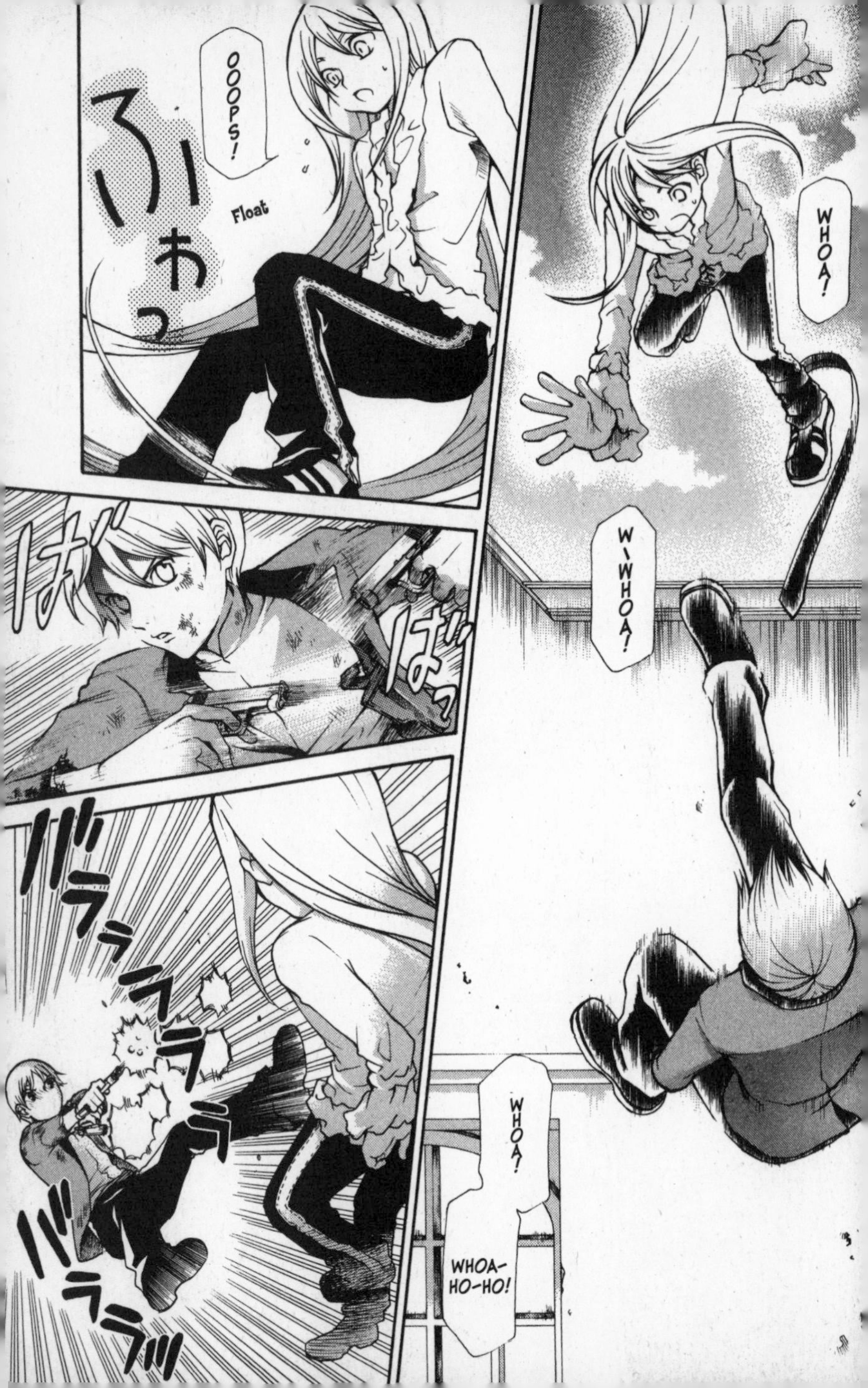
WHOA!
W-WHOA!
WHOA!
WHOA-HO-HO!
OOOPS!
ふわっ
Float
ばっ
ばっ

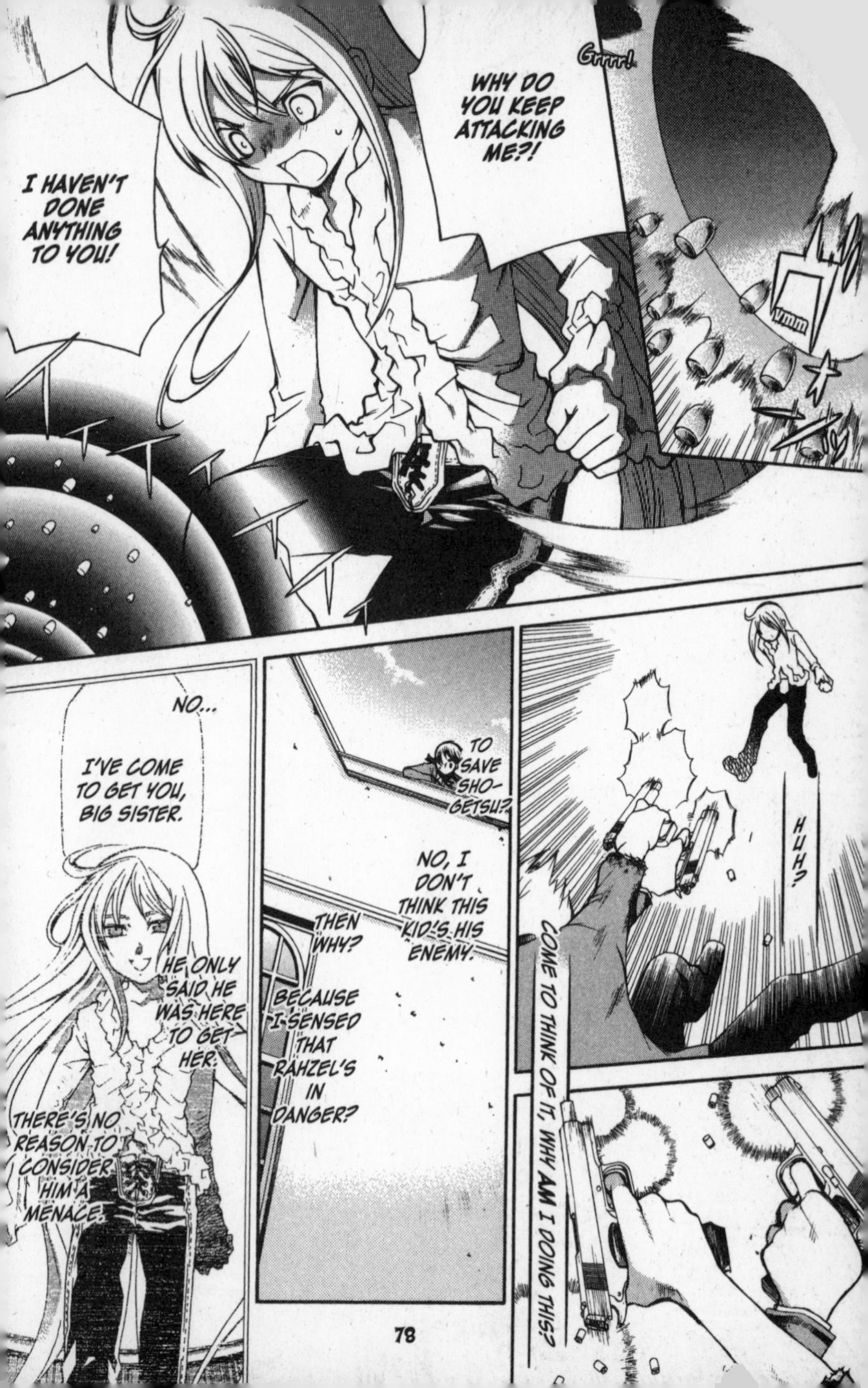
Grrrr!
WHY DO YOU KEEP ATTACKING ME?!
Vmm
I HAVEN'T DONE ANYTHING TO YOU!
HUH?
COME TO THINK OF IT, WHY AM I DOING THIS?
TO SAVE SHO-GETSU?
NO, I DON'T THINK THIS KID'S HIS ENEMY.
THEN WHY?
BECAUSE I SENSED THAT RAHZEL'S IN DANGER?
NO...
I'VE COME TO GET YOU, BIG SISTER.
HE ONLY SAID HE WAS HERE TO GET HER.
THERE'S NO REASON TO CONSIDER HIM A MENACE.

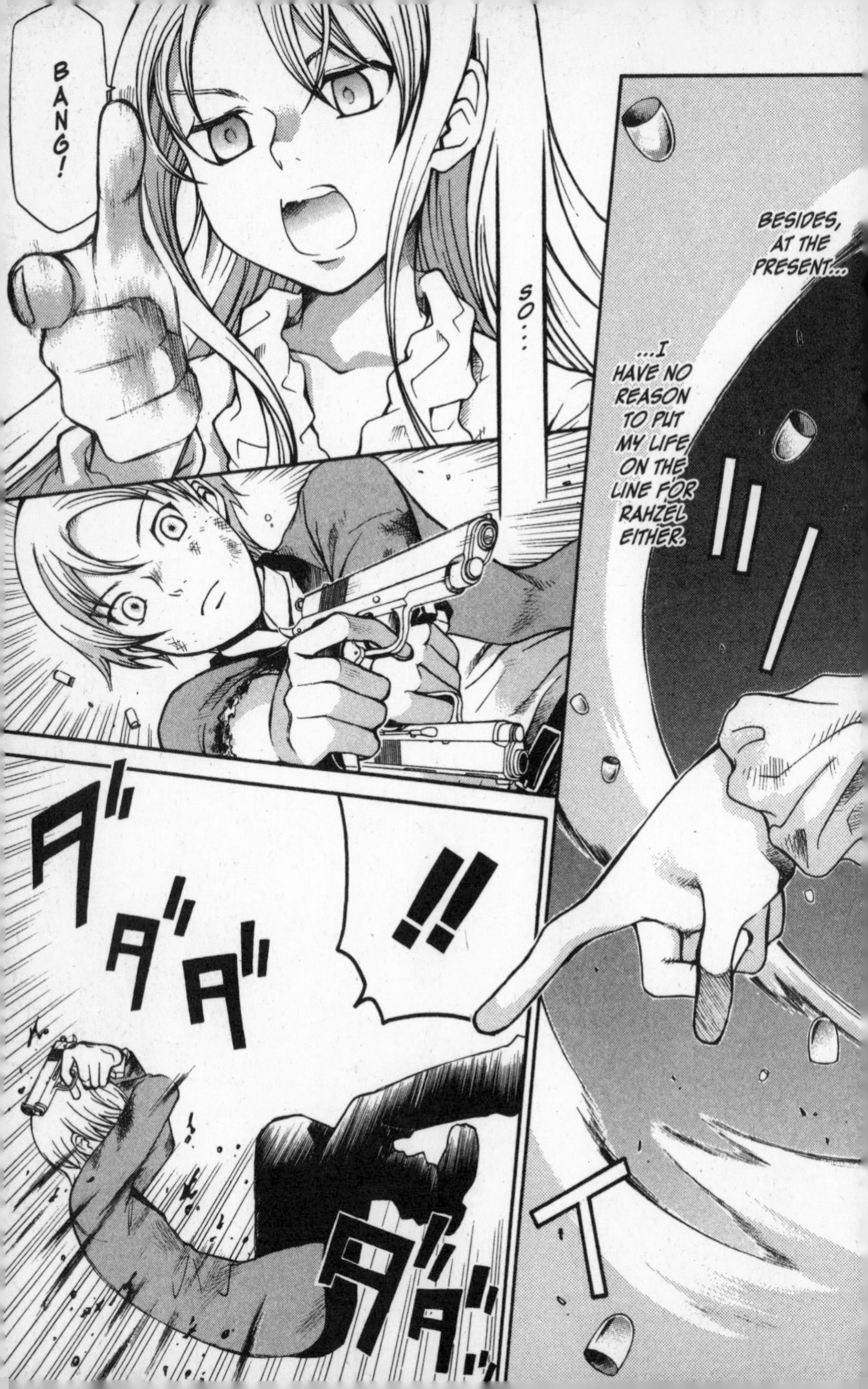
BESIDES, AT THE PRESENT...
...I HAVE NO REASON TO PUT MY LIFE ON THE LINE FOR RAHZEL EITHER.
SO...
BANG!
!!
ダダダ
ダダ

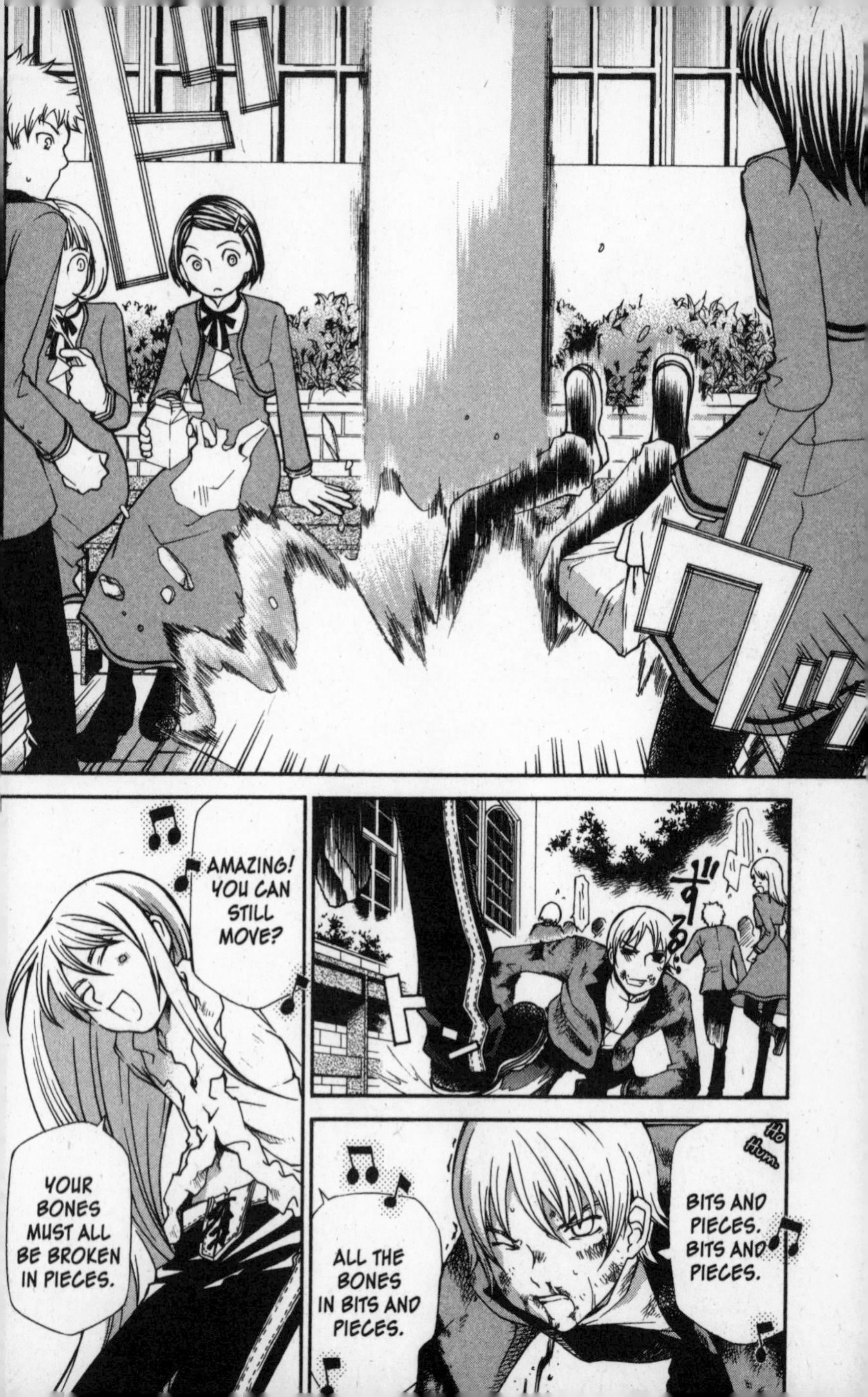
Ho Hum.
BITS AND PIECES. BITS AND PIECES.
ALL THE BONES IN BITS AND PIECES.
AMAZING! YOU CAN STILL MOVE?
YOUR BONES MUST ALL BE BROKEN IN PIECES.

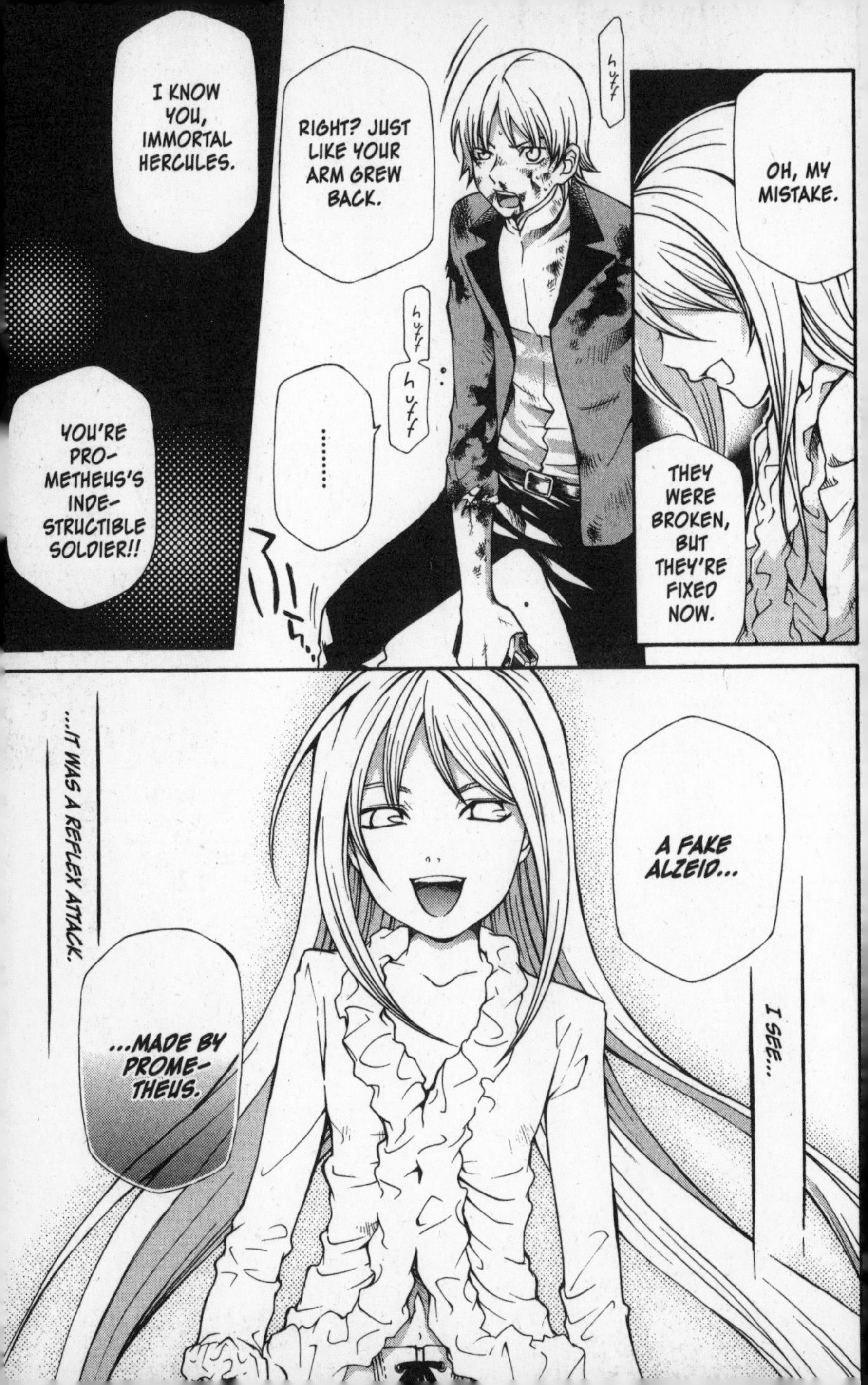
OH, MY MISTAKE.
THEY WERE BROKEN, BUT THEY'RE FIXED NOW.
huff
RIGHT? JUST LIKE YOUR ARM GREW BACK.
huff
huff
....
I KNOW YOU, IMMORTAL HERCULES.
YOU'RE PROMETHEUS'S INDESTRUCTIBLE SOLDIER!!
I SEE...
A FAKE ALZEID...
...MADE BY PROMETHEUS.
...IT WAS A REFLEX ATTACK.

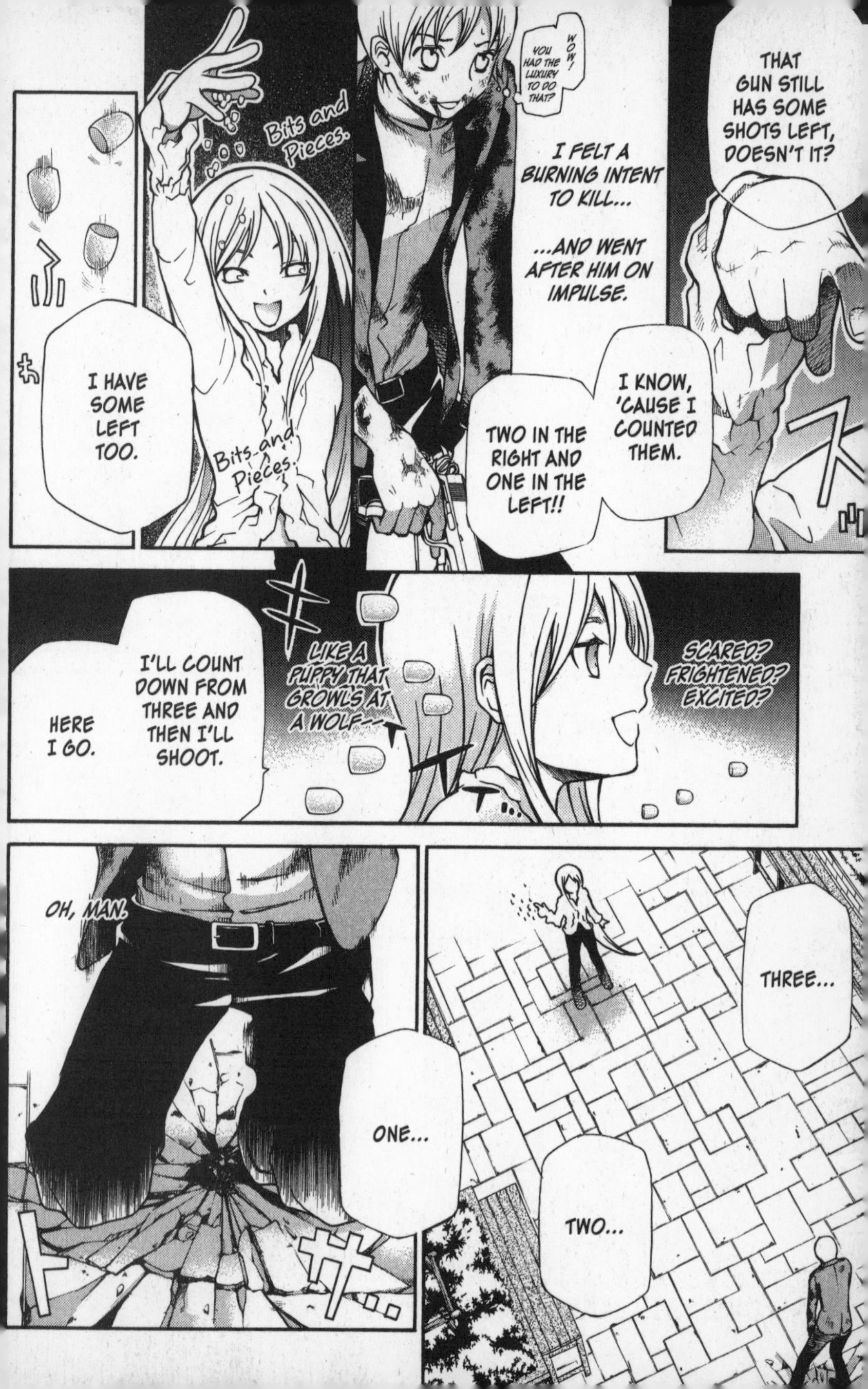
THAT GUN STILL HAS SOME SHOTS LEFT, DOESN'T IT?
WOW! YOU HAD THE LUXURY TO DO THAT?
I FELT A BURNING INTENT TO KILL...
...AND WENT AFTER HIM ON IMPULSE.
I KNOW, 'CAUSE I COUNTED THEM.
TWO IN THE RIGHT AND ONE IN THE LEFT!!
Bits and Pieces.
Bits and Pieces.
I HAVE SOME LEFT TOO.
SCARED? FRIGHTENED? EXCITED?
LIKE A PUPPY THAT GROWLS AT A WOLF--
I'LL COUNT DOWN FROM THREE AND THEN I'LL SHOOT.
HERE I GO.
THREE...
TWO...
ONE...
OH, MAN.

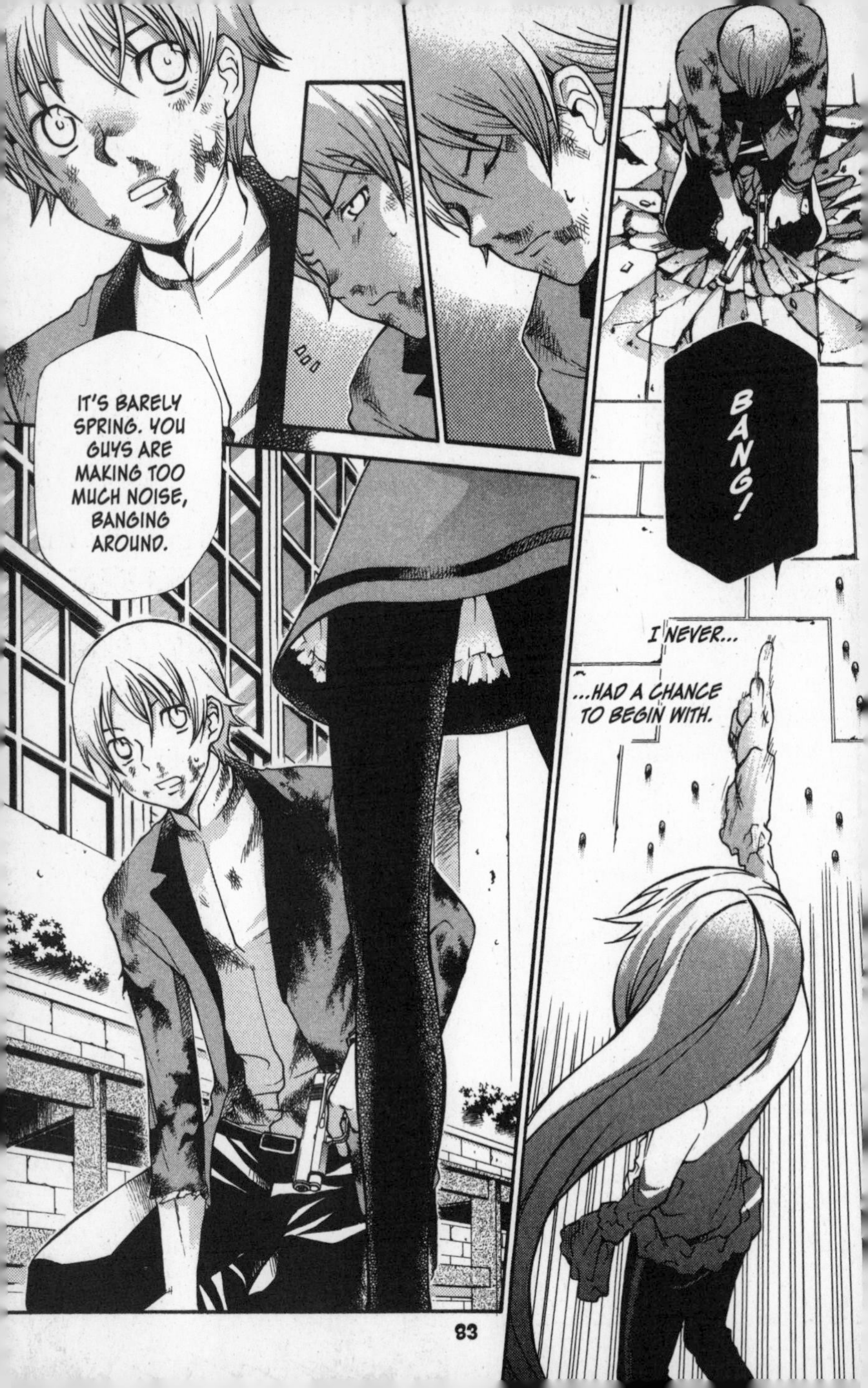
BANG!
I NEVER...
...HAD A CHANCE TO BEGIN WITH.
IT'S BARELY SPRING. YOU GUYS ARE MAKING TOO MUCH NOISE, BANGING AROUND.

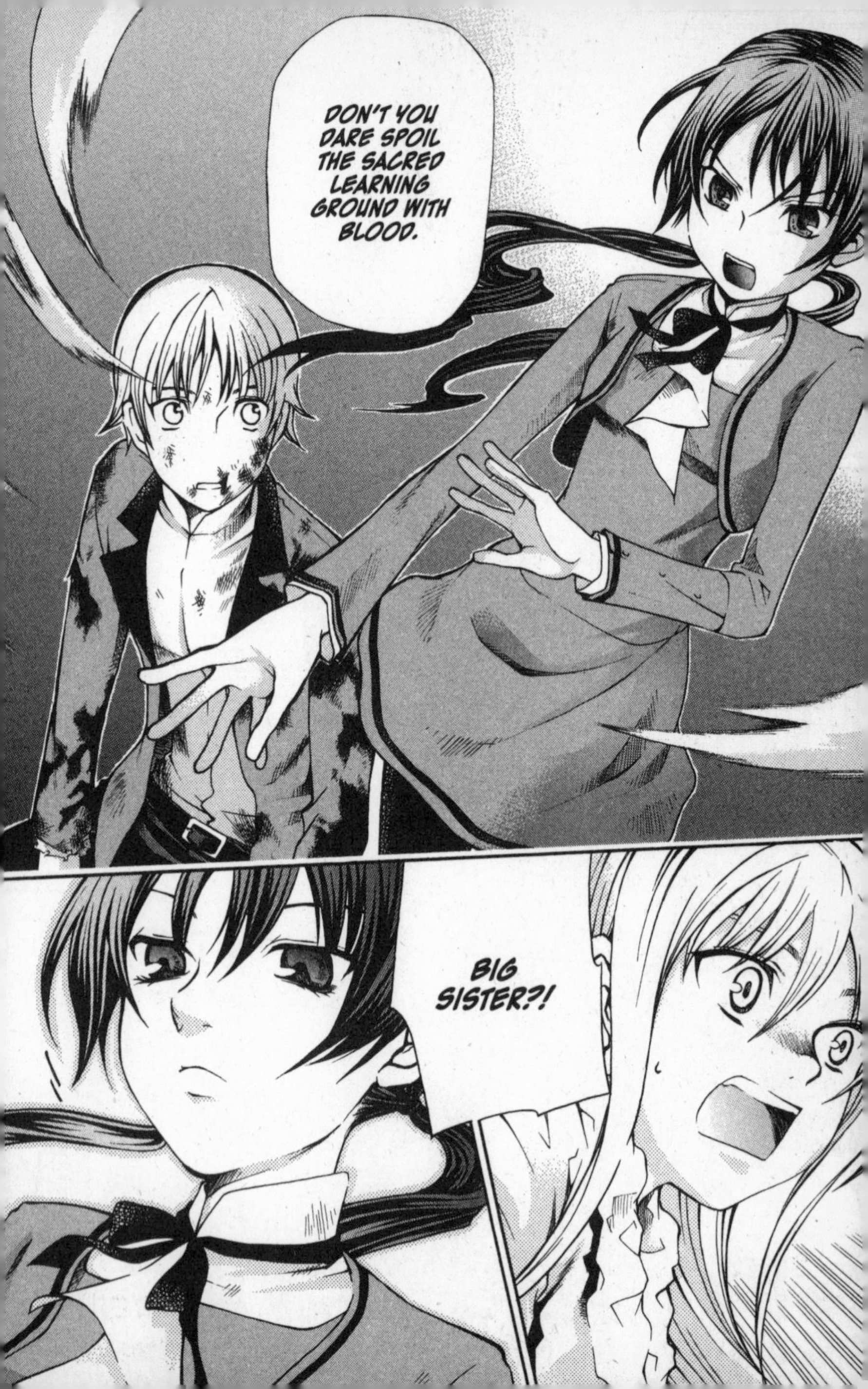
DON'T YOU DARE SPOIL THE SACRED LEARNING GROUND WITH BLOOD.
BIG SISTER?!

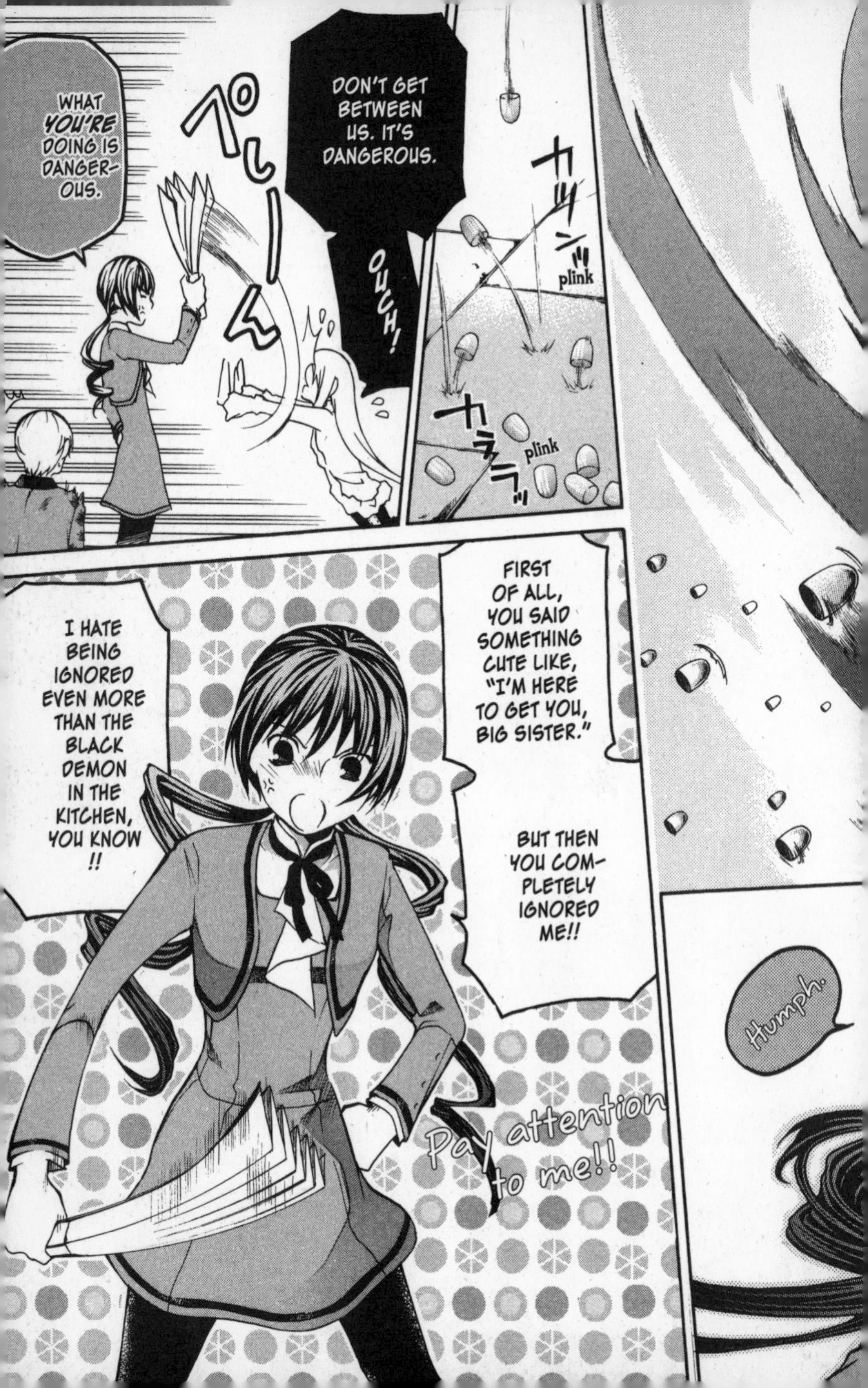
plink
plink
DON'T GET BETWEEN US. IT'S DANGEROUS.
WHAT YOU'RE DOING IS DANGER-OUS.
OUCH!
Humph.
FIRST OF ALL, YOU SAID SOMETHING CUTE LIKE, "I'M HERE TO GET YOU, BIG SISTER."
BUT THEN YOU COM-PLETELY IGNORED ME!!
I HATE BEING IGNORED EVEN MORE THAN THE BLACK DEMON IN THE KITCHEN, YOU KNOW!!
Pay attention to me!!

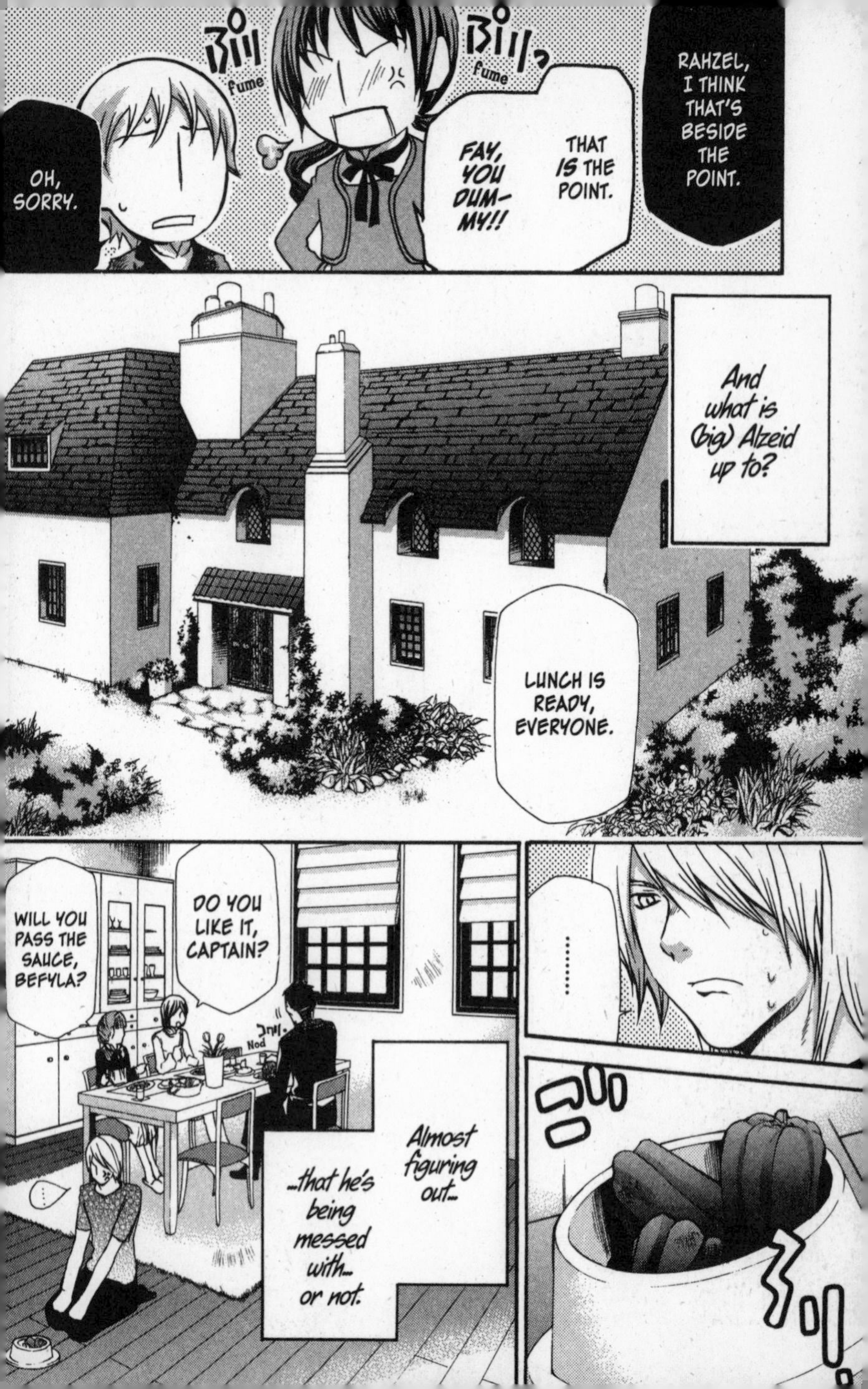
RAHZEL, I THINK THAT'S BESIDE THE POINT.
THAT *IS* THE POINT.
fume
FAY, YOU DUMM-MY!!
fume
OH, SORRY.
And what is (big) Alzeid up to?
LUNCH IS READY, EVERYONE.
......
DO YOU LIKE IT, CAPTAIN?
WILL YOU PASS THE SAUCE, BEFYLA?
Nod
Almost figuring out...
...that he's being messed with... or not.
...

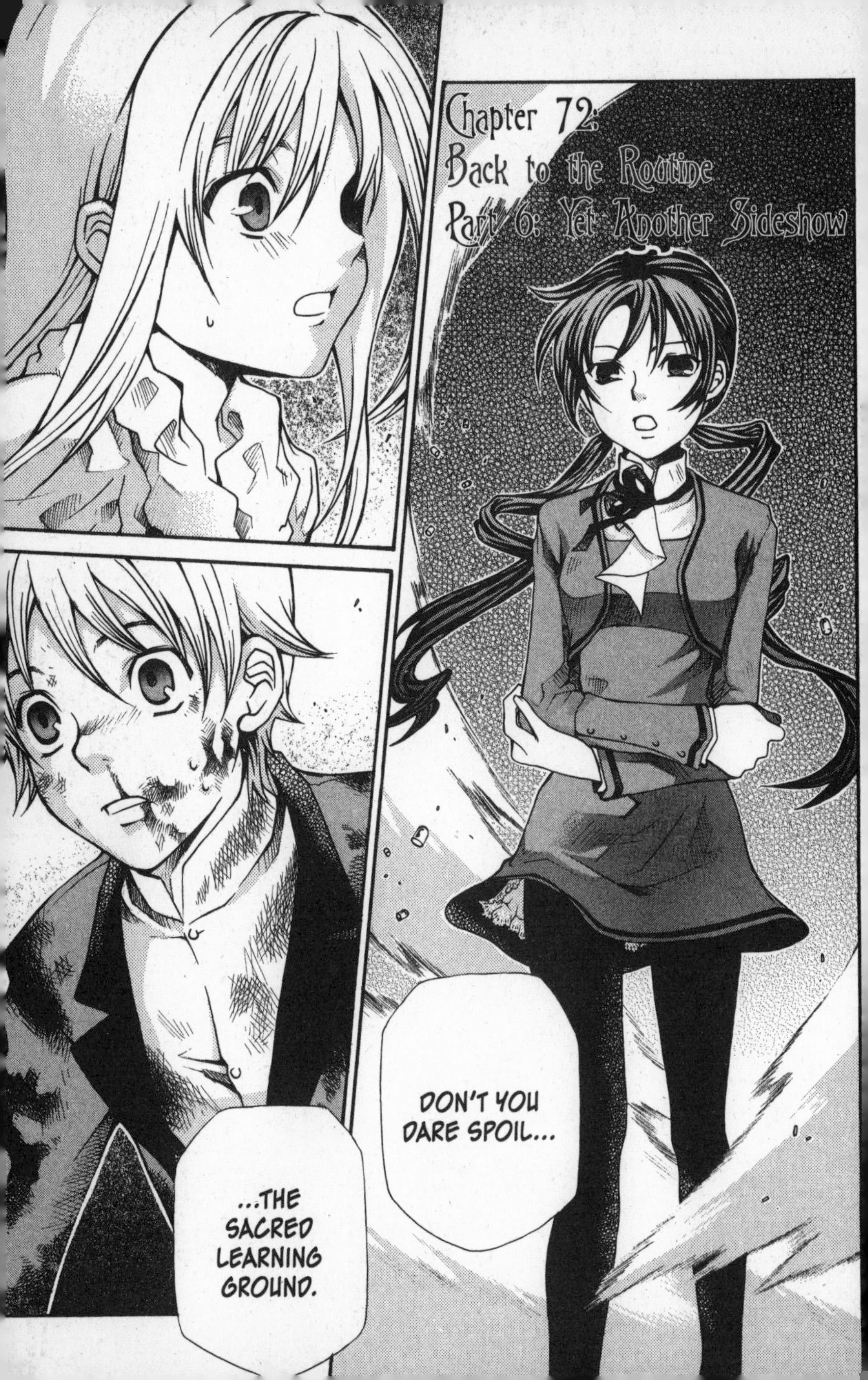
Chapter 72:
Back to the Routine
Part 6: Yet Another Sideshow
DON'T YOU DARE SPOIL...
...THE SACRED LEARNING GROUND.

Chapter 72:
Back to the Routine
Part 6: Yet Another Sideshow

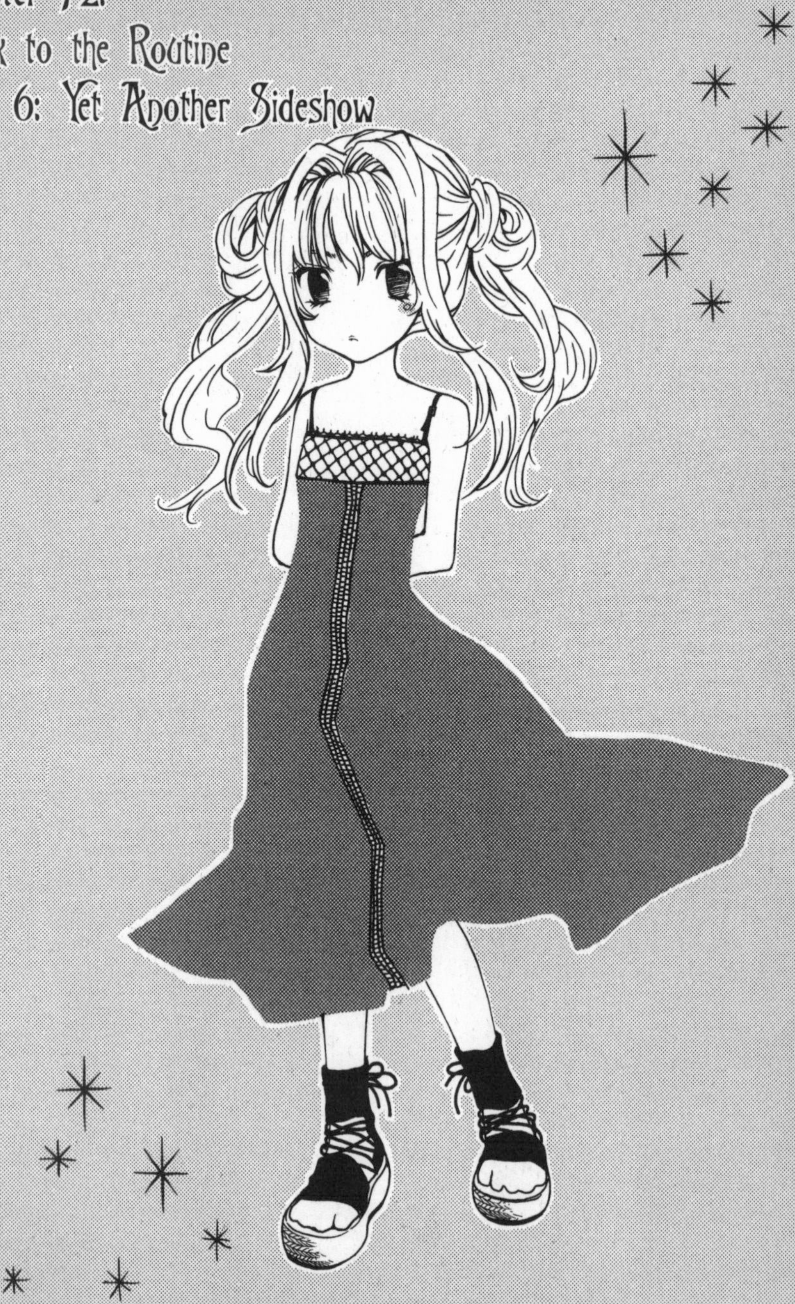

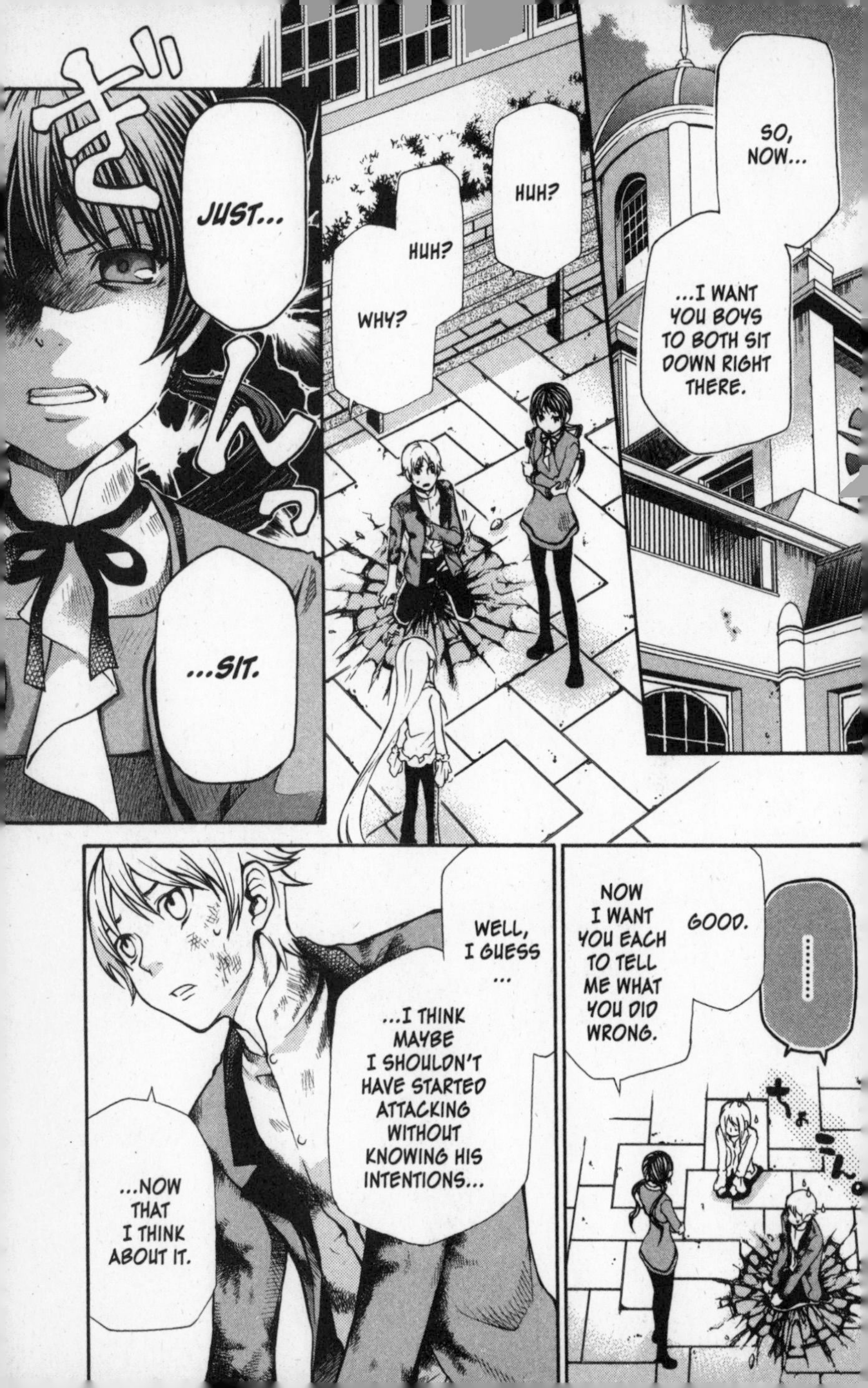
SO, NOW...
...I WANT YOU BOYS TO BOTH SIT DOWN RIGHT THERE.
HUH?
HUH?
WHY?
JUST...
...SIT.
GOOD.
NOW I WANT YOU EACH TO TELL ME WHAT YOU DID WRONG.
......
WELL, I GUESS ...
...I THINK MAYBE I SHOULDN'T HAVE STARTED ATTACKING WITHOUT KNOWING HIS INTENTIONS...
...NOW THAT I THINK ABOUT IT.

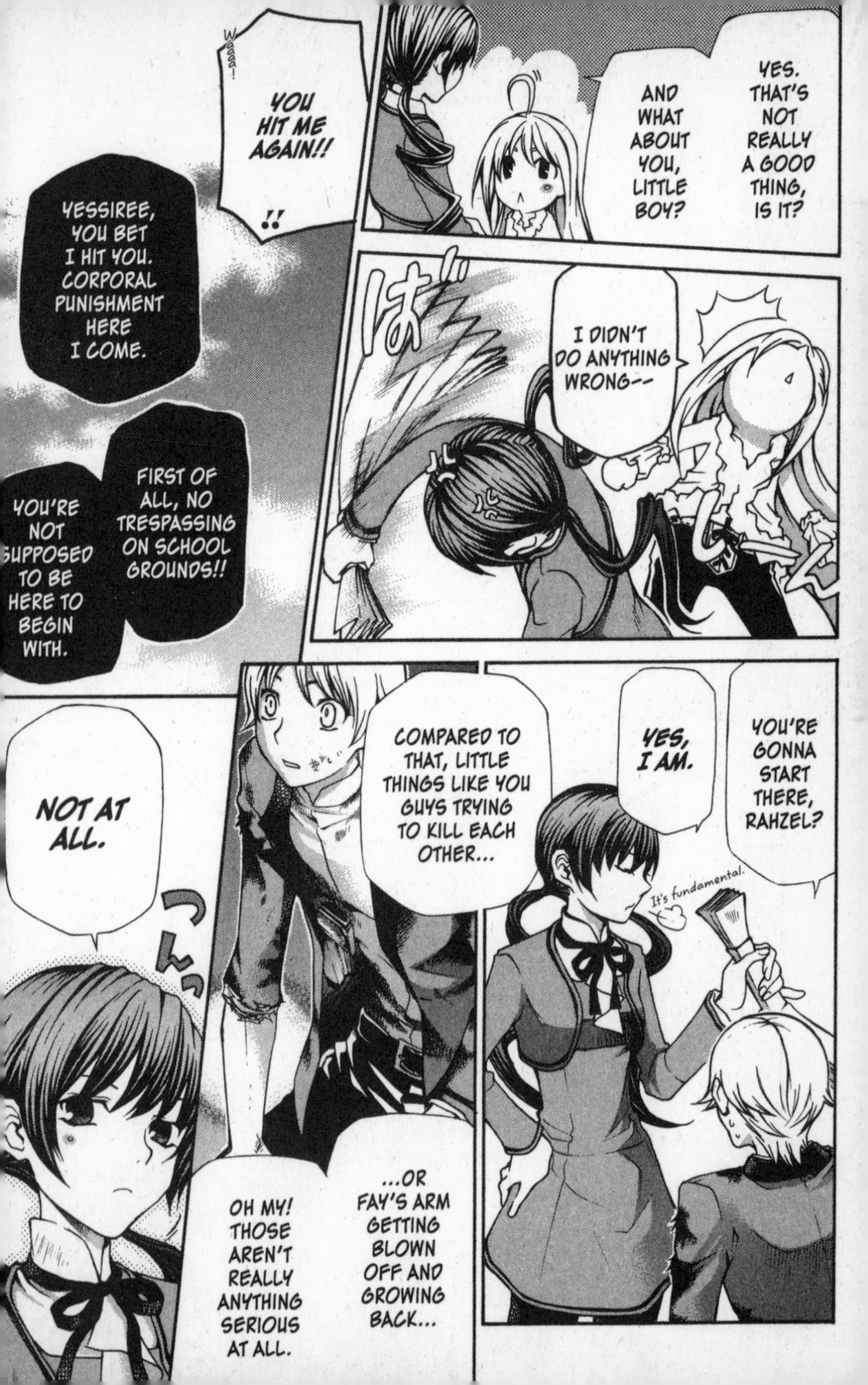
YES. THAT'S NOT REALLY A GOOD THING, IS IT?
AND WHAT ABOUT YOU, LITTLE BOY?
I DIDN'T DO ANYTHING WRONG--
YOU HIT ME AGAIN!!
!!
YESSIREE, YOU BET I HIT YOU. CORPORAL PUNISHMENT HERE I COME.
FIRST OF ALL, NO TRESPASSING ON SCHOOL GROUNDS!!
YOU'RE NOT SUPPOSED TO BE HERE TO BEGIN WITH.
YOU'RE GONNA START THERE, RAHZEL?
YES, I AM.
It's fundamental.
COMPARED TO THAT, LITTLE THINGS LIKE YOU GUYS TRYING TO KILL EACH OTHER...
...OR FAY'S ARM GETTING BLOWN OFF AND GROWING BACK...
OH MY! THOSE AREN'T REALLY ANYTHING SERIOUS AT ALL.
NOT AT ALL.

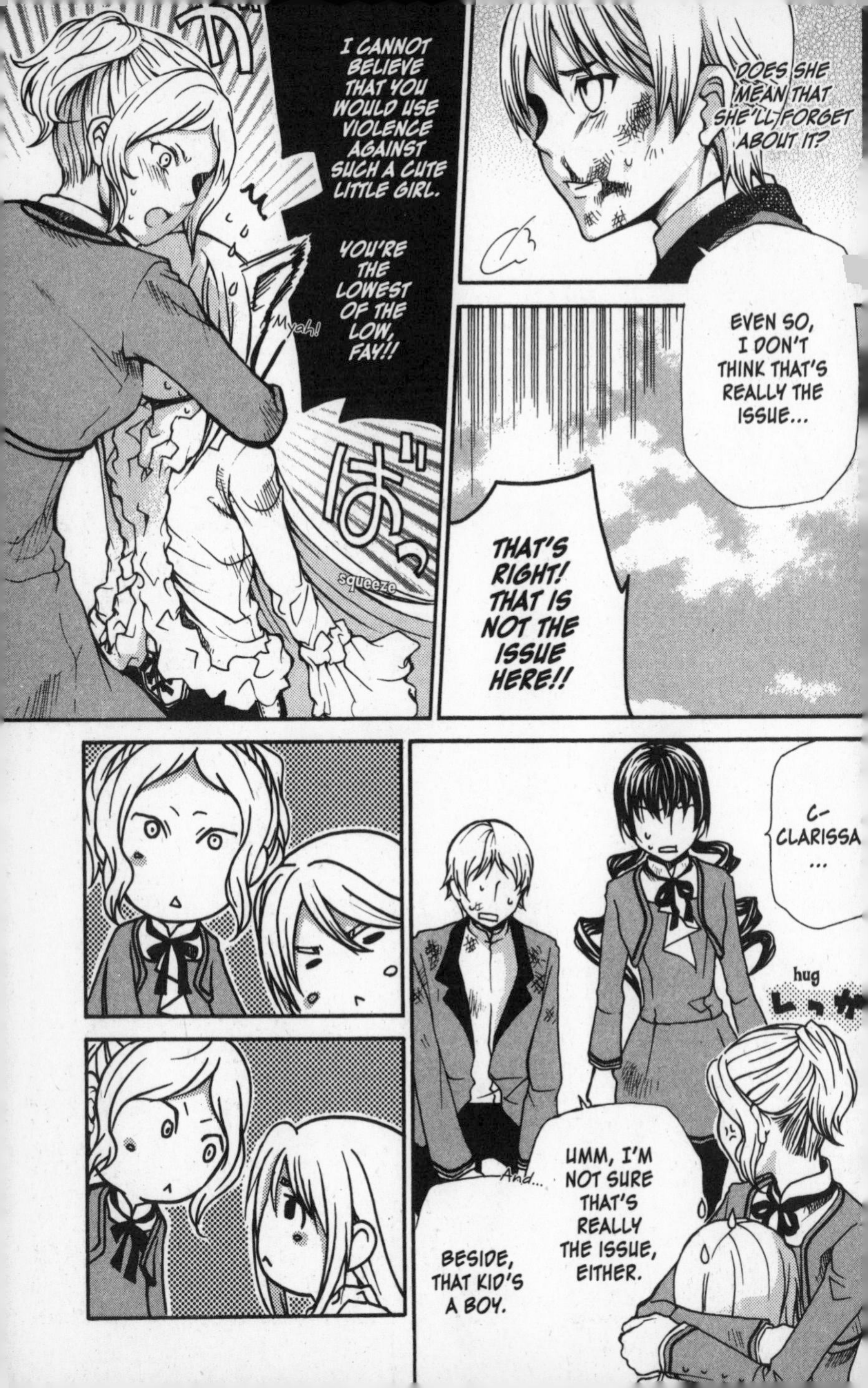
DOES SHE MEAN THAT SHE'LL FORGET ABOUT IT?
EVEN SO, I DON'T THINK THAT'S REALLY THE ISSUE...
THAT'S RIGHT! THAT IS NOT THE ISSUE HERE!!
I CANNOT BELIEVE THAT YOU WOULD USE VIOLENCE AGAINST SUCH A CUTE LITTLE GIRL.
YOU'RE THE LOWEST OF THE LOW, FAY!!
Myah!
squeeze
C-CLARISSA...
hug
UMM, I'M NOT SURE THAT'S REALLY THE ISSUE, EITHER.
And...
BESIDE, THAT KID'S A BOY.

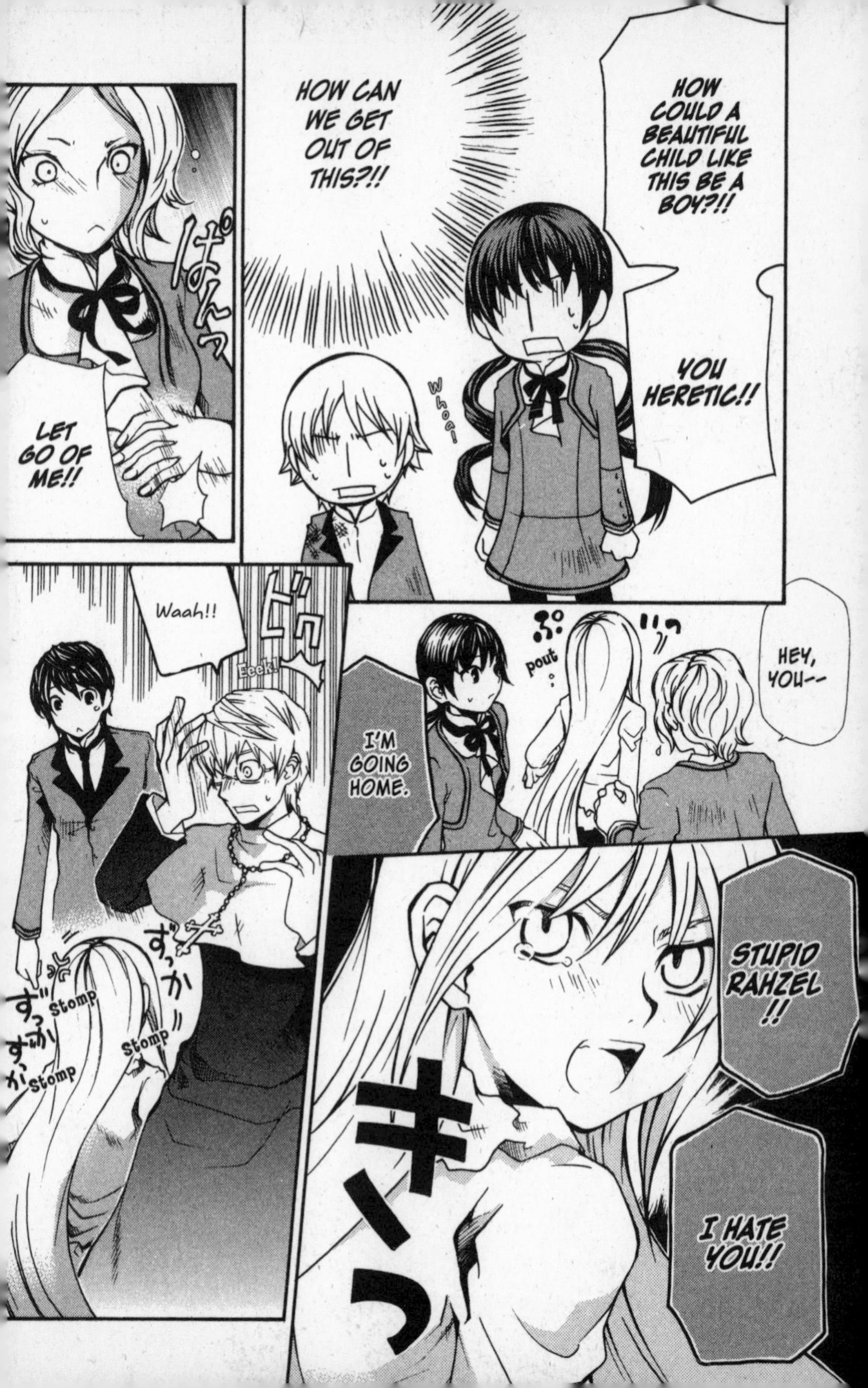
HOW COULD A BEAUTIFUL CHILD LIKE THIS BE A BOY?!!
HOW CAN WE GET OUT OF THIS?!!
YOU HERETIC!!
Whoa!
ぱんっ
LET GO OF ME!!
HEY, YOU--
ぷいっ
pout
I'M GOING HOME.
STUPID RAHZEL!!
I HATE YOU!!
キーっ
Waah!!
ビクッ
Eeek!
ずかずか
Stomp
Stomp
Stomp

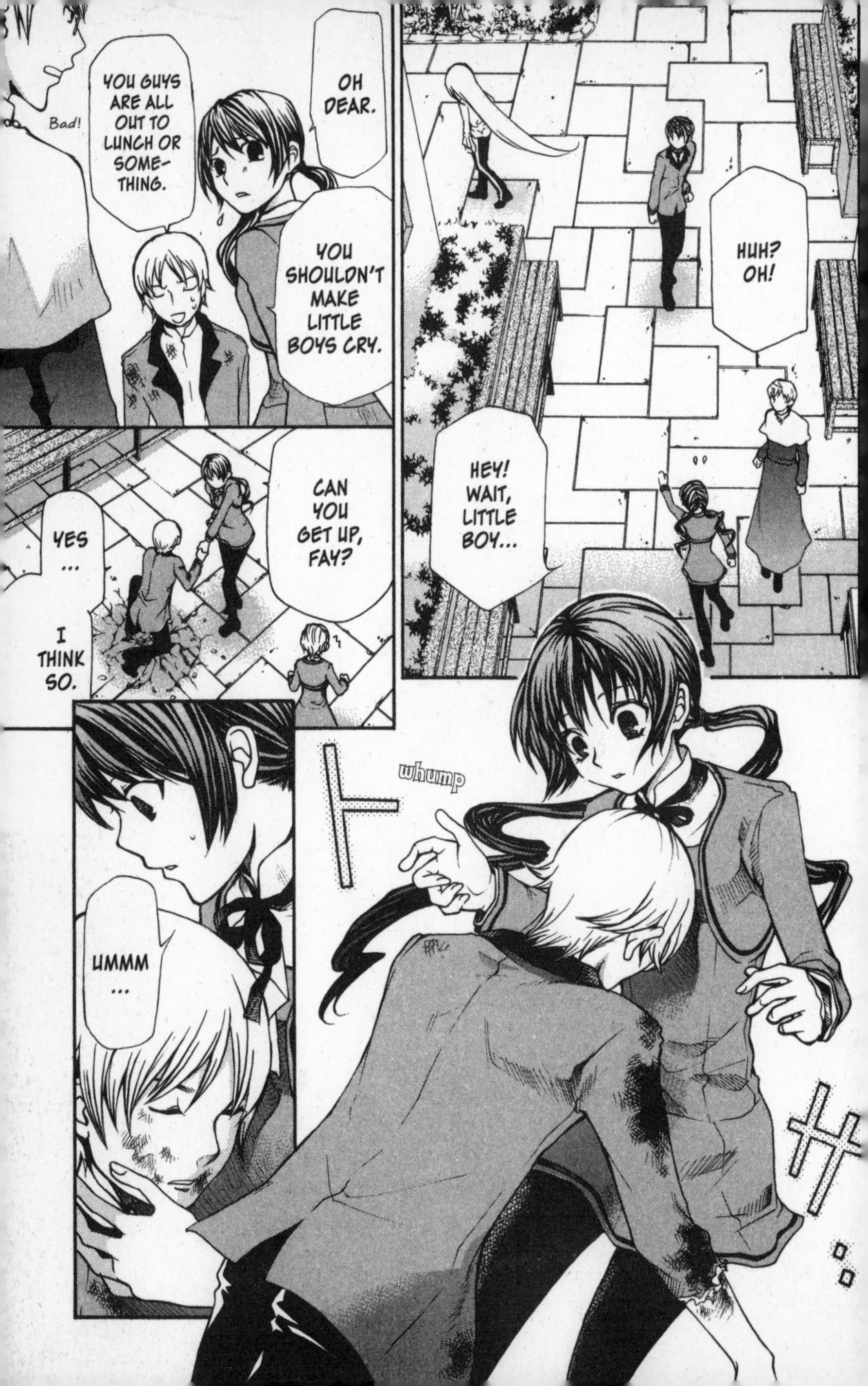
HUH? OH!
HEY! WAIT, LITTLE BOY...
OH DEAR.
YOU GUYS ARE ALL OUT TO LUNCH OR SOME-THING.
Bad!
YOU SHOULDN'T MAKE LITTLE BOYS CRY.
CAN YOU GET UP, FAY?
YES ... I THINK SO.
whump
UMMM ...

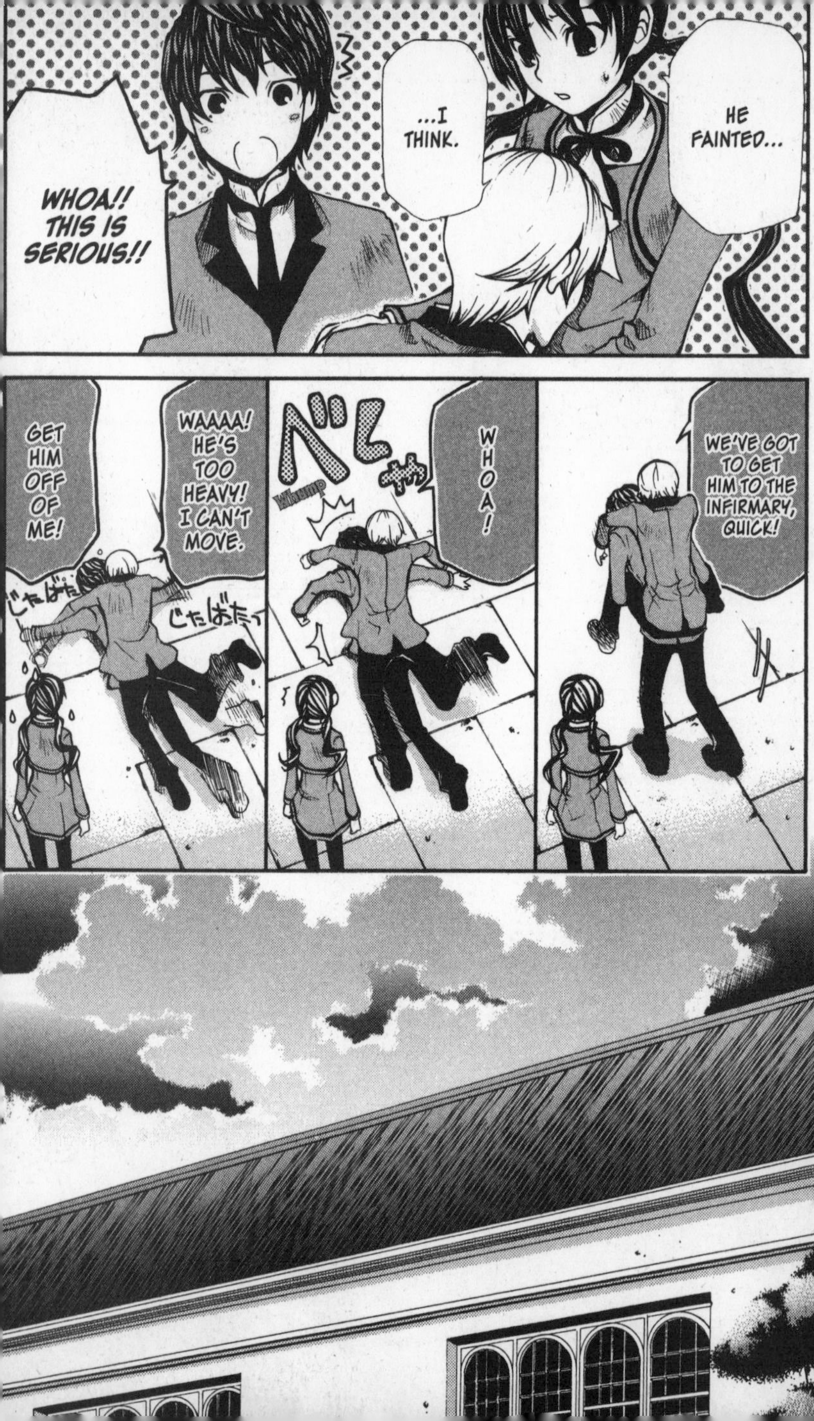
HE FAINTED...
...I THINK.
WHOA!! THIS IS SERIOUS!!
WE'VE GOT TO GET HIM TO THE INFIRMARY, QUICK!
WHOA!
Whump
WAAAA! HE'S TOO HEAVY! I CAN'T MOVE.
GET HIM OFF OF ME!

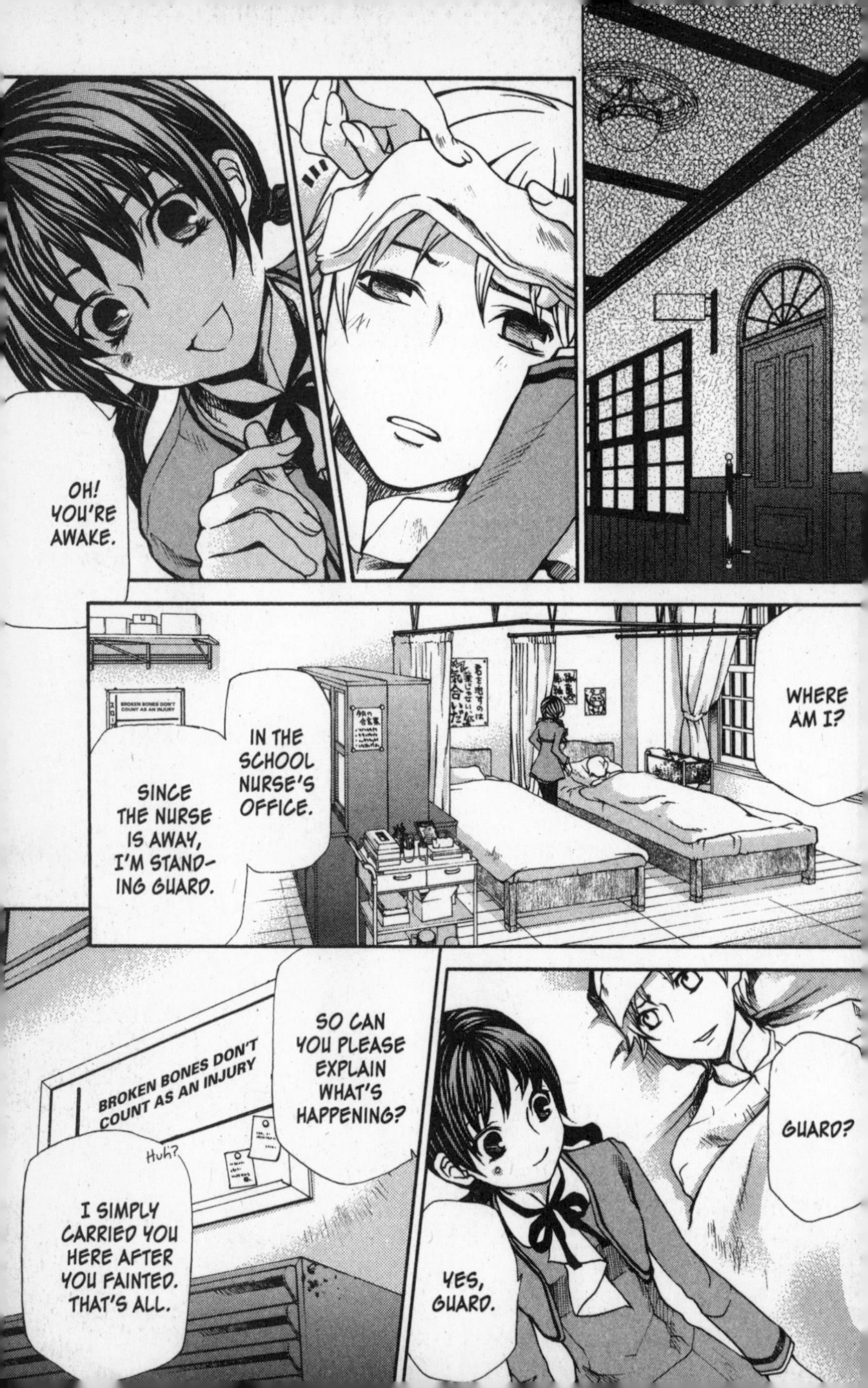
OH! YOU'RE AWAKE.
WHERE AM I?
IN THE SCHOOL NURSE'S OFFICE.
SINCE THE NURSE IS AWAY, I'M STANDING-ING GUARD.
BROKEN BONES DON'T COUNT AS AN INJURY
GUARD?
YES, GUARD.
SO CAN YOU PLEASE EXPLAIN WHAT'S HAPPENING?
BROKEN BONES DON'T COUNT AS AN INJURY
Huh?
I SIMPLY CARRIED YOU HERE AFTER YOU FAINTED. THAT'S ALL.

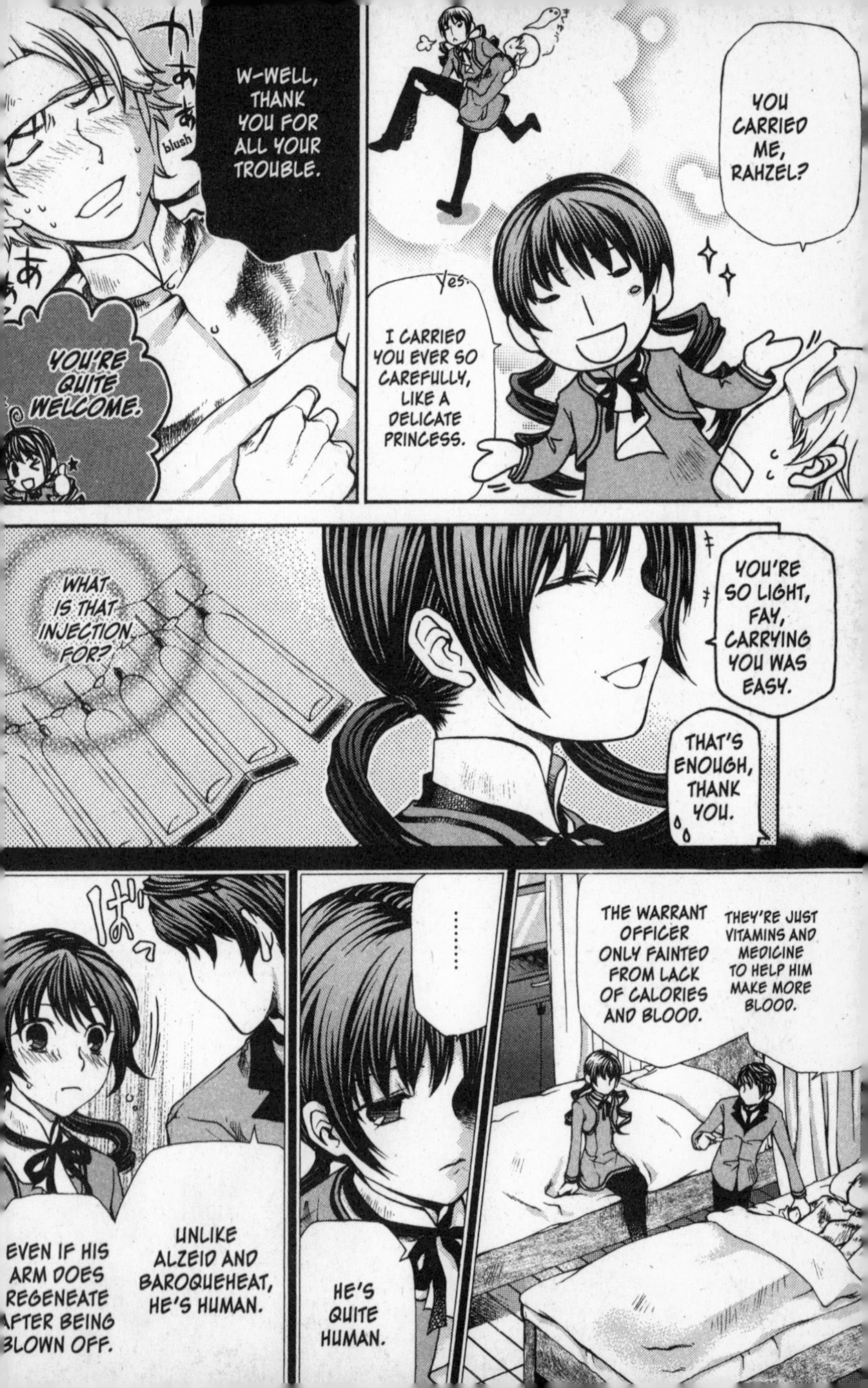
YOU CARRIED ME, RAHZEL?
Yes.
I CARRIED YOU EVER SO CAREFULLY, LIKE A DELICATE PRINCESS.
W-WELL, THANK YOU FOR ALL YOUR TROUBLE.
blush
YOU'RE QUITE WELCOME.
YOU'RE SO LIGHT, FAY, CARRYING YOU WAS EASY.
THAT'S ENOUGH, THANK YOU.
WHAT IS THAT INJECTION FOR?
THE WARRANT OFFICER ONLY FAINTED FROM LACK OF CALORIES AND BLOOD.
THEY'RE JUST VITAMINS AND MEDICINE TO HELP HIM MAKE MORE BLOOD.
......
HE'S QUITE HUMAN.
UNLIKE ALZEID AND BAROQUEHEAT, HE'S HUMAN.
EVEN IF HIS ARM DOES REGENEATE AFTER BEING BLOWN OFF.

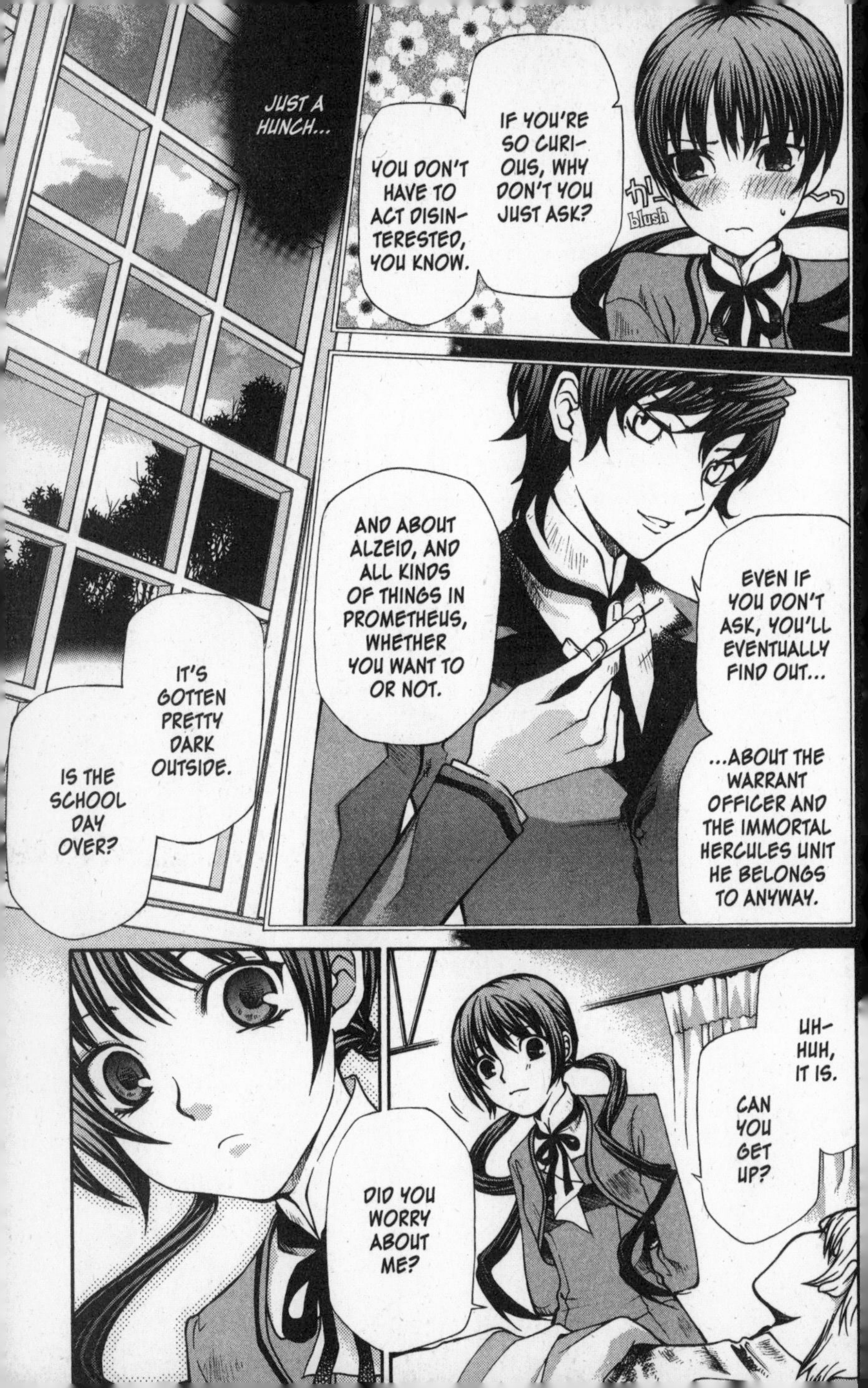
IF YOU'RE SO CURIOUS, WHY DON'T YOU JUST ASK?
YOU DON'T HAVE TO ACT DISINTERESTED, YOU KNOW.
blush
EVEN IF YOU DON'T ASK, YOU'LL EVENTUALLY FIND OUT...
...ABOUT THE WARRANT OFFICER AND THE IMMORTAL HERCULES UNIT HE BELONGS TO ANYWAY.
AND ABOUT ALZEID, AND ALL KINDS OF THINGS IN PROMETHEUS, WHETHER YOU WANT TO OR NOT.
JUST A HUNCH...
IT'S GOTTEN PRETTY DARK OUTSIDE.
IS THE SCHOOL DAY OVER?
UH-HUH, IT IS.
CAN YOU GET UP?
DID YOU WORRY ABOUT ME?

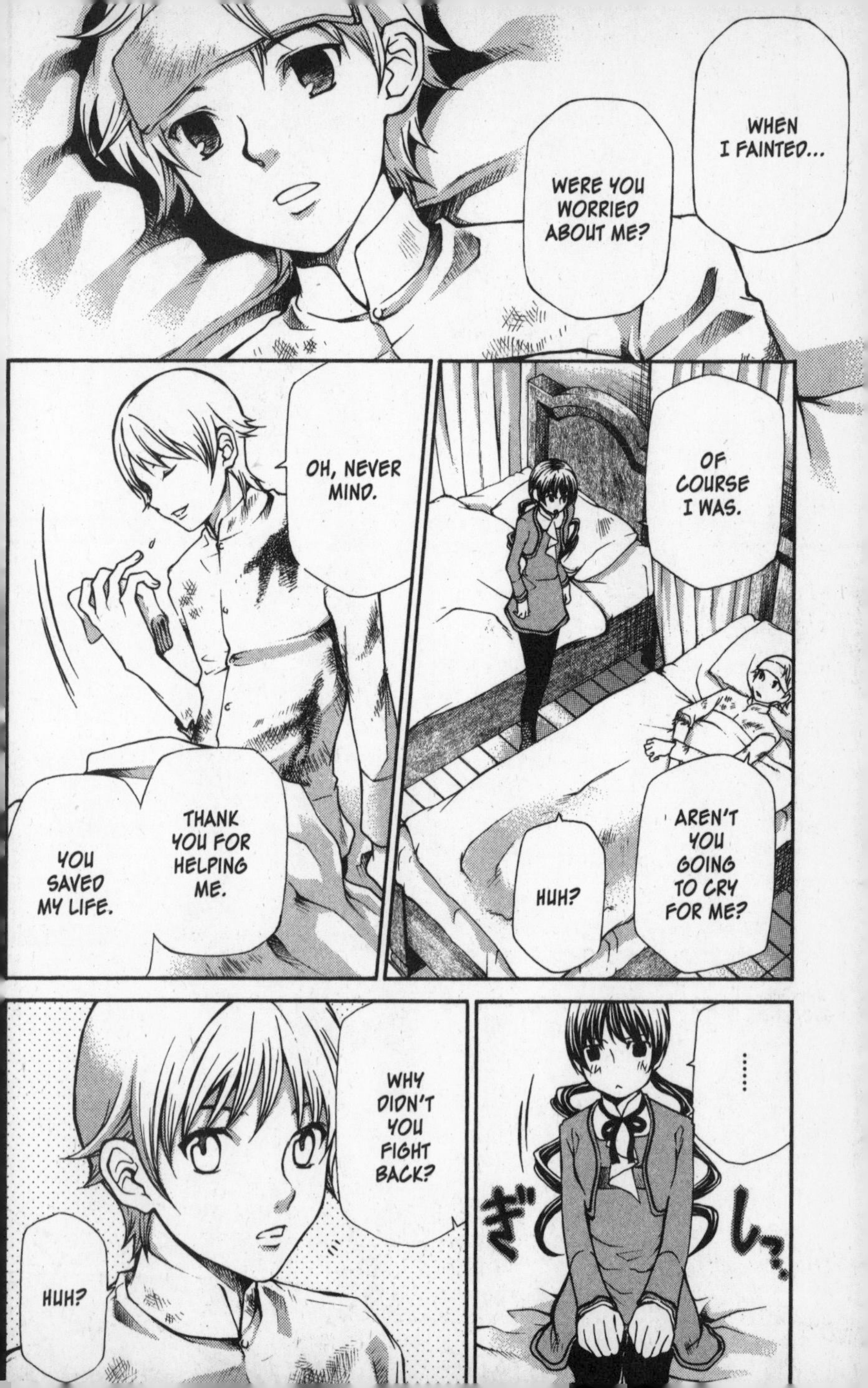
WHEN I FAINTED...
WERE YOU WORRIED ABOUT ME?
OF COURSE I WAS.
AREN'T YOU GOING TO CRY FOR ME?
HUH?
OH, NEVER MIND.
THANK YOU FOR HELPING ME.
YOU SAVED MY LIFE.
......
ぎしっ
WHY DIDN'T YOU FIGHT BACK?
HUH?

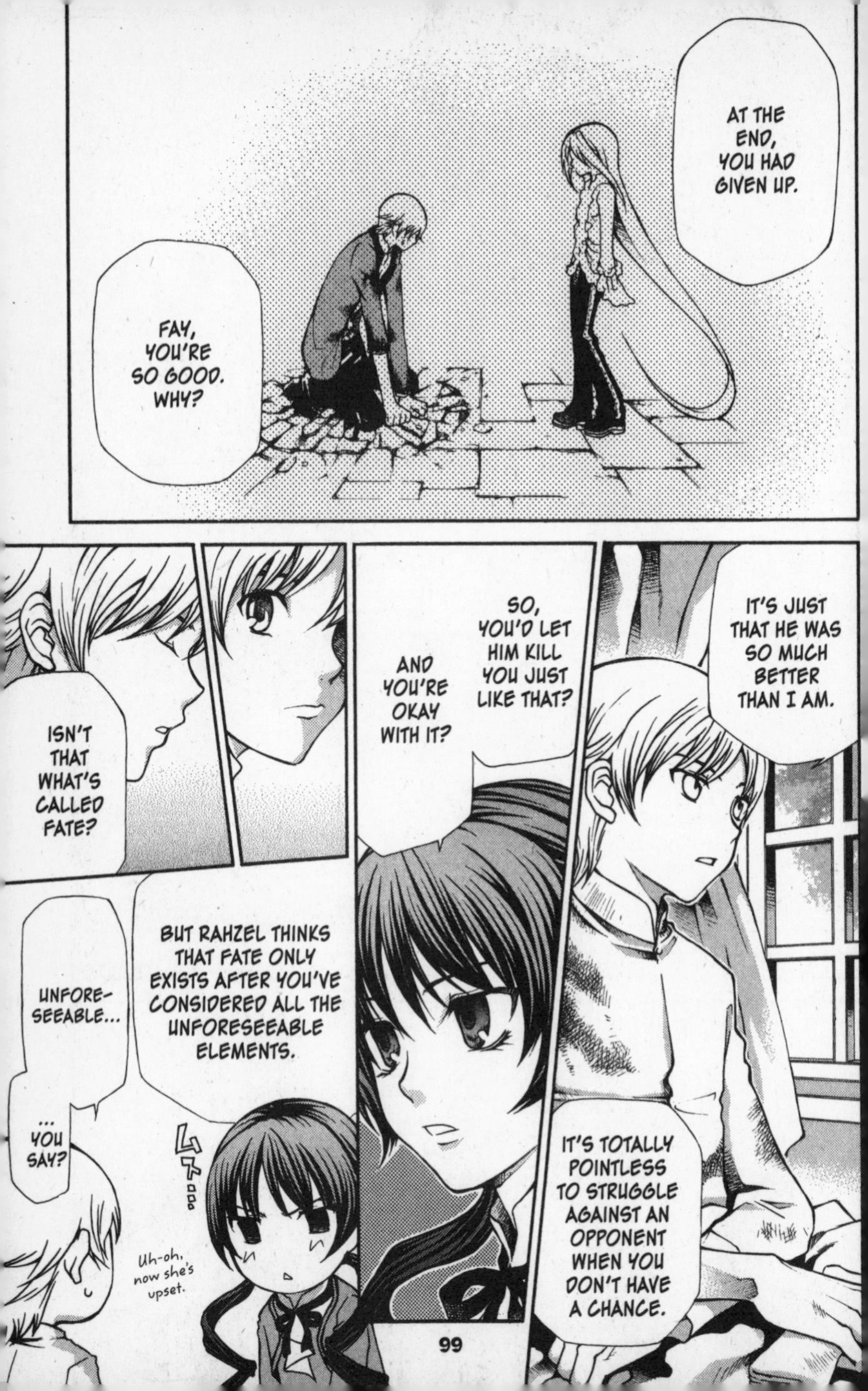
AT THE END, YOU HAD GIVEN UP.
FAY, YOU'RE SO GOOD. WHY?
IT'S JUST THAT HE WAS SO MUCH BETTER THAN I AM.
IT'S TOTALLY POINTLESS TO STRUGGLE AGAINST AN OPPONENT WHEN YOU DON'T HAVE A CHANCE.
SO, YOU'D LET HIM KILL YOU JUST LIKE THAT?
AND YOU'RE OKAY WITH IT?
ISN'T THAT WHAT'S CALLED FATE?
BUT RAHZEL THINKS THAT FATE ONLY EXISTS AFTER YOU'VE CONSIDERED ALL THE UNFORESEEABLE ELEMENTS.
UNFORE-SEEABLE...
... YOU SAY?
ムス
Uh-oh, now she's upset.

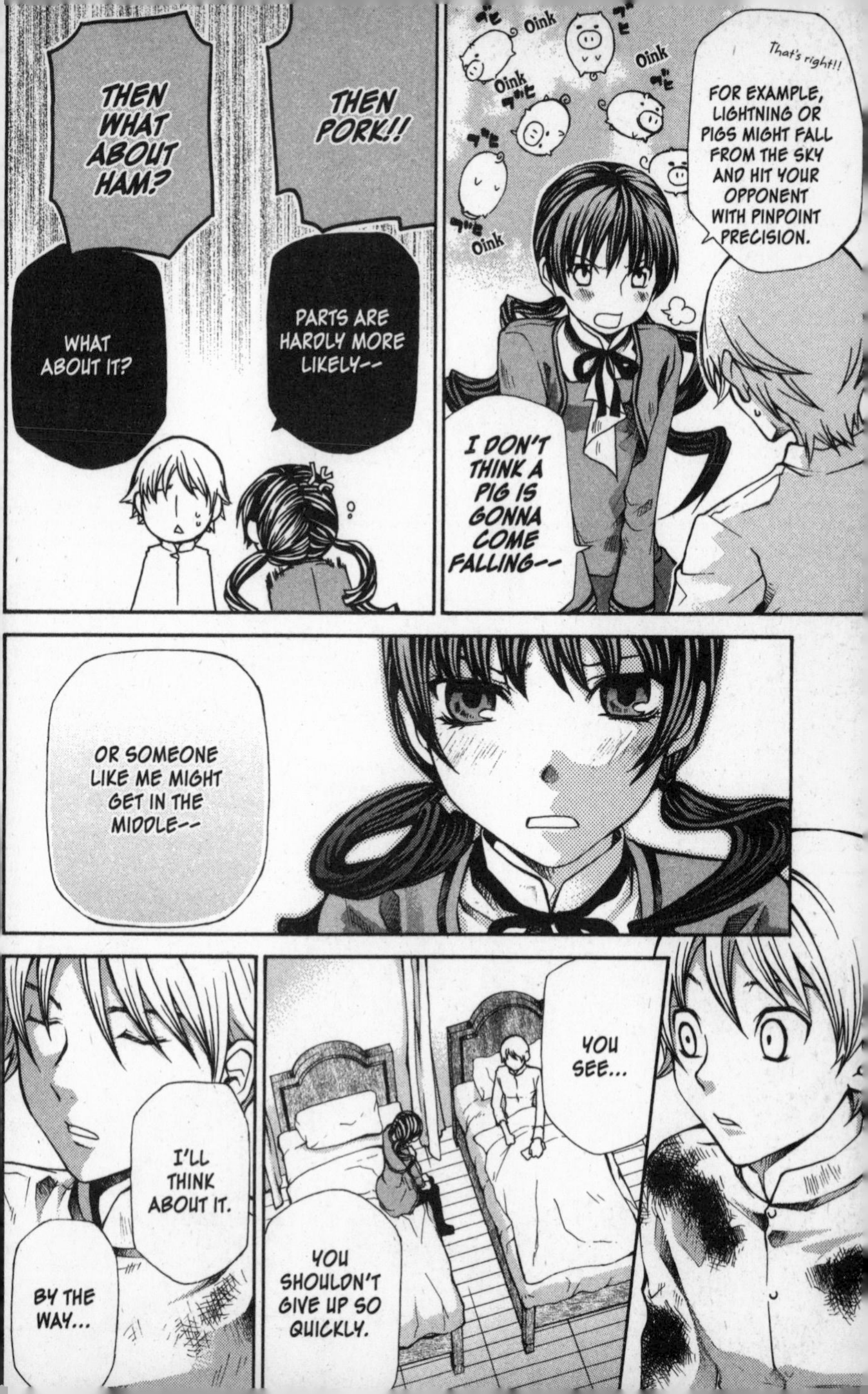

Oink
Oink
Oink
Oink
That's right!!
FOR EXAMPLE, LIGHTNING OR PIGS MIGHT FALL FROM THE SKY AND HIT YOUR OPPONENT WITH PINPOINT PRECISION.
I DON'T THINK A PIG IS GONNA COME FALLING--
THEN PORK!!
PARTS ARE HARDLY MORE LIKELY--
THEN WHAT ABOUT HAM?
WHAT ABOUT IT?
OR SOMEONE LIKE ME MIGHT GET IN THE MIDDLE--
YOU SEE...
YOU SHOULDN'T GIVE UP SO QUICKLY.
I'LL THINK ABOUT IT.
BY THE WAY...

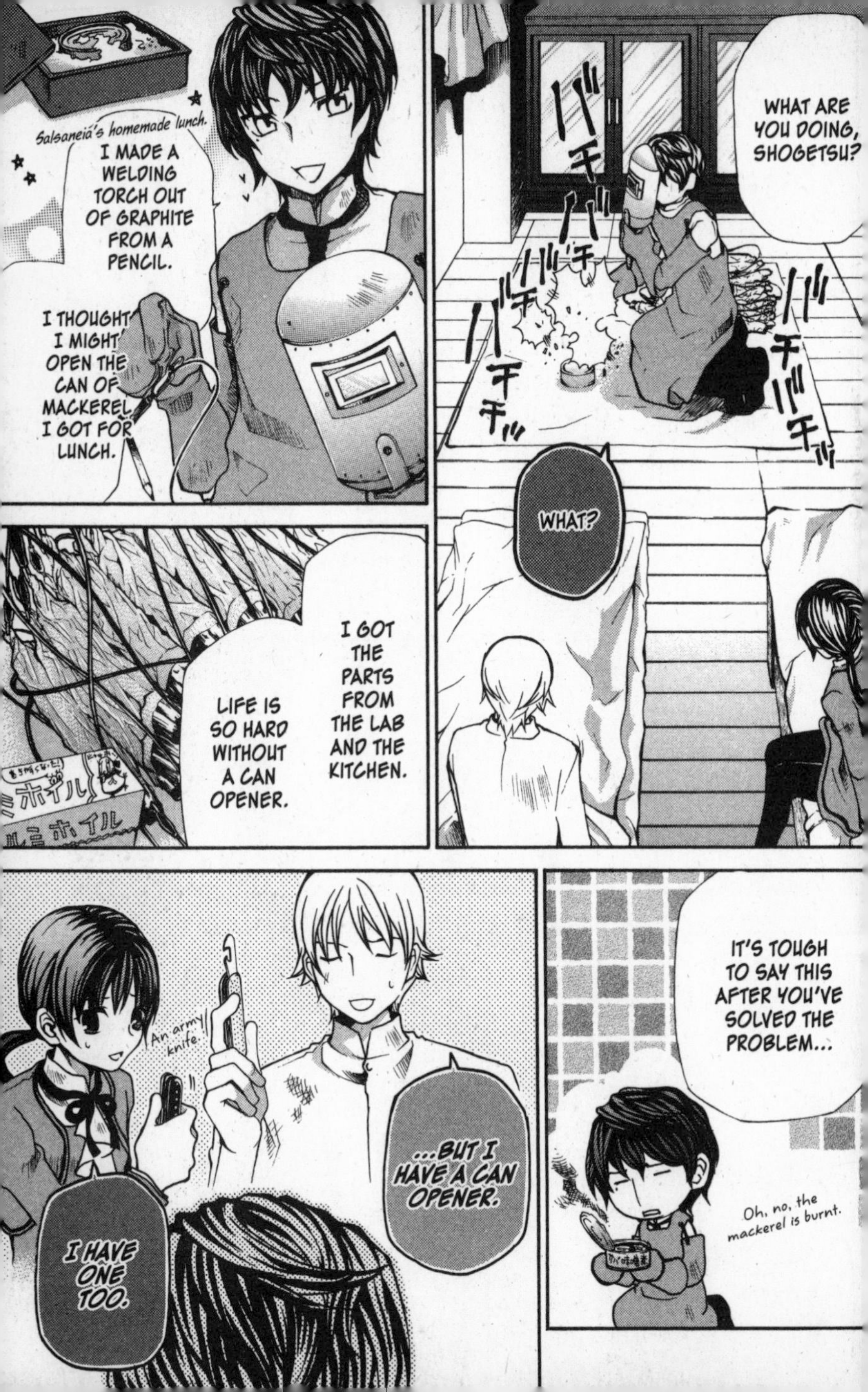
WHAT ARE YOU DOING, SHOGETSU?
Salsaneia's homemade lunch.
I MADE A WELDING TORCH OUT OF GRAPHITE FROM A PENCIL.
I THOUGHT I MIGHT OPEN THE CAN OF MACKEREL I GOT FOR LUNCH.
WHAT?
I GOT THE PARTS FROM THE LAB AND THE KITCHEN.
LIFE IS SO HARD WITHOUT A CAN OPENER.
IT'S TOUGH TO SAY THIS AFTER YOU'VE SOLVED THE PROBLEM...
Oh, no, the mackerel is burnt.
...BUT I HAVE A CAN OPENER.
An army knife.
I HAVE ONE TOO.

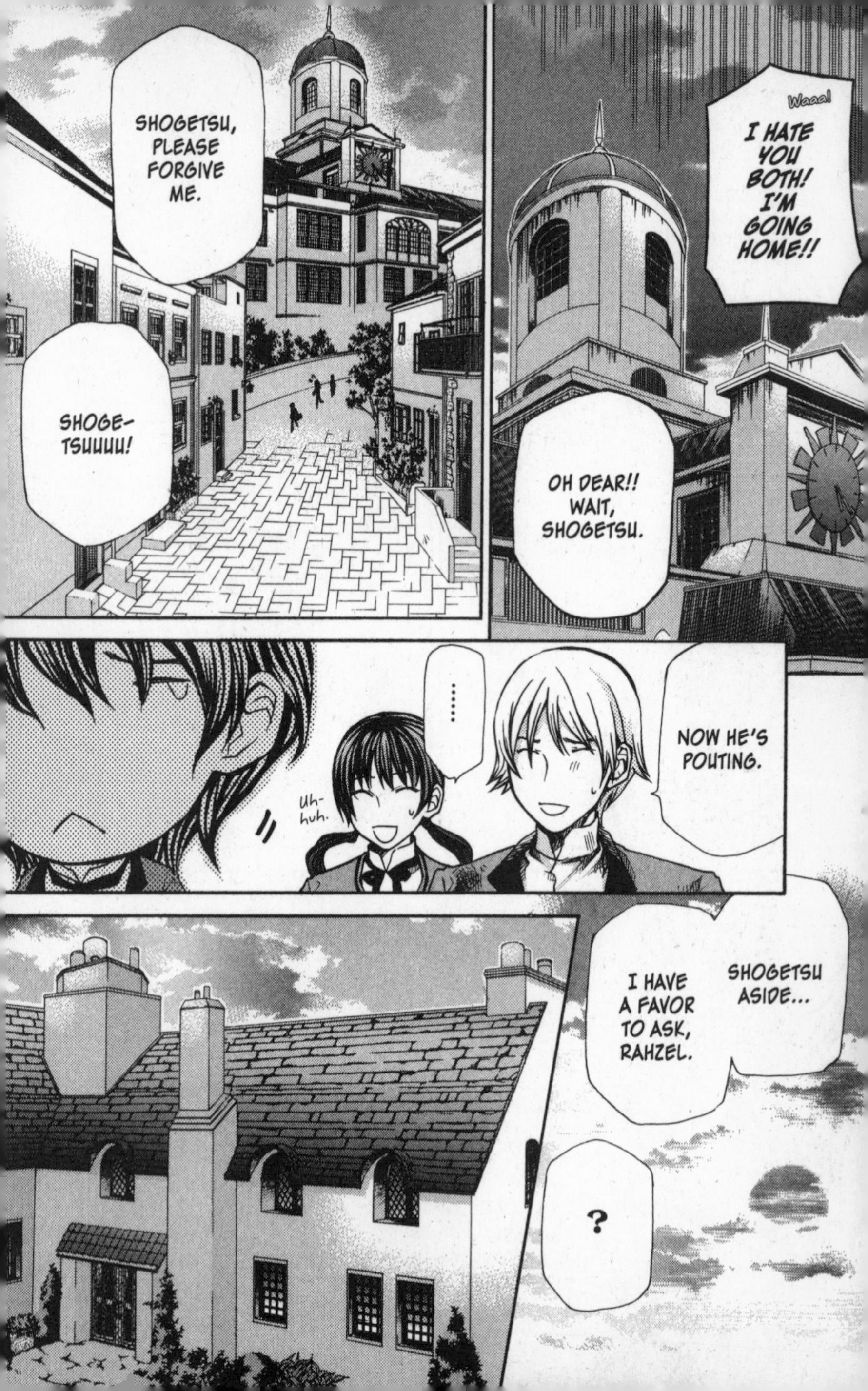
Waaa!
I HATE YOU BOTH! I'M GOING HOME!!
OH DEAR!! WAIT, SHOGETSU.
SHOGETSU, PLEASE FORGIVE ME.
SHOGE-TSUUUU!
NOW HE'S POUTING.
......
Uh-huh.
SHOGETSU ASIDE...
I HAVE A FAVOR TO ASK, RAHZEL.
?

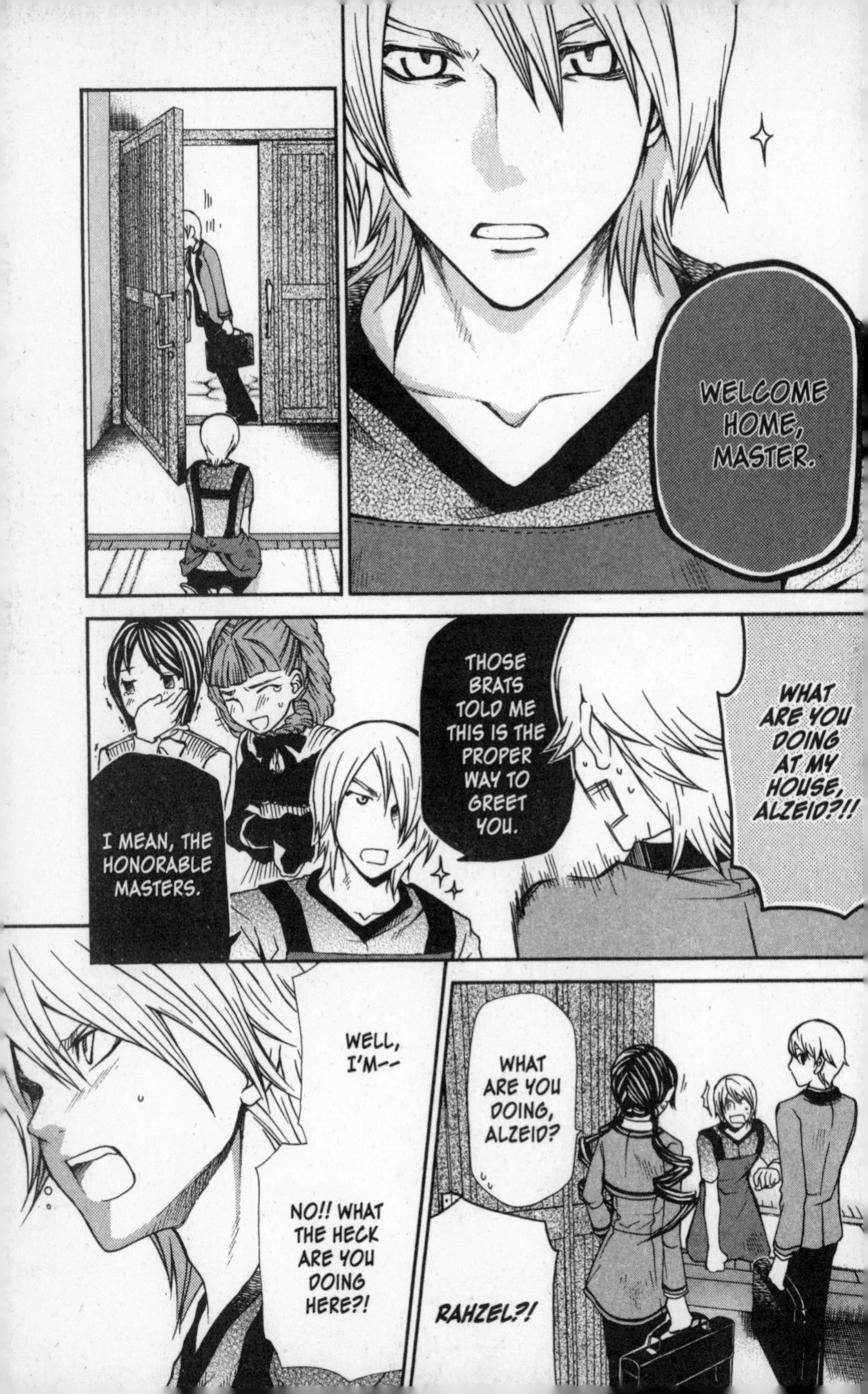
WELCOME HOME, MASTER.
WHAT ARE YOU DOING AT MY HOUSE, ALZEID?!!
THOSE BRATS TOLD ME THIS IS THE PROPER WAY TO GREET YOU.
I MEAN, THE HONORABLE MASTERS.
WHAT ARE YOU DOING, ALZEID?
RAHZEL?!
WELL, I'M--
NO!! WHAT THE HECK ARE YOU DOING HERE?!

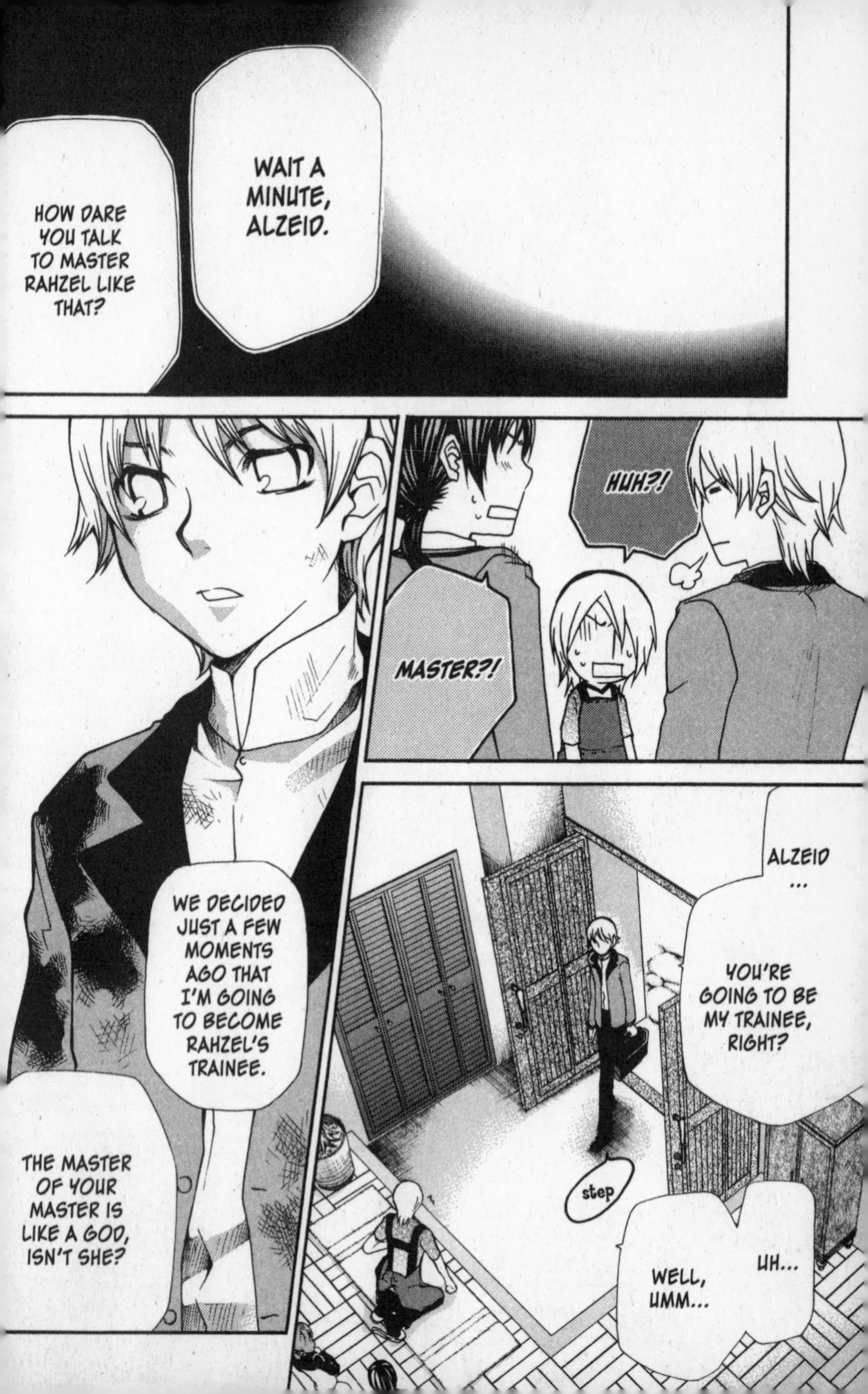
WAIT A MINUTE, ALZEID.
HOW DARE YOU TALK TO MASTER RAHZEL LIKE THAT?
HUH?!
MASTER?!
ALZEID...
YOU'RE GOING TO BE MY TRAINEE, RIGHT?
step
UH...
WELL, UMM...
WE DECIDED JUST A FEW MOMENTS AGO THAT I'M GOING TO BECOME RAHZEL'S TRAINEE.
THE MASTER OF YOUR MASTER IS LIKE A GOD, ISN'T SHE?

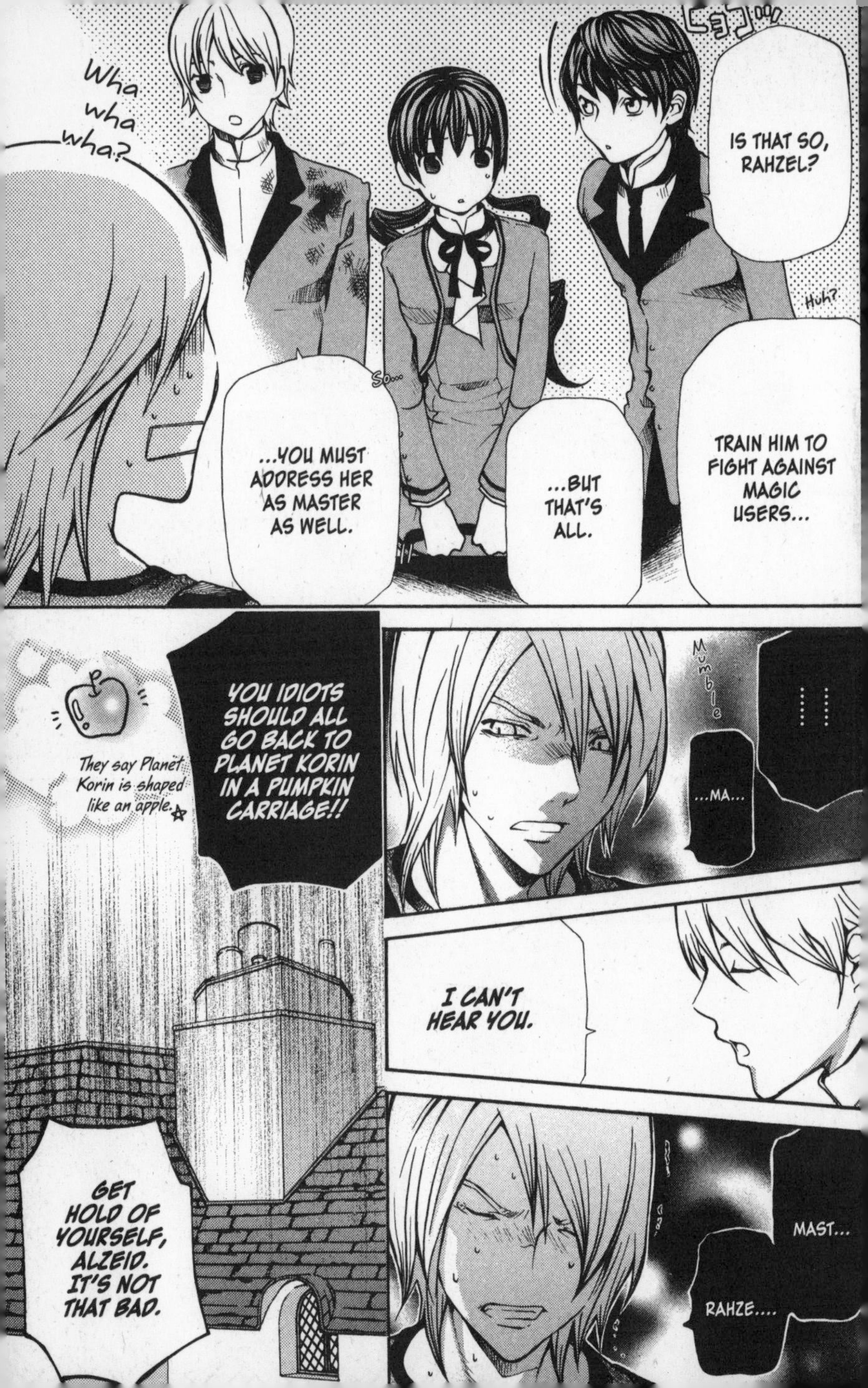
IS THAT SO, RAHZEL?
Huh?
TRAIN HIM TO FIGHT AGAINST MAGIC USERS...
...BUT THAT'S ALL.
So...
...YOU MUST ADDRESS HER AS MASTER AS WELL.
Wha wha wha?
Mumble
......
...MA...
I CAN'T HEAR YOU.
MAST...
RAHZE....
YOU IDIOTS SHOULD ALL GO BACK TO PLANET KORIN IN A PUMPKIN CARRIAGE!!
They say Planet Korin is shaped like an apple.☆
GET HOLD OF YOURSELF, ALZEID. IT'S NOT THAT BAD.

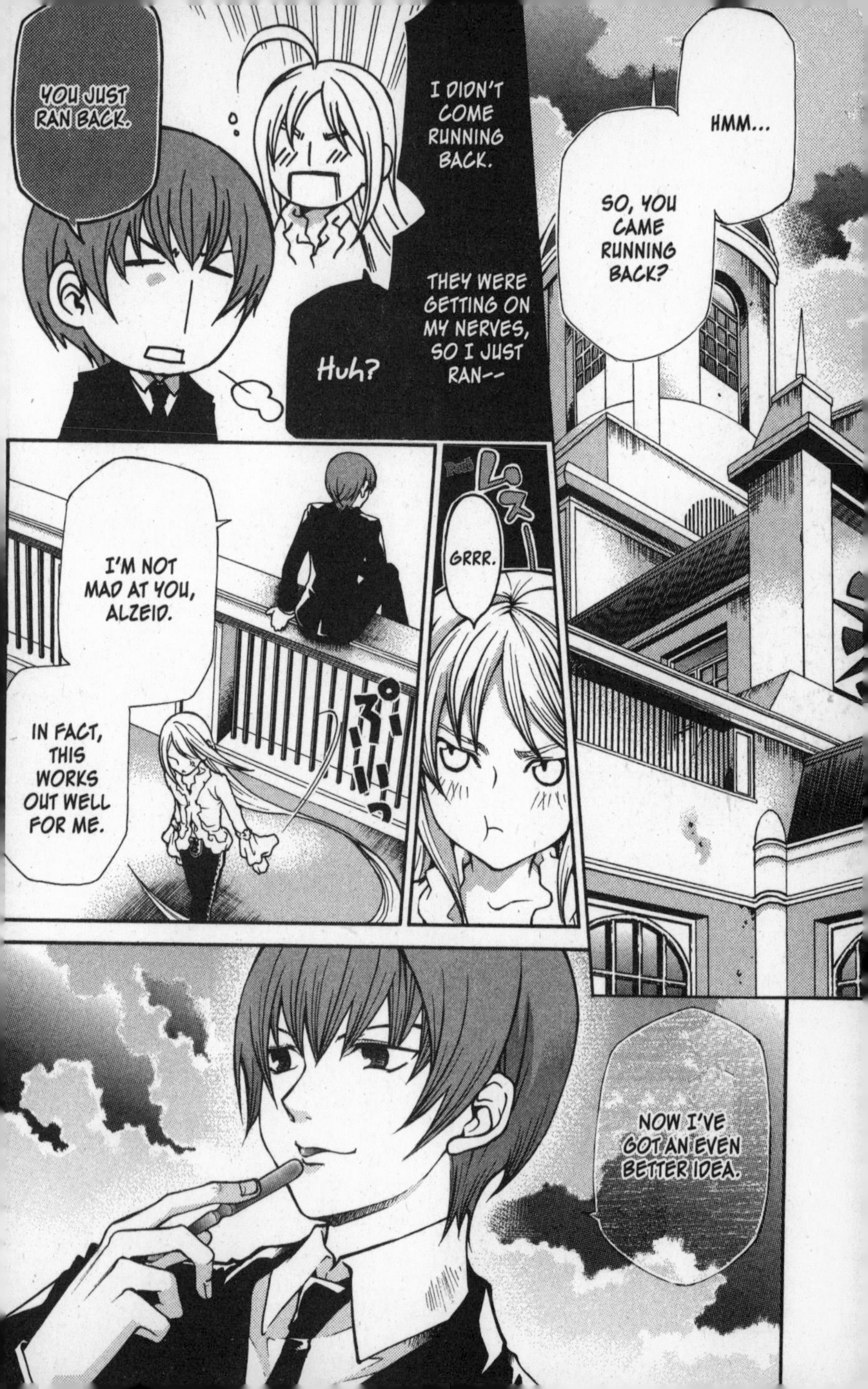
HMM...
SO, YOU CAME RUNNING BACK?
I DIDN'T COME RUNNING BACK.
THEY WERE GETTING ON MY NERVES, SO I JUST RAN--
Huh?
YOU JUST RAN BACK.
Pout
GRRR.
I'M NOT MAD AT YOU, ALZEID.
IN FACT, THIS WORKS OUT WELL FOR ME.
NOW I'VE GOT AN EVEN BETTER IDEA.

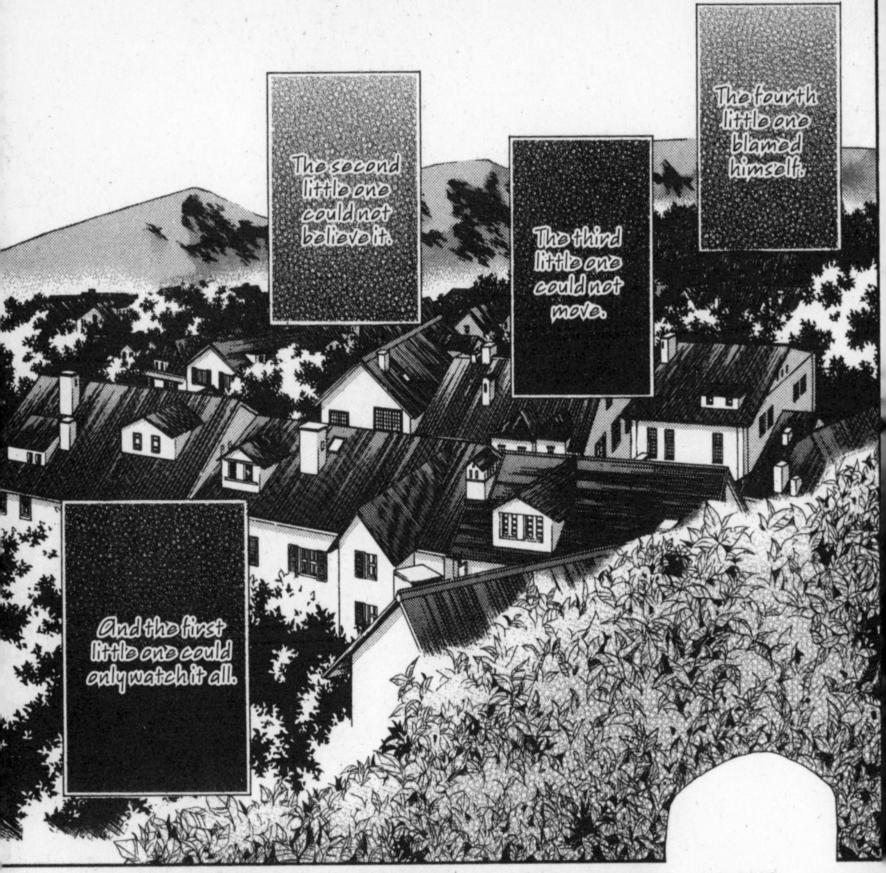
The second little one could not believe it.
The third little one could not move.
The fourth little one blamed himself.
And the first little one could only watch it all.

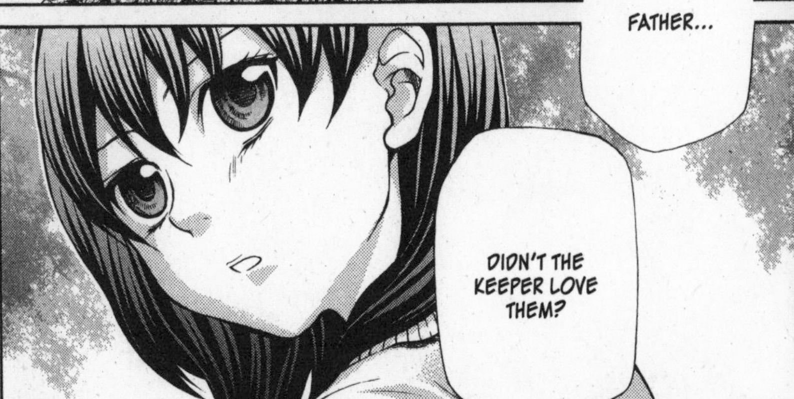
FATHER...
DIDN'T THE KEEPER LOVE THEM?

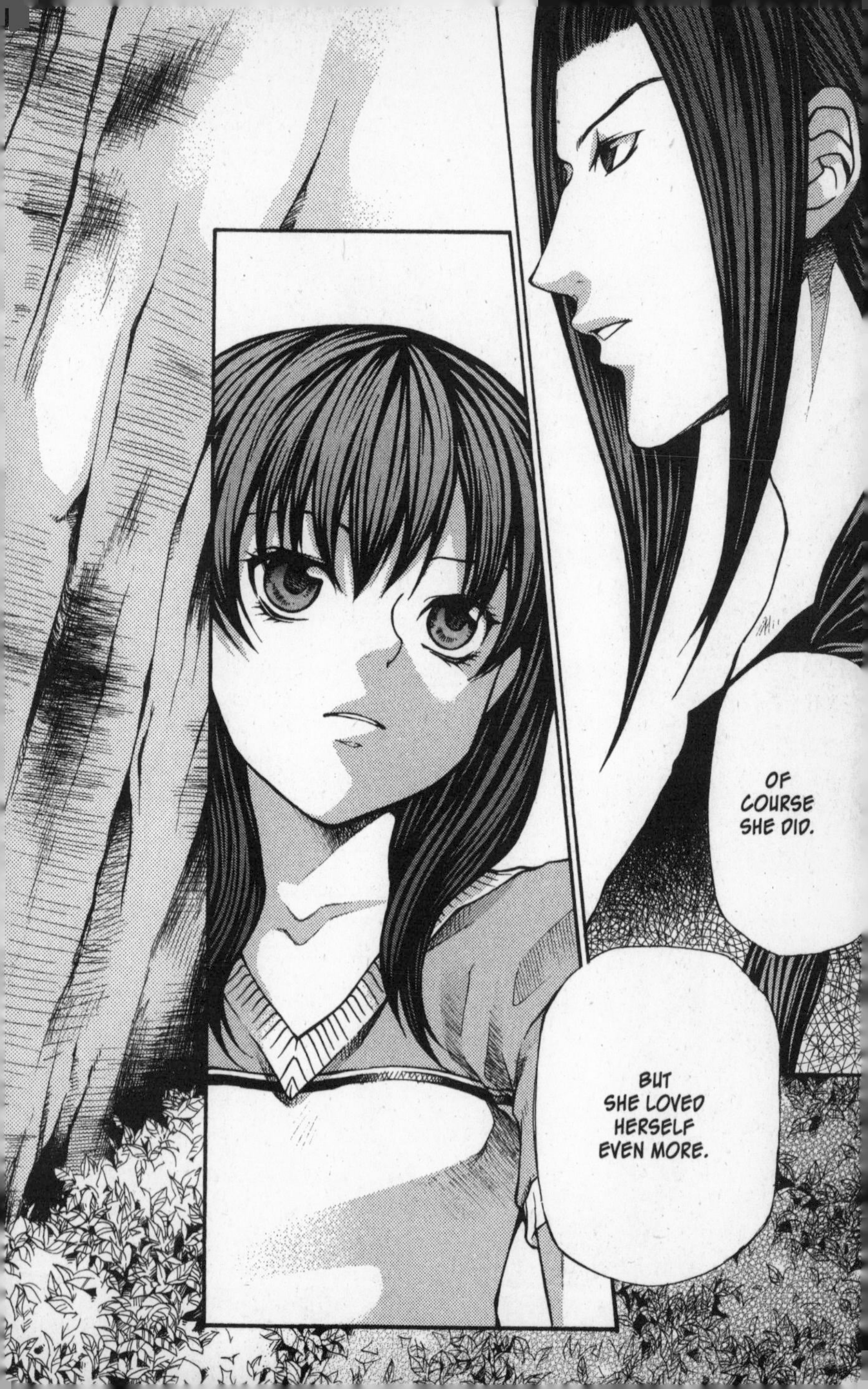
OF COURSE SHE DID.
BUT SHE LOVED HERSELF EVEN MORE.

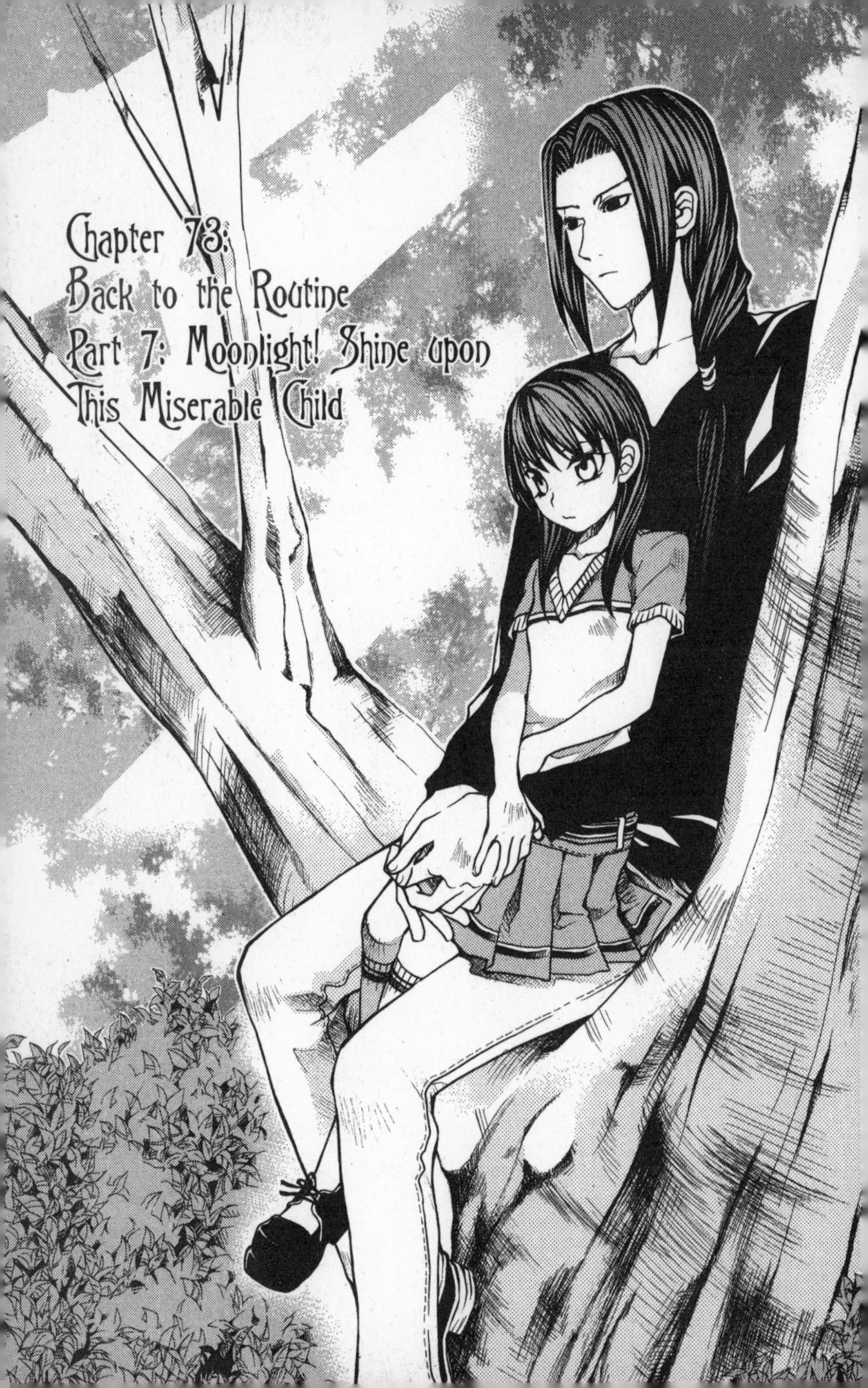
Chapter 73:
Back to the Routine
Part 7: Moonlight! Shine upon
This Miserable Child

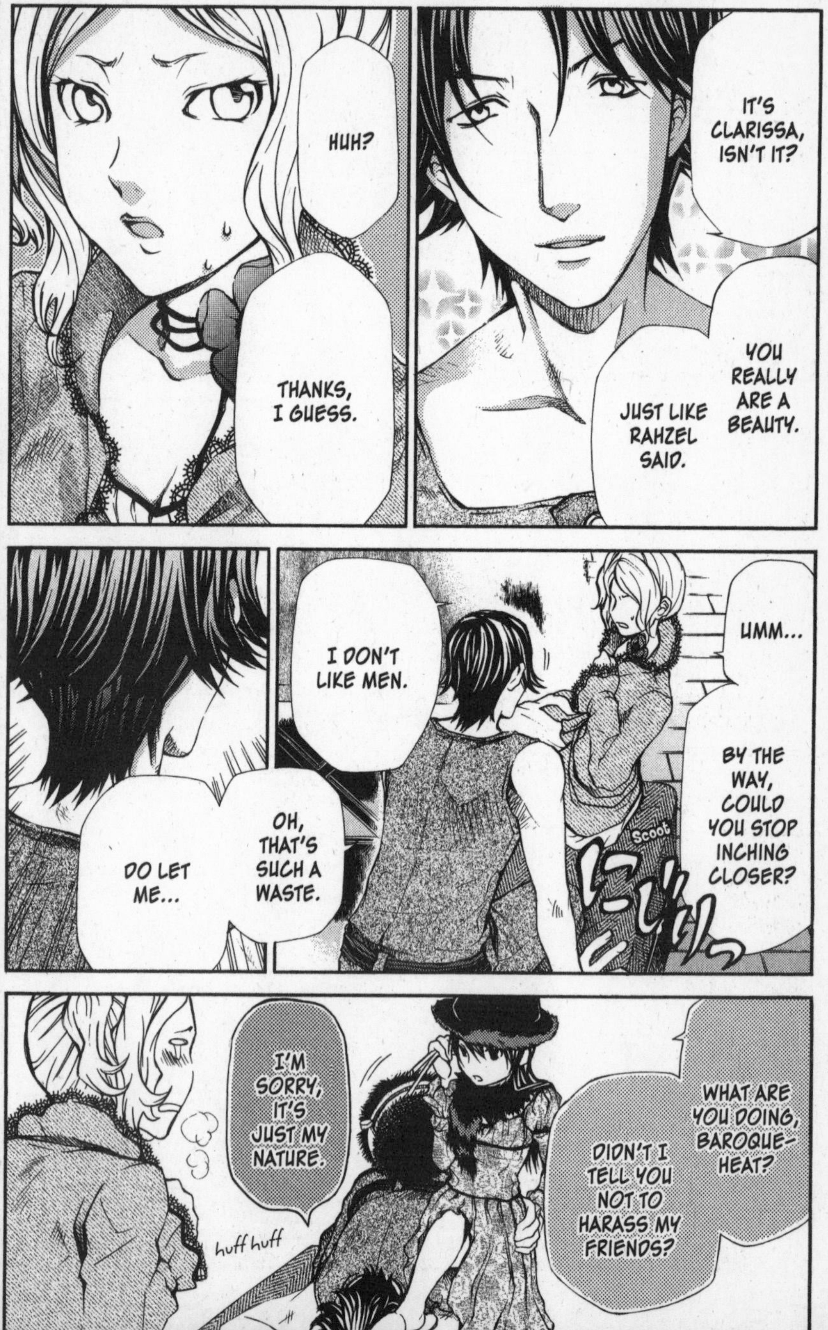
IT'S CLARISSA, ISN'T IT?
YOU REALLY ARE A BEAUTY.
JUST LIKE RAHZEL SAID.
HUH?
THANKS, I GUESS.
UMM...
BY THE WAY, COULD YOU STOP INCHING CLOSER?
Scoot
I DON'T LIKE MEN.
OH, THAT'S SUCH A WASTE.
DO LET ME...
WHAT ARE YOU DOING, BAROQUE-HEAT?
DIDN'T I TELL YOU NOT TO HARASS MY FRIENDS?
I'M SORRY, IT'S JUST MY NATURE.
huff huff

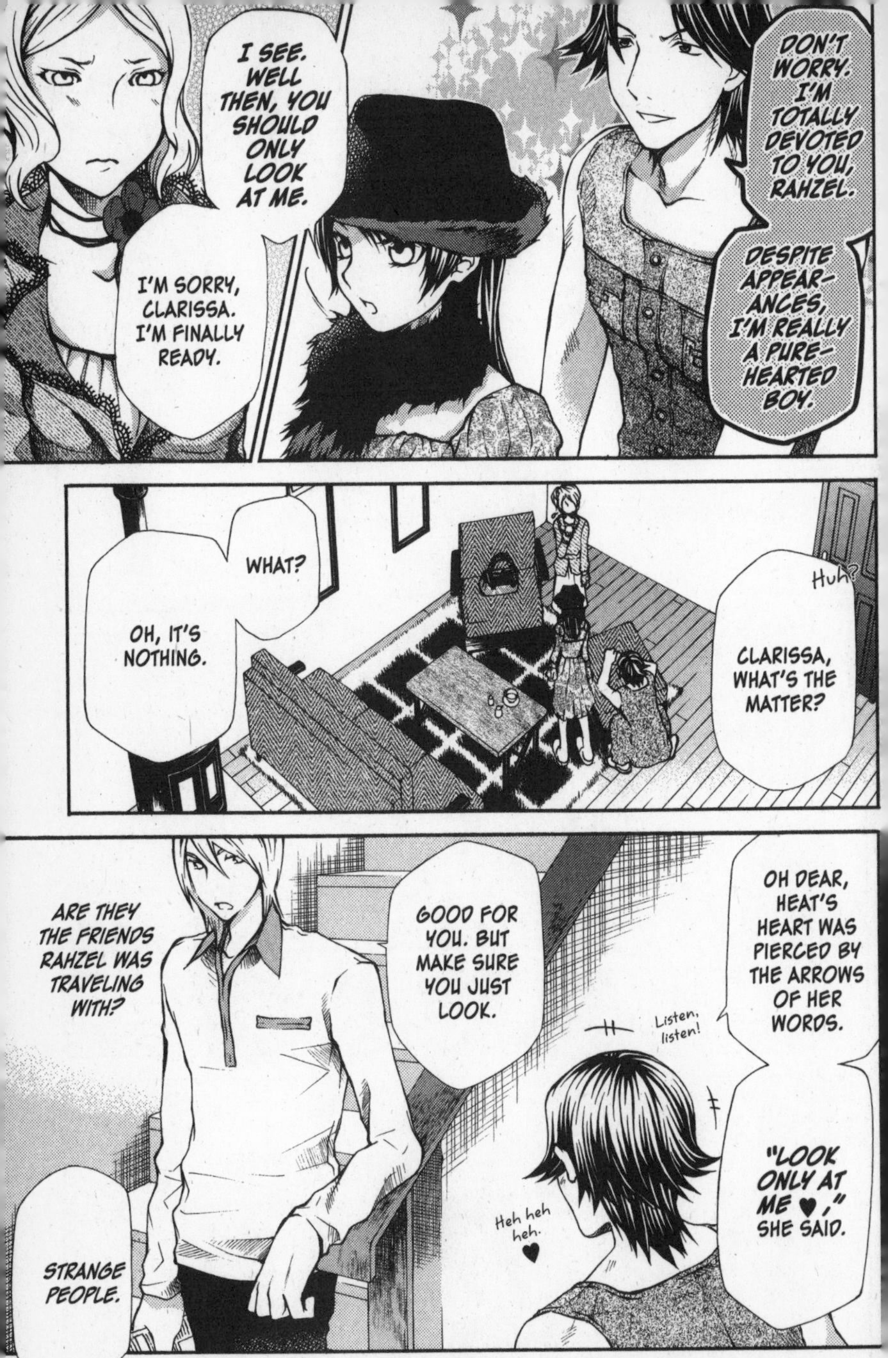
DON'T WORRY. I'M TOTALLY DEVOTED TO YOU, RAHZEL.
DESPITE APPEARANCES, I'M REALLY A PURE-HEARTED BOY.
I SEE. WELL THEN, YOU SHOULD ONLY LOOK AT ME.
I'M SORRY, CLARISSA. I'M FINALLY READY.
Huh?
CLARISSA, WHAT'S THE MATTER?
WHAT?
OH, IT'S NOTHING.
OH DEAR, HEAT'S HEART WAS PIERCED BY THE ARROWS OF HER WORDS.
"LOOK ONLY AT ME ♥," SHE SAID.
Listen, listen!
Heh heh heh. ♥
GOOD FOR YOU. BUT MAKE SURE YOU JUST LOOK.
ARE THEY THE FRIENDS RAHZEL WAS TRAVELING WITH?
STRANGE PEOPLE.

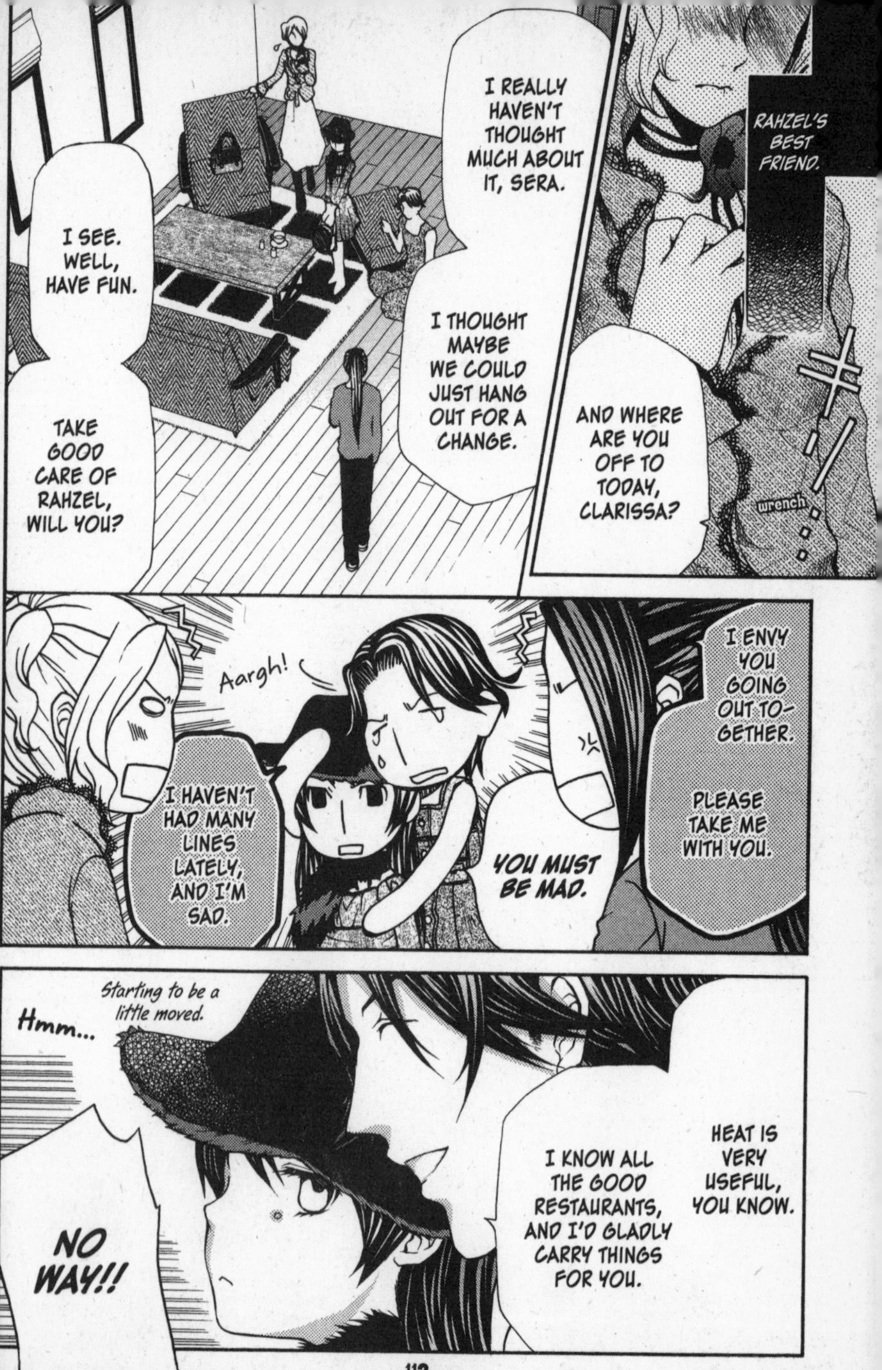
RAHZEL'S BEST FRIEND.
wrench
AND WHERE ARE YOU OFF TO TODAY, CLARISSA?
I REALLY HAVEN'T THOUGHT MUCH ABOUT IT, SERA.
I THOUGHT MAYBE WE COULD JUST HANG OUT FOR A CHANGE.
I SEE. WELL, HAVE FUN.
TAKE GOOD CARE OF RAHZEL, WILL YOU?
I ENVY YOU GOING OUT TO-GETHER.
PLEASE TAKE ME WITH YOU.
YOU MUST BE MAD.
Aargh!
I HAVEN'T HAD MANY LINES LATELY, AND I'M SAD.
HEAT IS VERY USEFUL, YOU KNOW.
I KNOW ALL THE GOOD RESTAURANTS, AND I'D GLADLY CARRY THINGS FOR YOU.
Starting to be a little moved.
Hmm...
NO WAY!!

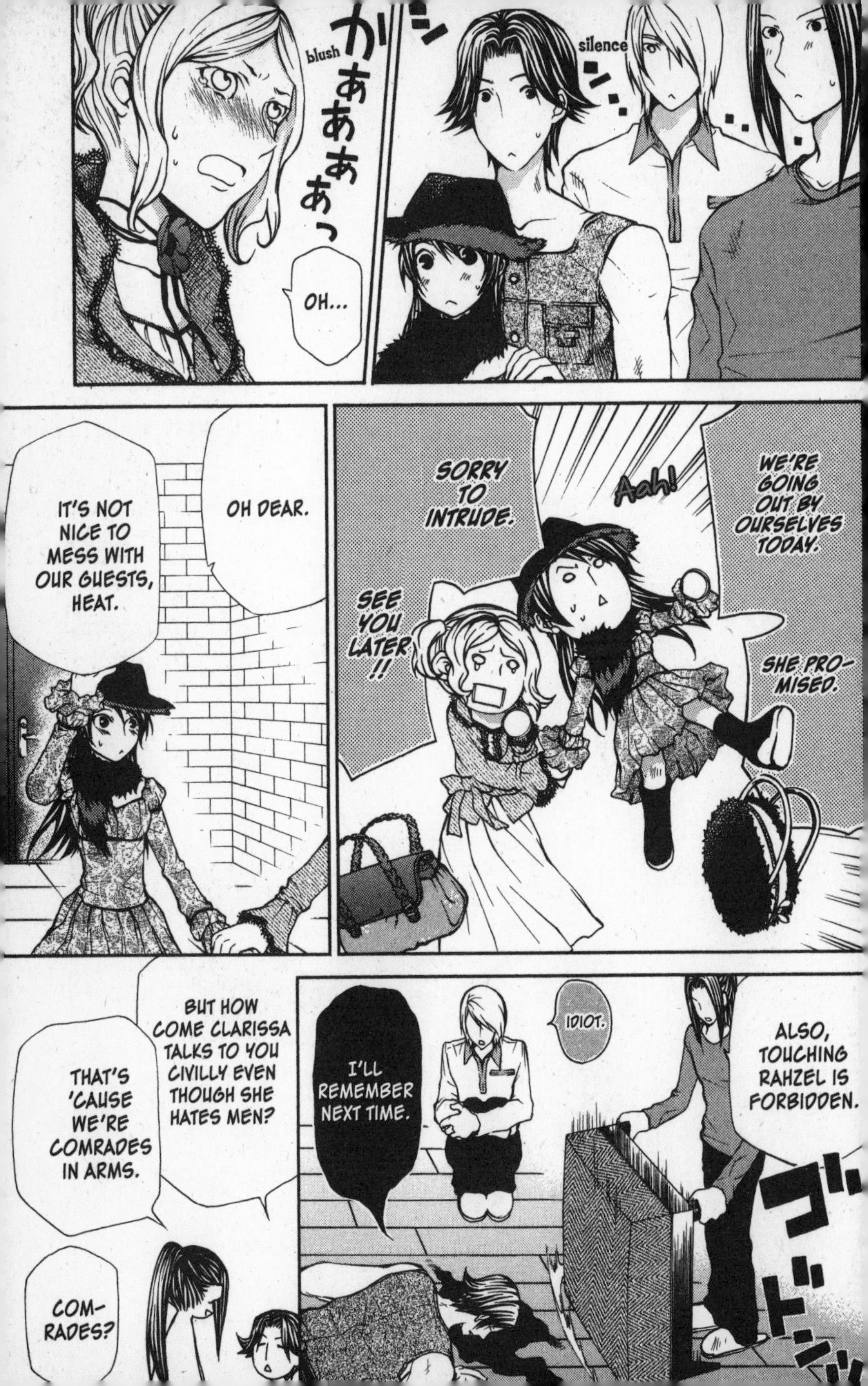
silence
blush
かあああっ
OH...
WE'RE GOING OUT BY OURSELVES TODAY.
Aah!
SORRY TO INTRUDE.
SHE PRO-MISED.
SEE YOU LATER!!
OH DEAR.
IT'S NOT NICE TO MESS WITH OUR GUESTS, HEAT.
ALSO, TOUCHING RAHZEL IS FORBIDDEN.
IDIOT.
I'LL REMEMBER NEXT TIME.
BUT HOW COME CLARISSA TALKS TO YOU CIVILLY EVEN THOUGH SHE HATES MEN?
THAT'S 'CAUSE WE'RE COMRADES IN ARMS.
COM-RADES?

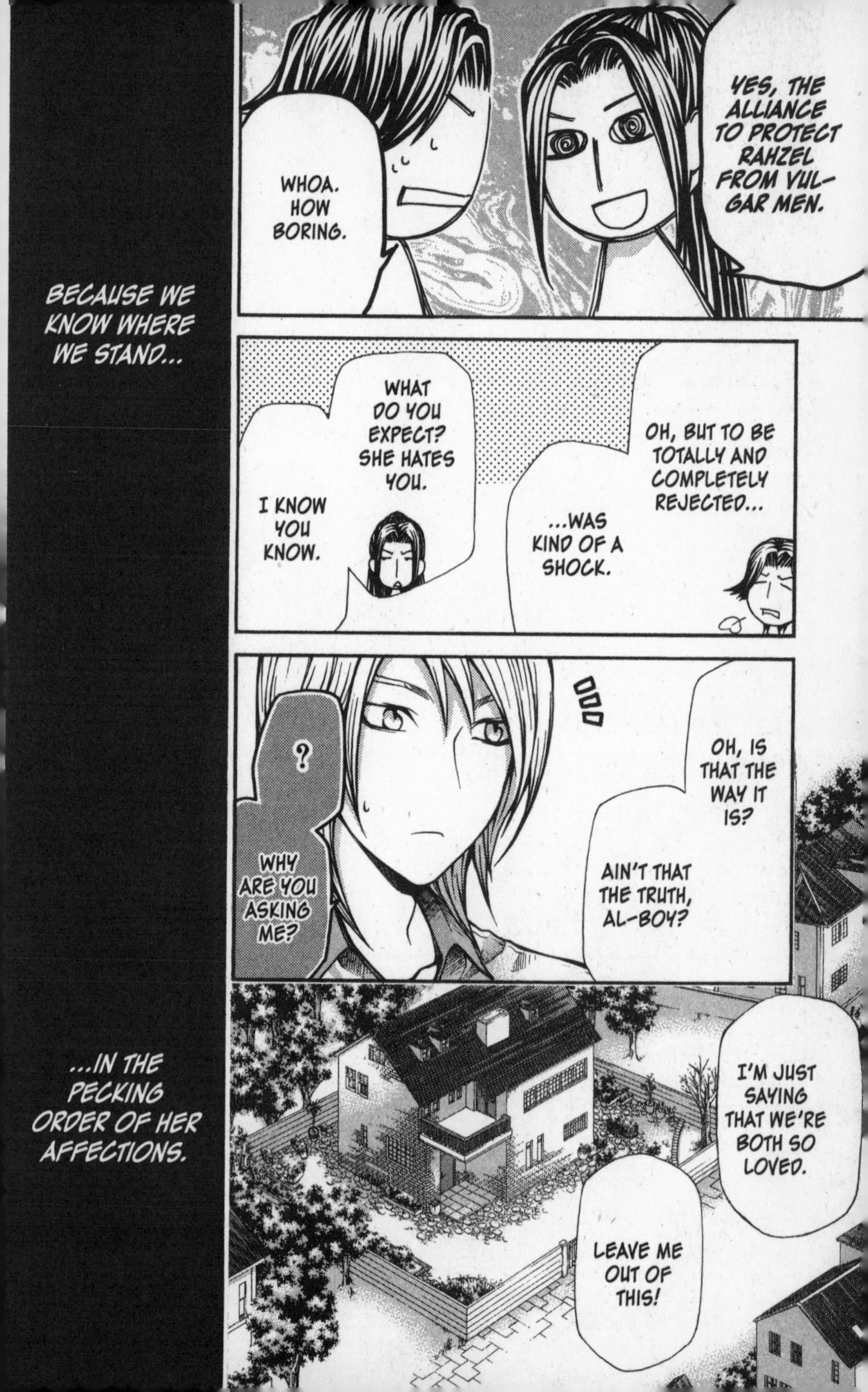
YES, THE ALLIANCE TO PROTECT RAHZEL FROM VUL-GAR MEN.
WHOA. HOW BORING.
OH, BUT TO BE TOTALLY AND COMPLETELY REJECTED...
...WAS KIND OF A SHOCK.
WHAT DO YOU EXPECT? SHE HATES YOU.
I KNOW YOU KNOW.
OH, IS THAT THE WAY IT IS?
AIN'T THAT THE TRUTH, AL-BOY?
?
WHY ARE YOU ASKING ME?
I'M JUST SAYING THAT WE'RE BOTH SO LOVED.
LEAVE ME OUT OF THIS!
BECAUSE WE KNOW WHERE WE STAND...
...IN THE PECKING ORDER OF HER AFFECTIONS.

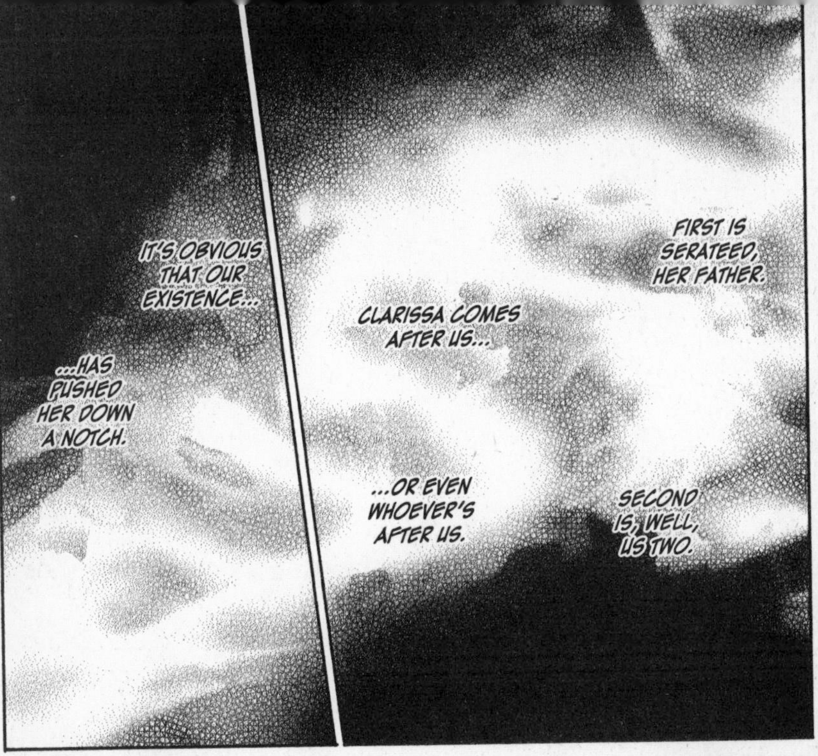
FIRST IS SERATEED, HER FATHER.
SECOND IS, WELL, US TWO.
CLARISSA COMES AFTER US...
...OR EVEN WHOEVER'S AFTER US.
IT'S OBVIOUS THAT OUR EXISTENCE...
...HAS PUSHED HER DOWN A NOTCH.

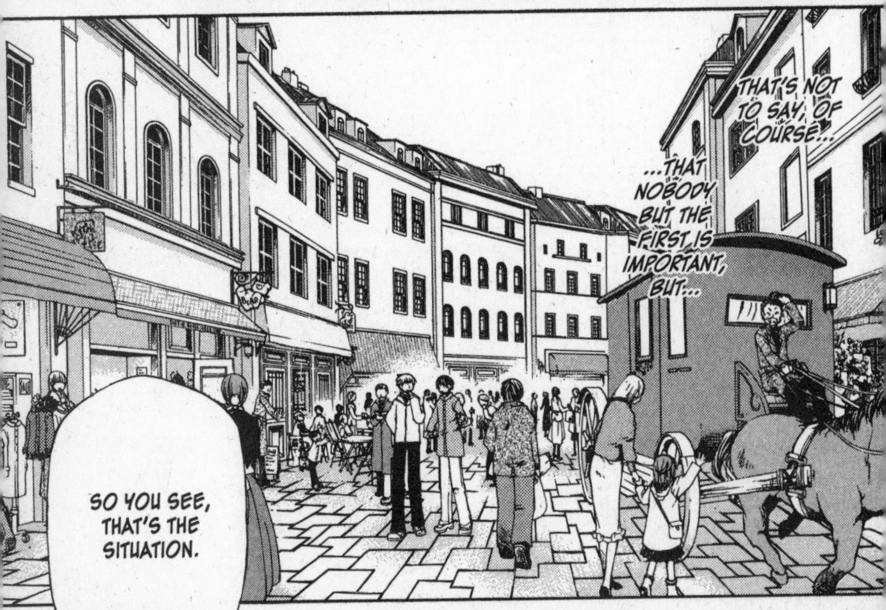
THAT'S NOT TO SAY, OF COURSE...
...THAT NOBODY BUT THE FIRST IS IMPORTANT, BUT...
SO YOU SEE, THAT'S THE SITUATION.

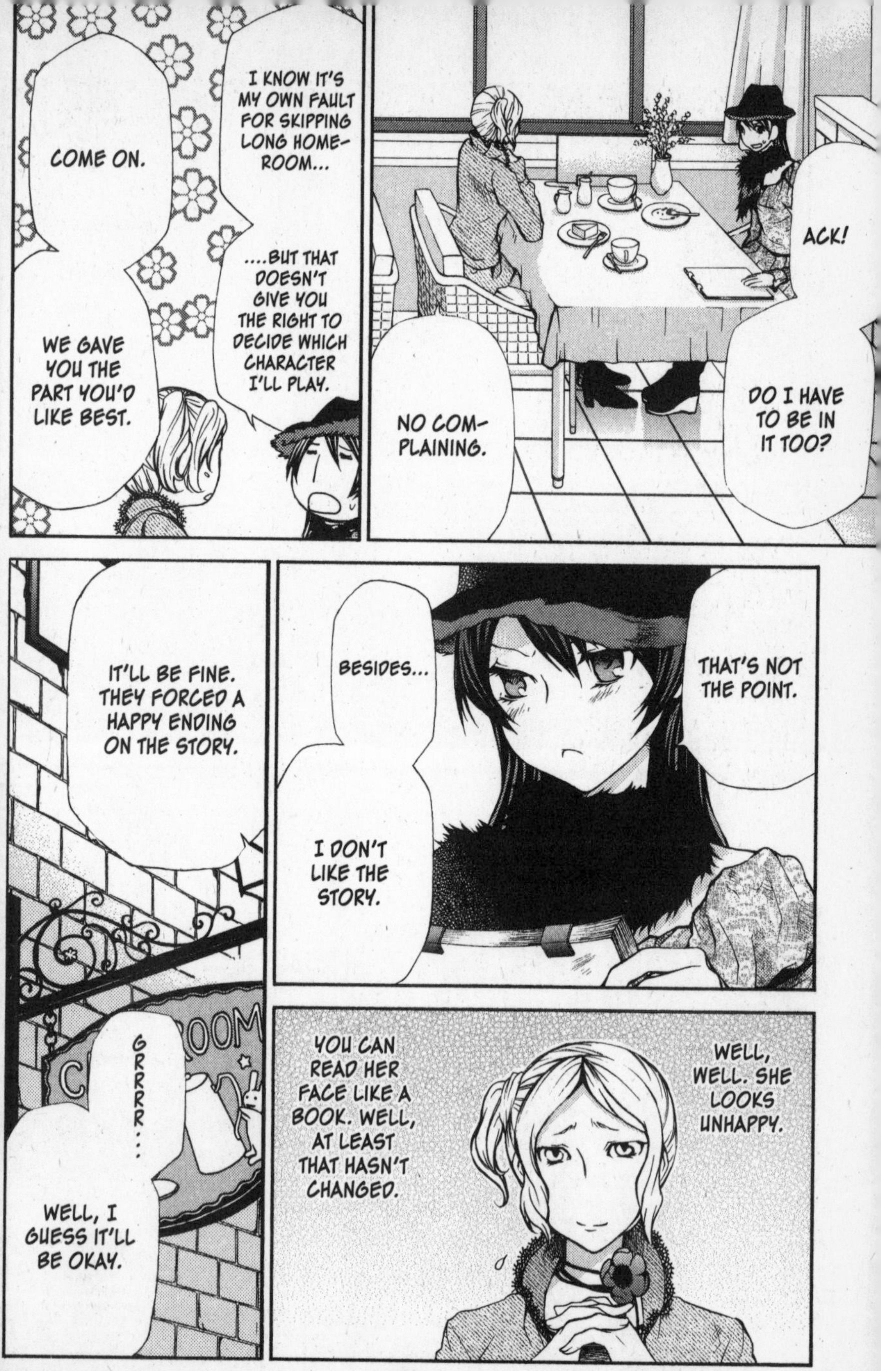
ACK!
DO I HAVE TO BE IN IT TOO?
NO COM-PLAINING.
I KNOW IT'S MY OWN FAULT FOR SKIPPING LONG HOME-ROOM...
....BUT THAT DOESN'T GIVE YOU THE RIGHT TO DECIDE WHICH CHARACTER I'LL PLAY.
COME ON.
WE GAVE YOU THE PART YOU'D LIKE BEST.
THAT'S NOT THE POINT.
BESIDES...
I DON'T LIKE THE STORY.
WELL, WELL. SHE LOOKS UNHAPPY.
YOU CAN READ HER FACE LIKE A BOOK. WELL, AT LEAST THAT HASN'T CHANGED.
IT'LL BE FINE. THEY FORCED A HAPPY ENDING ON THE STORY.
GRRRR...
WELL, I GUESS IT'LL BE OKAY.

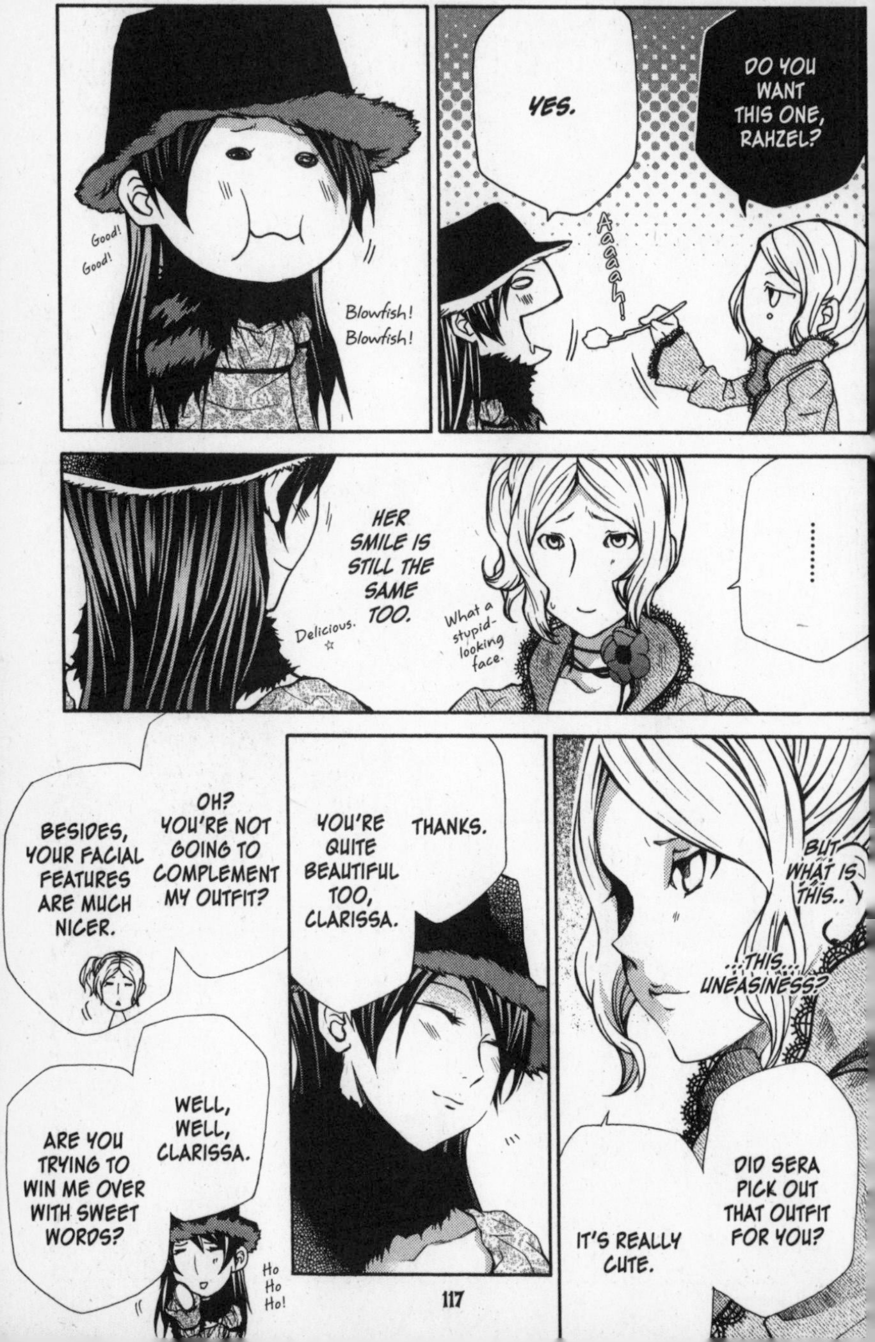
DO YOU WANT THIS ONE, RAHZEL?
YES.
Aaaah!
Good! Good!
Blowfish! Blowfish!
......
What a stupid-looking face.
HER SMILE IS STILL THE SAME TOO.
Delicious. ☆
BUT WHAT IS THIS..
...THIS... UNEASINESS?
DID SERA PICK OUT THAT OUTFIT FOR YOU?
IT'S REALLY CUTE.
THANKS.
YOU'RE QUITE BEAUTIFUL TOO, CLARISSA.
OH? YOU'RE NOT GOING TO COMPLEMENT MY OUTFIT?
BESIDES, YOUR FACIAL FEATURES ARE MUCH NICER.
WELL, WELL, CLARISSA.
ARE YOU TRYING TO WIN ME OVER WITH SWEET WORDS?
Ho Ho Ho!

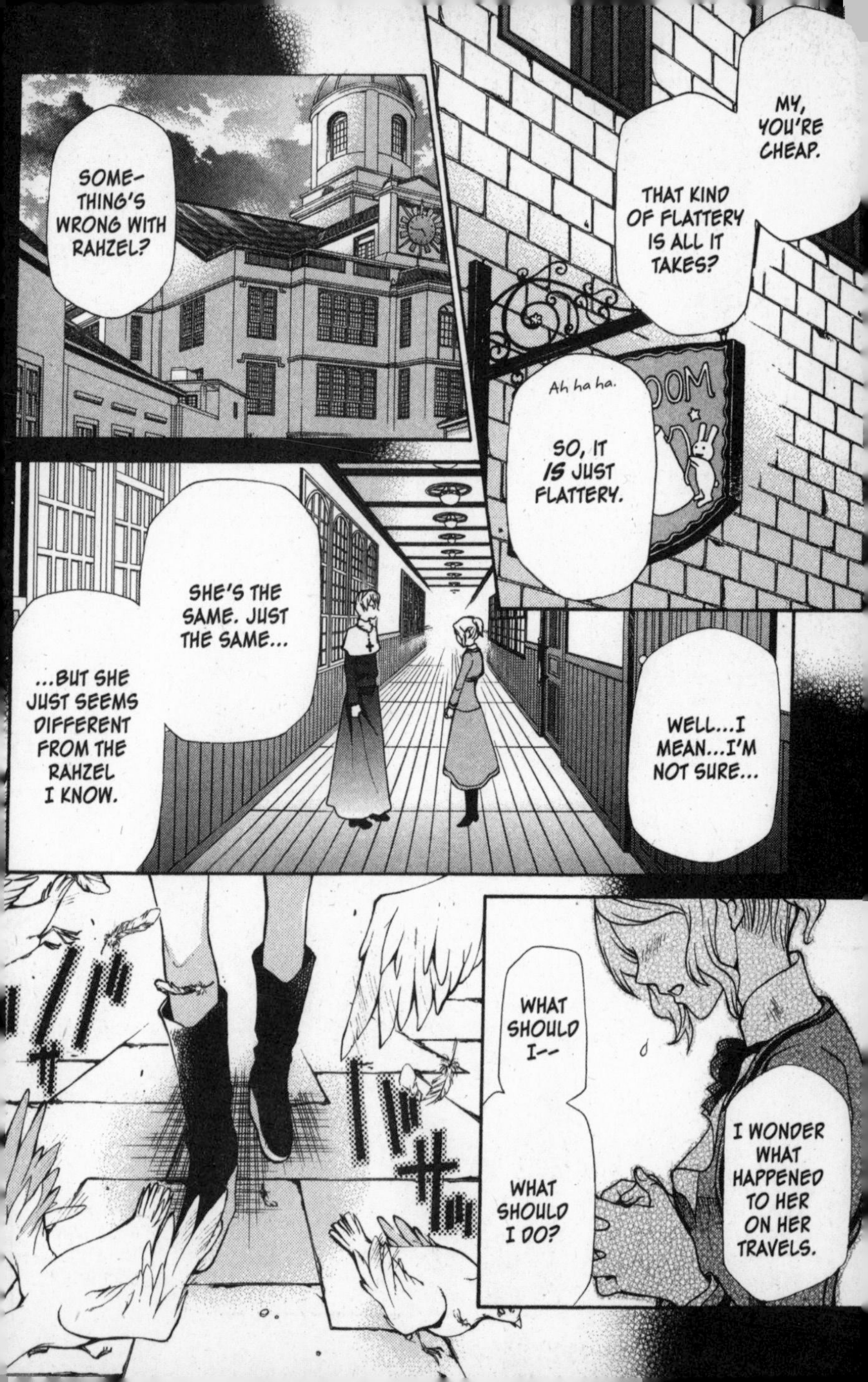
MY, YOU'RE CHEAP.
THAT KIND OF FLATTERY IS ALL IT TAKES?
Ah ha ha.
SO, IT *IS* JUST FLATTERY.
SOME-THING'S WRONG WITH RAHZEL?
SHE'S THE SAME. JUST THE SAME...
...BUT SHE JUST SEEMS DIFFERENT FROM THE RAHZEL I KNOW.
WELL...I MEAN...I'M NOT SURE...
I WONDER WHAT HAPPENED TO HER ON HER TRAVELS.
WHAT SHOULD I--
WHAT SHOULD I DO?

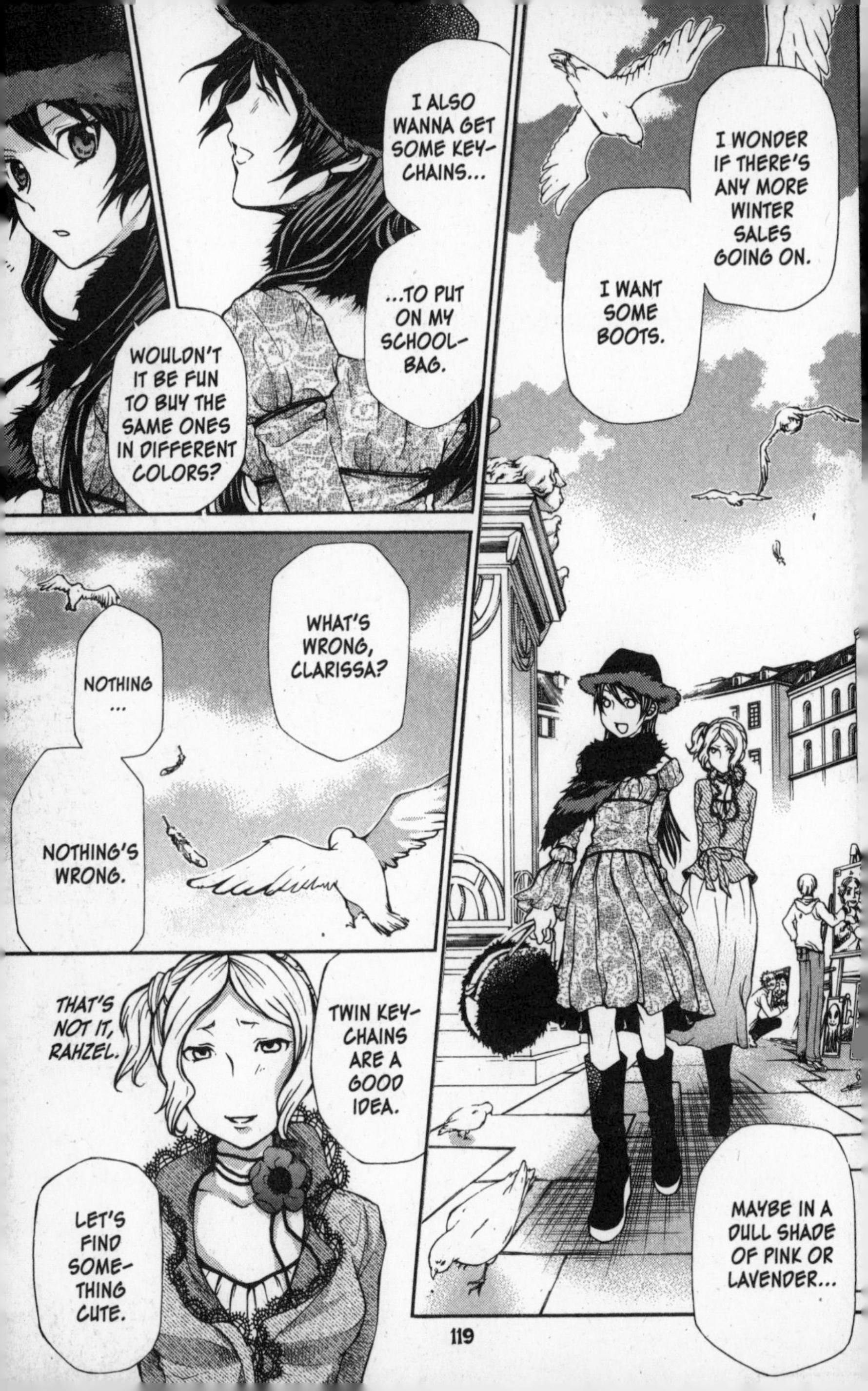
I WONDER IF THERE'S ANY MORE WINTER SALES GOING ON.
I WANT SOME BOOTS.
MAYBE IN A DULL SHADE OF PINK OR LAVENDER...
I ALSO WANNA GET SOME KEY-CHAINS...
...TO PUT ON MY SCHOOL-BAG.
WOULDN'T IT BE FUN TO BUY THE SAME ONES IN DIFFERENT COLORS?
WHAT'S WRONG, CLARISSA?
NOTHING...
NOTHING'S WRONG.
TWIN KEY-CHAINS ARE A GOOD IDEA.
THAT'S NOT IT, RAHZEL.
LET'S FIND SOME-THING CUTE.

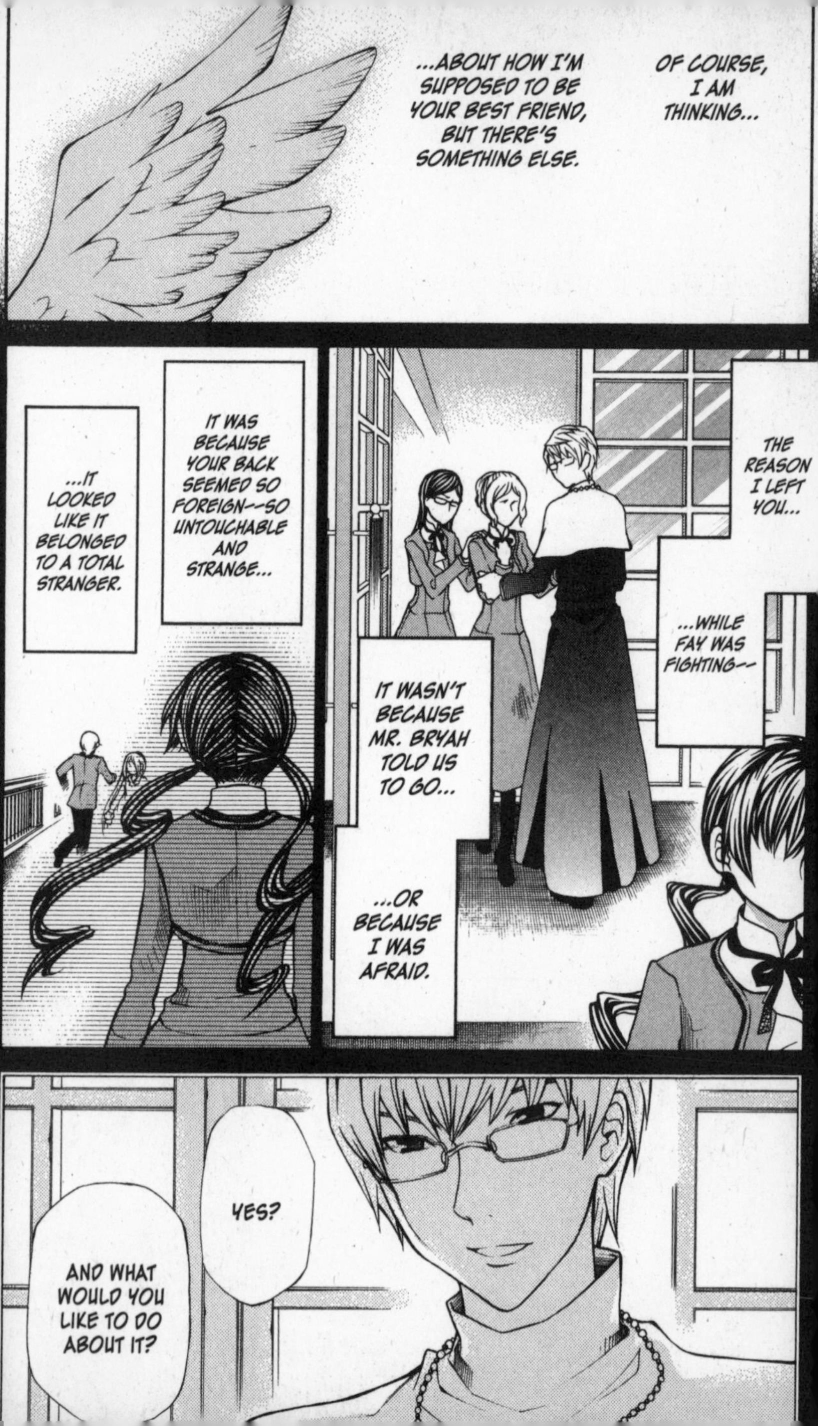
OF COURSE, I AM THINKING...
...ABOUT HOW I'M SUPPOSED TO BE YOUR BEST FRIEND, BUT THERE'S SOMETHING ELSE.
THE REASON I LEFT YOU...
...WHILE FAY WAS FIGHTING--
IT WASN'T BECAUSE MR. BRYAH TOLD US TO GO...
...OR BECAUSE I WAS AFRAID.
IT WAS BECAUSE YOUR BACK SEEMED SO FOREIGN--SO UNTOUCHABLE AND STRANGE...
...IT LOOKED LIKE IT BELONGED TO A TOTAL STRANGER.
YES?
AND WHAT WOULD YOU LIKE TO DO ABOUT IT?

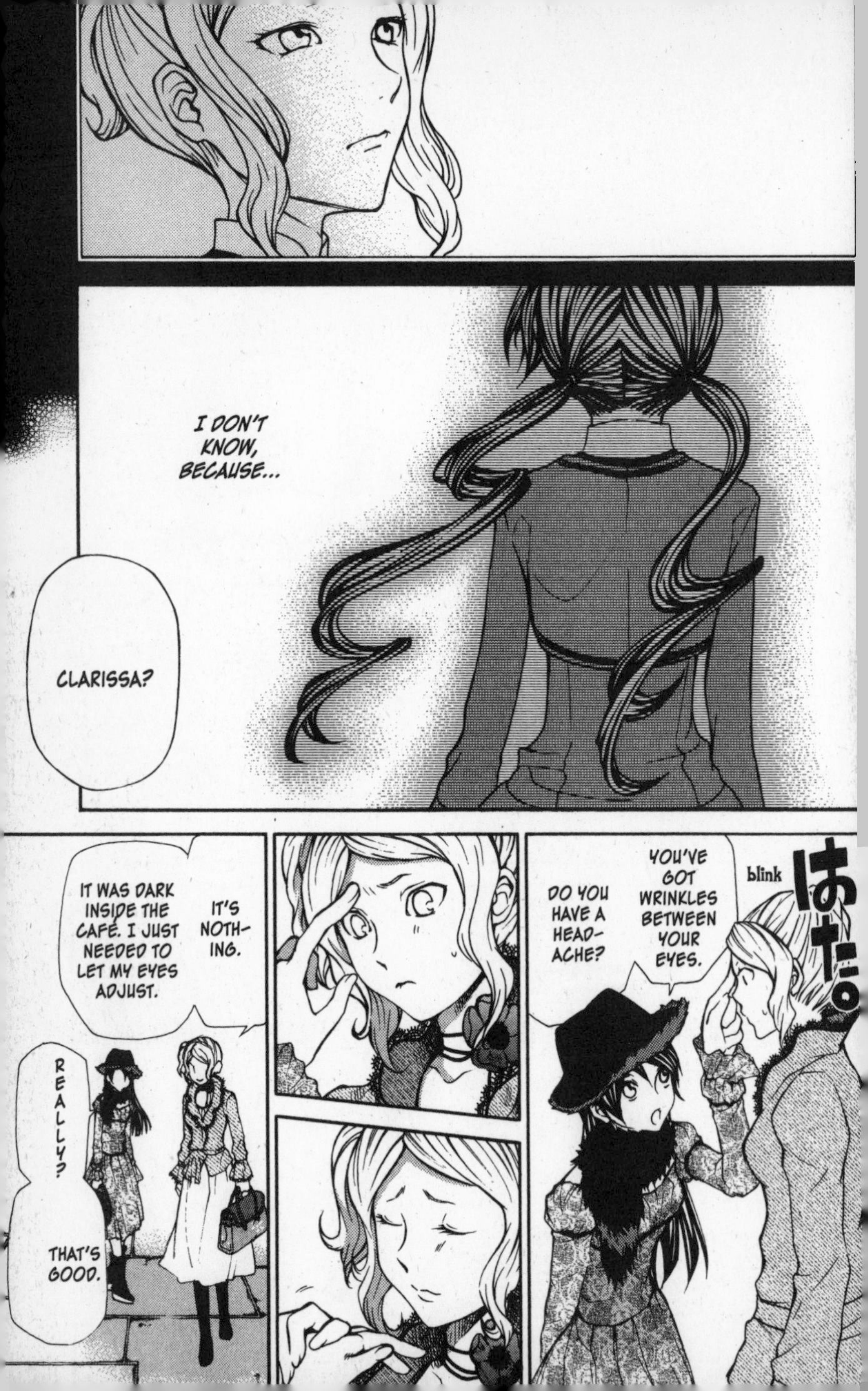
I DON'T KNOW, BECAUSE...
CLARISSA?
blink
YOU'VE GOT WRINKLES BETWEEN YOUR EYES.
DO YOU HAVE A HEAD-ACHE?
IT'S NOTH-ING.
IT WAS DARK INSIDE THE CAFÉ. I JUST NEEDED TO LET MY EYES ADJUST.
REALLY?
THAT'S GOOD.

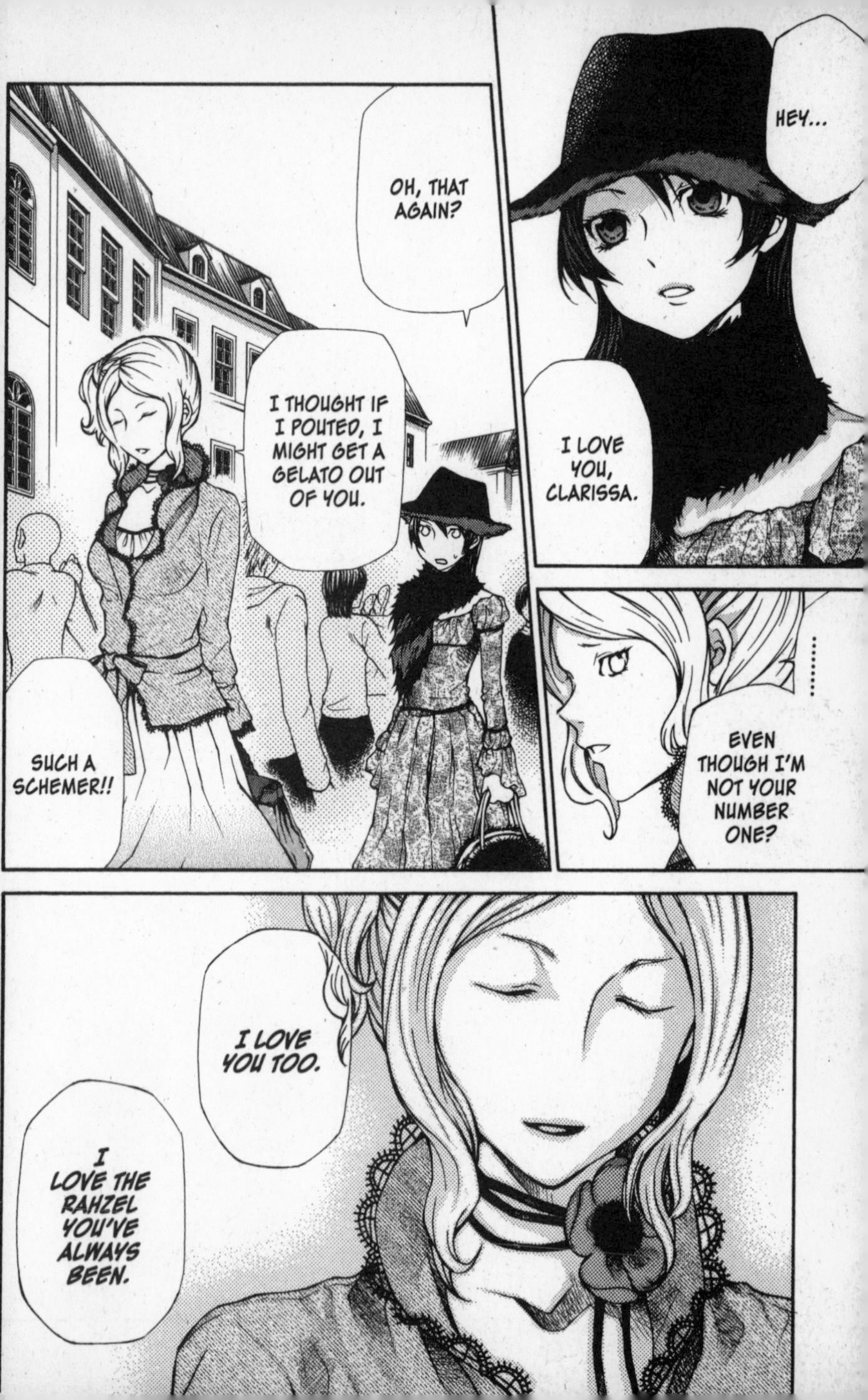
HEY...
I LOVE YOU, CLARISSA.
......
EVEN THOUGH I'M NOT YOUR NUMBER ONE?
OH, THAT AGAIN?
I THOUGHT IF I POUTED, I MIGHT GET A GELATO OUT OF YOU.
SUCH A SCHEMER!!
I LOVE YOU TOO.
I LOVE THE RAHZEL YOU'VE ALWAYS BEEN.

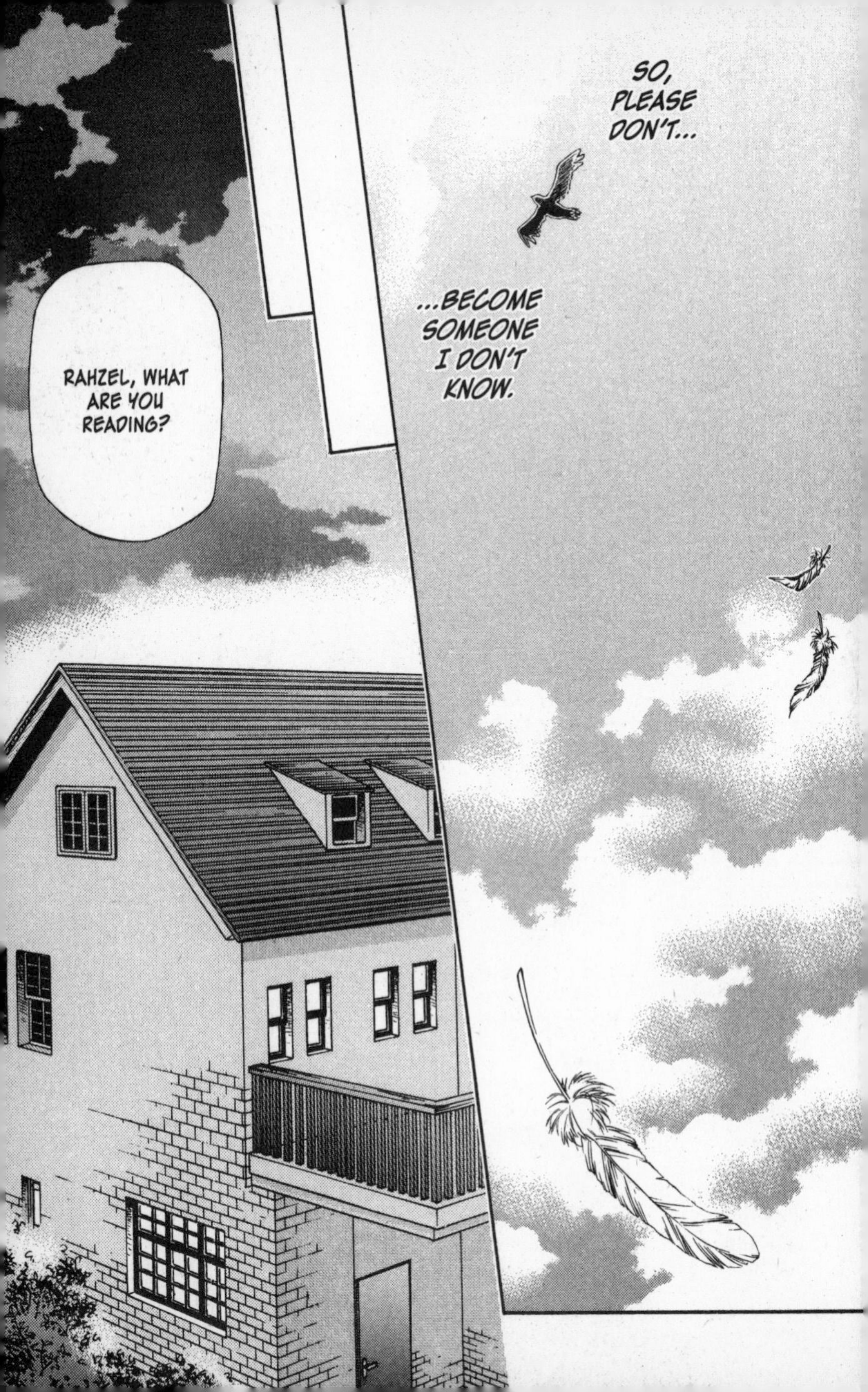
SO, PLEASE DON'T...
...BECOME SOMEONE I DON'T KNOW.
RAHZEL, WHAT ARE YOU READING?

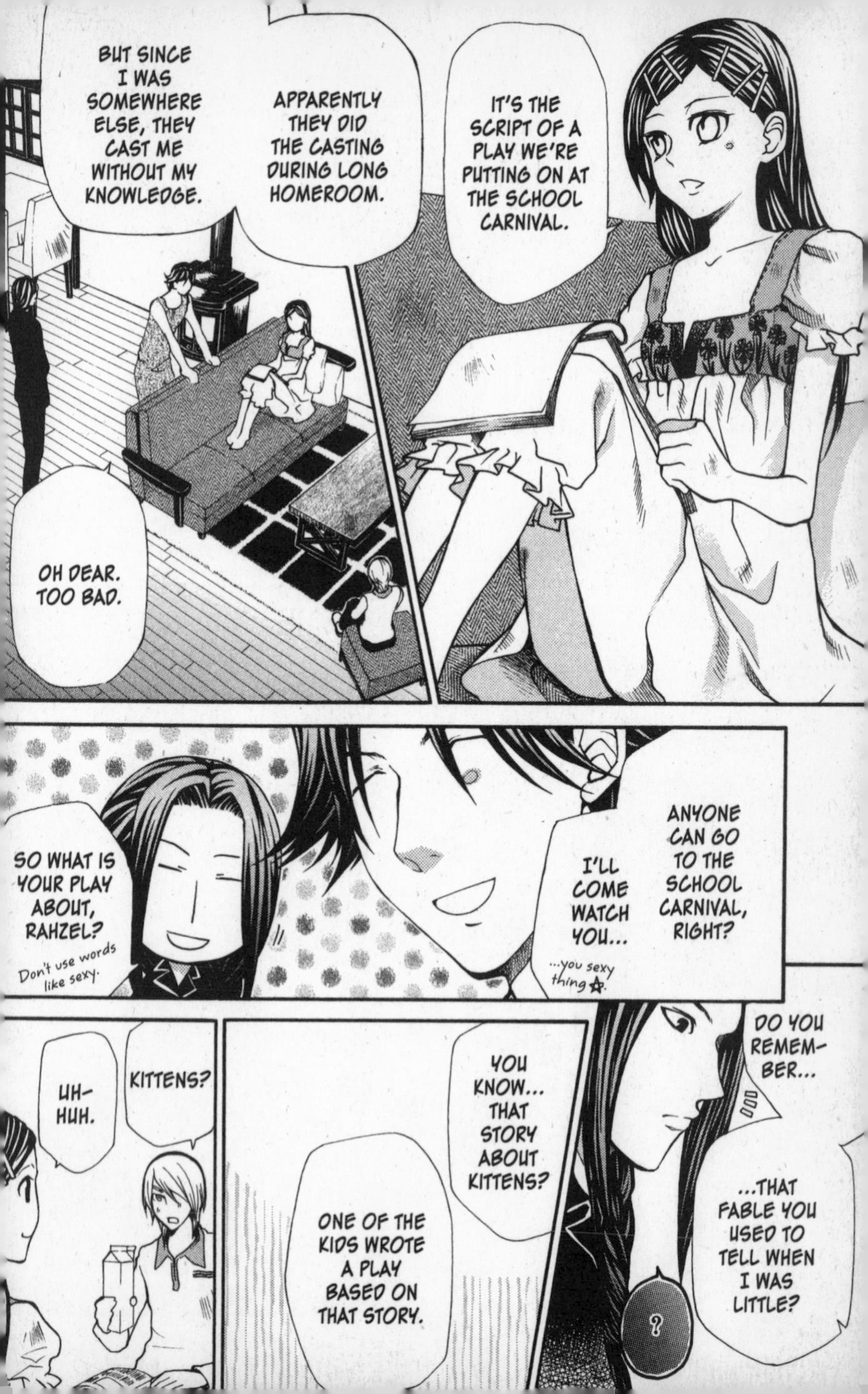
IT'S THE SCRIPT OF A PLAY WE'RE PUTTING ON AT THE SCHOOL CARNIVAL.
APPARENTLY THEY DID THE CASTING DURING LONG HOMEROOM.
BUT SINCE I WAS SOMEWHERE ELSE, THEY CAST ME WITHOUT MY KNOWLEDGE.
OH DEAR. TOO BAD.
ANYONE CAN GO TO THE SCHOOL CARNIVAL, RIGHT?
I'LL COME WATCH YOU...
...you sexy thing☆.
SO WHAT IS YOUR PLAY ABOUT, RAHZEL?
Don't use words like sexy.
DO YOU REMEMBER...
...THAT FABLE YOU USED TO TELL WHEN I WAS LITTLE?
?
YOU KNOW... THAT STORY ABOUT KITTENS?
ONE OF THE KIDS WROTE A PLAY BASED ON THAT STORY.
KITTENS?
UH-HUH.

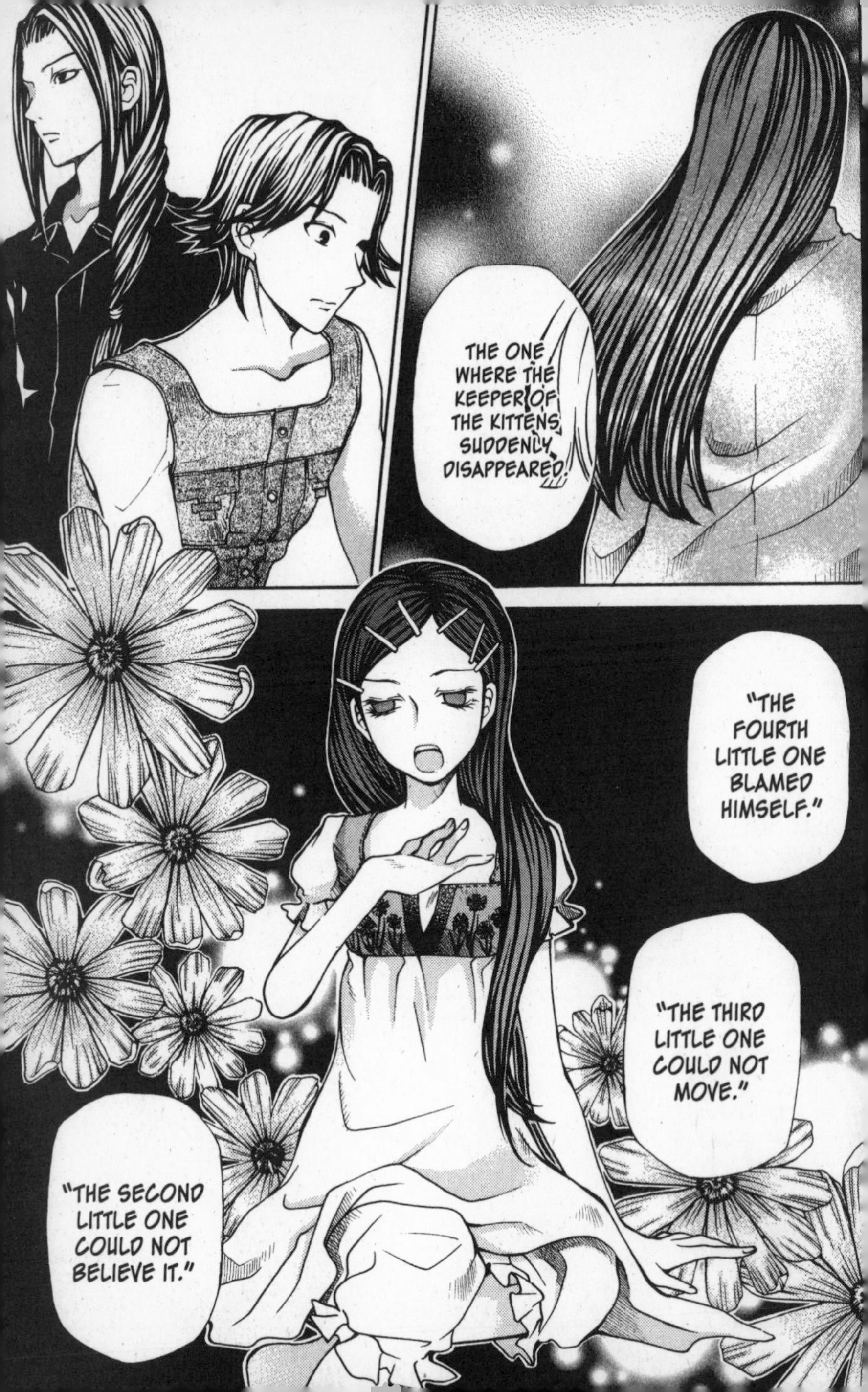
THE ONE WHERE THE KEEPER OF THE KITTENS SUDDENLY DISAPPEARED.
"THE FOURTH LITTLE ONE BLAMED HIMSELF."
"THE THIRD LITTLE ONE COULD NOT MOVE."
"THE SECOND LITTLE ONE COULD NOT BELIEVE IT."

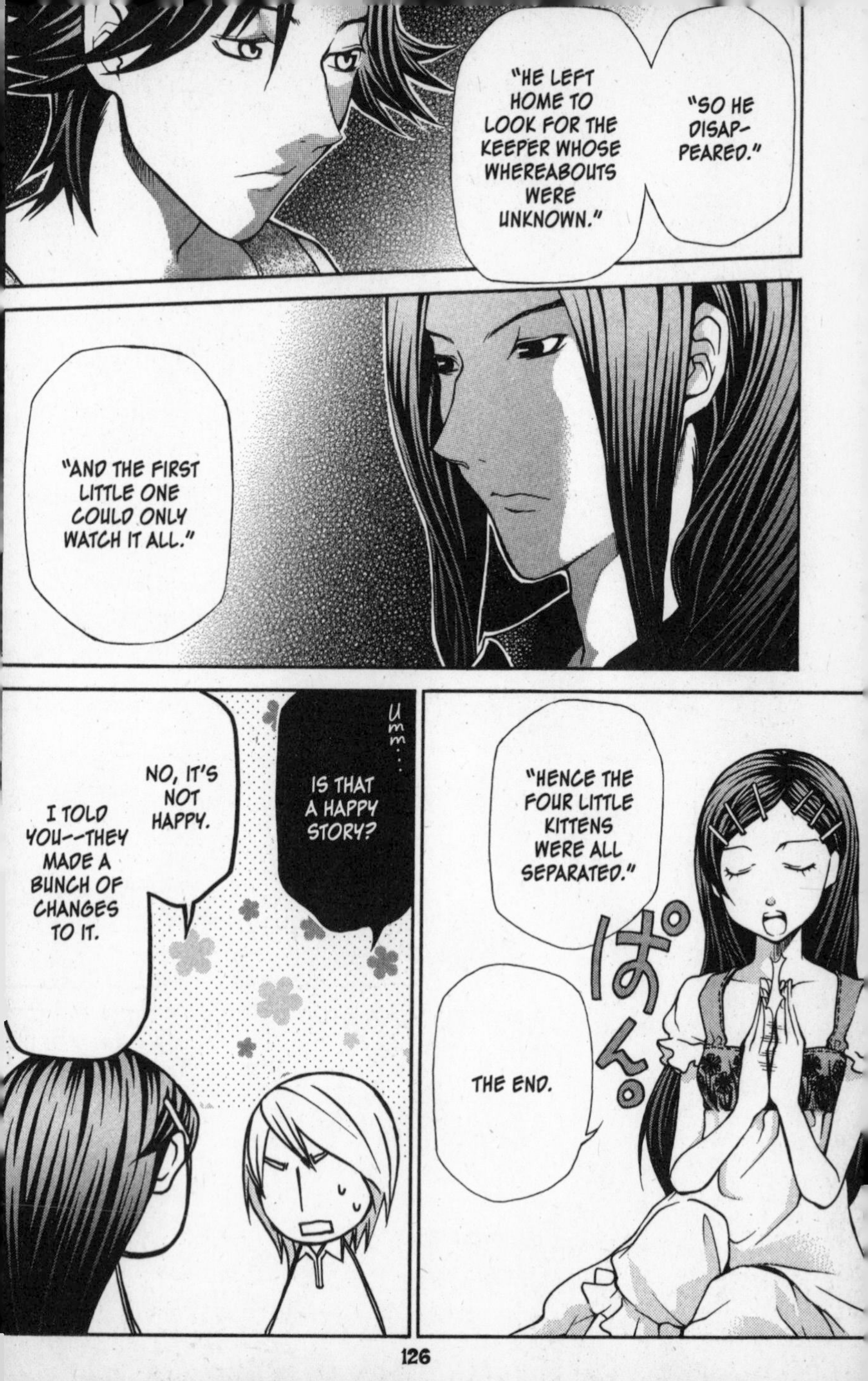
"SO HE DISAP-PEARED."
"HE LEFT HOME TO LOOK FOR THE KEEPER WHOSE WHEREABOUTS WERE UNKNOWN."
"AND THE FIRST LITTLE ONE COULD ONLY WATCH IT ALL."
"HENCE THE FOUR LITTLE KITTENS WERE ALL SEPARATED."
ぱん。
THE END.
Umm...
IS THAT A HAPPY STORY?
NO, IT'S NOT HAPPY.
I TOLD YOU--THEY MADE A BUNCH OF CHANGES TO IT.

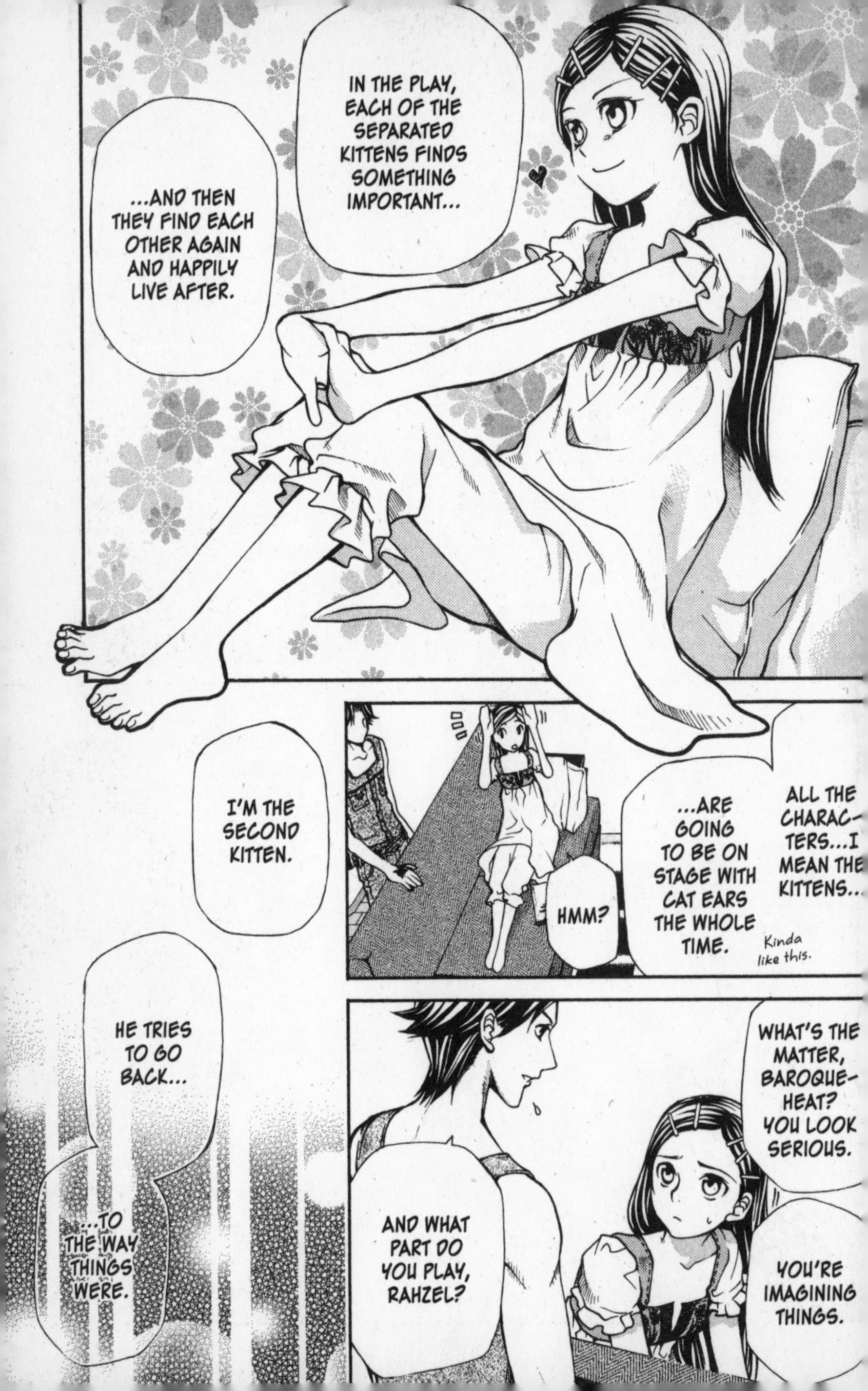
IN THE PLAY, EACH OF THE SEPARATED KITTENS FINDS SOMETHING IMPORTANT...
...AND THEN THEY FIND EACH OTHER AGAIN AND HAPPILY LIVE AFTER.
ALL THE CHARAC-TERS...I MEAN THE KITTENS...
...ARE GOING TO BE ON STAGE WITH CAT EARS THE WHOLE TIME.
Kinda like this.
HMM?
I'M THE SECOND KITTEN.
WHAT'S THE MATTER, BAROQUE-HEAT? YOU LOOK SERIOUS.
YOU'RE IMAGINING THINGS.
AND WHAT PART DO YOU PLAY, RAHZEL?
HE TRIES TO GO BACK...
...TO THE WAY THINGS WERE.

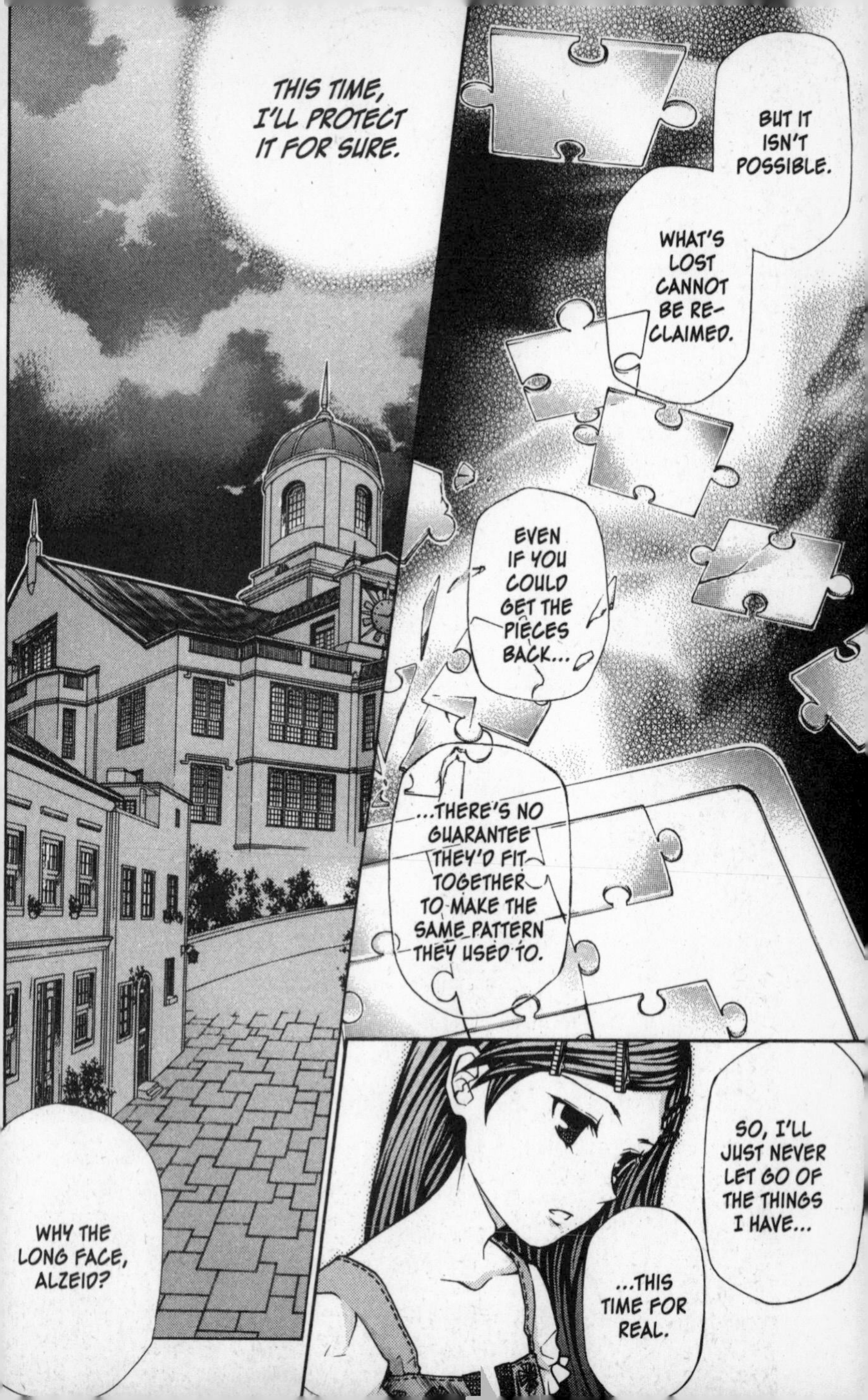
BUT IT ISN'T POSSIBLE.
WHAT'S LOST CANNOT BE RE-CLAIMED.
EVEN IF YOU COULD GET THE PIECES BACK...
...THERE'S NO GUARANTEE THEY'D FIT TOGETHER TO MAKE THE SAME PATTERN THEY USED TO.
SO, I'LL JUST NEVER LET GO OF THE THINGS I HAVE...
...THIS TIME FOR REAL.
THIS TIME, I'LL PROTECT IT FOR SURE.
WHY THE LONG FACE, ALZEID?

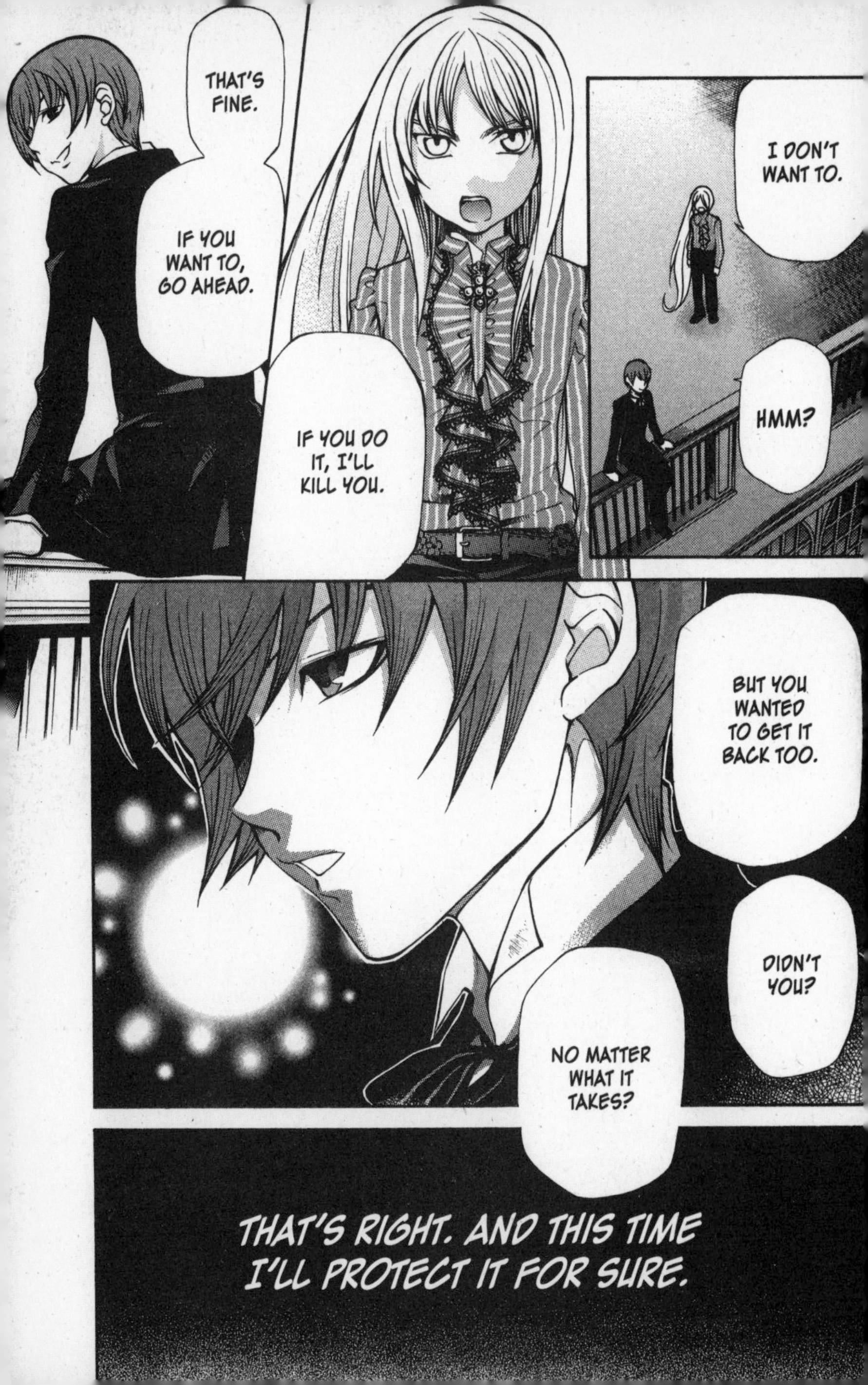
I DON'T WANT TO.
HMM?
IF YOU DO IT, I'LL KILL YOU.
THAT'S FINE.
IF YOU WANT TO, GO AHEAD.
BUT YOU WANTED TO GET IT BACK TOO.
DIDN'T YOU?
NO MATTER WHAT IT TAKES?
THAT'S RIGHT. AND THIS TIME I'LL PROTECT IT FOR SURE.

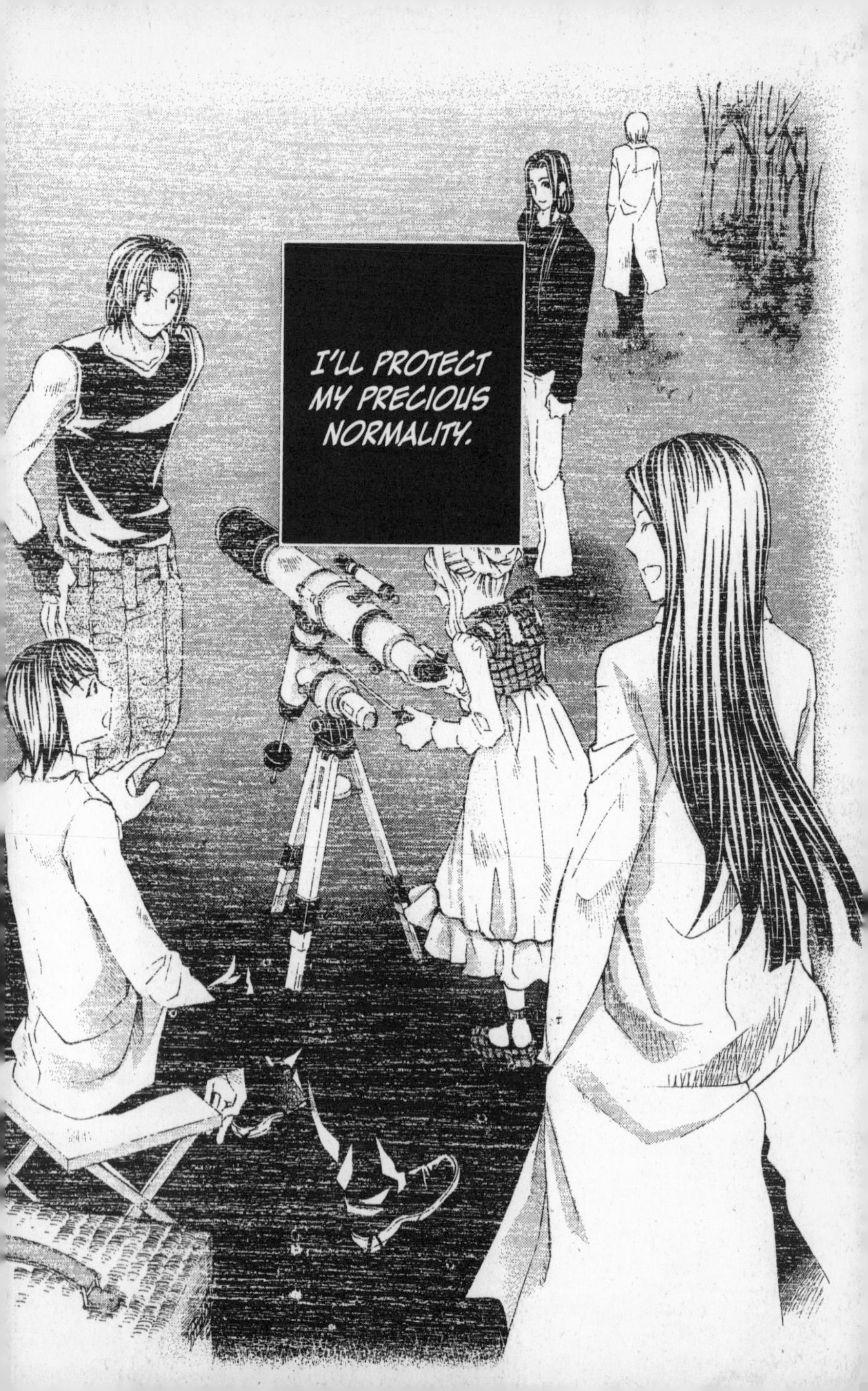
I'LL PROTECT MY PRECIOUS NORMALITY.

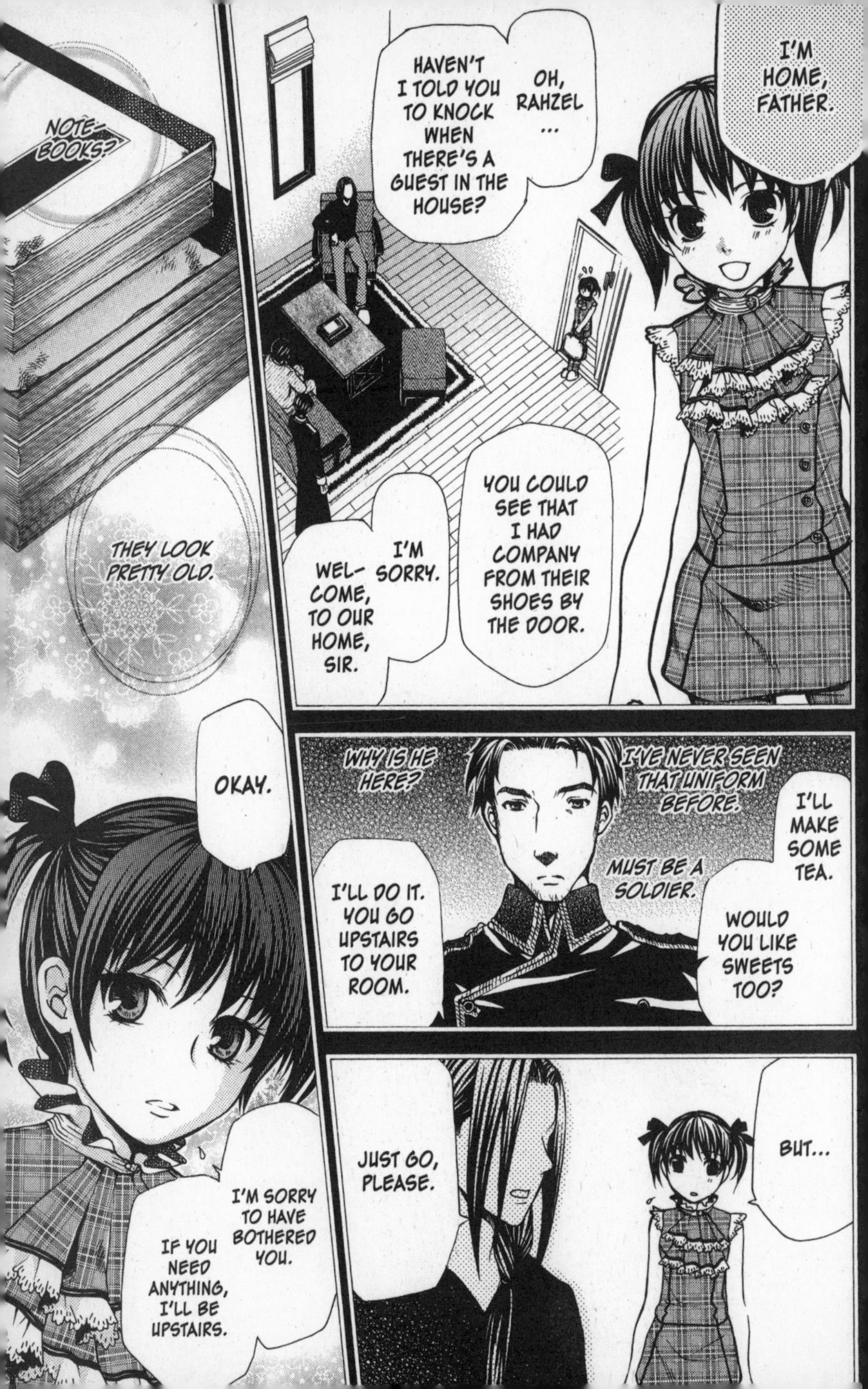
I'M HOME, FATHER.
OH, RAHZEL...
HAVEN'T I TOLD YOU TO KNOCK WHEN THERE'S A GUEST IN THE HOUSE?
YOU COULD SEE THAT I HAD COMPANY FROM THEIR SHOES BY THE DOOR.
I'M SORRY.
WEL-COME, TO OUR HOME, SIR.
NOTE-BOOKS?
THEY LOOK PRETTY OLD.
I'LL MAKE SOME TEA.
I'VE NEVER SEEN THAT UNIFORM BEFORE.
WOULD YOU LIKE SWEETS TOO?
WHY IS HE HERE?
MUST BE A SOLDIER.
I'LL DO IT. YOU GO UPSTAIRS TO YOUR ROOM.
BUT...
JUST GO, PLEASE.
OKAY.
I'M SORRY TO HAVE BOTHERED YOU.
IF YOU NEED ANYTHING, I'LL BE UPSTAIRS.

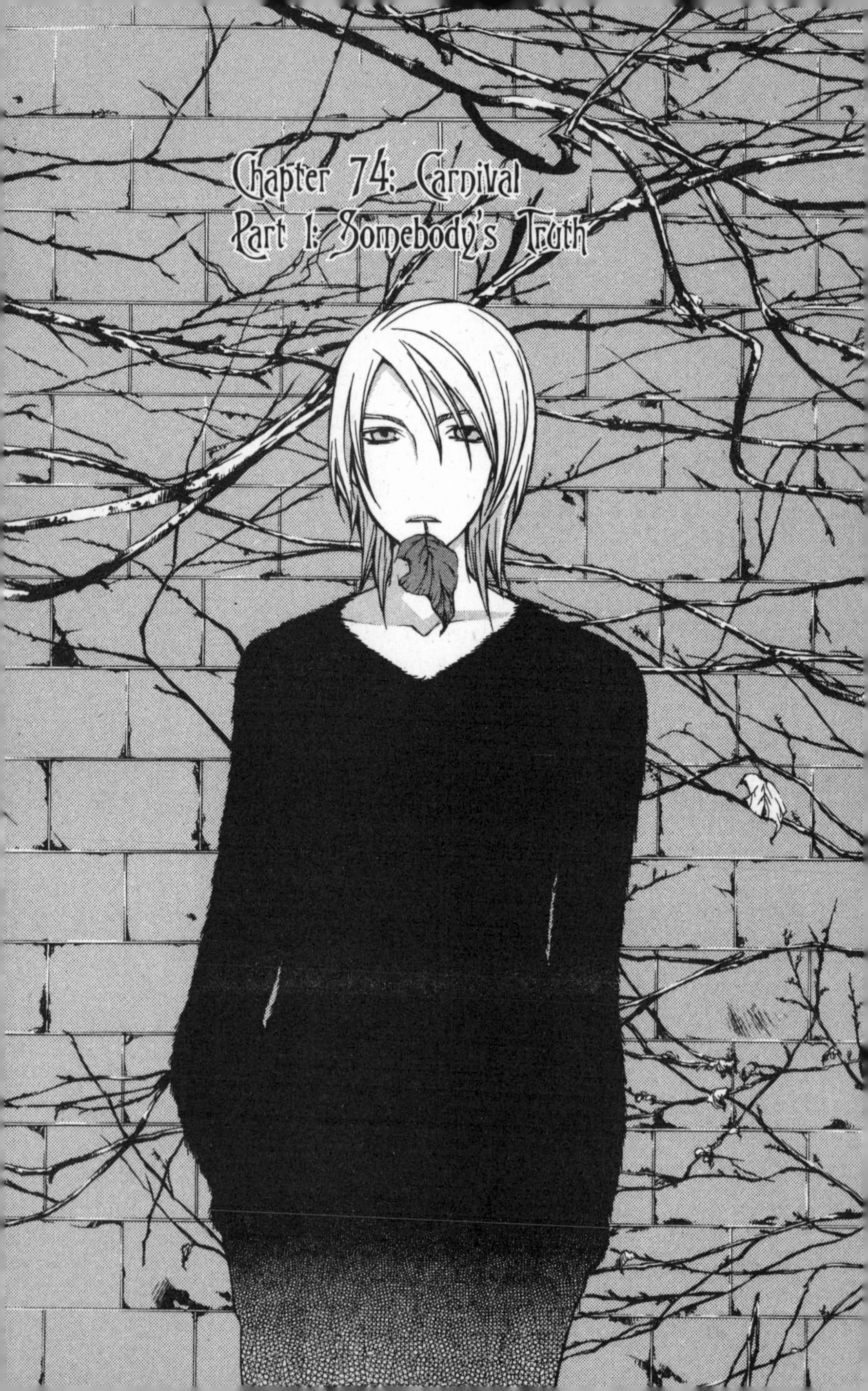
Chapter 74: Carnival
Part 1: Somebody's Truth

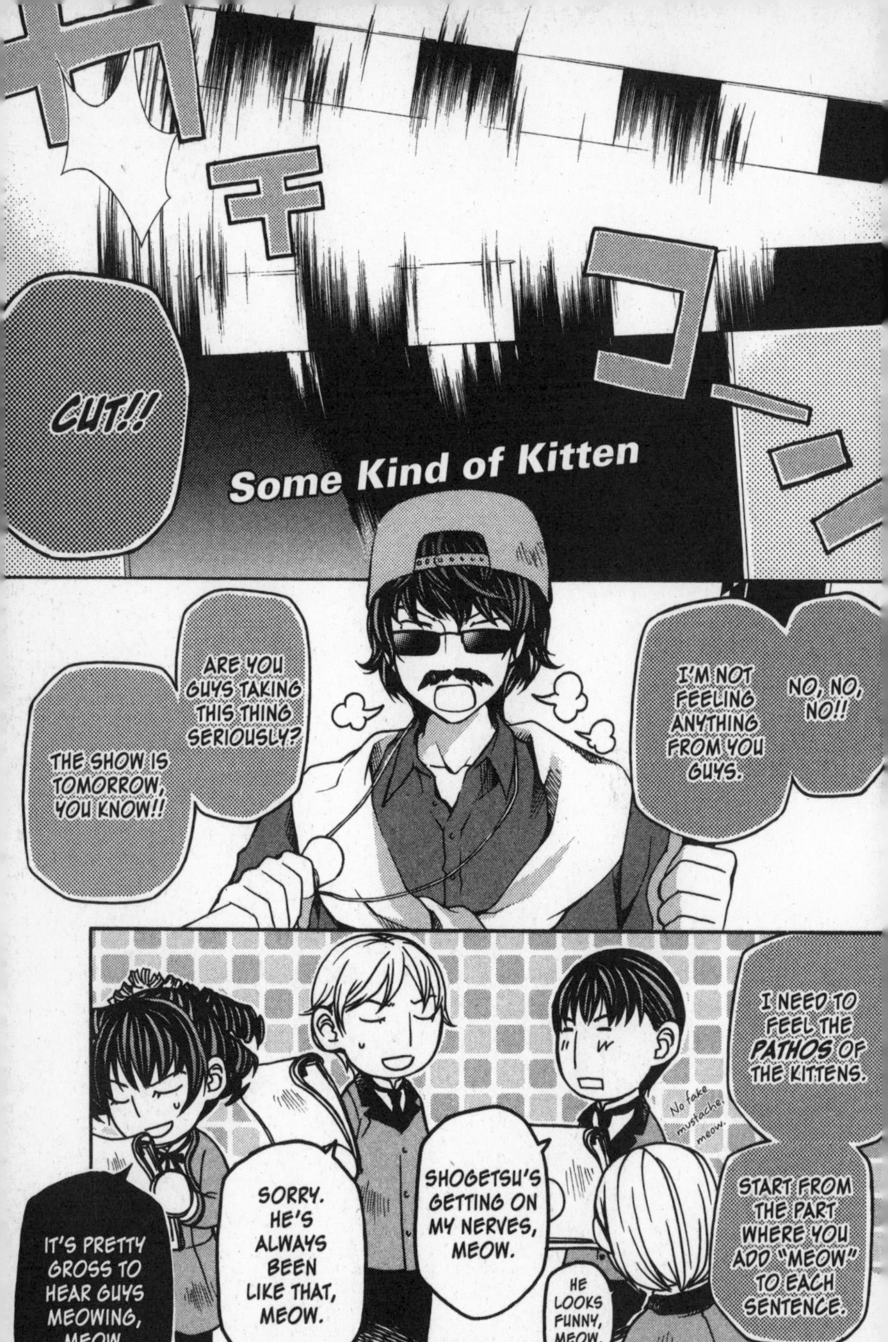
CUT!!
Some Kind of Kitten
NO, NO, NO!!
I'M NOT FEELING ANYTHING FROM YOU GUYS.
ARE YOU GUYS TAKING THIS THING SERIOUSLY?
THE SHOW IS TOMORROW, YOU KNOW!!
I NEED TO FEEL THE *PATHOS* OF THE KITTENS.
START FROM THE PART WHERE YOU ADD "MEOW" TO EACH SENTENCE.
No fake mustache, meow.
HE LOOKS FUNNY, MEOW.
SHOGETSU'S GETTING ON MY NERVES, MEOW.
SORRY. HE'S ALWAYS BEEN LIKE THAT, MEOW.
IT'S PRETTY GROSS TO HEAR GUYS MEOWING, MEOW.

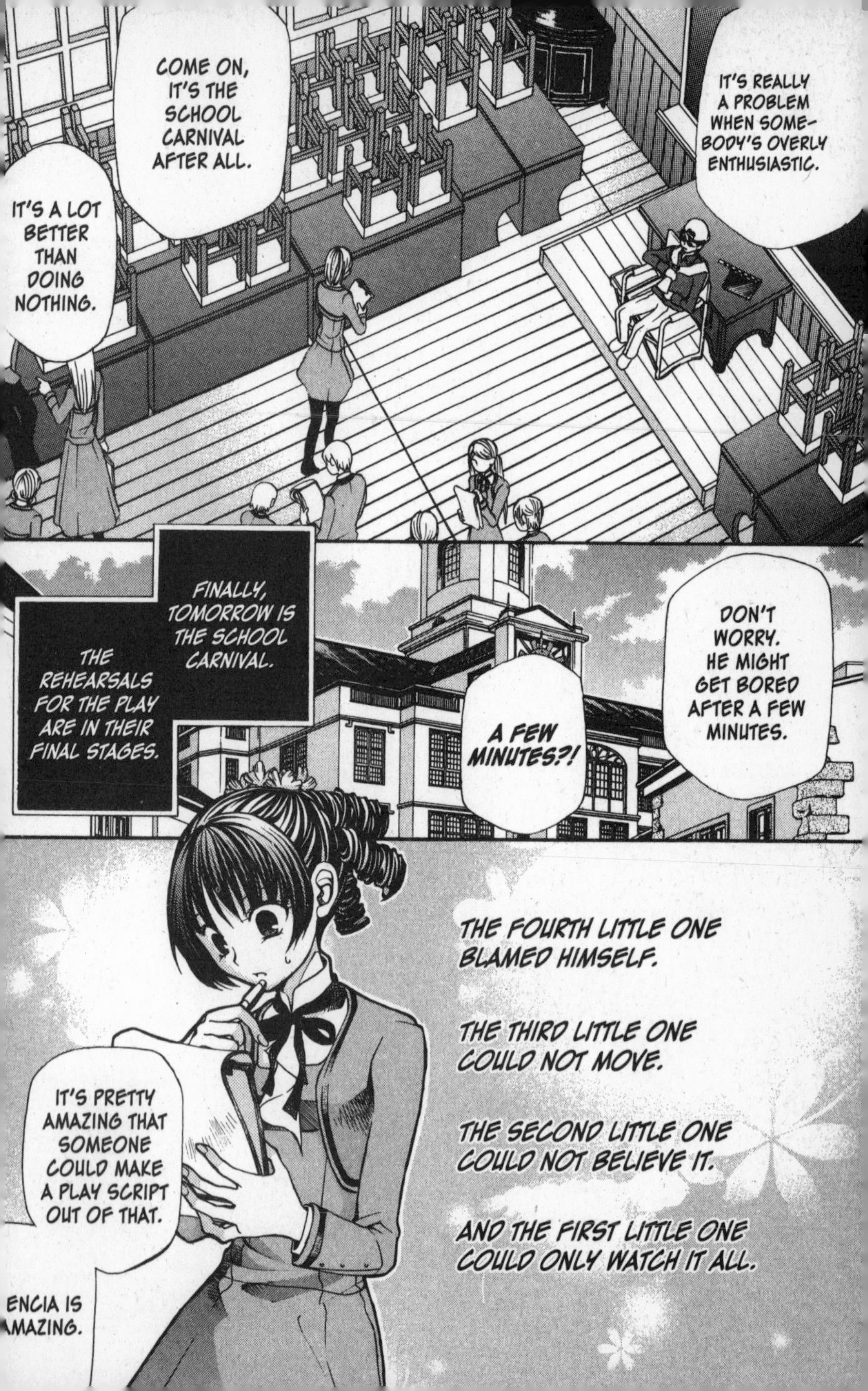
IT'S REALLY A PROBLEM WHEN SOME-BODY'S OVERLY ENTHUSIASTIC.
COME ON, IT'S THE SCHOOL CARNIVAL AFTER ALL.
IT'S A LOT BETTER THAN DOING NOTHING.
DON'T WORRY. HE MIGHT GET BORED AFTER A FEW MINUTES.
A FEW MINUTES?!
FINALLY, TOMORROW IS THE SCHOOL CARNIVAL.
THE REHEARSALS FOR THE PLAY ARE IN THEIR FINAL STAGES.
THE FOURTH LITTLE ONE BLAMED HIMSELF.
THE THIRD LITTLE ONE COULD NOT MOVE.
THE SECOND LITTLE ONE COULD NOT BELIEVE IT.
AND THE FIRST LITTLE ONE COULD ONLY WATCH IT ALL.
IT'S PRETTY AMAZING THAT SOMEONE COULD MAKE A PLAY SCRIPT OUT OF THAT.
ENCIA IS AMAZING.

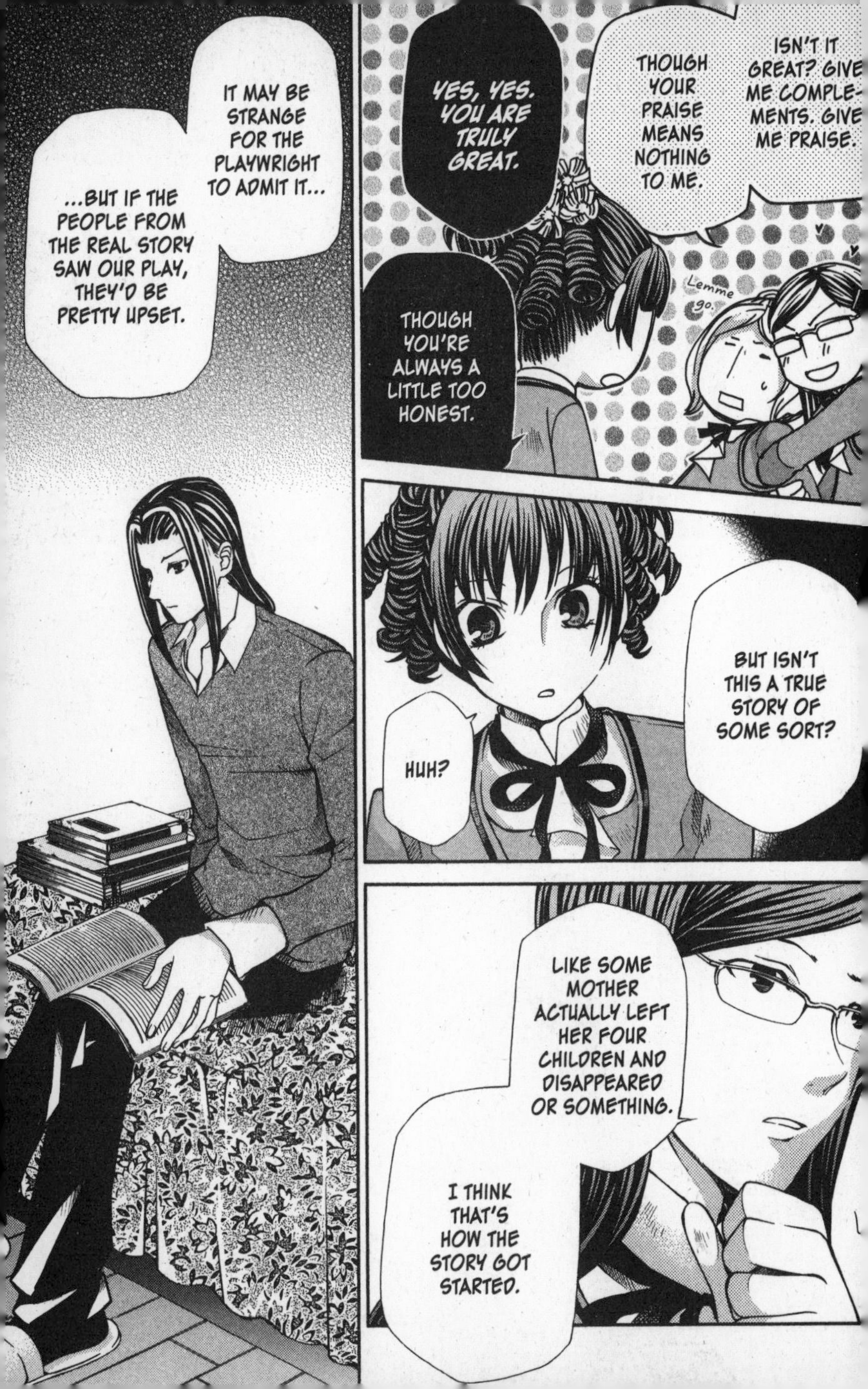
ISN'T IT GREAT? GIVE ME COMPLEMENTS. GIVE ME PRAISE.
THOUGH YOUR PRAISE MEANS NOTHING TO ME.
YES, YES. YOU ARE TRULY GREAT.
Lemme go.
THOUGH YOU'RE ALWAYS A LITTLE TOO HONEST.
BUT ISN'T THIS A TRUE STORY OF SOME SORT?
HUH?
LIKE SOME MOTHER ACTUALLY LEFT HER FOUR CHILDREN AND DISAPPEARED OR SOMETHING.
I THINK THAT'S HOW THE STORY GOT STARTED.
IT MAY BE STRANGE FOR THE PLAYWRIGHT TO ADMIT IT...
...BUT IF THE PEOPLE FROM THE REAL STORY SAW OUR PLAY, THEY'D BE PRETTY UPSET.

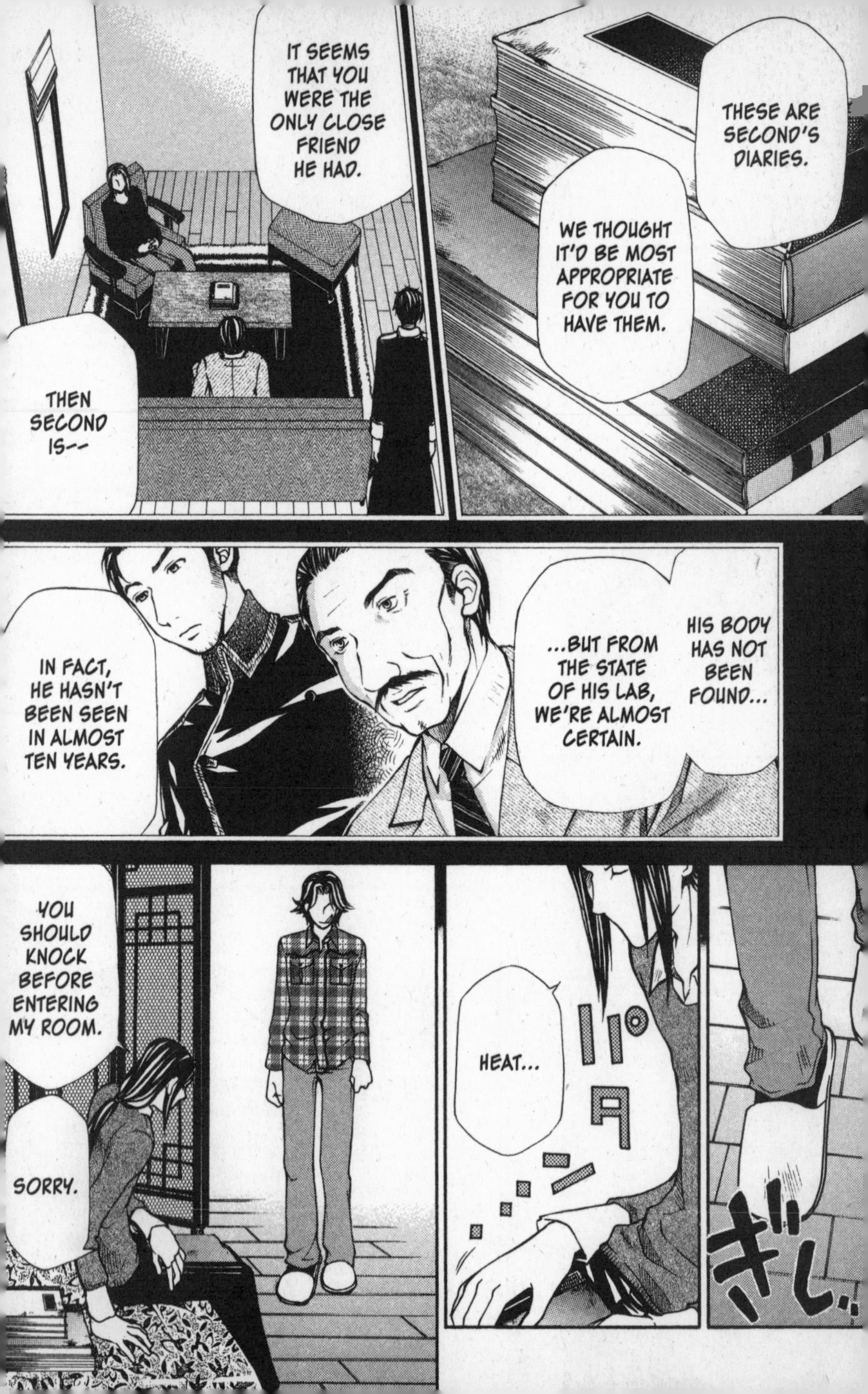
THESE ARE SECOND'S DIARIES.
WE THOUGHT IT'D BE MOST APPROPRIATE FOR YOU TO HAVE THEM.
IT SEEMS THAT YOU WERE THE ONLY CLOSE FRIEND HE HAD.
THEN SECOND IS--
HIS BODY HAS NOT BEEN FOUND...
...BUT FROM THE STATE OF HIS LAB, WE'RE ALMOST CERTAIN.
IN FACT, HE HASN'T BEEN SEEN IN ALMOST TEN YEARS.
きし..
HEAT...
YOU SHOULD KNOCK BEFORE ENTERING MY ROOM.
SORRY.

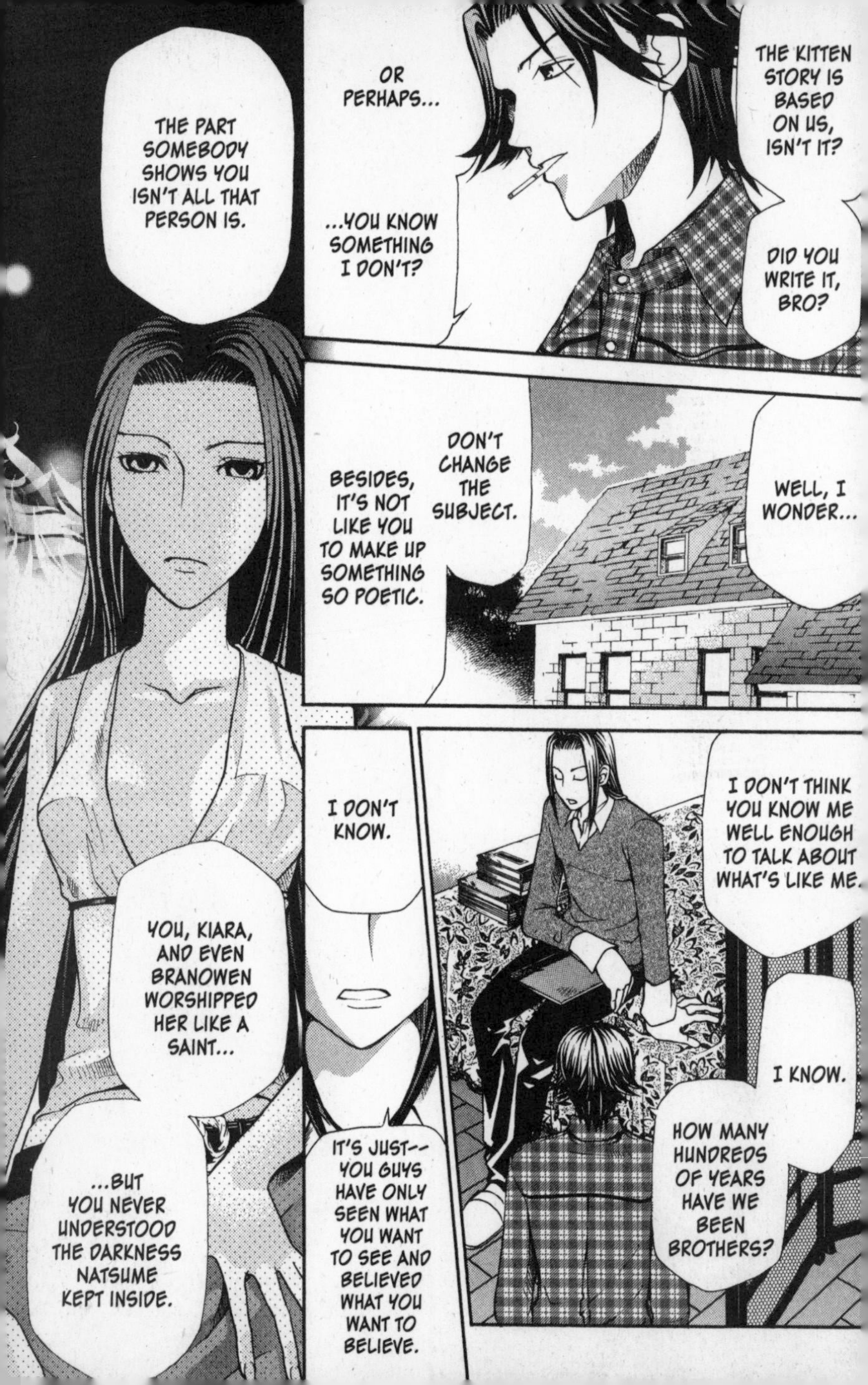
THE KITTEN STORY IS BASED ON US, ISN'T IT?
DID YOU WRITE IT, BRO?
OR PERHAPS...
...YOU KNOW SOMETHING I DON'T?
WELL, I WONDER...
DON'T CHANGE THE SUBJECT.
BESIDES, IT'S NOT LIKE YOU TO MAKE UP SOMETHING SO POETIC.
I DON'T THINK YOU KNOW ME WELL ENOUGH TO TALK ABOUT WHAT'S LIKE ME.
I KNOW.
HOW MANY HUNDREDS OF YEARS HAVE WE BEEN BROTHERS?
I DON'T KNOW.
IT'S JUST-- YOU GUYS HAVE ONLY SEEN WHAT YOU WANT TO SEE AND BELIEVED WHAT YOU WANT TO BELIEVE.
THE PART SOMEBODY SHOWS YOU ISN'T ALL THAT PERSON IS.
YOU, KIARA, AND EVEN BRANOWEN WORSHIPPED HER LIKE A SAINT...
...BUT YOU NEVER UNDERSTOOD THE DARKNESS NATSUME KEPT INSIDE.

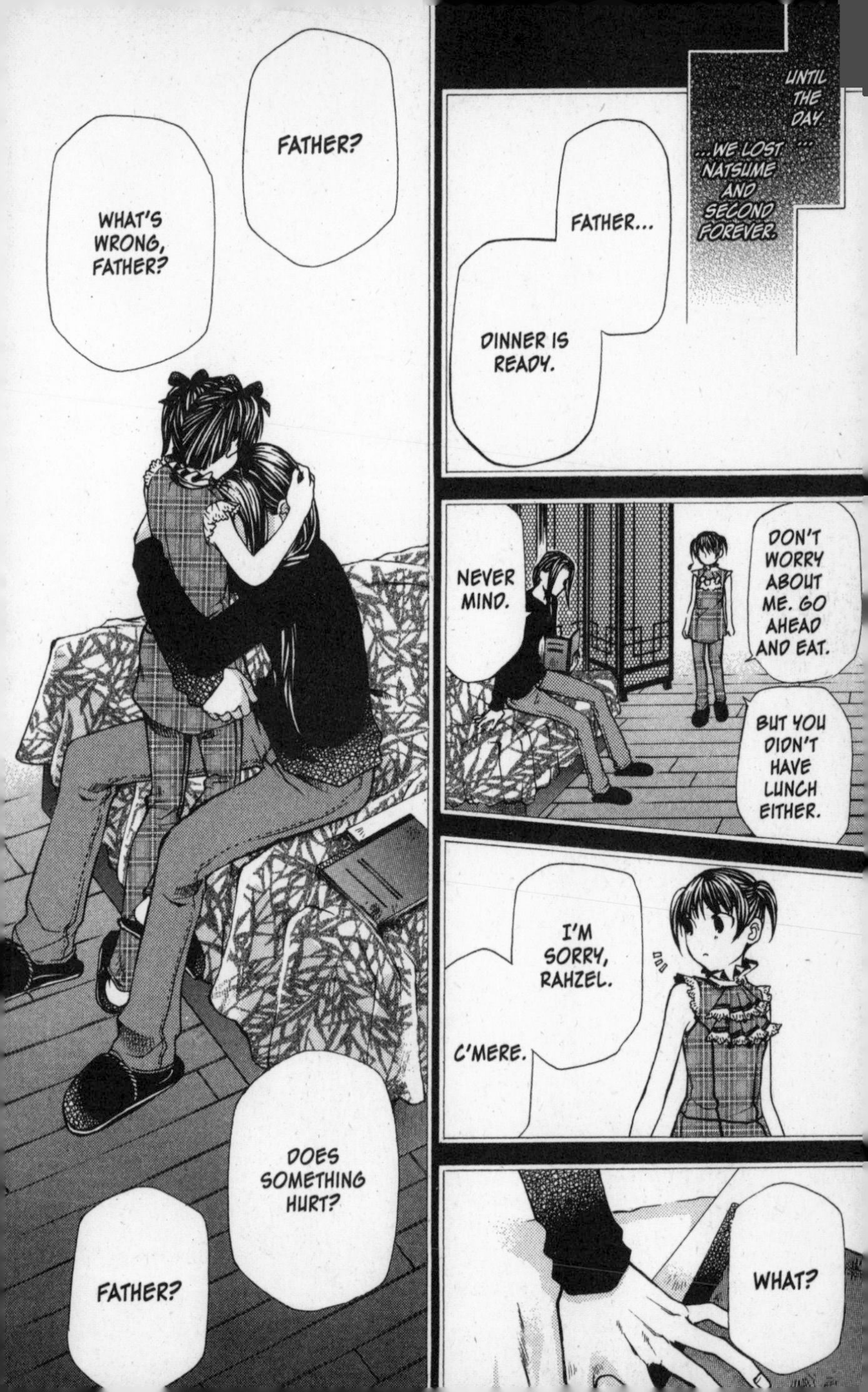
UNTIL THE DAY...
...WE LOST NATSUME AND SECOND FOREVER.
FATHER...
DINNER IS READY.
DON'T WORRY ABOUT ME. GO AHEAD AND EAT.
BUT YOU DIDN'T HAVE LUNCH EITHER.
NEVER MIND.
I'M SORRY, RAHZEL.
C'MERE.
WHAT?
FATHER?
WHAT'S WRONG, FATHER?
DOES SOMETHING HURT?
FATHER?

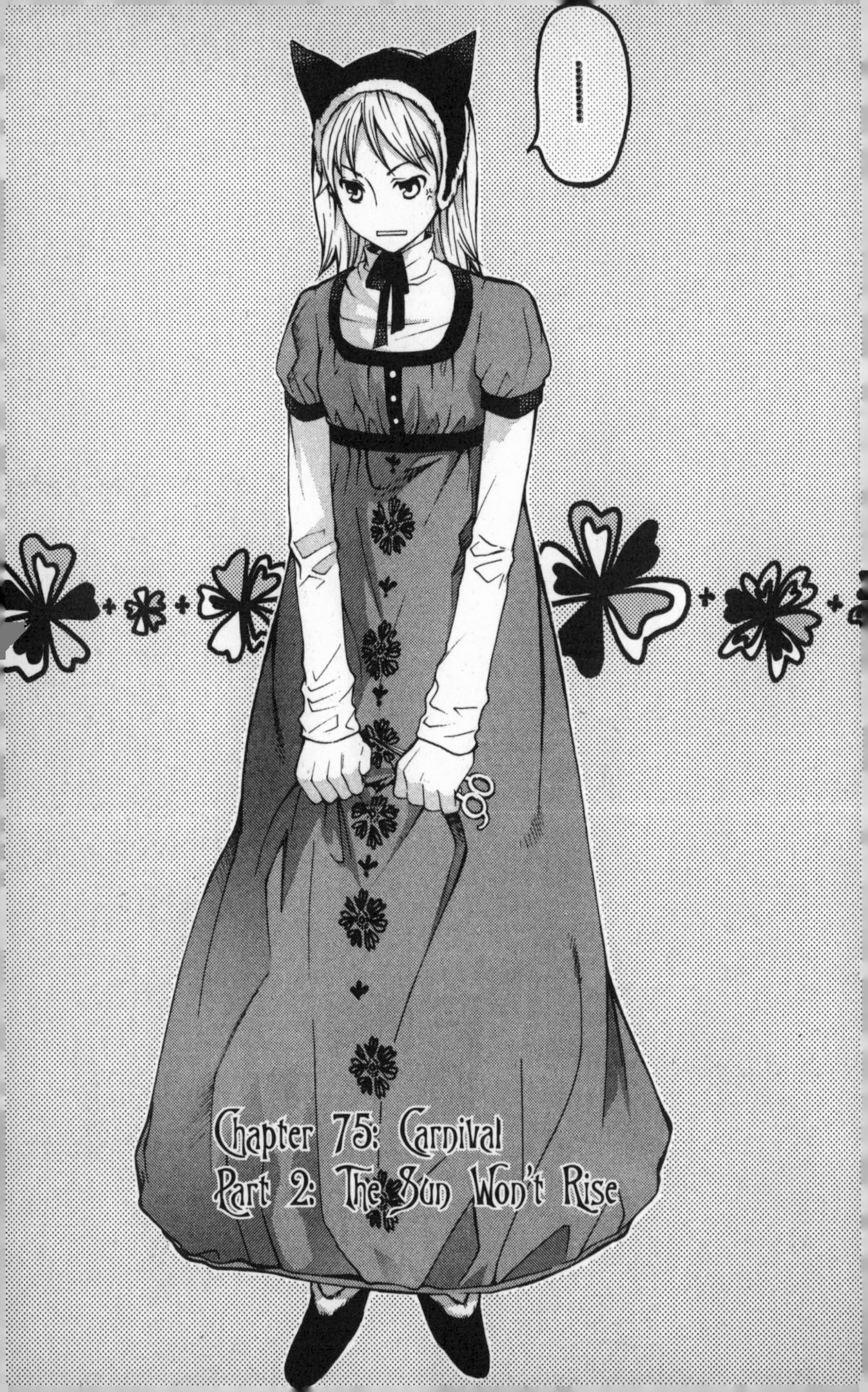
Chapter 75: Carnival
Part 2: The Sun Won't Rise

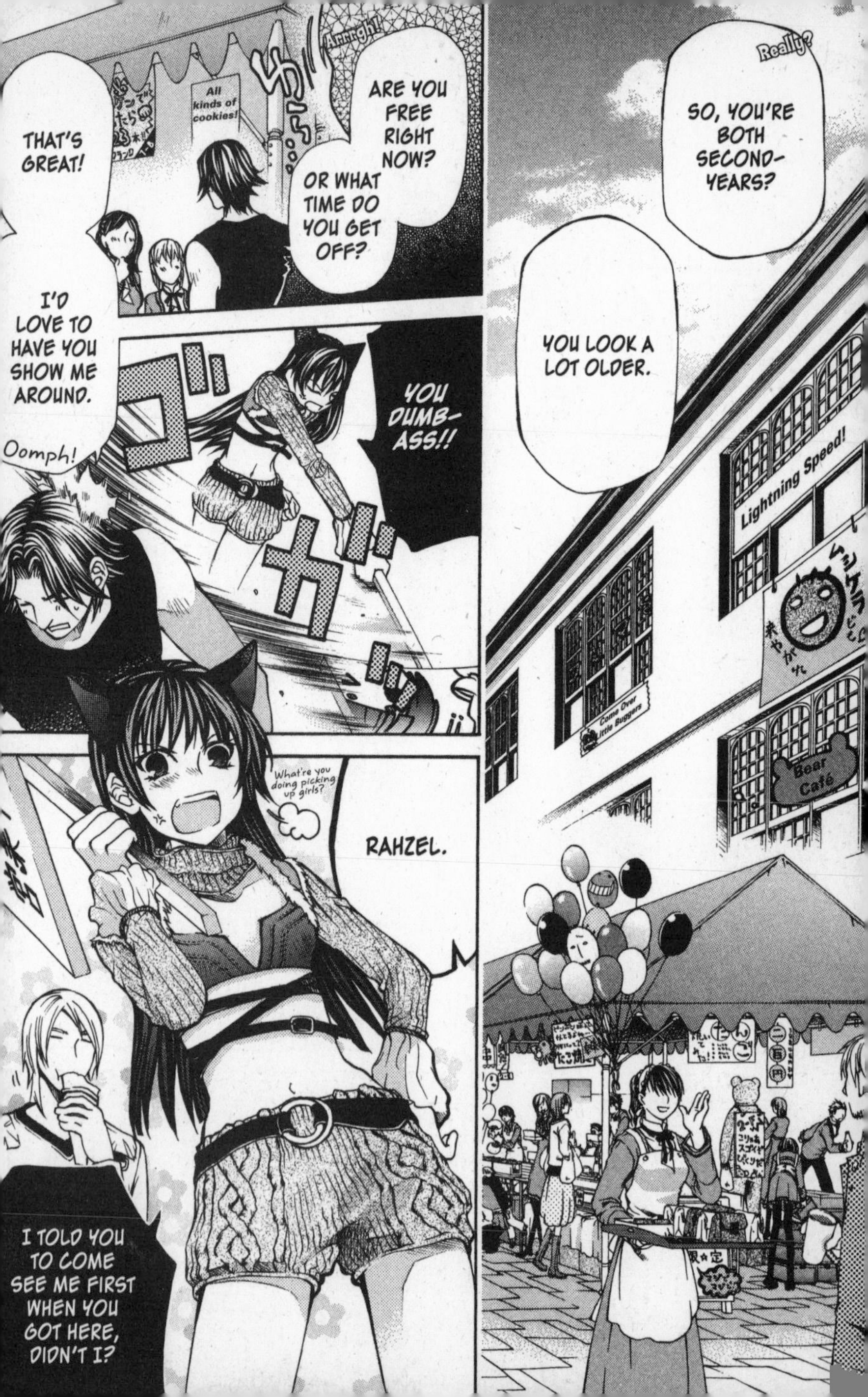
Really?
SO, YOU'RE BOTH SECOND-YEARS?
YOU LOOK A LOT OLDER.
Lightning Speed!
Come Over Little Buggers
Bear Café
Arrrgh!
ARE YOU FREE RIGHT NOW?
OR WHAT TIME DO YOU GET OFF?
All kinds of cookies!
THAT'S GREAT!
I'D LOVE TO HAVE YOU SHOW ME AROUND.
YOU DUMB-ASS!!
Oomph!
What're you doing picking up girls?
RAHZEL.
I TOLD YOU TO COME SEE ME FIRST WHEN YOU GOT HERE, DIDN'T I?

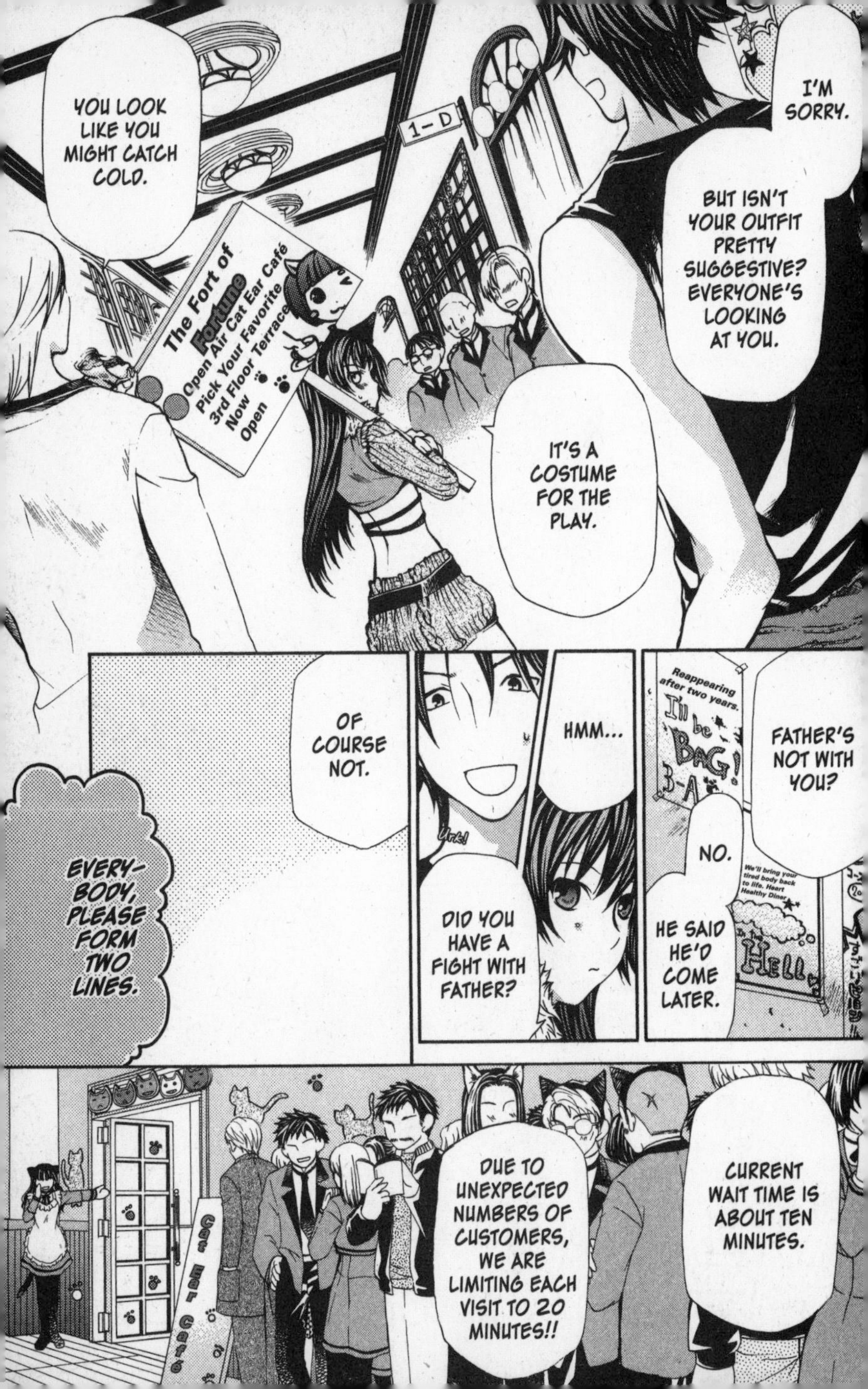
I'M SORRY.
BUT ISN'T YOUR OUTFIT PRETTY SUGGESTIVE? EVERYONE'S LOOKING AT YOU.
YOU LOOK LIKE YOU MIGHT CATCH COLD.
1-D
The Fort of Fortune Open Air Cat Ear Café Pick Your Favorite 3rd Floor Terrace Now Open
IT'S A COSTUME FOR THE PLAY.
Reappearing after two years. I'll be BACK! 3-A
FATHER'S NOT WITH YOU?
NO.
HE SAID HE'D COME LATER.
We'll bring your tired body back to life. Heart Healthy Diner
To the Hell
HMM...
Urk!
DID YOU HAVE A FIGHT WITH FATHER?
OF COURSE NOT.
EVERY-BODY, PLEASE FORM TWO LINES.
CURRENT WAIT TIME IS ABOUT TEN MINUTES.
DUE TO UNEXPECTED NUMBERS OF CUSTOMERS, WE ARE LIMITING EACH VISIT TO 20 MINUTES!!
Cat Ear Café

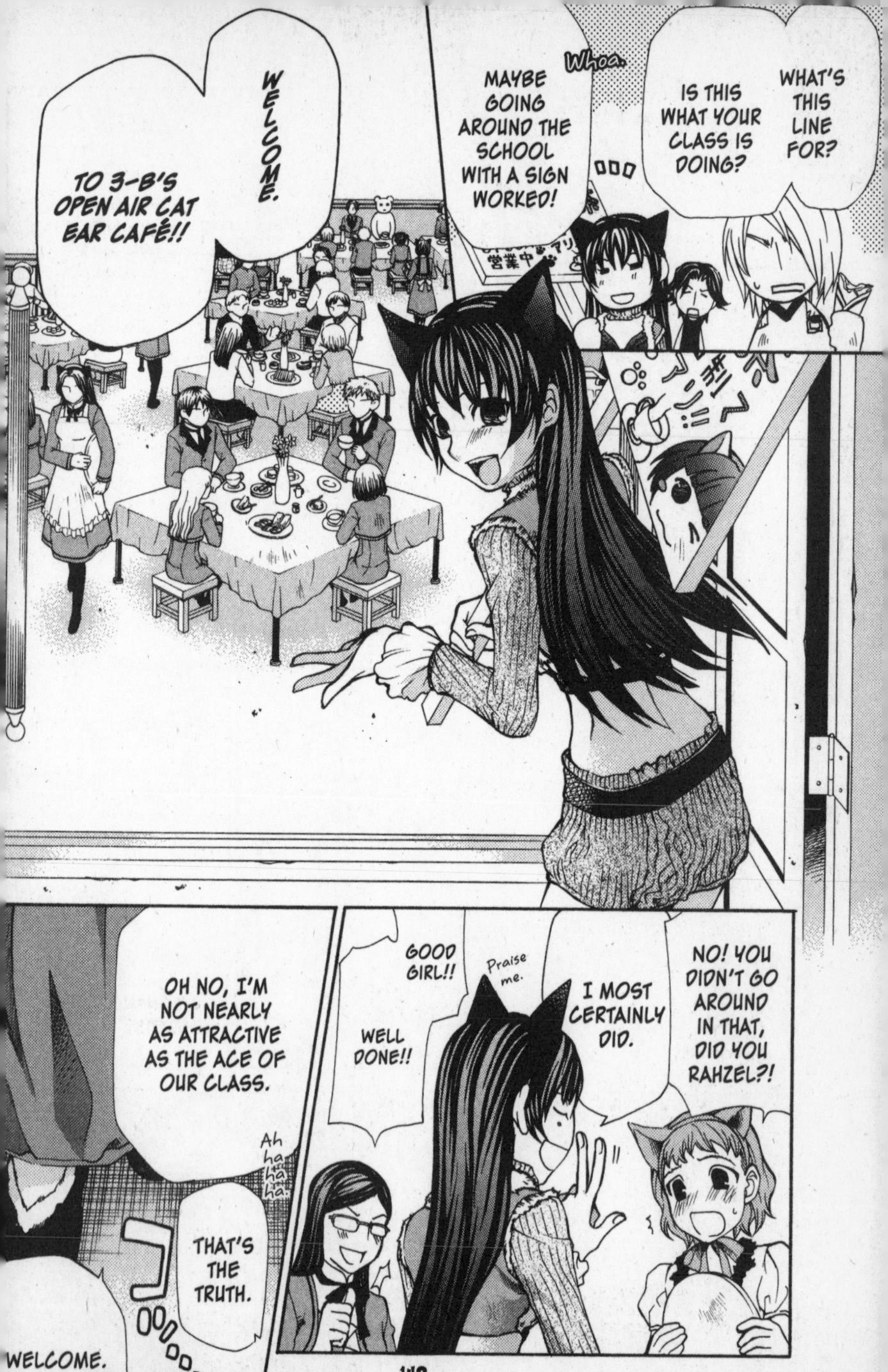
WHAT'S THIS LINE FOR?
IS THIS WHAT YOUR CLASS IS DOING?
Whoa.
MAYBE GOING AROUND THE SCHOOL WITH A SIGN WORKED!
WELCOME.
TO 3-B'S OPEN AIR CAT EAR CAFÉ!!
NO! YOU DIDN'T GO AROUND IN THAT, DID YOU RAHZEL?!
I MOST CERTAINLY DID.
Praise me.
GOOD GIRL!!
WELL DONE!!
OH NO, I'M NOT NEARLY AS ATTRACTIVE AS THE ACE OF OUR CLASS.
Ah ha ha ha ha.
THAT'S THE TRUTH.
WELCOME.

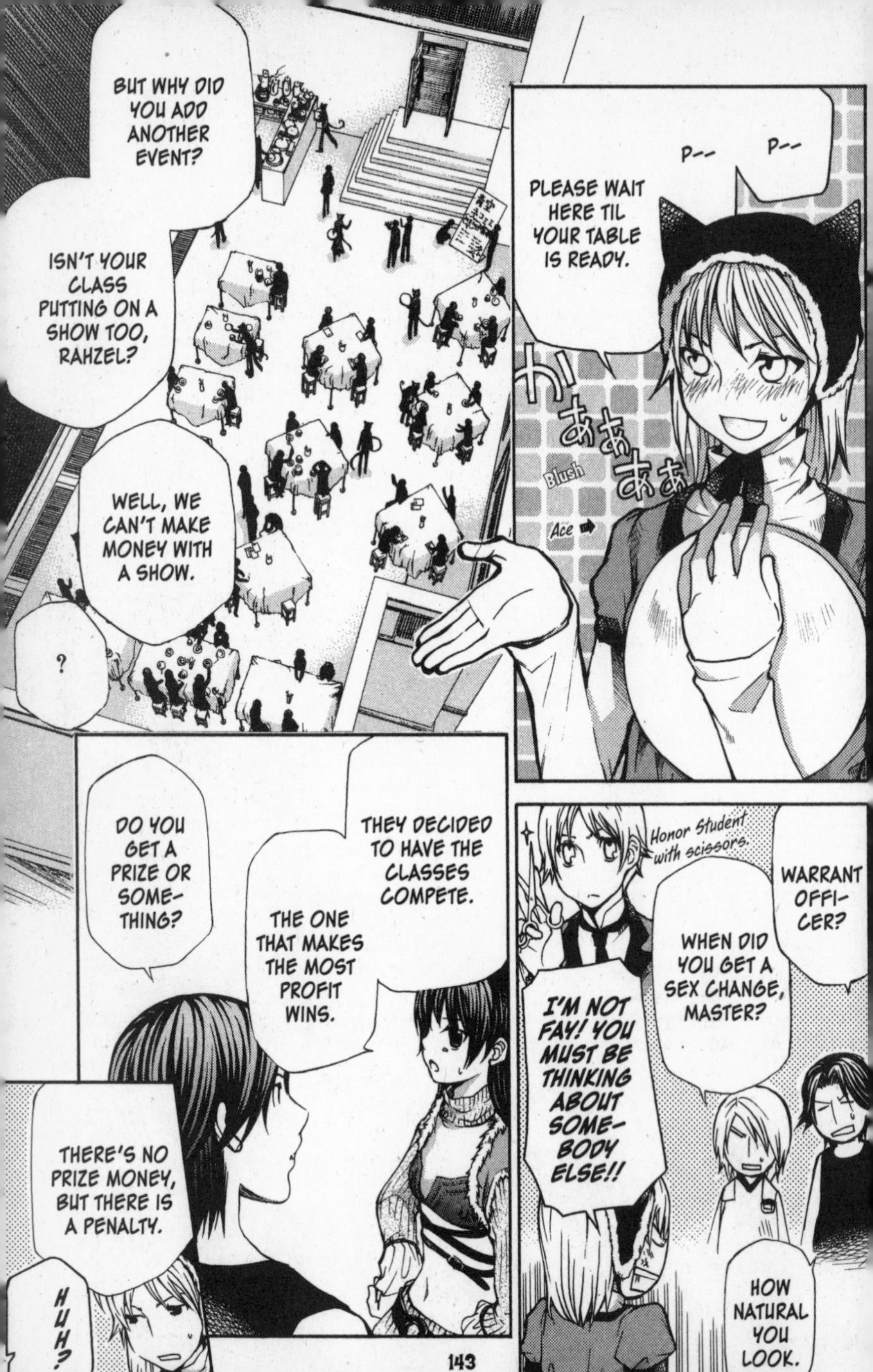
P-- P--
PLEASE WAIT HERE TIL YOUR TABLE IS READY.
かあああ
Blush
Ace
BUT WHY DID YOU ADD ANOTHER EVENT?
ISN'T YOUR CLASS PUTTING ON A SHOW TOO, RAHZEL?
WELL, WE CAN'T MAKE MONEY WITH A SHOW.
?
WARRANT OFFICER?
WHEN DID YOU GET A SEX CHANGE, MASTER?
Honor Student with scissors.
I'M NOT FAY! YOU MUST BE THINKING ABOUT SOMEBODY ELSE!!
HOW NATURAL YOU LOOK.
DO YOU GET A PRIZE OR SOMETHING?
THEY DECIDED TO HAVE THE CLASSES COMPETE.
THE ONE THAT MAKES THE MOST PROFIT WINS.
THERE'S NO PRIZE MONEY, BUT THERE IS A PENALTY.
HUH?

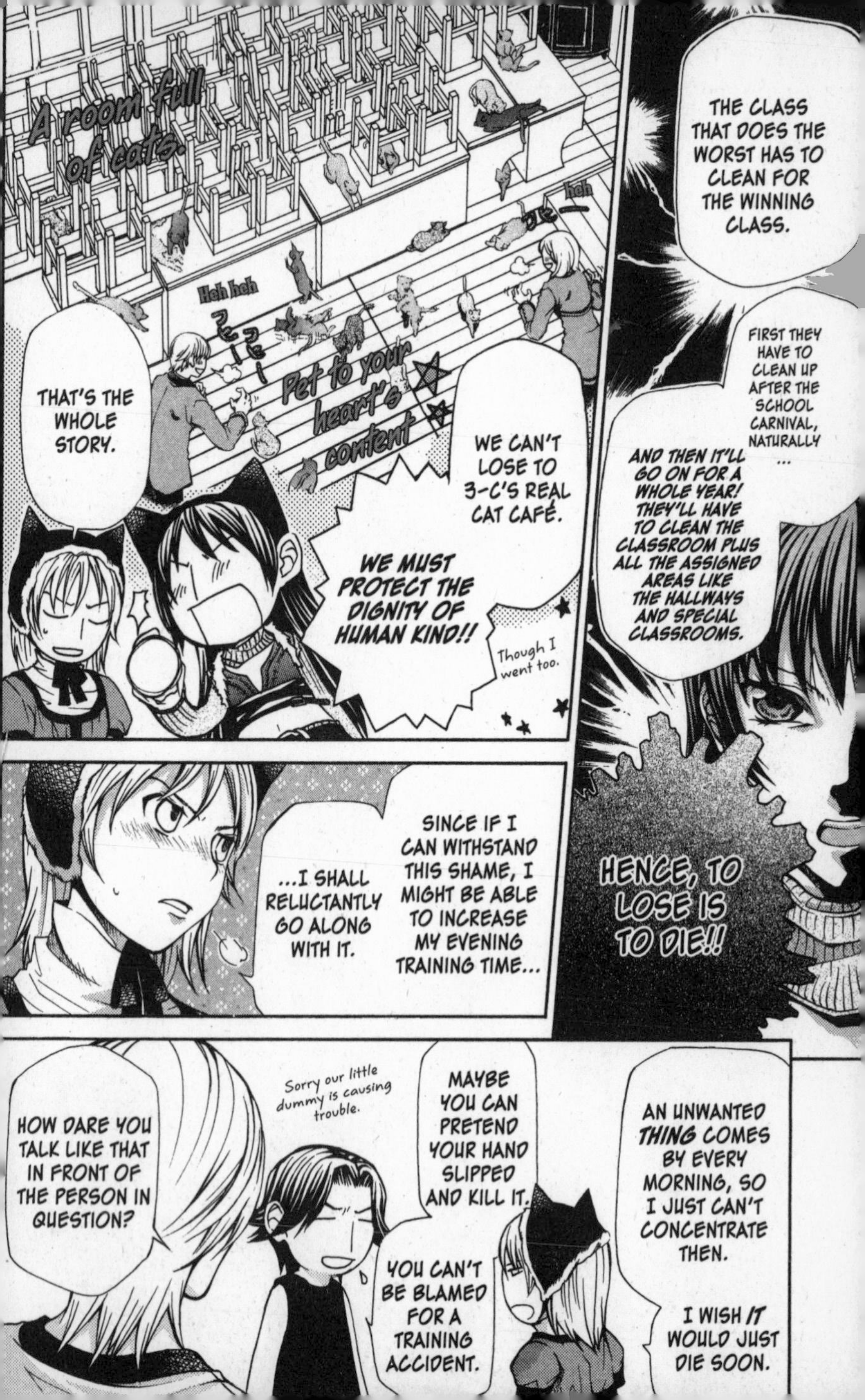
THE CLASS THAT DOES THE WORST HAS TO CLEAN FOR THE WINNING CLASS.
FIRST THEY HAVE TO CLEAN UP AFTER THE SCHOOL CARNIVAL, NATURALLY...
AND THEN IT'LL GO ON FOR A WHOLE YEAR! THEY'LL HAVE TO CLEAN THE CLASSROOM PLUS ALL THE ASSIGNED AREAS LIKE THE HALLWAYS AND SPECIAL CLASSROOMS.
HENCE, TO LOSE IS TO DIE!!
heh
A room full of cats.
Heh heh
Pet to your heart's content
WE CAN'T LOSE TO 3-C'S REAL CAT CAFÉ.
WE MUST PROTECT THE DIGNITY OF HUMAN KIND!!
Though I went too.
THAT'S THE WHOLE STORY.
SINCE IF I CAN WITHSTAND THIS SHAME, I MIGHT BE ABLE TO INCREASE MY EVENING TRAINING TIME...
...I SHALL RELUCTANTLY GO ALONG WITH IT.
AN UNWANTED *THING* COMES BY EVERY MORNING, SO I JUST CAN'T CONCENTRATE THEN.
I WISH *IT* WOULD JUST DIE SOON.
MAYBE YOU CAN PRETEND YOUR HAND SLIPPED AND KILL IT.
YOU CAN'T BE BLAMED FOR A TRAINING ACCIDENT.
Sorry our little dummy is causing trouble.
HOW DARE YOU TALK LIKE THAT IN FRONT OF THE PERSON IN QUESTION?

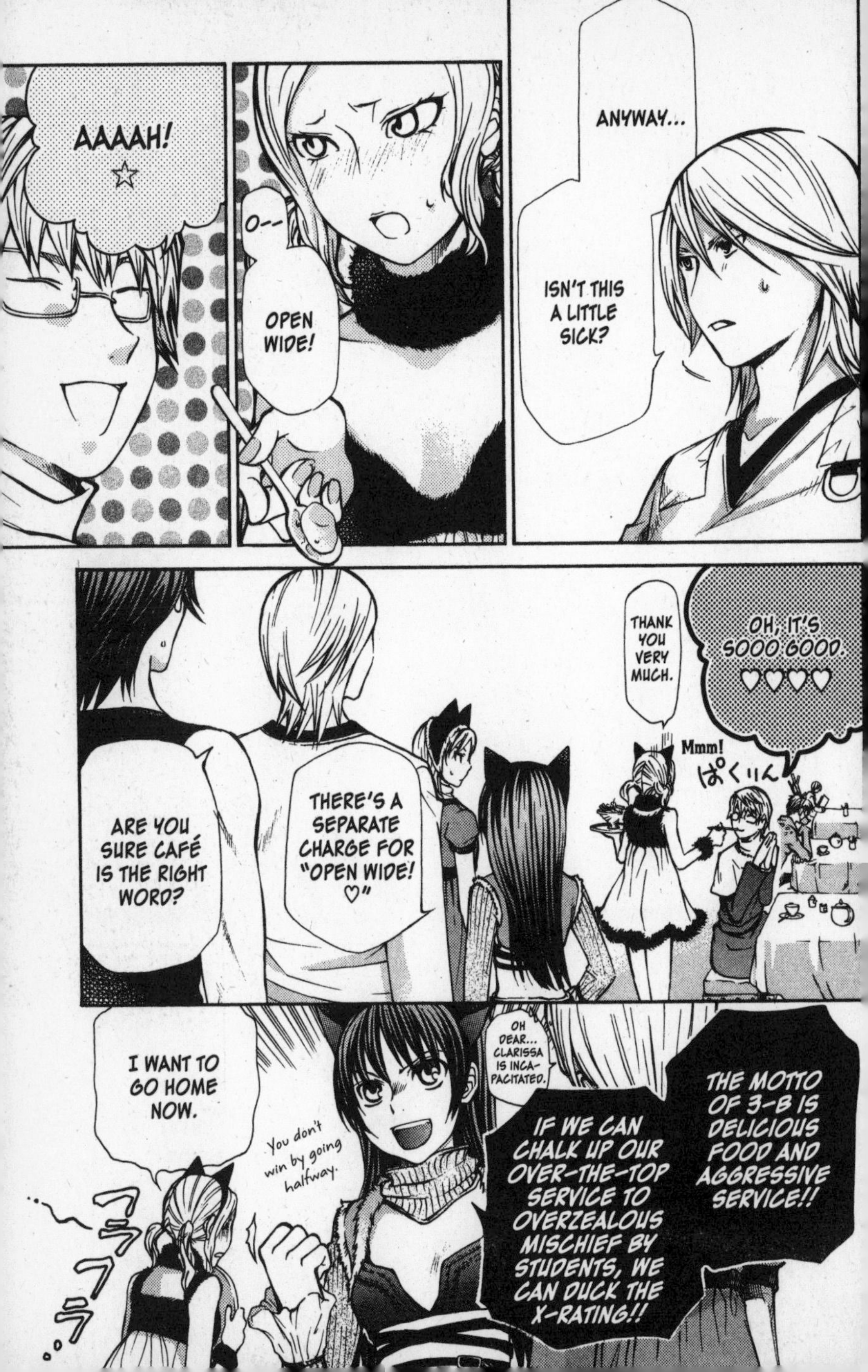
ANYWAY...
ISN'T THIS A LITTLE SICK?
O--
OPEN WIDE!
AAAAH! ☆
OH, IT'S SOOO GOOD. ♥♥♥♥
THANK YOU VERY MUCH.
Mmm!
ぱくりん
THERE'S A SEPARATE CHARGE FOR "OPEN WIDE! ♡"
ARE YOU SURE CAFÉ IS THE RIGHT WORD?
THE MOTTO OF 3-B IS DELICIOUS FOOD AND AGGRESSIVE SERVICE!!
IF WE CAN CHALK UP OUR OVER-THE-TOP SERVICE TO OVERZEALOUS MISCHIEF BY STUDENTS, WE CAN DUCK THE X-RATING!!
OH DEAR... CLARISSA IS INCA-PACITATED.
You don't win by going halfway.
I WANT TO GO HOME NOW.
フラフラ

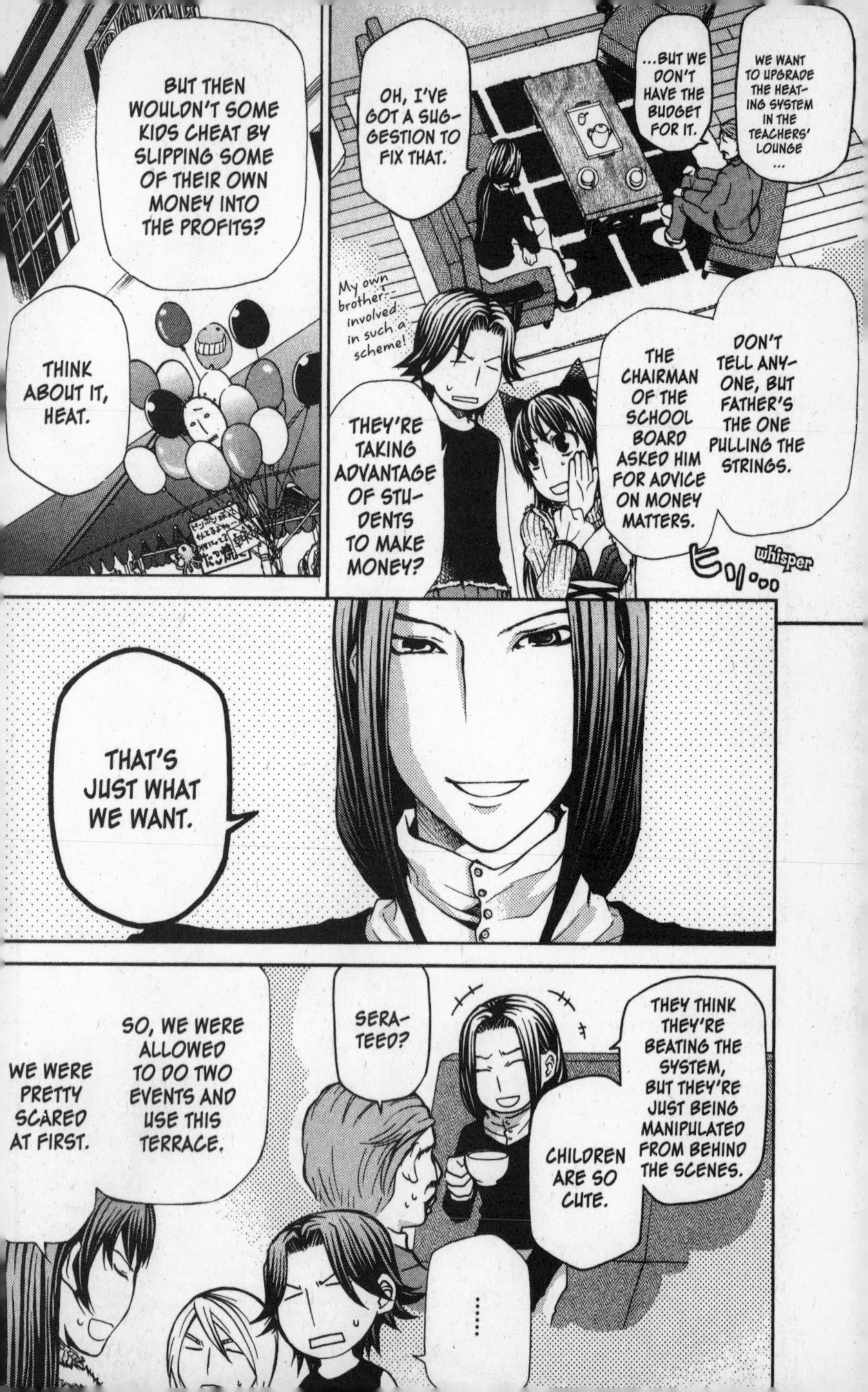
WE WANT TO UPGRADE THE HEATING SYSTEM IN THE TEACHERS' LOUNGE ...
...BUT WE DON'T HAVE THE BUDGET FOR IT.
OH, I'VE GOT A SUGGESTION TO FIX THAT.
DON'T TELL ANYONE, BUT FATHER'S THE ONE PULLING THE STRINGS.
THE CHAIRMAN OF THE SCHOOL BOARD ASKED HIM FOR ADVICE ON MONEY MATTERS.
whisper
My own brother-- involved in such a scheme!
THEY'RE TAKING ADVANTAGE OF STUDENTS TO MAKE MONEY?
BUT THEN WOULDN'T SOME KIDS CHEAT BY SLIPPING SOME OF THEIR OWN MONEY INTO THE PROFITS?
THINK ABOUT IT, HEAT.
THAT'S JUST WHAT WE WANT.
THEY THINK THEY'RE BEATING THE SYSTEM, BUT THEY'RE JUST BEING MANIPULATED FROM BEHIND THE SCENES.
SERATEED?
CHILDREN ARE SO CUTE.
SO, WE WERE ALLOWED TO DO TWO EVENTS AND USE THIS TERRACE.
WE WERE PRETTY SCARED AT FIRST.
......

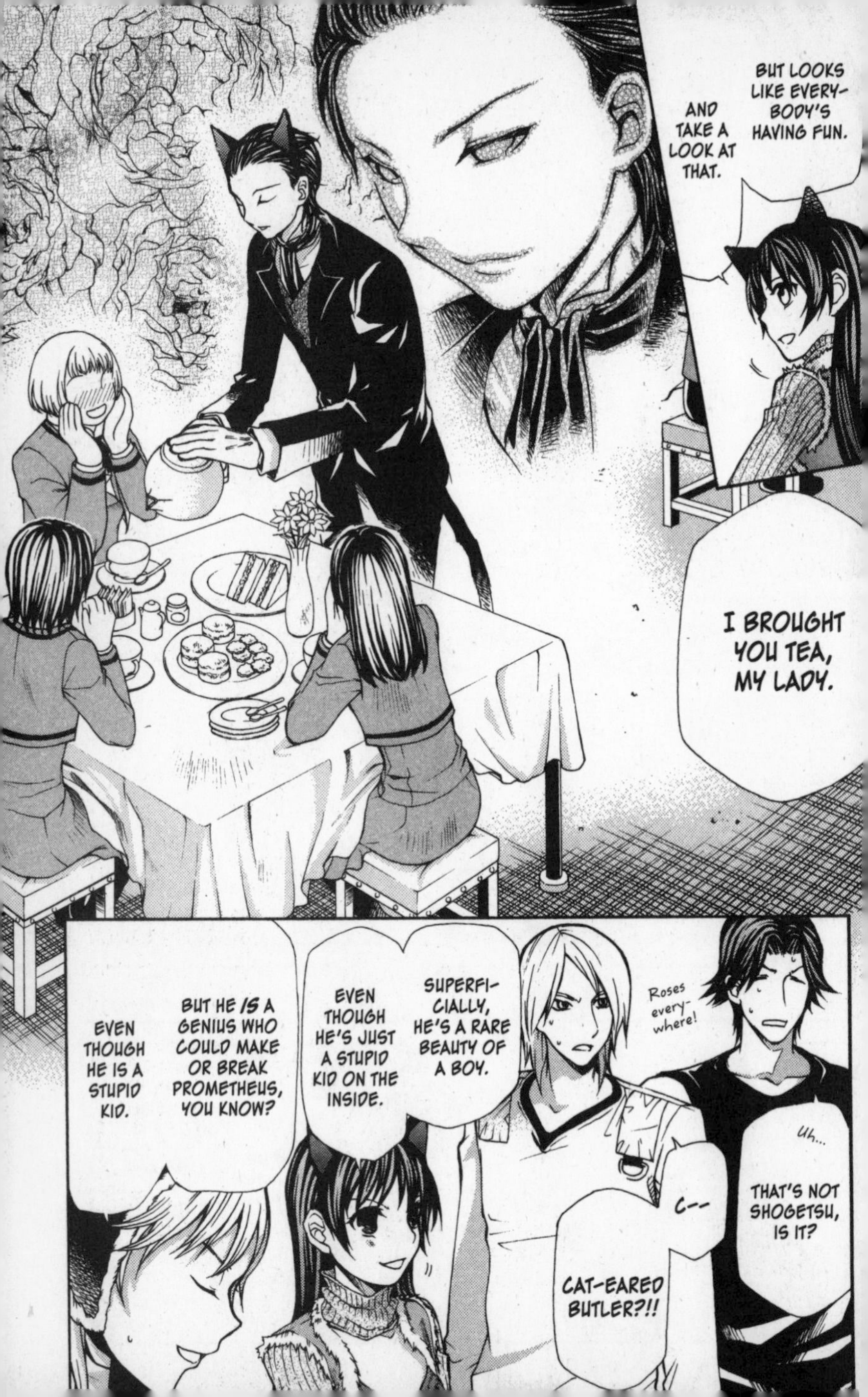

BUT LOOKS LIKE EVERY-BODY'S HAVING FUN.
AND TAKE A LOOK AT THAT.
I BROUGHT YOU TEA, MY LADY.
Roses every-where!
Uh...
THAT'S NOT SHOGETSU, IS IT?
C--
CAT-EARED BUTLER?!!
SUPERFI-CIALLY, HE'S A RARE BEAUTY OF A BOY.
EVEN THOUGH HE'S JUST A STUPID KID ON THE INSIDE.
BUT HE *IS* A GENIUS WHO COULD MAKE OR BREAK PROMETHEUS, YOU KNOW?
EVEN THOUGH HE IS A STUPID KID.

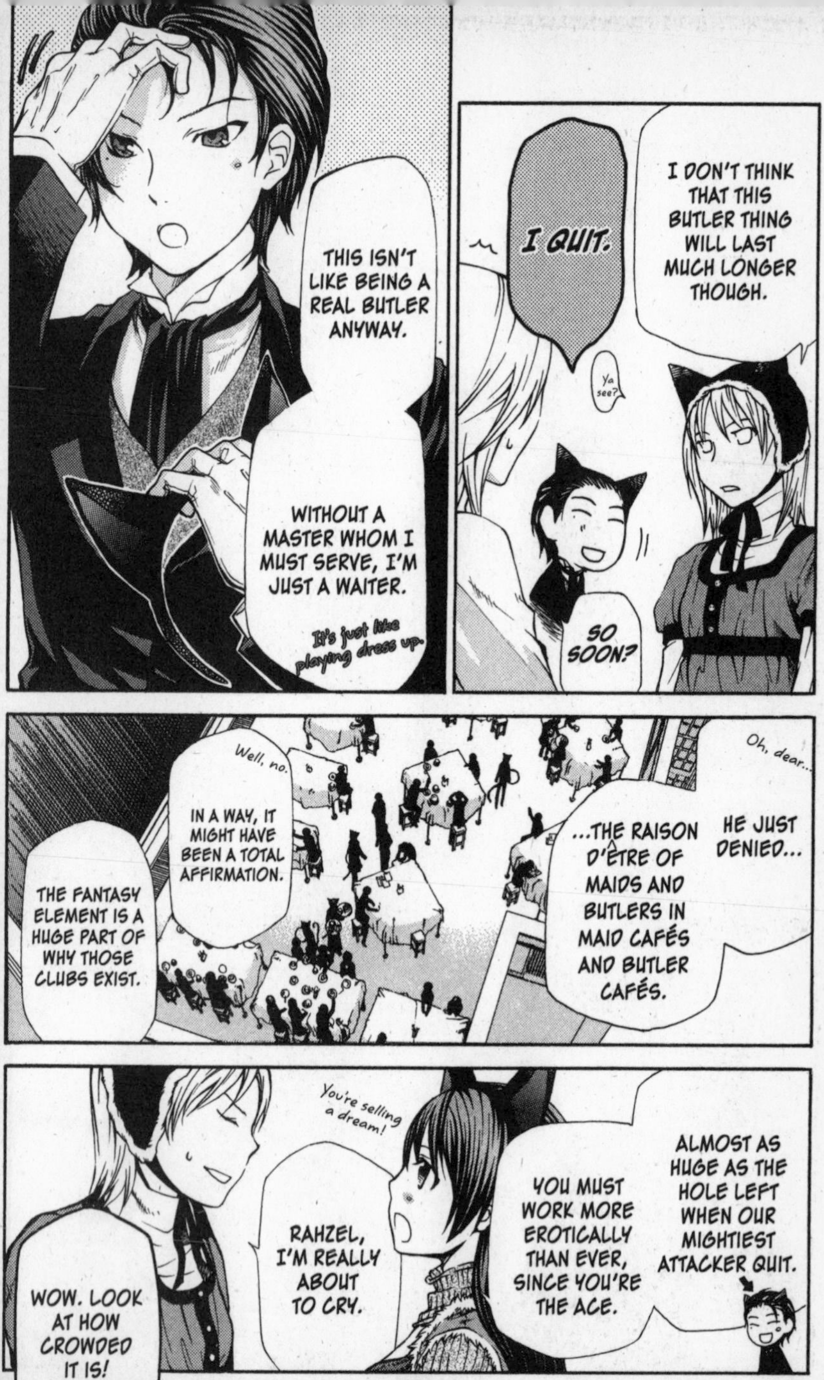
I DON'T THINK THAT THIS BUTLER THING WILL LAST MUCH LONGER THOUGH.
I QUIT.
Ya see?
SO SOON?
THIS ISN'T LIKE BEING A REAL BUTLER ANYWAY.
WITHOUT A MASTER WHOM I MUST SERVE, I'M JUST A WAITER.
It's just like playing dress up.
Oh, dear...
HE JUST DENIED...
...THE RAISON D'ÊTRE OF MAIDS AND BUTLERS IN MAID CAFÉS AND BUTLER CAFÉS.
Well, no.
IN A WAY, IT MIGHT HAVE BEEN A TOTAL AFFIRMATION.
THE FANTASY ELEMENT IS A HUGE PART OF WHY THOSE CLUBS EXIST.
ALMOST AS HUGE AS THE HOLE LEFT WHEN OUR MIGHTIEST ATTACKER QUIT.
YOU MUST WORK MORE EROTICALLY THAN EVER, SINCE YOU'RE THE ACE.
You're selling a dream!
RAHZEL, I'M REALLY ABOUT TO CRY.
WOW. LOOK AT HOW CROWDED IT IS!

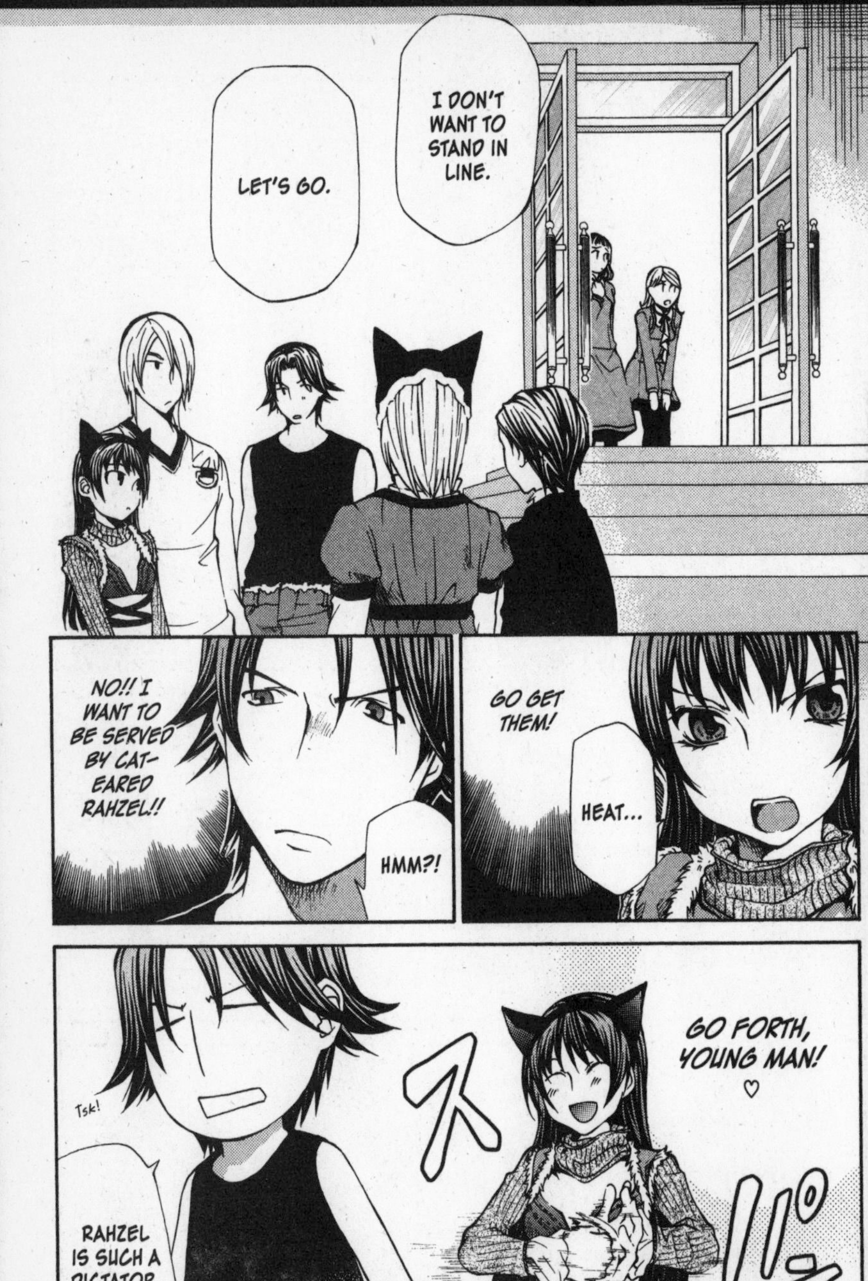
I DON'T WANT TO STAND IN LINE.
LET'S GO.
GO GET THEM!
HEAT...
NO!! I WANT TO BE SERVED BY CAT-EARED RAHZEL!!
HMM?!
GO FORTH, YOUNG MAN! ♡
パッ
ス
Tsk!
RAHZEL IS SUCH A DICTATOR.

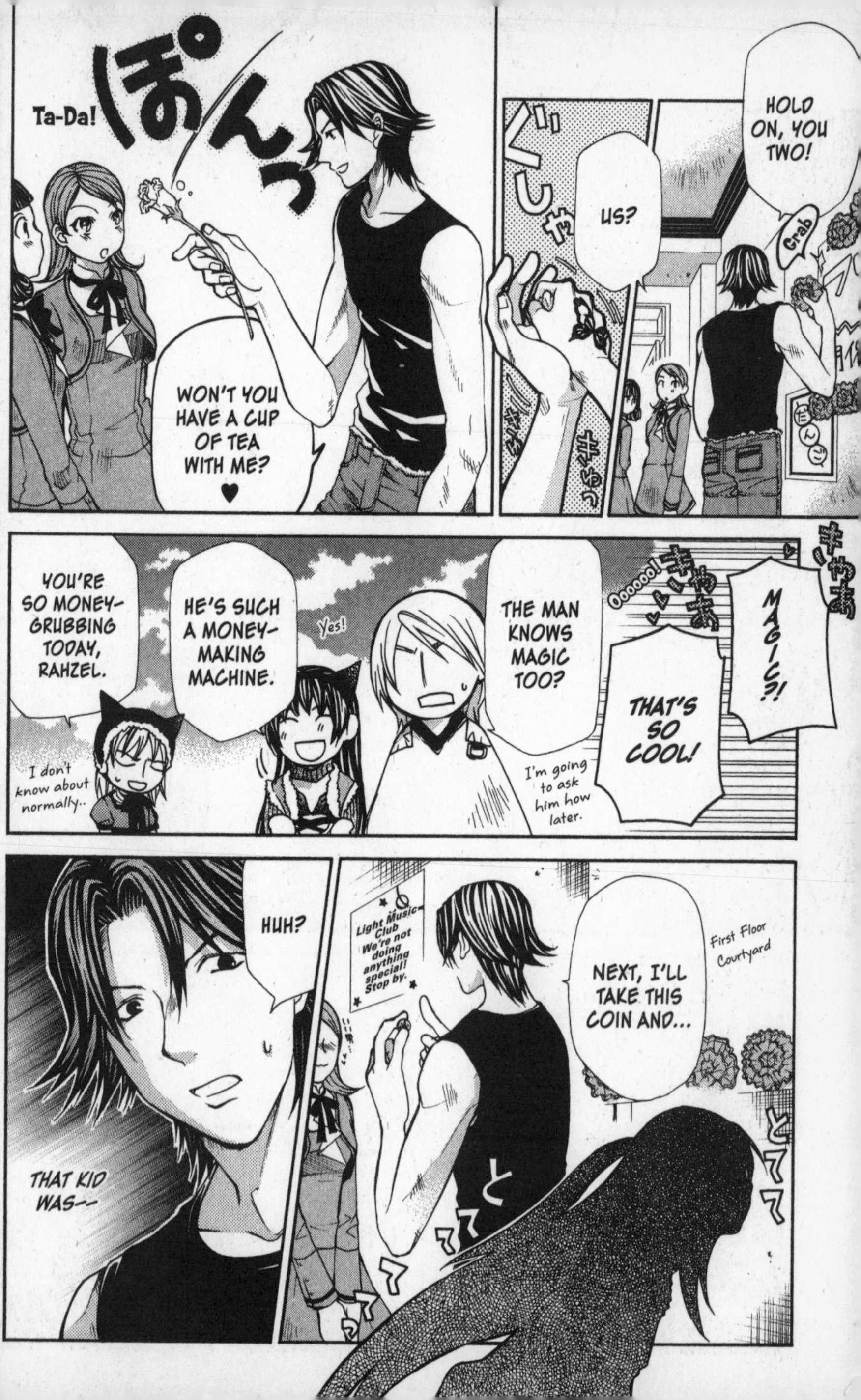
HOLD ON, YOU TWO!
Grab
US?
Ta-Da!
WON'T YOU HAVE A CUP OF TEA WITH ME? ♥
MAGIC?!
THAT'S SO COOL!
Oooooo!
THE MAN KNOWS MAGIC TOO?
I'm going to ask him how later.
Yes!
HE'S SUCH A MONEY-MAKING MACHINE.
YOU'RE SO MONEY-GRUBBING TODAY, RAHZEL.
I don't know about normally..
First Floor Courtyard
NEXT, I'LL TAKE THIS COIN AND...
Light Music Club We're not doing anything special! Stop by.
HUH?
THAT KID WAS--

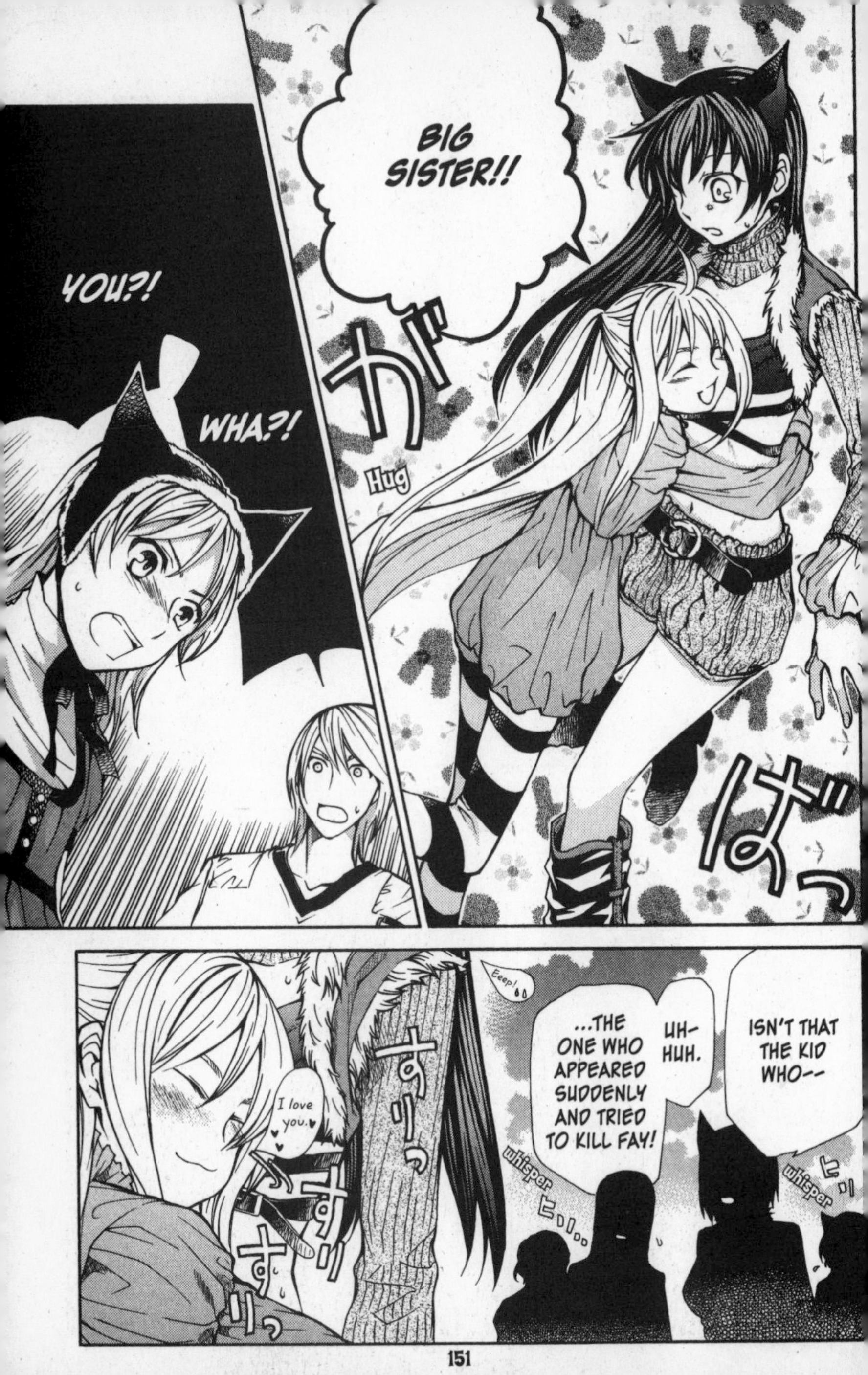
BIG SISTER!!
Hug
YOU?!
WHA?!
ISN'T THAT THE KID WHO--
UH-HUH.
...THE ONE WHO APPEARED SUDDENLY AND TRIED TO KILL FAY!
whisper
whisper
Eeep!
I love you.♥

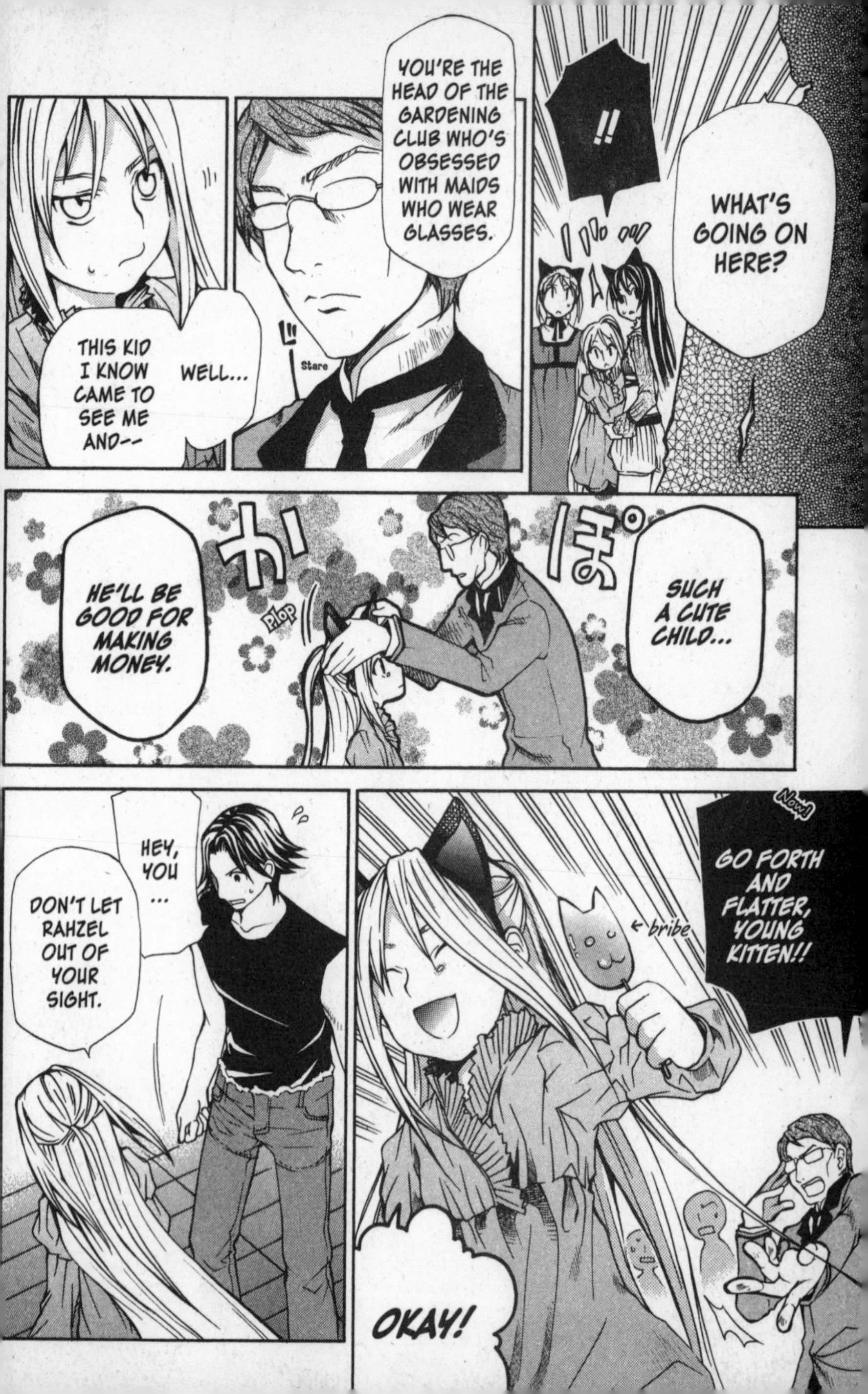
!!
WHAT'S GOING ON HERE?
YOU'RE THE HEAD OF THE GARDENING CLUB WHO'S OBSESSED WITH MAIDS WHO WEAR GLASSES.
Stare
WELL...
THIS KID I KNOW CAME TO SEE ME AND--
SUCH A CUTE CHILD...
かぽ
Plop
HE'LL BE GOOD FOR MAKING MONEY.
Now!
GO FORTH AND FLATTER, YOUNG KITTEN!!
bribe
OKAY!
HEY, YOU ...
DON'T LET RAHZEL OUT OF YOUR SIGHT.

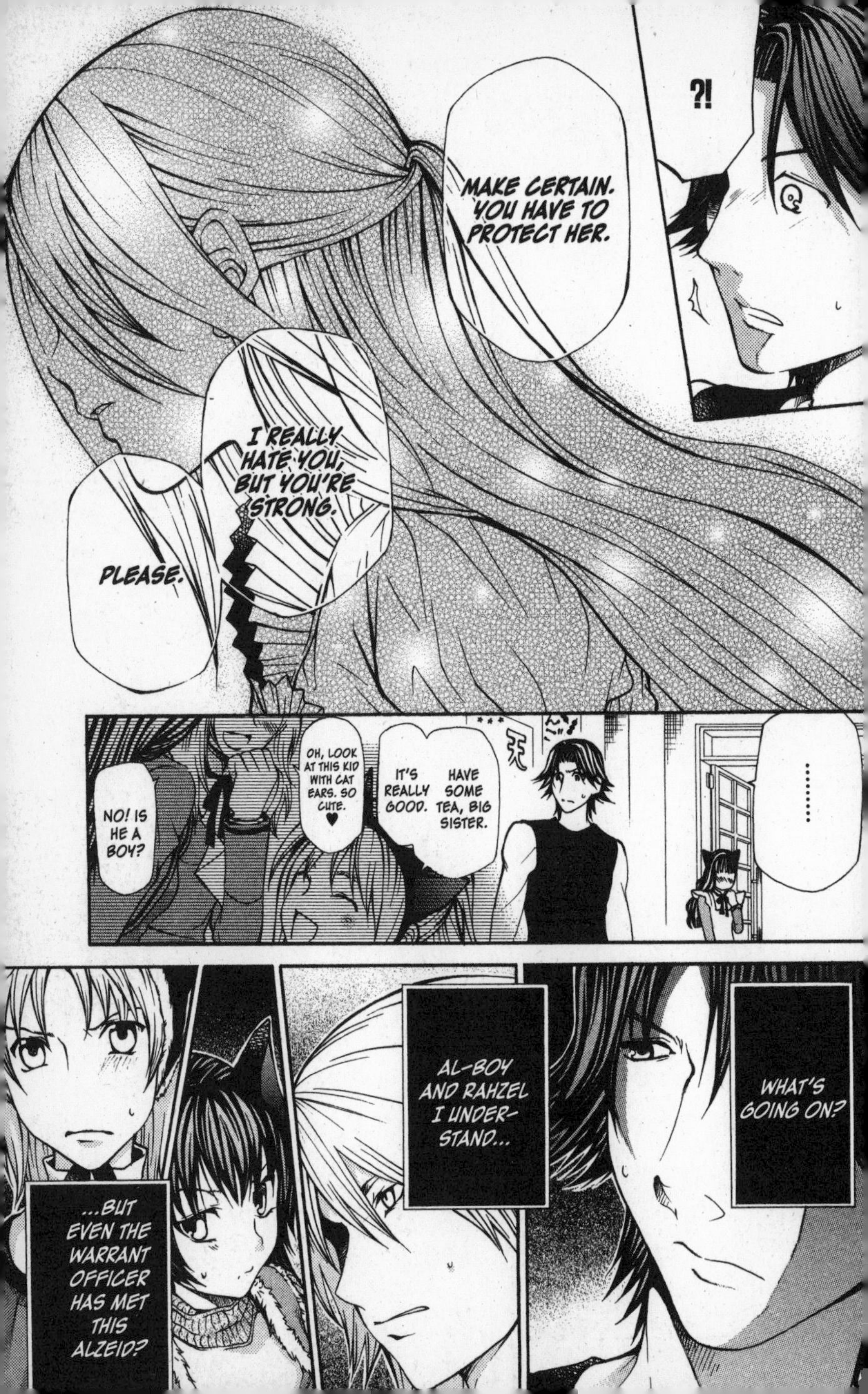
?!
MAKE CERTAIN. YOU HAVE TO PROTECT HER.
I REALLY HATE YOU, BUT YOU'RE STRONG.
PLEASE.
......
HAVE SOME TEA, BIG SISTER.
IT'S REALLY GOOD.
OH, LOOK AT THIS KID WITH CAT EARS. SO CUTE. ♥
NO! IS HE A BOY?
WHAT'S GOING ON?
AL-BOY AND RAHZEL I UNDER-STAND...
...BUT EVEN THE WARRANT OFFICER HAS MET THIS ALZEID?

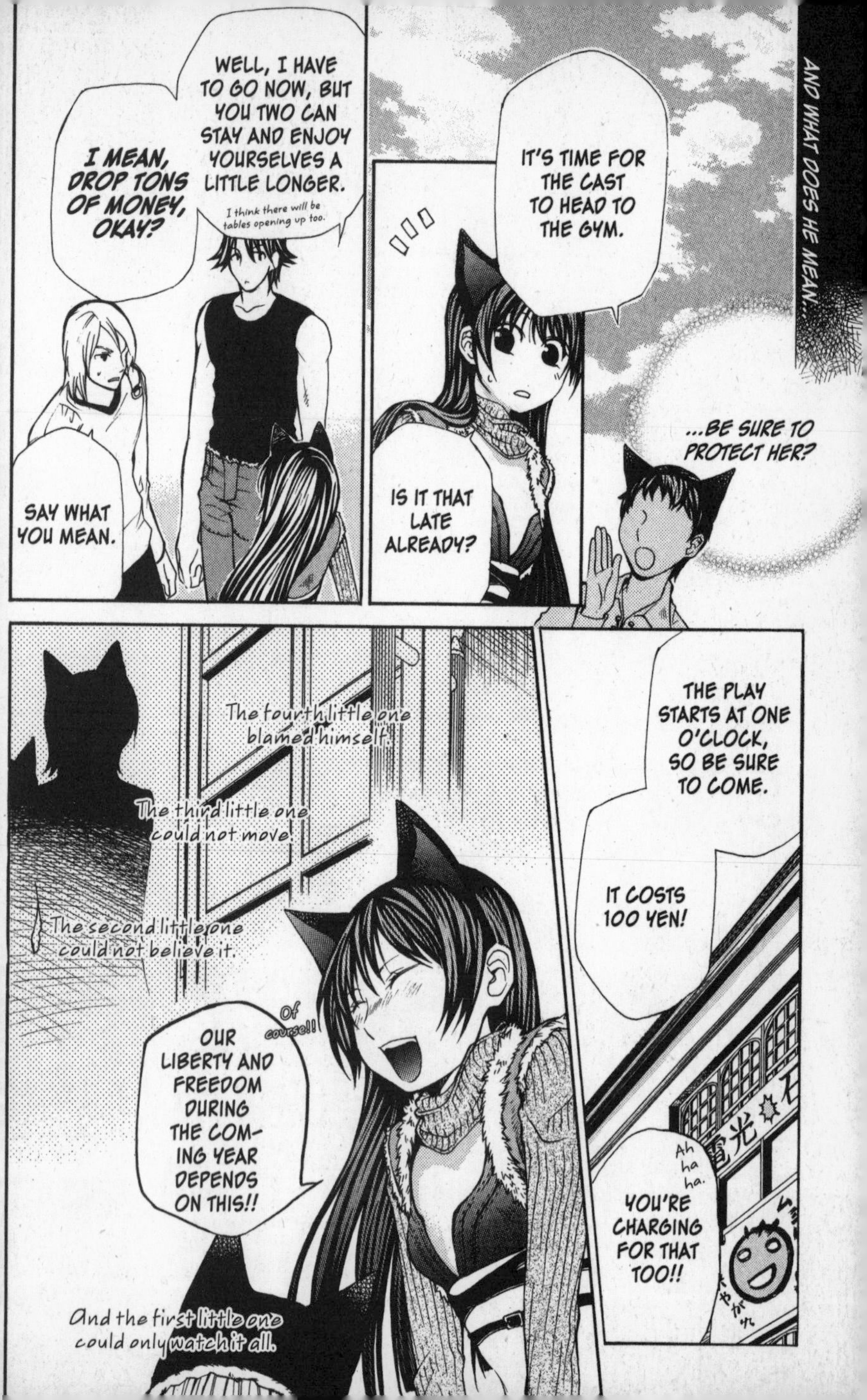
AND WHAT DOES HE MEAN...
...BE SURE TO PROTECT HER?
IT'S TIME FOR THE CAST TO HEAD TO THE GYM.
IS IT THAT LATE ALREADY?
WELL, I HAVE TO GO NOW, BUT YOU TWO CAN STAY AND ENJOY YOURSELVES A LITTLE LONGER.
I think there will be tables opening up too.
I MEAN, DROP TONS OF MONEY, OKAY?
SAY WHAT YOU MEAN.
THE PLAY STARTS AT ONE O'CLOCK, SO BE SURE TO COME.
IT COSTS 100 YEN!
Ah ha ha.
YOU'RE CHARGING FOR THAT TOO!!
Of course!!
OUR LIBERTY AND FREEDOM DURING THE COMING YEAR DEPENDS ON THIS!!
The fourth little one blamed himself.
The third little one could not move.
The second little one could not believe it.
And the first little one could only watch it all.

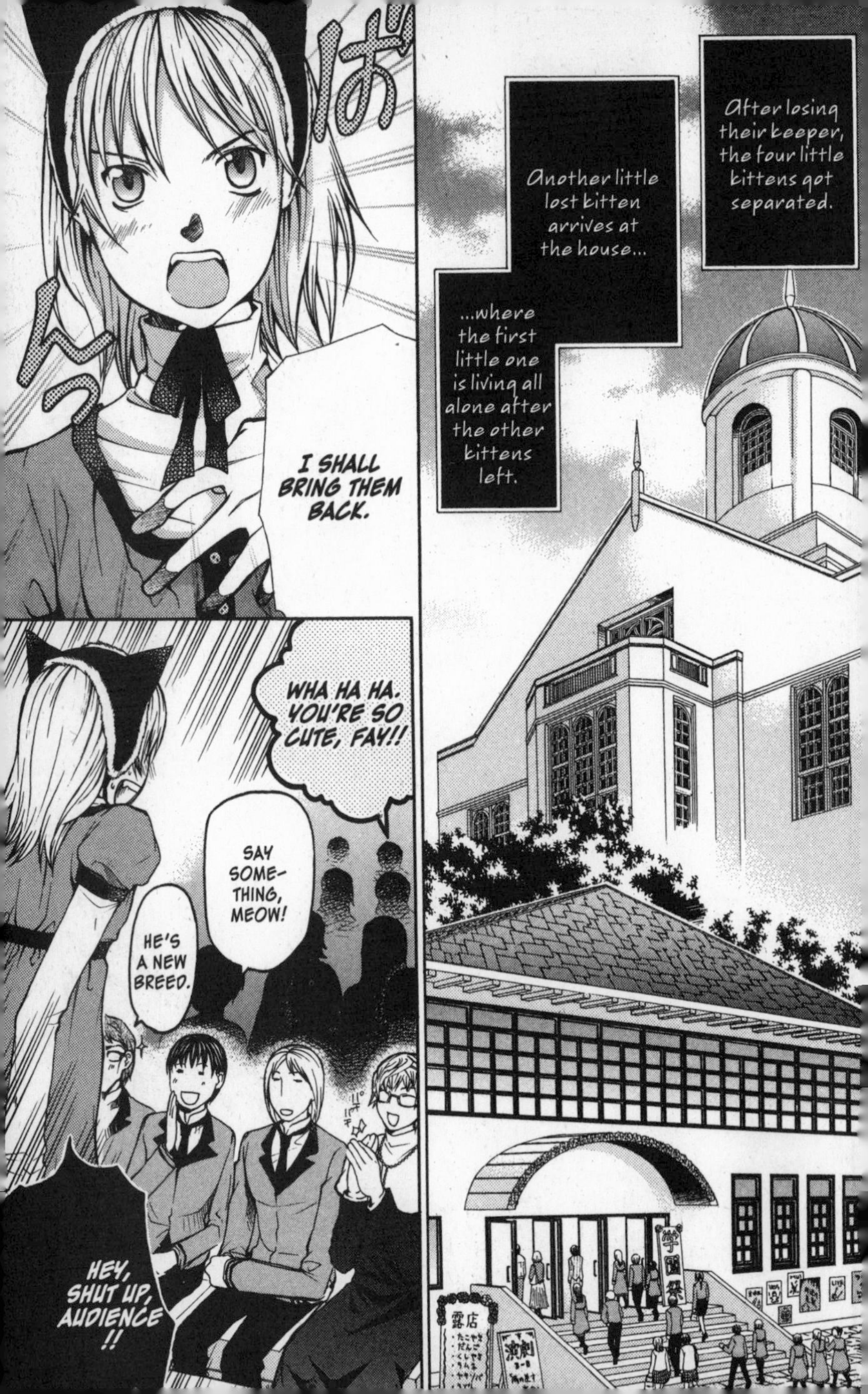
After losing their keeper, the four little kittens got separated.
Another little lost kitten arrives at the house...
...where the first little one is living all alone after the other kittens left.
露店
I SHALL BRING THEM BACK.
WHA HA HA. YOU'RE SO CUTE, FAY!!
SAY SOME-THING, MEOW!
HE'S A NEW BREED.
HEY, SHUT UP, AUDIENCE!!

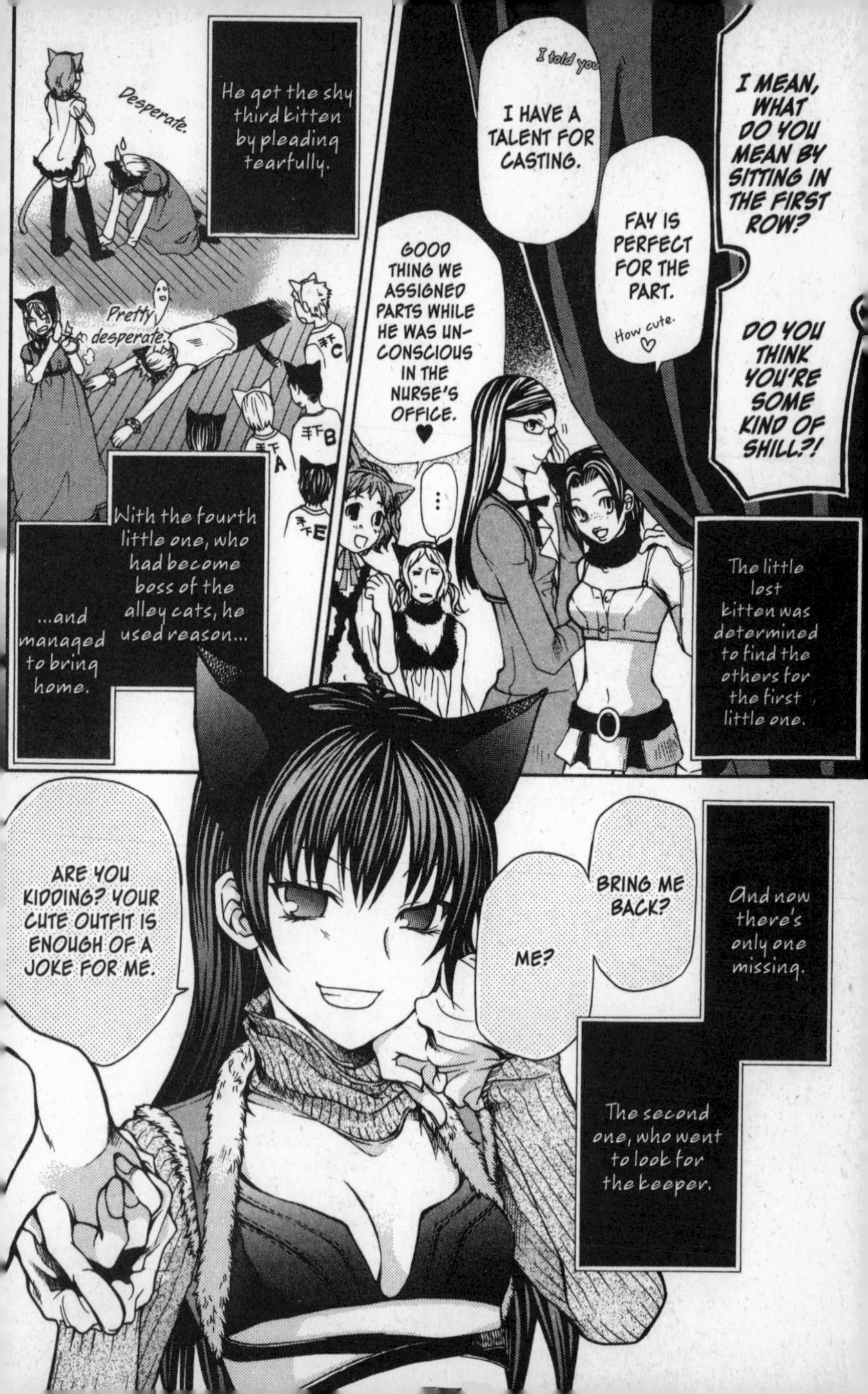
I MEAN, WHAT DO YOU MEAN BY SITTING IN THE FIRST ROW?
DO YOU THINK YOU'RE SOME KIND OF SHILL?!
The little lost kitten was determined to find the others for the first little one.
I told you
I HAVE A TALENT FOR CASTING.
FAY IS PERFECT FOR THE PART.
How cute.
GOOD THING WE ASSIGNED PARTS WHILE HE WAS UN-CONSCIOUS IN THE NURSE'S OFFICE.
...
He got the shy third kitten by pleading tearfully.
Desperate.
Pretty desperate.
With the fourth little one, who had become boss of the alley cats, he used reason...
...and managed to bring home.
And now there's only one missing.
The second one, who went to look for the keeper.
BRING ME BACK?
ME?
ARE YOU KIDDING? YOUR CUTE OUTFIT IS ENOUGH OF A JOKE FOR ME.

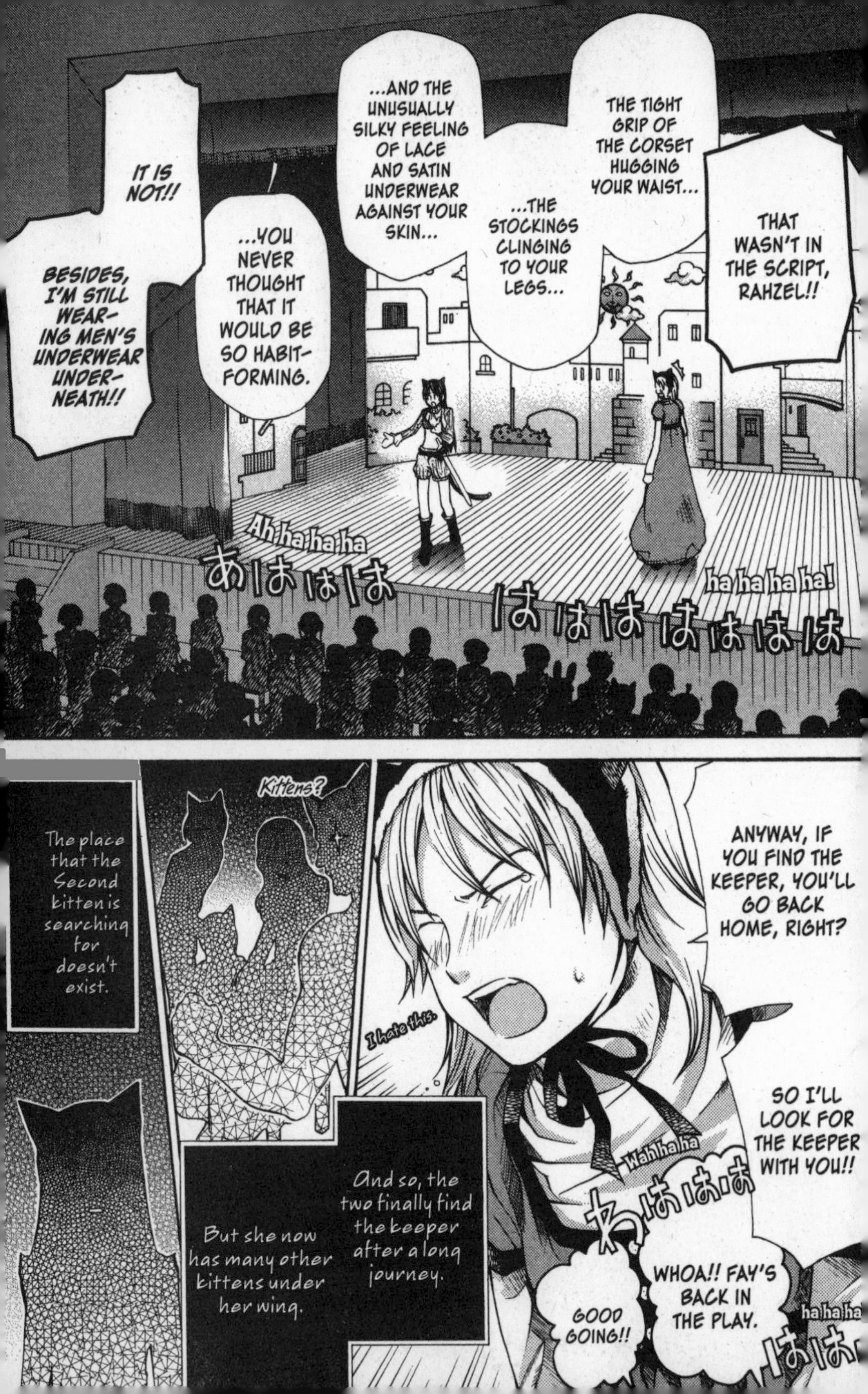
THAT WASN'T IN THE SCRIPT, RAHZEL!!
THE TIGHT GRIP OF THE CORSET HUGGING YOUR WAIST...
...THE STOCKINGS CLINGING TO YOUR LEGS...
...AND THE UNUSUALLY SILKY FEELING OF LACE AND SATIN UNDERWEAR AGAINST YOUR SKIN...
...YOU NEVER THOUGHT THAT IT WOULD BE SO HABIT-FORMING.
IT IS NOT!!
BESIDES, I'M STILL WEARING MEN'S UNDERWEAR UNDERNEATH!!
ははははははは
ha ha ha ha!
あははは
Ah ha ha ha
ANYWAY, IF YOU FIND THE KEEPER, YOU'LL GO BACK HOME, RIGHT?
SO I'LL LOOK FOR THE KEEPER WITH YOU!!
I hate this.
わぁはぁ
Wah ha ha
WHOA!! FAY'S BACK IN THE PLAY.
GOOD GOING!!
はぁは
ha ha ha
Kittens?
And so, the two finally find the keeper after a long journey.
But she now has many other kittens under her wing.
The place that the Second kitten is searching for doesn't exist.

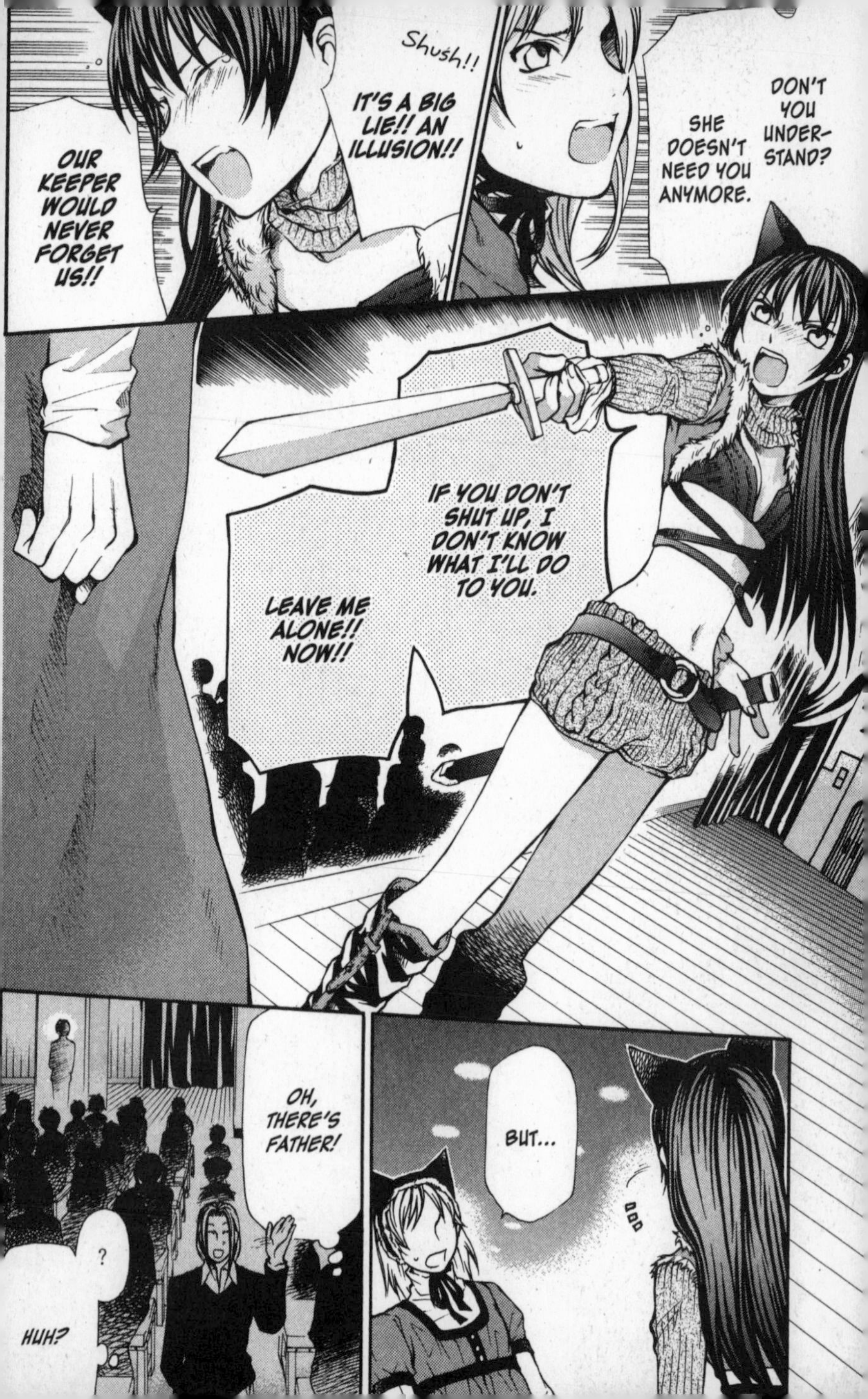
DON'T YOU UNDERSTAND?
SHE DOESN'T NEED YOU ANYMORE.
Shush!!
IT'S A BIG LIE!! AN ILLUSION!!
OUR KEEPER WOULD NEVER FORGET US!!
IF YOU DON'T SHUT UP, I DON'T KNOW WHAT I'LL DO TO YOU.
LEAVE ME ALONE!! NOW!!
BUT...
OH, THERE'S FATHER!
?
HUH?

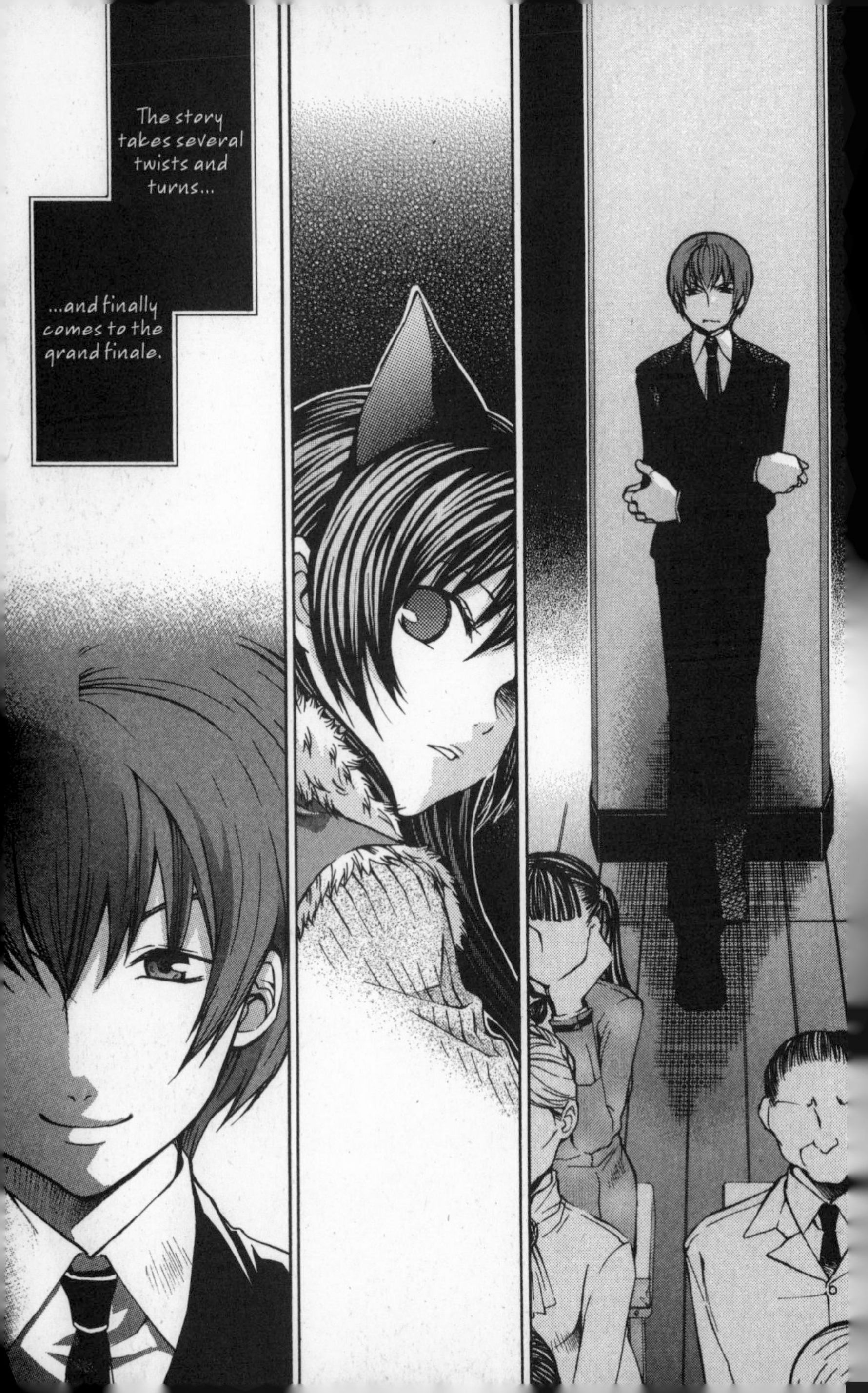
The story takes several twists and turns...
...and finally comes to the grand finale.

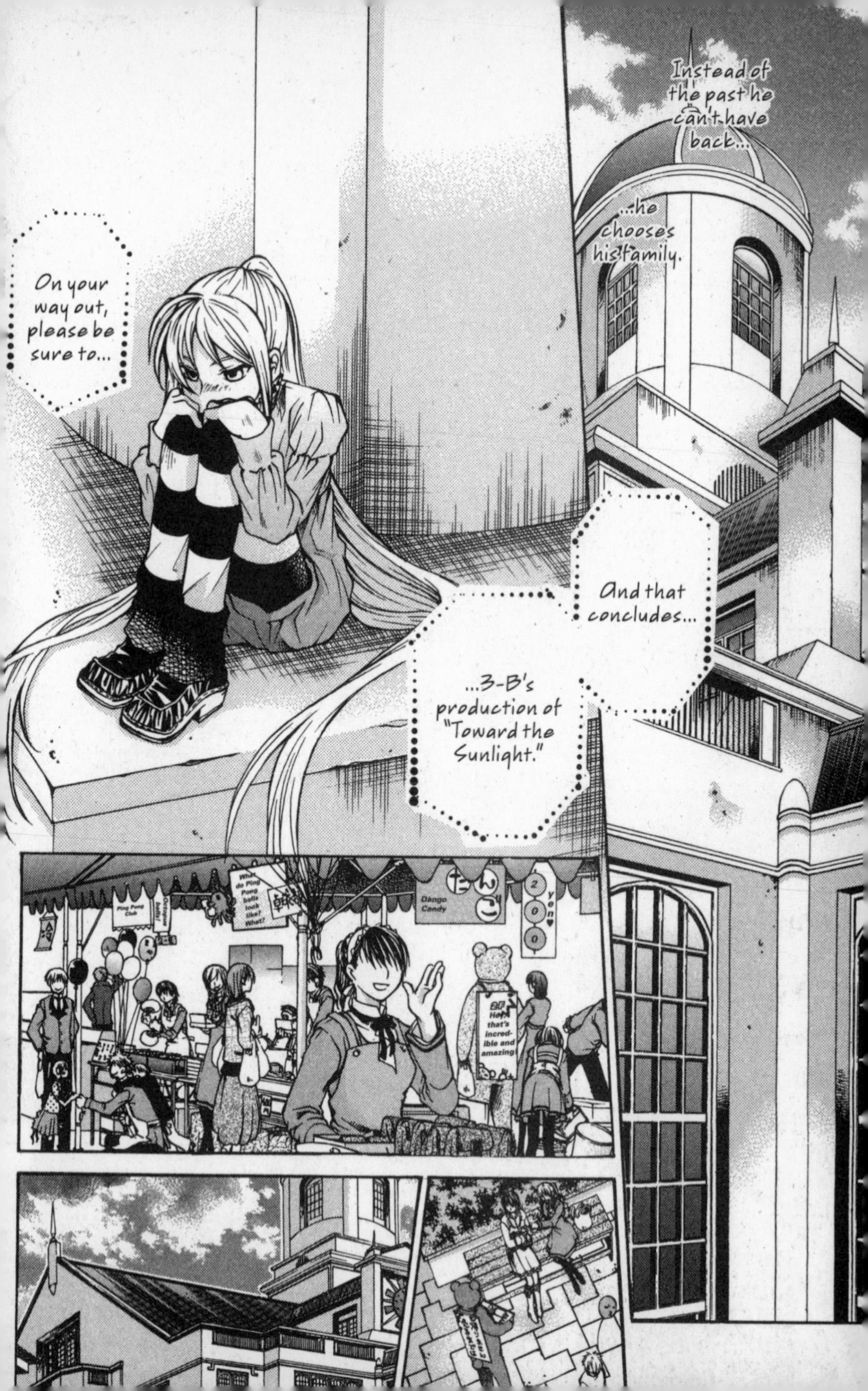
Instead of the past he can't have back...
...he chooses his family.
On your way out, please be sure to...
And that concludes...
...3-B's production of "Toward the Sunlight."
2F Hey, that's incredible and amazing!
200 yen♥
Dango Candy
What do Ping Pong balls look like? What?
Octopus balls!
Ping Pong Club

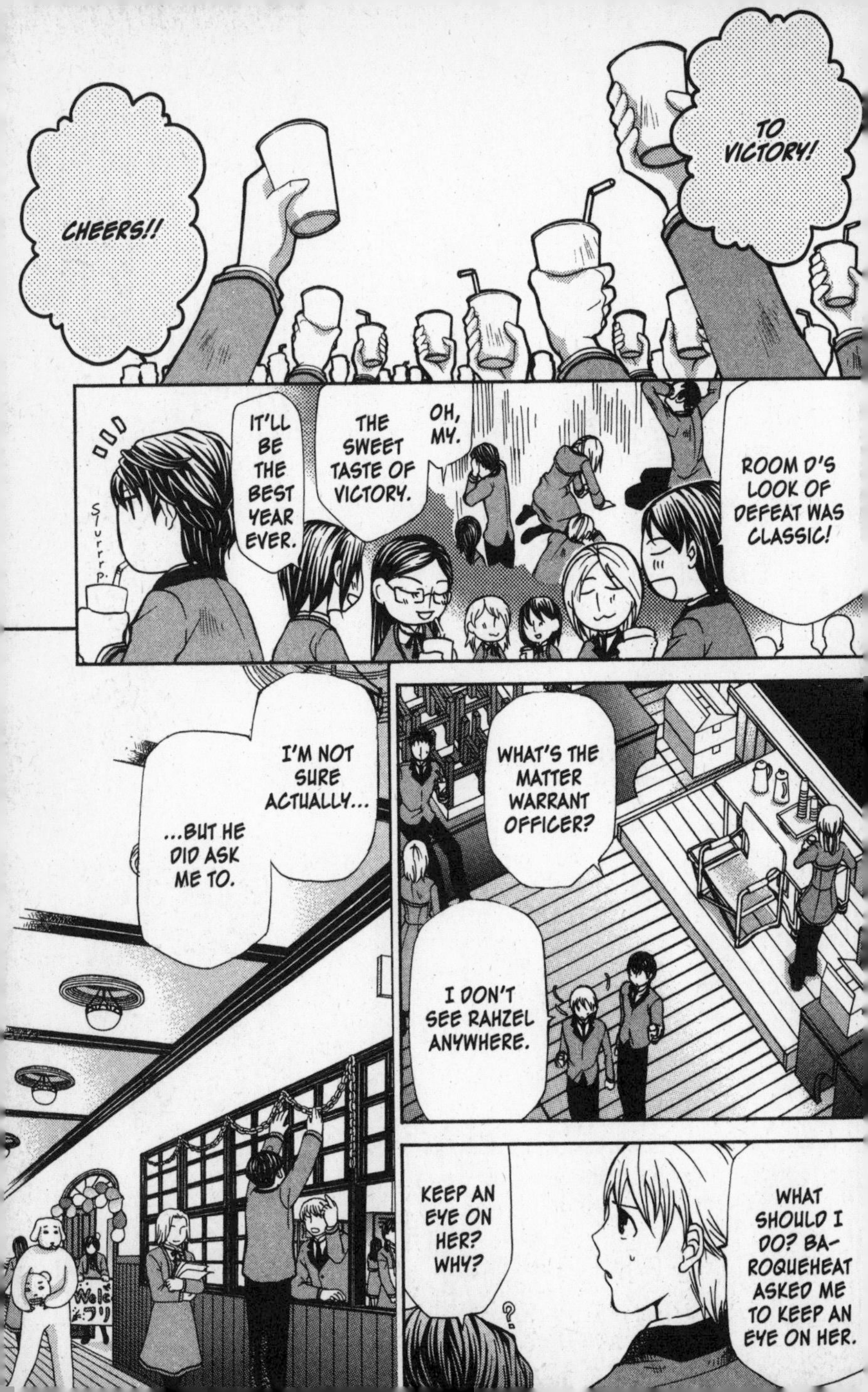
TO VICTORY!
CHEERS!!
ROOM D'S LOOK OF DEFEAT WAS CLASSIC!
OH, MY.
THE SWEET TASTE OF VICTORY.
IT'LL BE THE BEST YEAR EVER.
Slurrrp.
WHAT'S THE MATTER WARRANT OFFICER?
I DON'T SEE RAHZEL ANYWHERE.
WHAT SHOULD I DO? BA-ROQUEHEAT ASKED ME TO KEEP AN EYE ON HER.
KEEP AN EYE ON HER? WHY?
I'M NOT SURE ACTUALLY...
...BUT HE DID ASK ME TO.

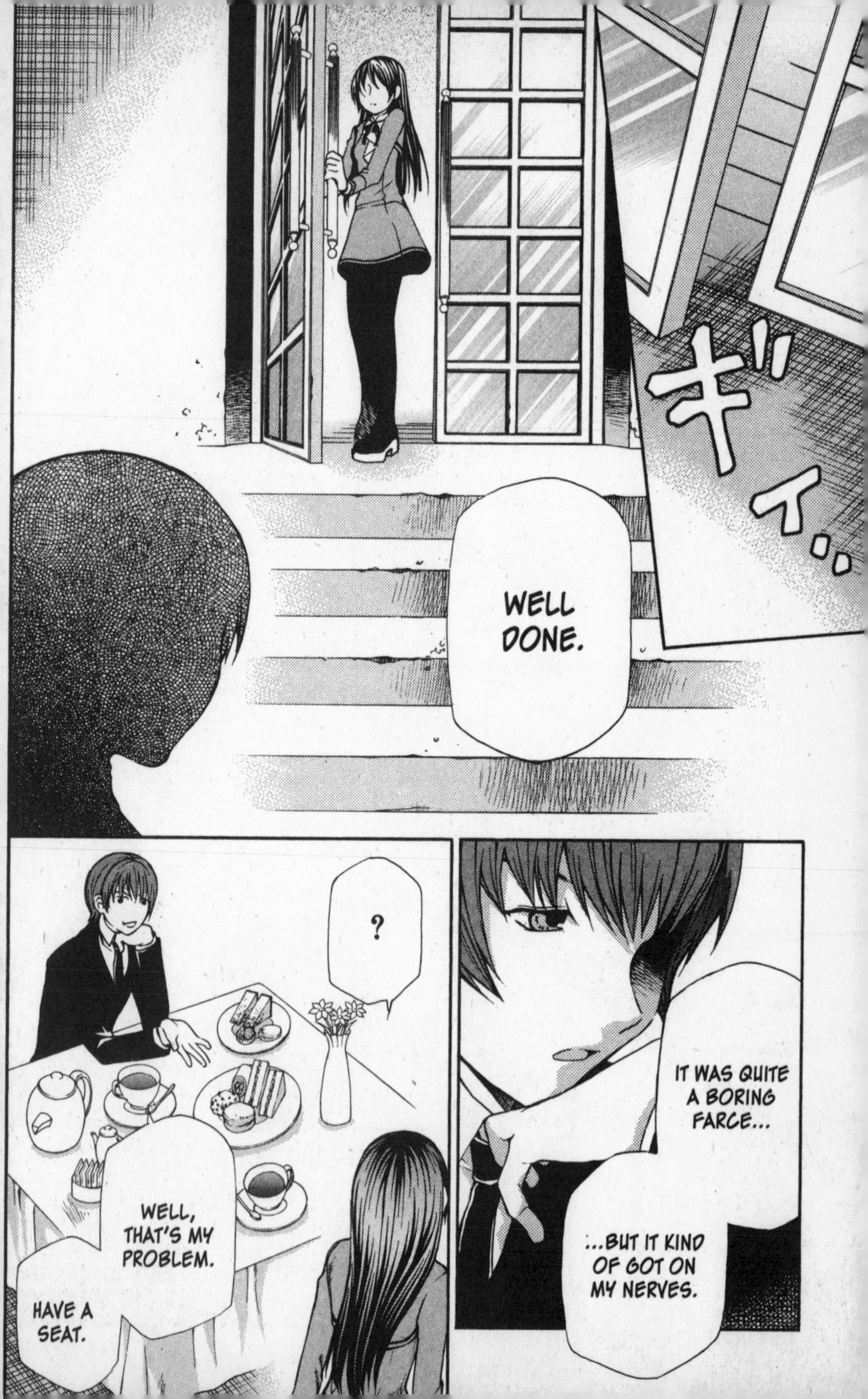
ギィ..
WELL DONE.
IT WAS QUITE A BORING FARCE...
...BUT IT KIND OF GOT ON MY NERVES.
?
WELL, THAT'S MY PROBLEM.
HAVE A SEAT.

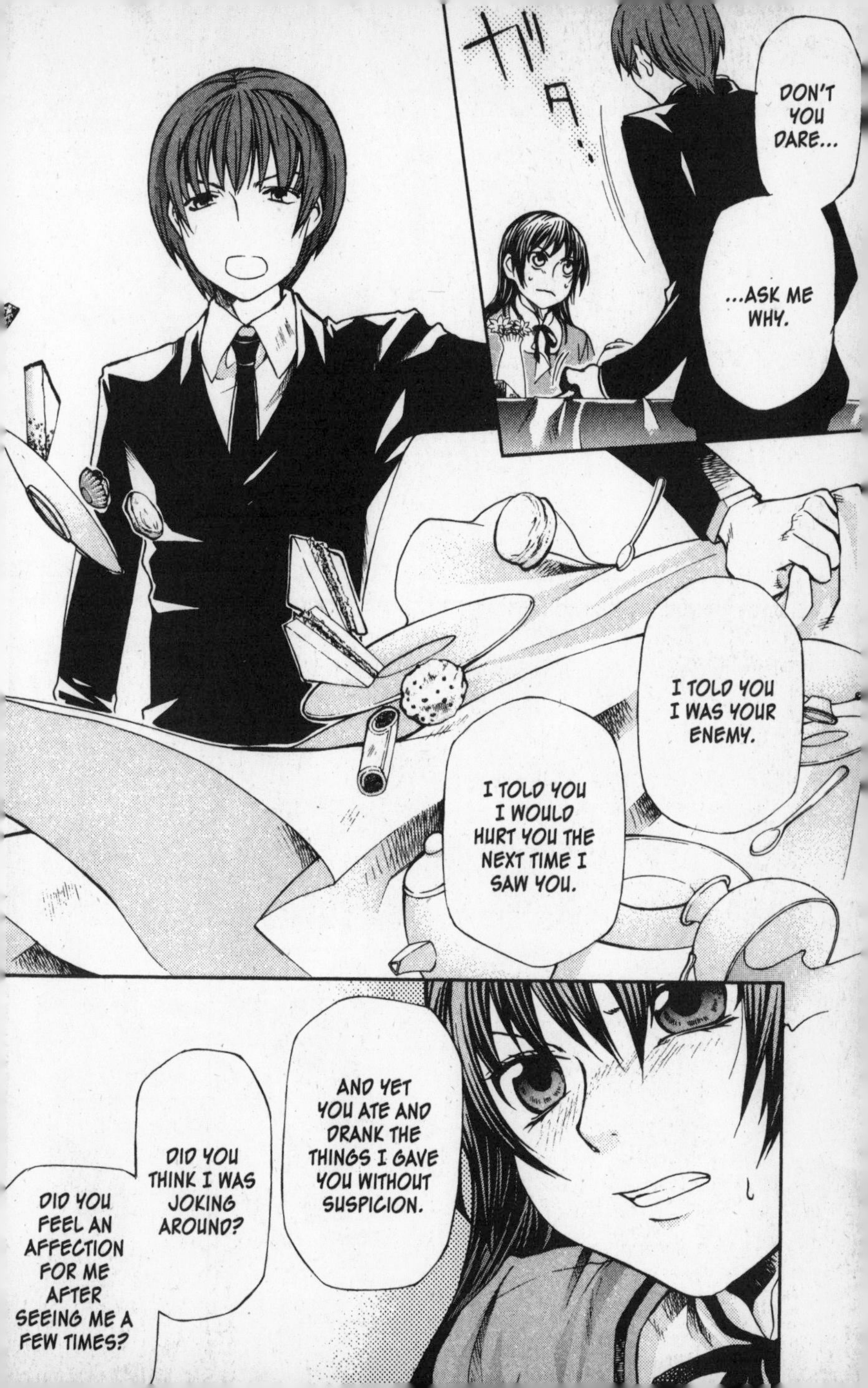
ガタ・・
DON'T YOU DARE...
...ASK ME WHY.
I TOLD YOU I WAS YOUR ENEMY.
I TOLD YOU I WOULD HURT YOU THE NEXT TIME I SAW YOU.
AND YET YOU ATE AND DRANK THE THINGS I GAVE YOU WITHOUT SUSPICION.
DID YOU THINK I WAS JOKING AROUND?
DID YOU FEEL AN AFFECTION FOR ME AFTER SEEING ME A FEW TIMES?

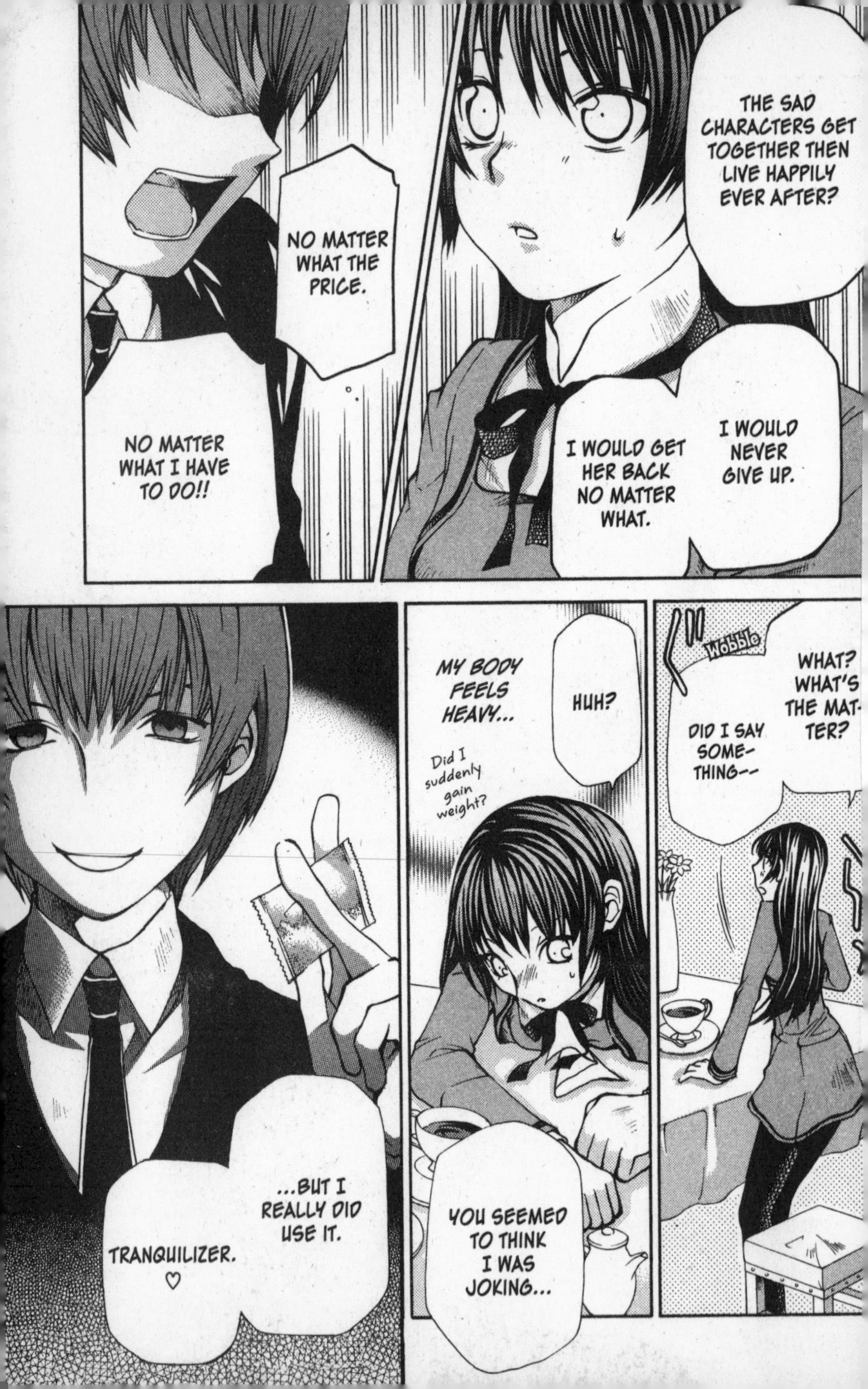
THE SAD CHARACTERS GET TOGETHER THEN LIVE HAPPILY EVER AFTER?
I WOULD NEVER GIVE UP.
I WOULD GET HER BACK NO MATTER WHAT.
NO MATTER WHAT THE PRICE.
NO MATTER WHAT I HAVE TO DO!!
Wobble
WHAT? WHAT'S THE MAT-TER?
DID I SAY SOME-THING--
HUH?
MY BODY FEELS HEAVY...
Did I suddenly gain weight?
YOU SEEMED TO THINK I WAS JOKING...
...BUT I REALLY DID USE IT.
TRANQUILIZER. ♡

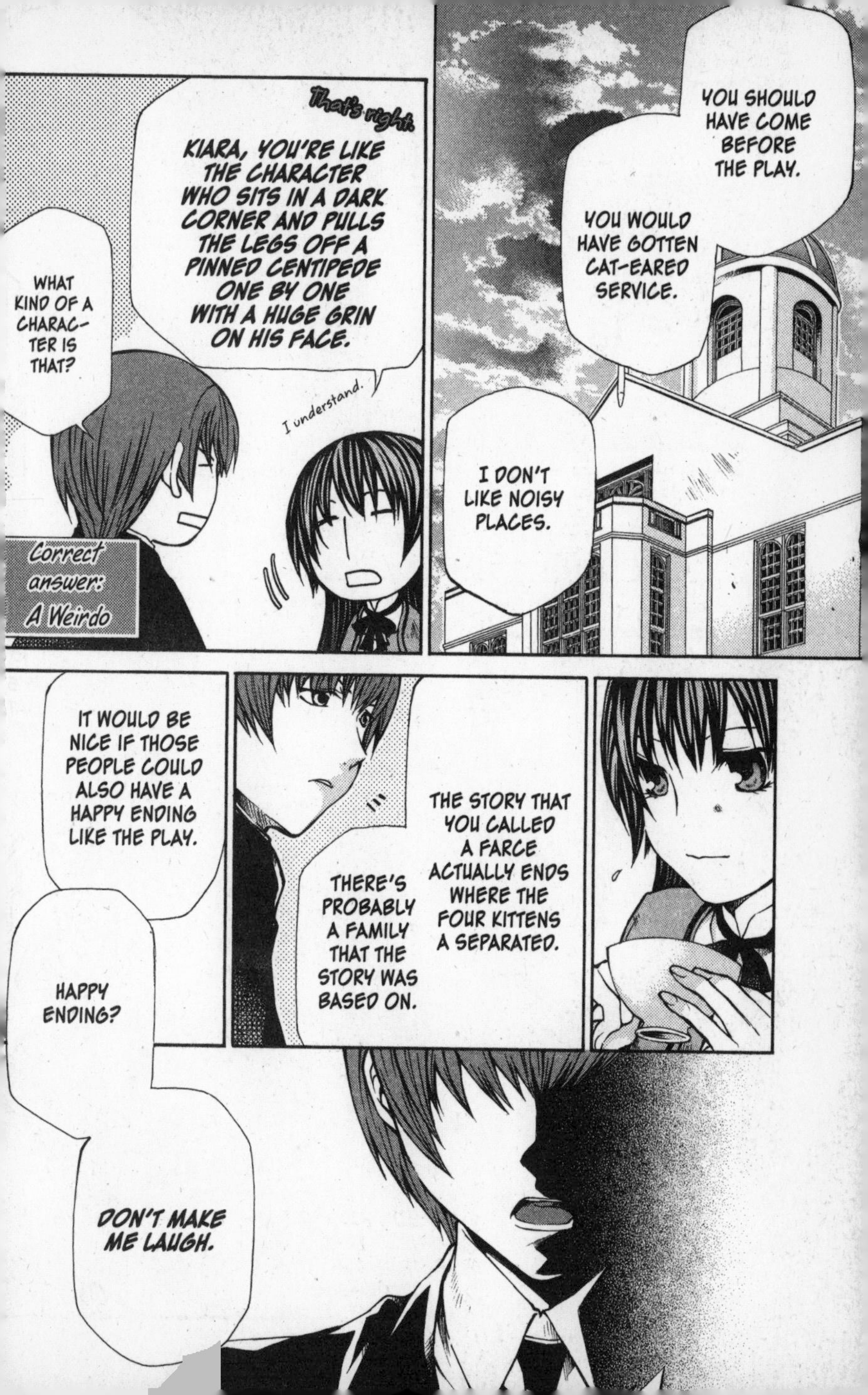
YOU SHOULD HAVE COME BEFORE THE PLAY.
YOU WOULD HAVE GOTTEN CAT-EARED SERVICE.
I DON'T LIKE NOISY PLACES.
That's right.
KIARA, YOU'RE LIKE THE CHARACTER WHO SITS IN A DARK CORNER AND PULLS THE LEGS OFF A PINNED CENTIPEDE ONE BY ONE WITH A HUGE GRIN ON HIS FACE.
I understand.
WHAT KIND OF A CHARAC-TER IS THAT?
Correct answer: A Weirdo
THE STORY THAT YOU CALLED A FARCE ACTUALLY ENDS WHERE THE FOUR KITTENS A SEPARATED.
THERE'S PROBABLY A FAMILY THAT THE STORY WAS BASED ON.
IT WOULD BE NICE IF THOSE PEOPLE COULD ALSO HAVE A HAPPY ENDING LIKE THE PLAY.
HAPPY ENDING?
DON'T MAKE ME LAUGH.

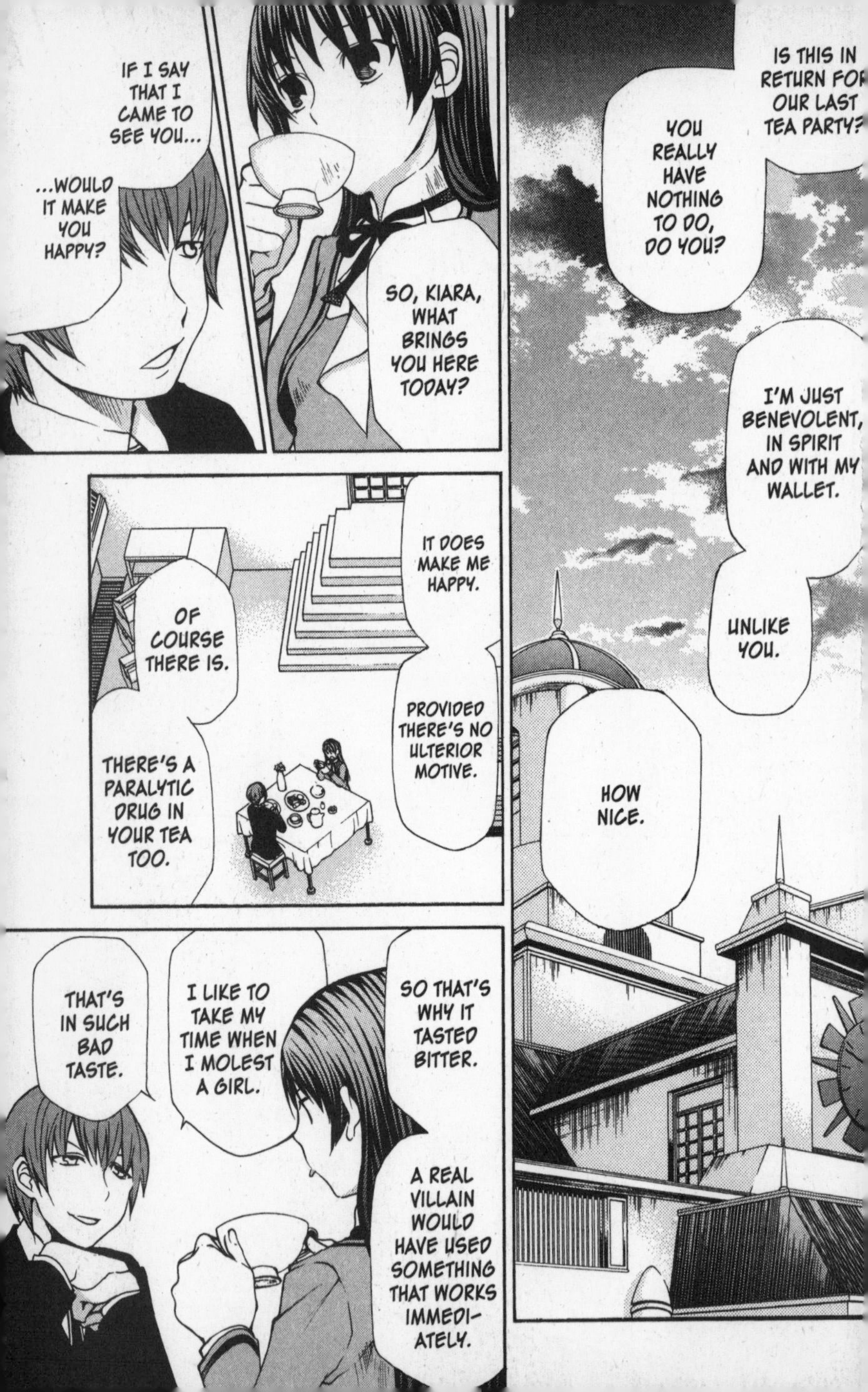
IS THIS IN RETURN FOR OUR LAST TEA PARTY?
YOU REALLY HAVE NOTHING TO DO, DO YOU?
I'M JUST BENEVOLENT, IN SPIRIT AND WITH MY WALLET.
UNLIKE YOU.
HOW NICE.
SO, KIARA, WHAT BRINGS YOU HERE TODAY?
IF I SAY THAT I CAME TO SEE YOU...
...WOULD IT MAKE YOU HAPPY?
IT DOES MAKE ME HAPPY.
PROVIDED THERE'S NO ULTERIOR MOTIVE.
OF COURSE THERE IS.
THERE'S A PARALYTIC DRUG IN YOUR TEA TOO.
SO THAT'S WHY IT TASTED BITTER.
A REAL VILLAIN WOULD HAVE USED SOMETHING THAT WORKS IMMEDIATELY.
I LIKE TO TAKE MY TIME WHEN I MOLEST A GIRL.
THAT'S IN SUCH BAD TASTE.

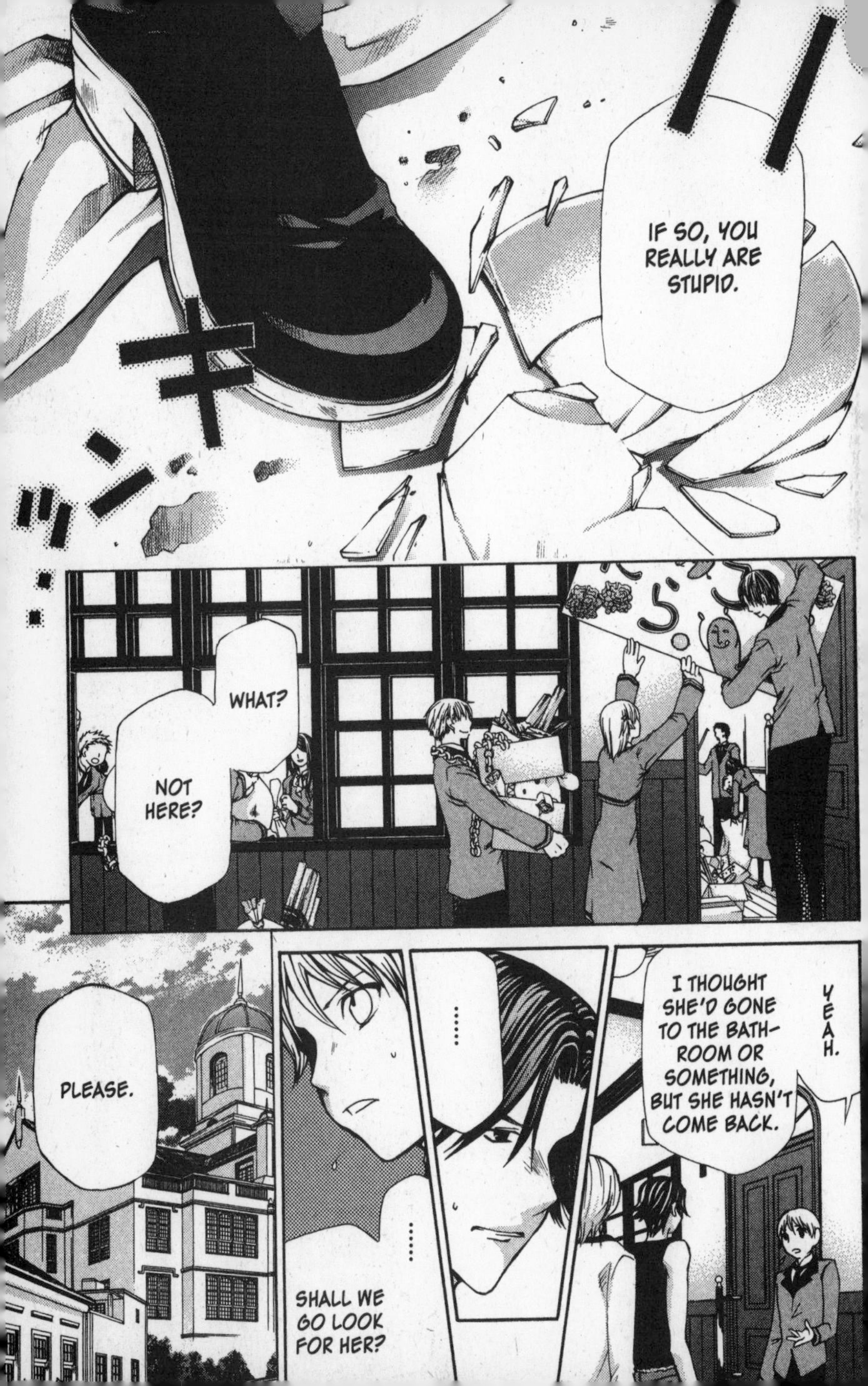
IF SO, YOU REALLY ARE STUPID.
WHAT?
NOT HERE?
YEAH.
I THOUGHT SHE'D GONE TO THE BATH-ROOM OR SOMETHING, BUT SHE HASN'T COME BACK.
......
......
SHALL WE GO LOOK FOR HER?
PLEASE.

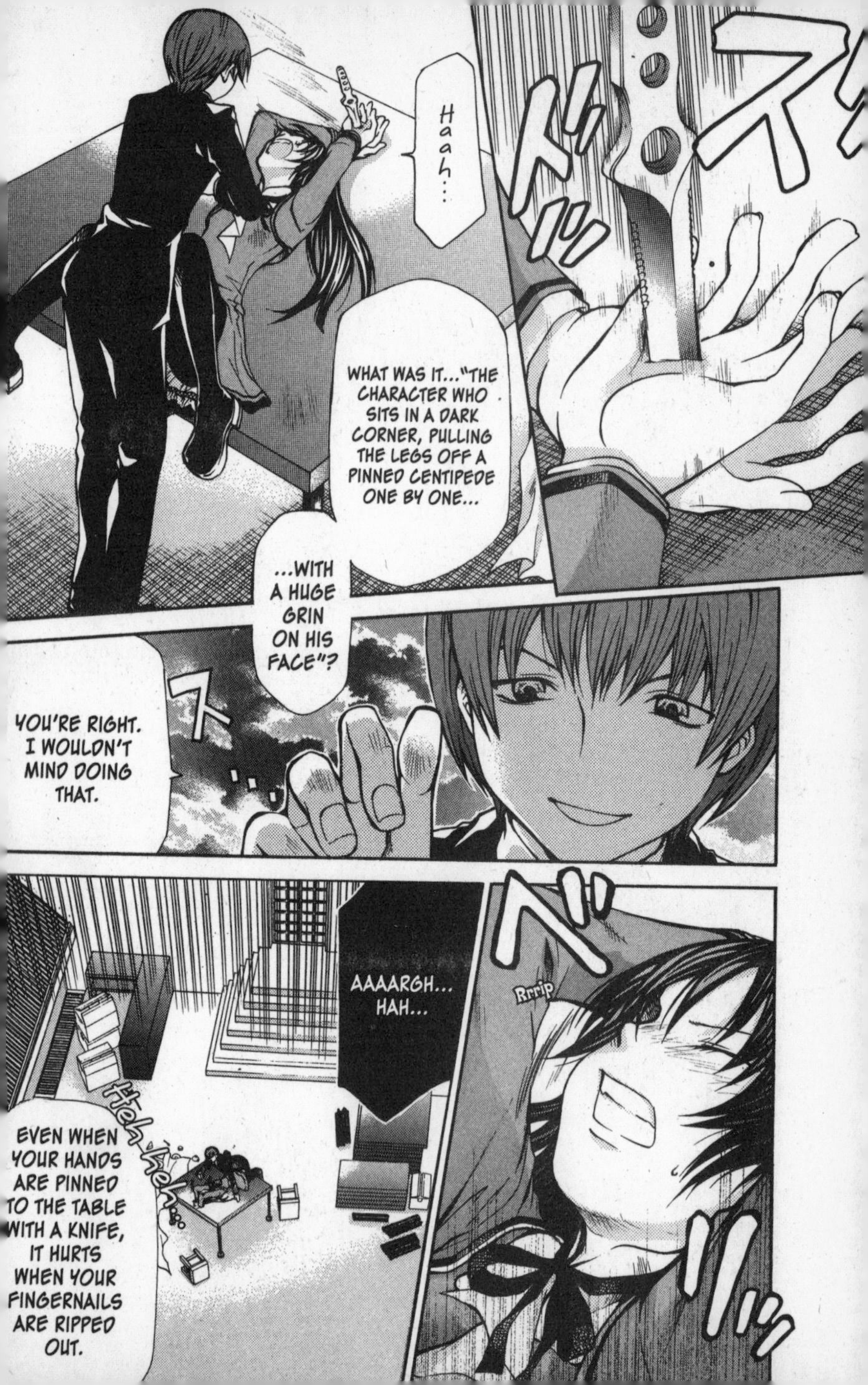
Haaah...
WHAT WAS IT..."THE CHARACTER WHO SITS IN A DARK CORNER, PULLING THE LEGS OFF A PINNED CENTIPEDE ONE BY ONE...
...WITH A HUGE GRIN ON HIS FACE"?
YOU'RE RIGHT. I WOULDN'T MIND DOING THAT.
Rrrip
AAAARGH... HAH...
Heh heh
EVEN WHEN YOUR HANDS ARE PINNED TO THE TABLE WITH A KNIFE, IT HURTS WHEN YOUR FINGERNAILS ARE RIPPED OUT.

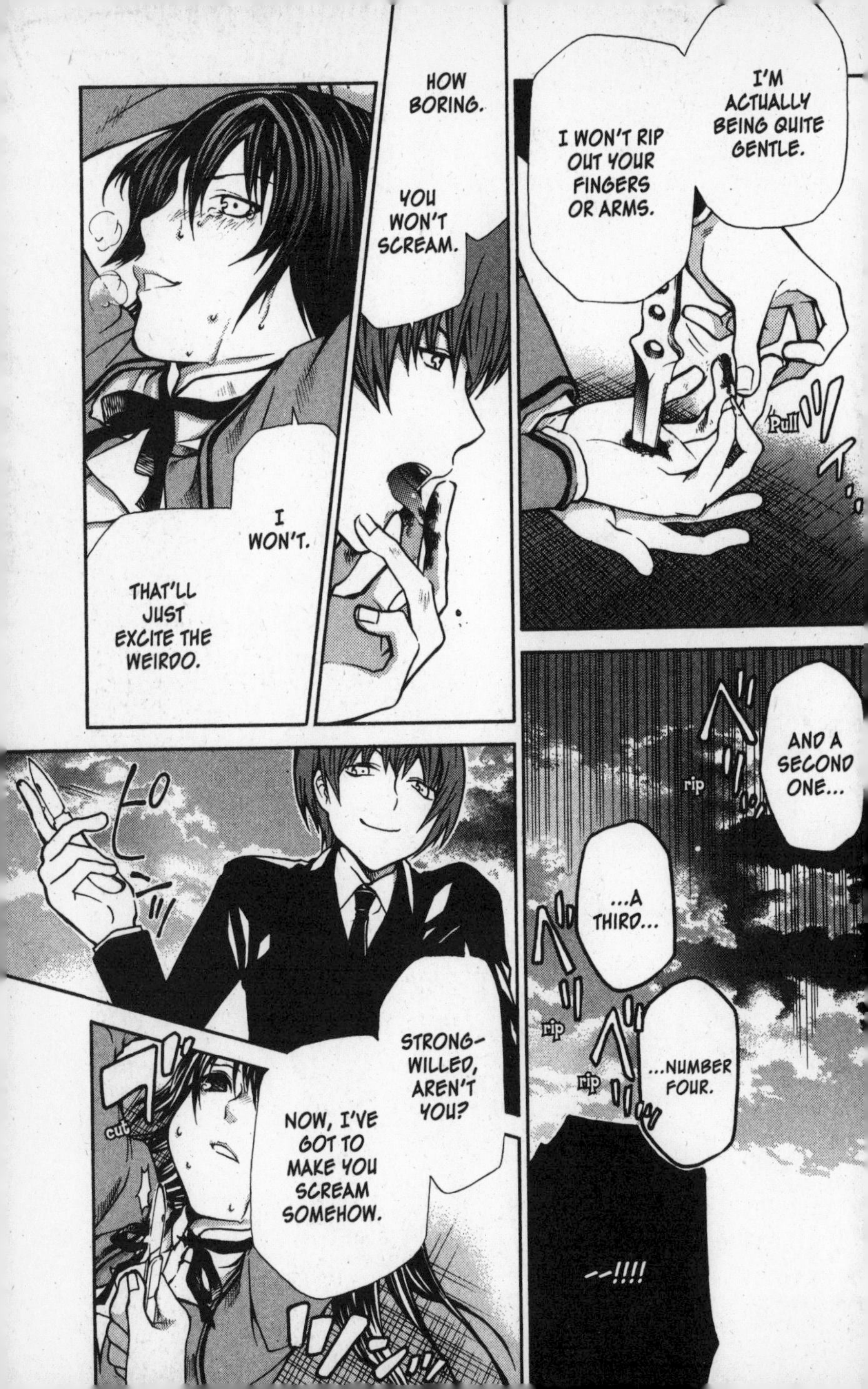
I'M ACTUALLY BEING QUITE GENTLE.
I WON'T RIP OUT YOUR FINGERS OR ARMS.
Pull
HOW BORING.
YOU WON'T SCREAM.
I WON'T.
THAT'LL JUST EXCITE THE WEIRDO.
AND A SECOND ONE...
rip
...A THIRD...
rip
rip
...NUMBER FOUR.
--!!!!
STRONG-WILLED, AREN'T YOU?
NOW, I'VE GOT TO MAKE YOU SCREAM SOMEHOW.
cut

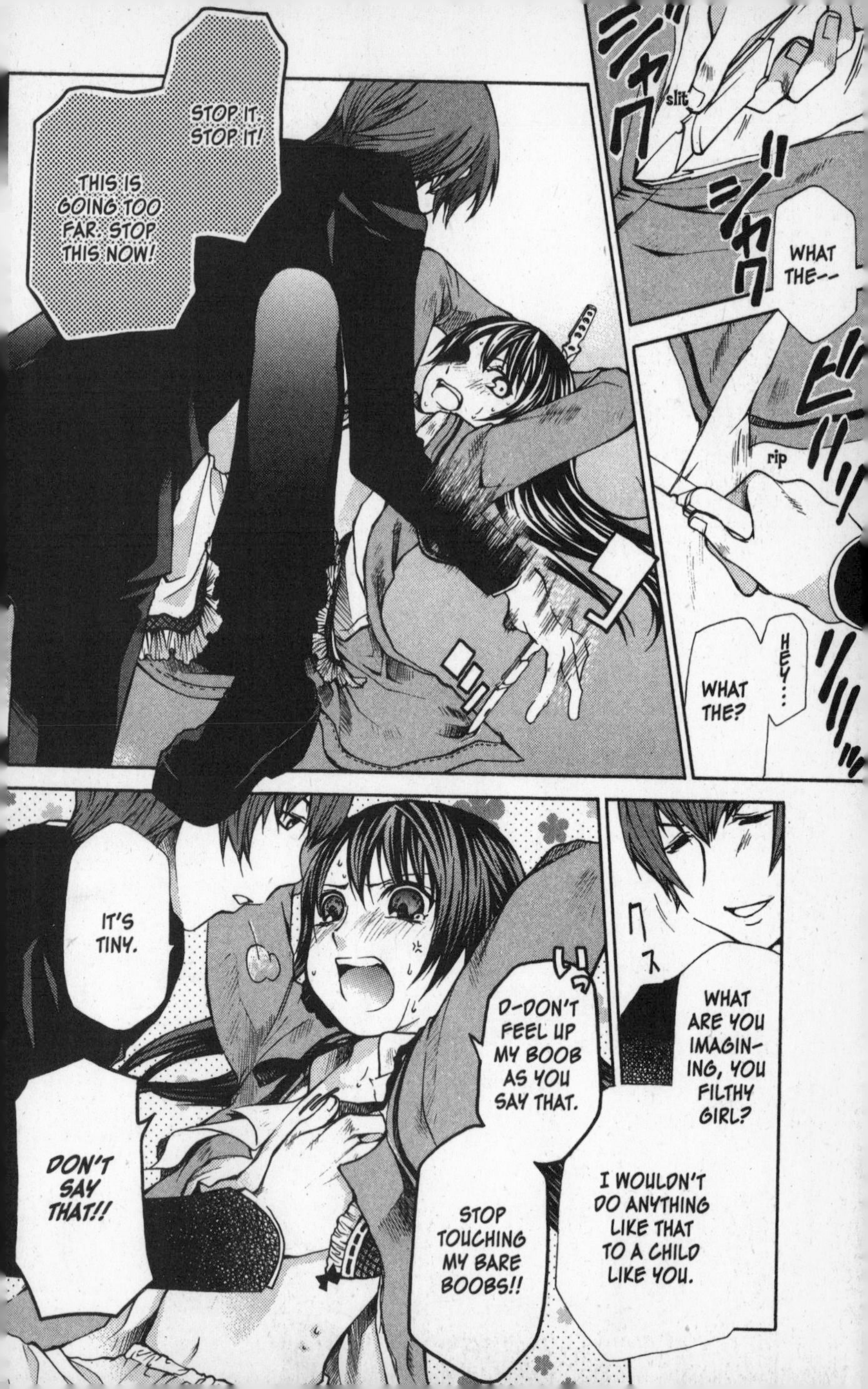
slit
WHAT THE--
rip
HEY...
WHAT THE?
STOP IT. STOP IT!
THIS IS GOING TOO FAR. STOP THIS NOW!
WHAT ARE YOU IMAGINING, YOU FILTHY GIRL?
I WOULDN'T DO ANYTHING LIKE THAT TO A CHILD LIKE YOU.
IT'S TINY.
D-DON'T FEEL UP MY BOOB AS YOU SAY THAT.
STOP TOUCHING MY BARE BOOBS!!
DON'T SAY THAT!!

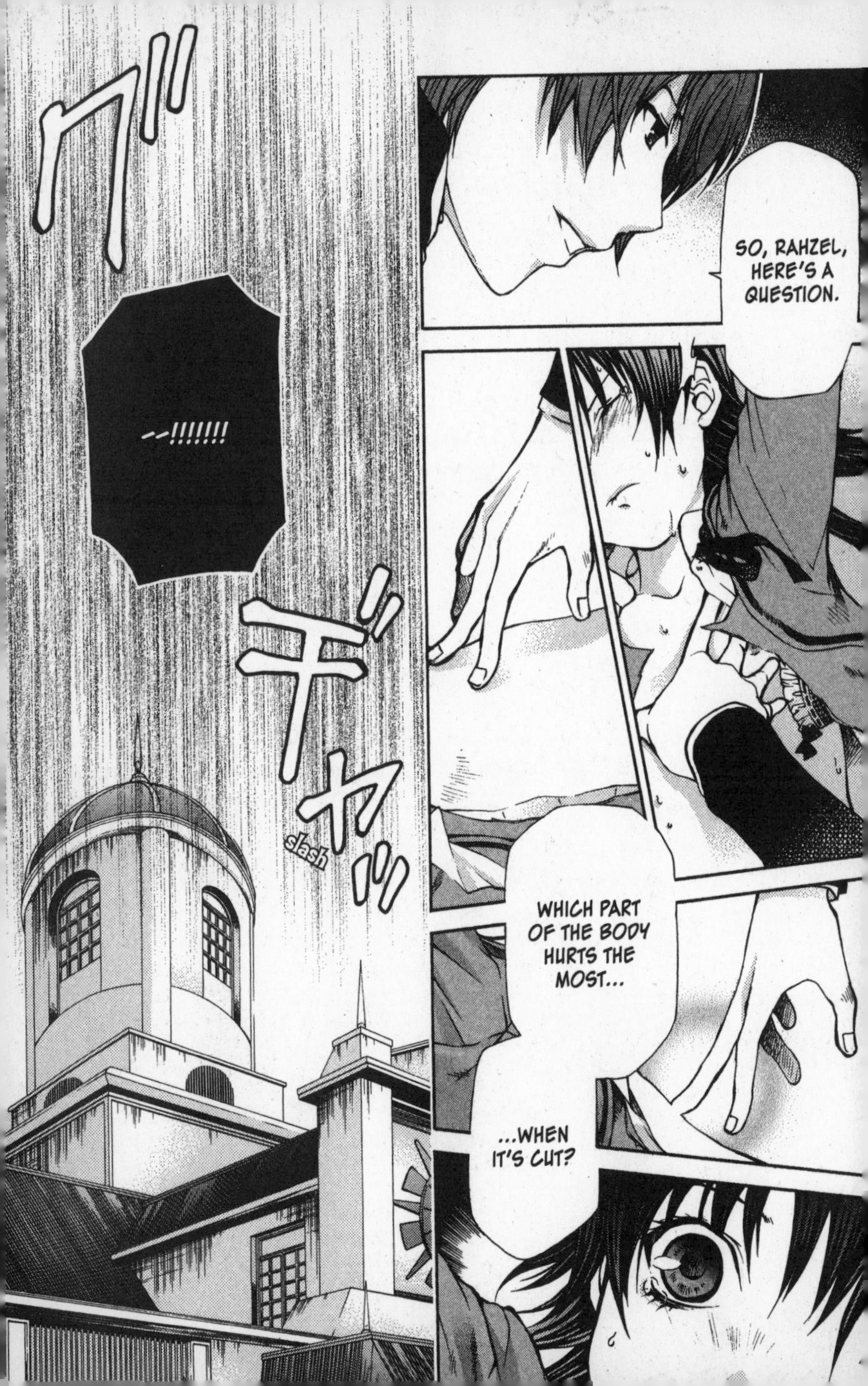
SO, RAHZEL, HERE'S A QUESTION.
WHICH PART OF THE BODY HURTS THE MOST...
...WHEN IT'S CUT?
グ
--!!!!!!!
ギャッ
slash

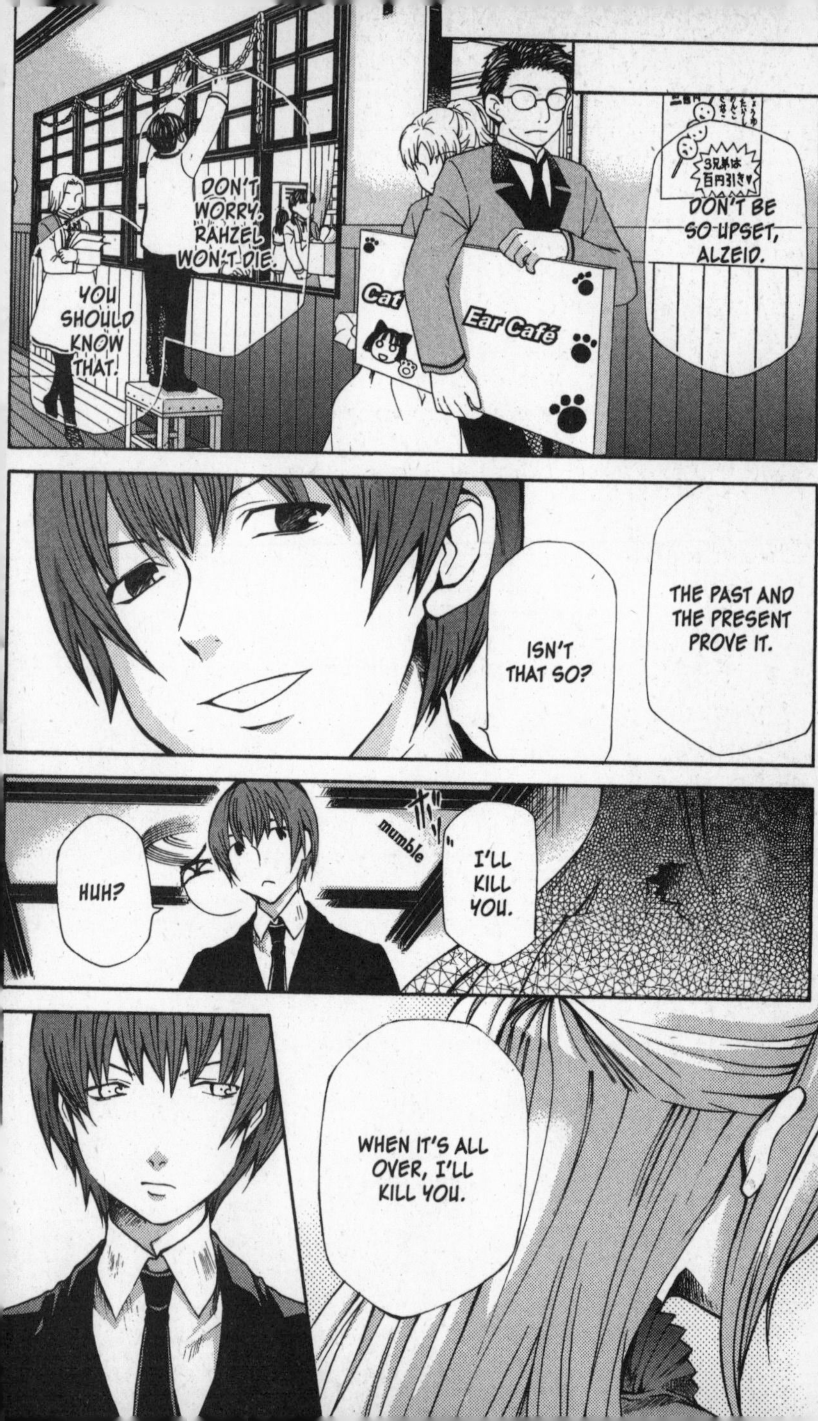
3兄弟は百円引き♥
DON'T BE SO UPSET, ALZEID.
Cat Ear Café
DON'T WORRY. RAHZEL WON'T DIE.
YOU SHOULD KNOW THAT!
THE PAST AND THE PRESENT PROVE IT.
ISN'T THAT SO?
I'LL KILL YOU.
mumble
HUH?
WHEN IT'S ALL OVER, I'LL KILL YOU.

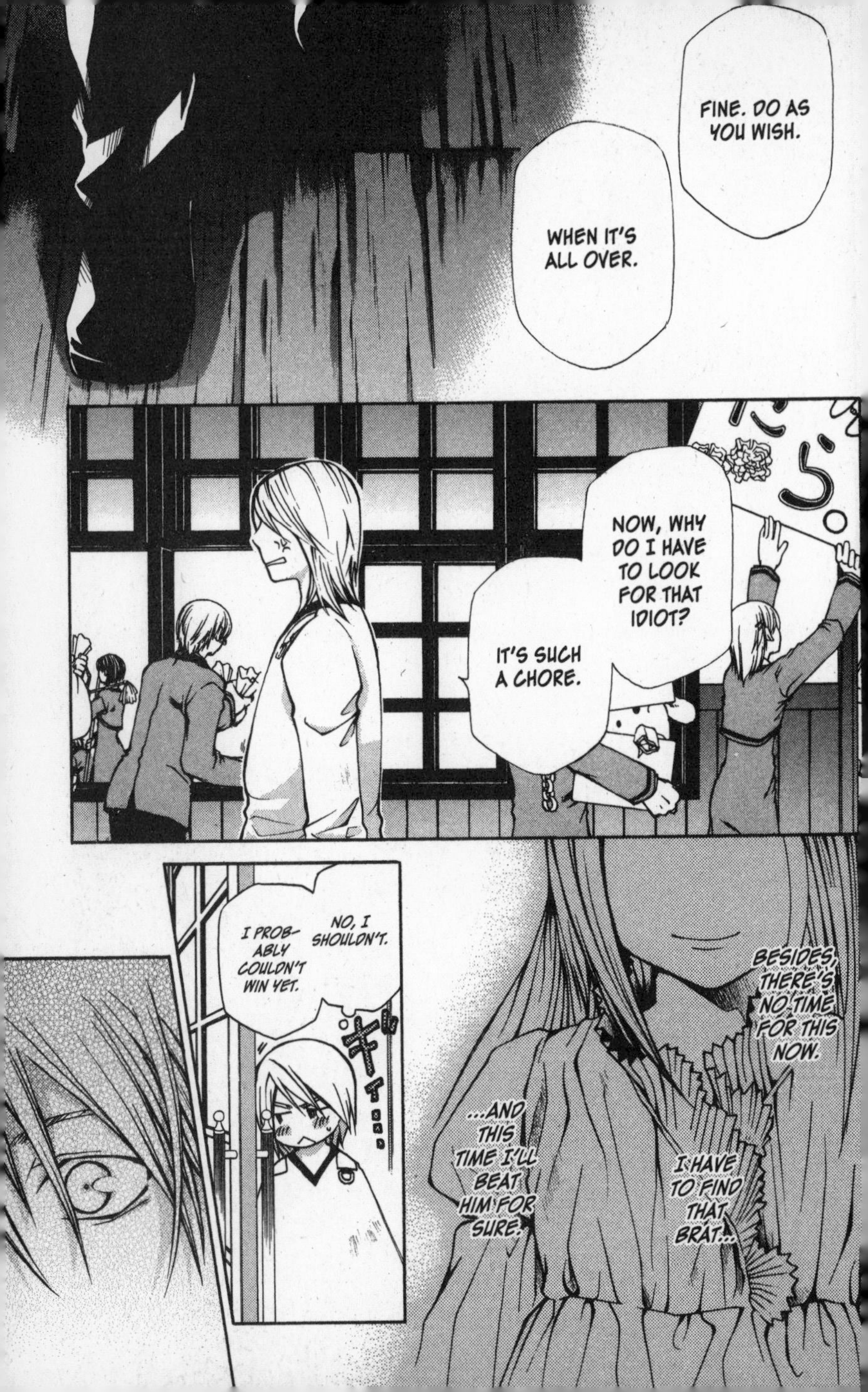
FINE. DO AS YOU WISH.
WHEN IT'S ALL OVER.
NOW, WHY DO I HAVE TO LOOK FOR THAT IDIOT?
IT'S SUCH A CHORE.
BESIDES, THERE'S NO TIME FOR THIS NOW.
I HAVE TO FIND THAT BRAT...
...AND THIS TIME I'LL BEAT HIM FOR SURE.
NO, I SHOULDN'T.
I PROBABLY COULDN'T WIN YET.

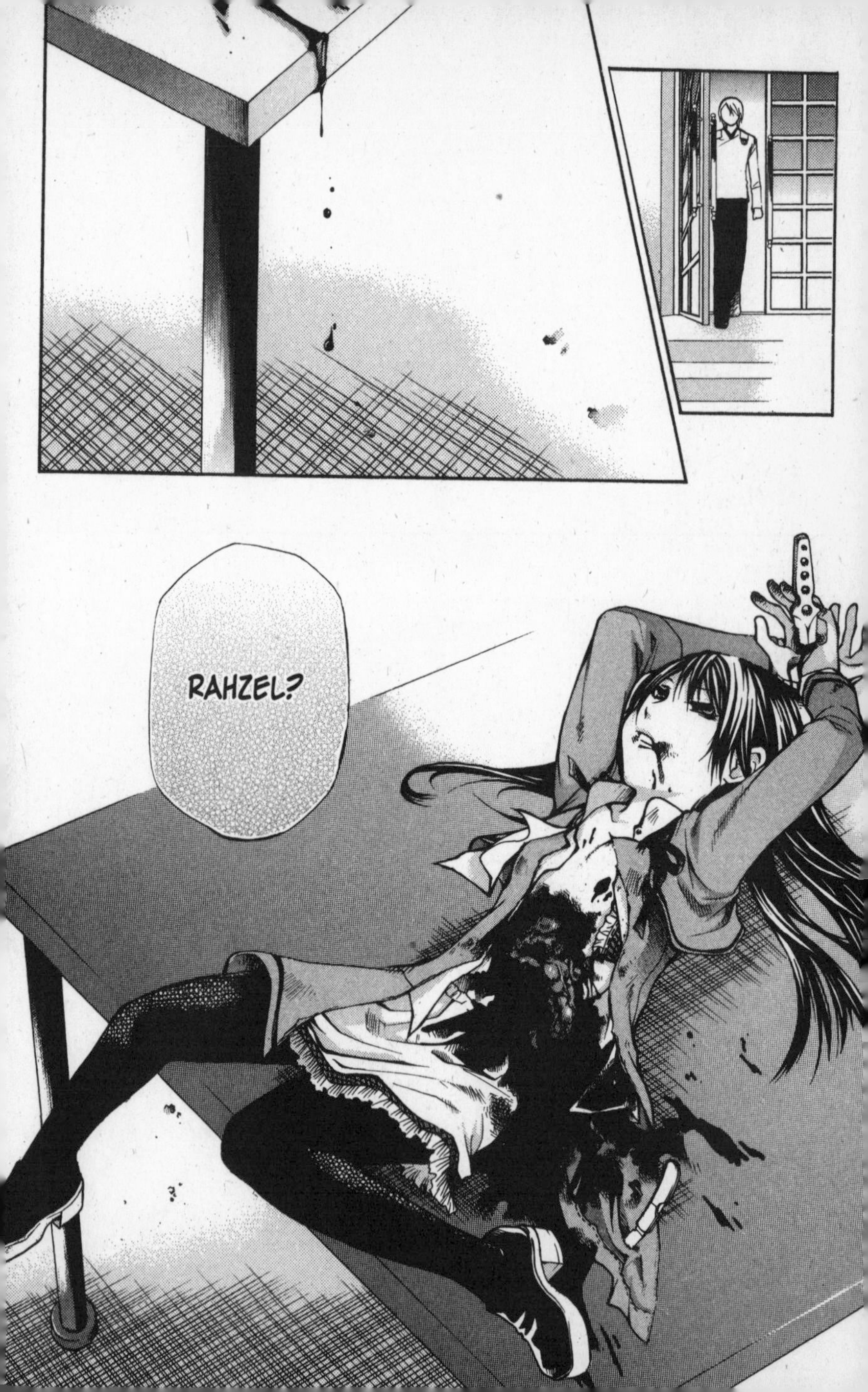
RAHZEL?

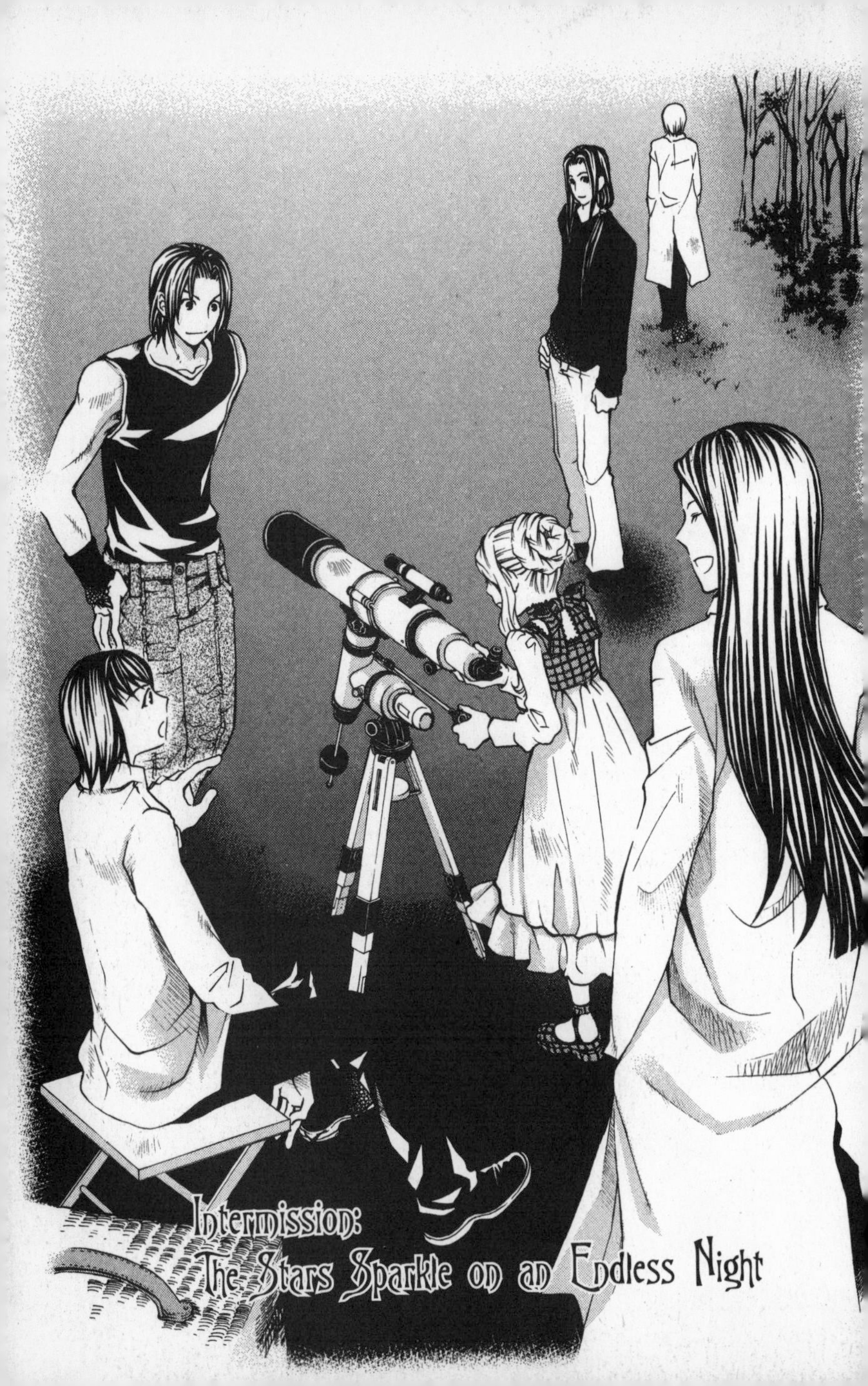
Intermission:
The Stars Sparkle on an Endless Night

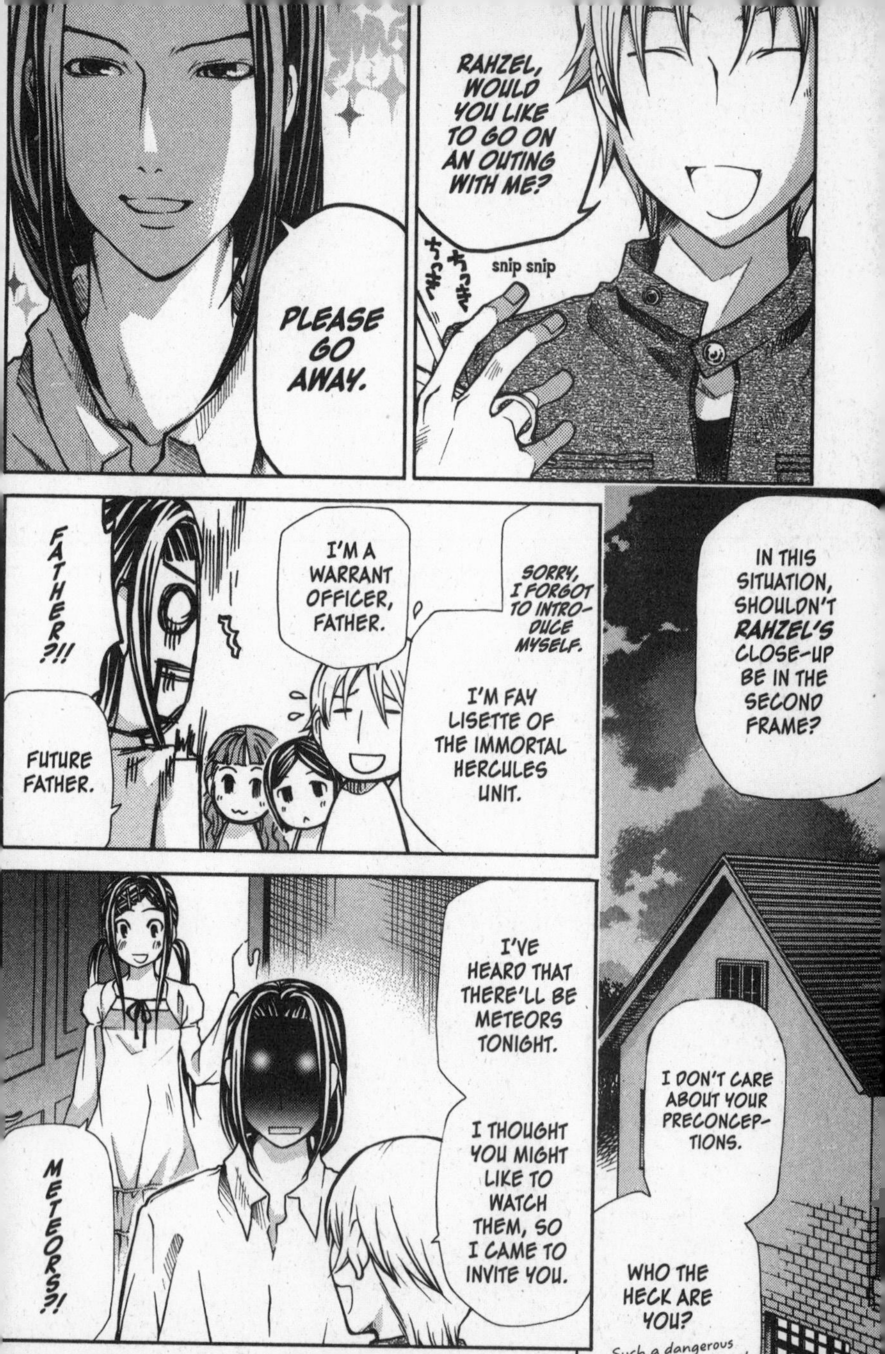
RAHZEL, WOULD YOU LIKE TO GO ON AN OUTING WITH ME?
ちっき ちっき
snip snip
PLEASE GO AWAY.
IN THIS SITUATION, SHOULDN'T RAHZEL'S CLOSE-UP BE IN THE SECOND FRAME?
I DON'T CARE ABOUT YOUR PRECONCEP-TIONS.
WHO THE HECK ARE YOU?
Such a dangerous child, running around with scissors.
SORRY, I FORGOT TO INTRO-DUCE MYSELF.
I'M FAY LISETTE OF THE IMMORTAL HERCULES UNIT.
I'M A WARRANT OFFICER, FATHER.
FATHER?!!
FUTURE FATHER.
I'VE HEARD THAT THERE'LL BE METEORS TONIGHT.
I THOUGHT YOU MIGHT LIKE TO WATCH THEM, SO I CAME TO INVITE YOU.
METEORS?!

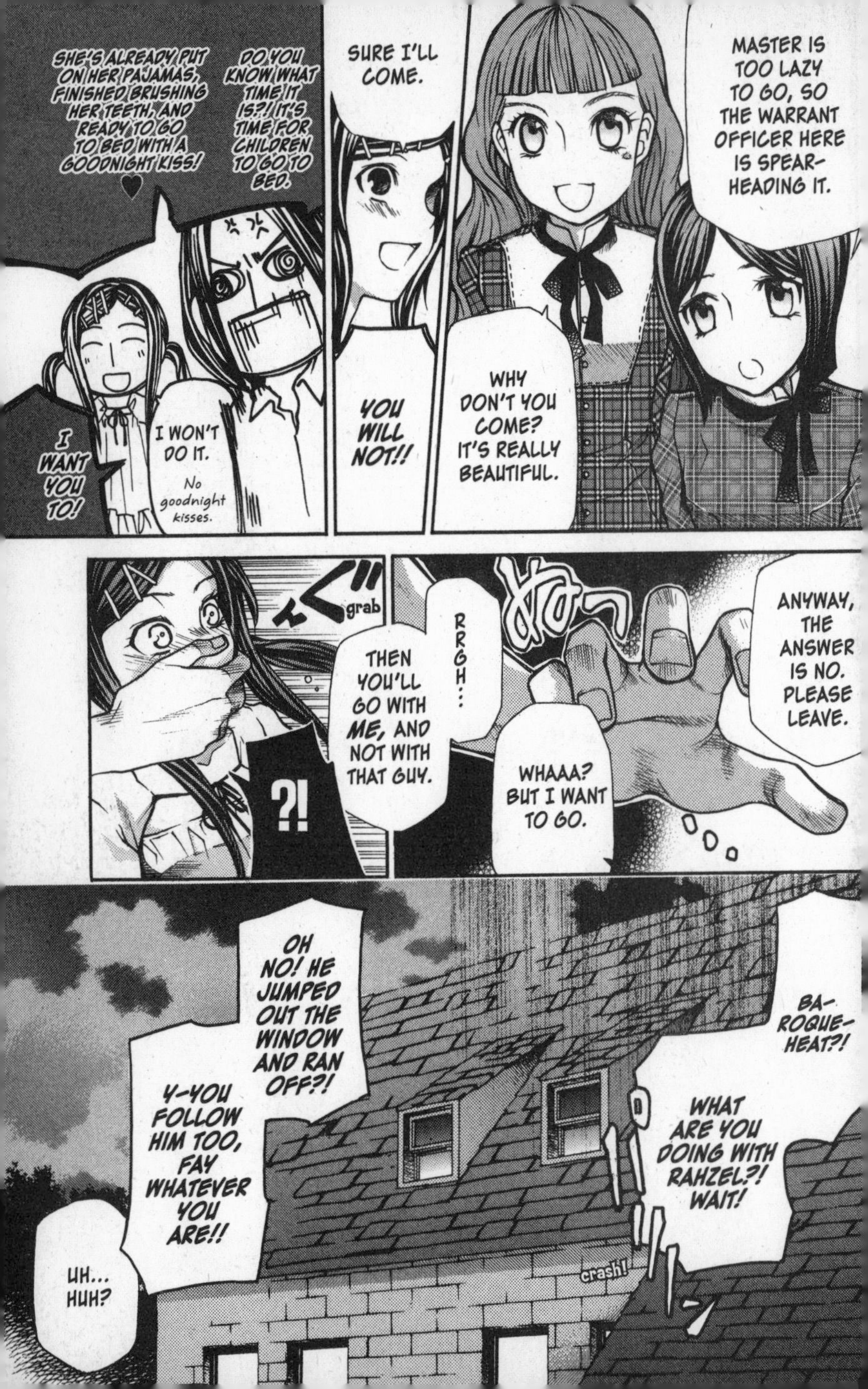

MASTER IS TOO LAZY TO GO, SO THE WARRANT OFFICER HERE IS SPEAR-HEADING IT.
WHY DON'T YOU COME? IT'S REALLY BEAUTIFUL.
SURE I'LL COME.
YOU WILL NOT!!
DO YOU KNOW WHAT TIME IT IS?! IT'S TIME FOR CHILDREN TO GO TO BED.
SHE'S ALREADY PUT ON HER PAJAMAS, FINISHED BRUSHING HER TEETH, AND READY TO GO TO BED WITH A GOODNIGHT KISS! ♥
I WON'T DO IT.
No goodnight kisses.
I WANT YOU TO!
ANYWAY, THE ANSWER IS NO. PLEASE LEAVE.
RRGH...
WHAAA? BUT I WANT TO GO.
THEN YOU'LL GO WITH ME, AND NOT WITH THAT GUY.
grab
?!
BA-ROQUE-HEAT?!
WHAT ARE YOU DOING WITH RAHZEL?! WAIT!
crash!
OH NO! HE JUMPED OUT THE WINDOW AND RAN OFF?!
Y-YOU FOLLOW HIM TOO, FAY WHATEVER YOU ARE!!
UH... HUH?

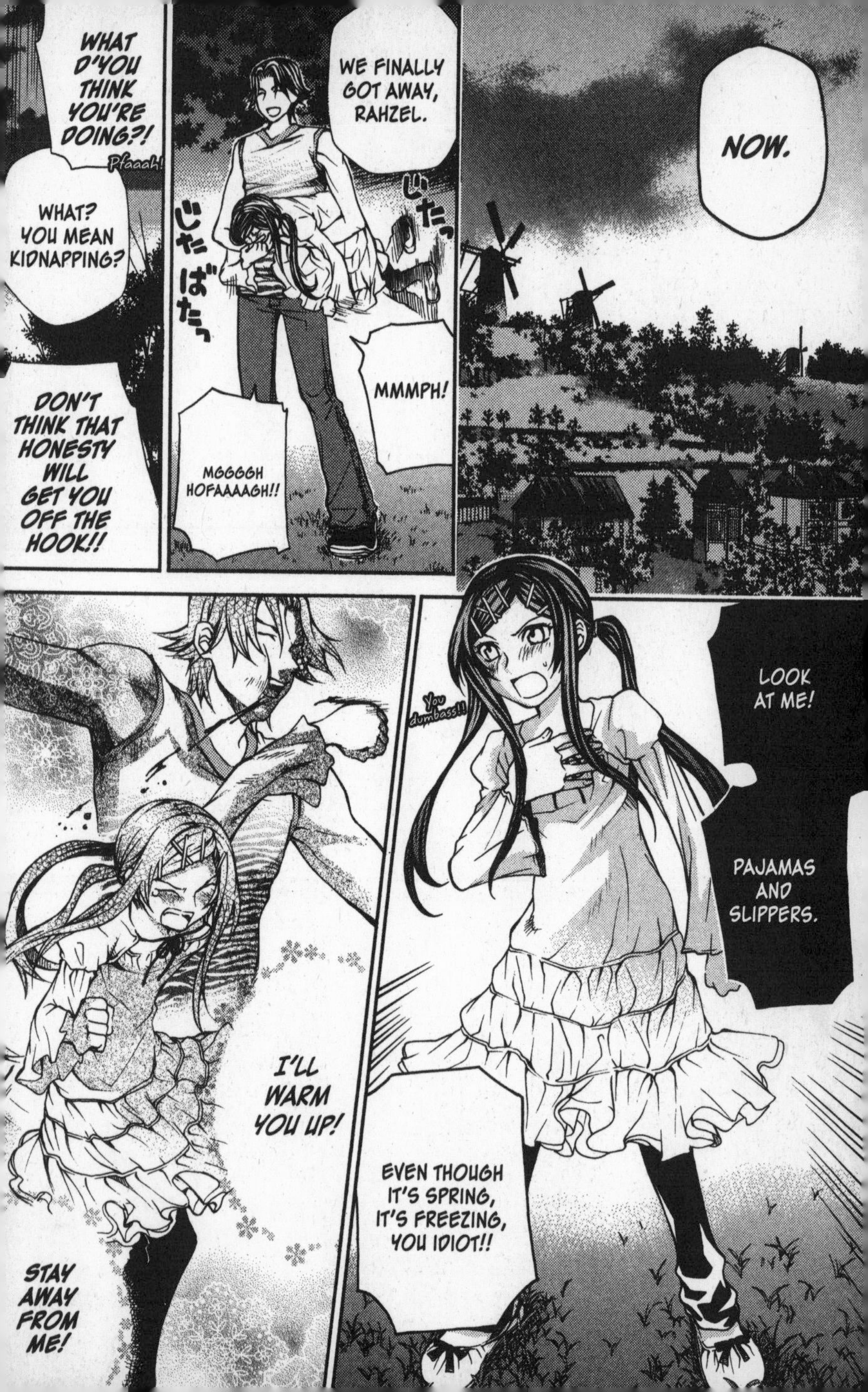
NOW.
WE FINALLY GOT AWAY, RAHZEL.
じたっ
じたばたっ
MMMPH!
MGGGGH HOFAAAAGH!!
WHAT D'YOU THINK YOU'RE DOING?!
Pfaaah!
WHAT? YOU MEAN KIDNAPPING?
DON'T THINK THAT HONESTY WILL GET YOU OFF THE HOOK!!
LOOK AT ME!
You dumbass!!
PAJAMAS AND SLIPPERS.
EVEN THOUGH IT'S SPRING, IT'S FREEZING, YOU IDIOT!!
I'LL WARM YOU UP!
STAY AWAY FROM ME!

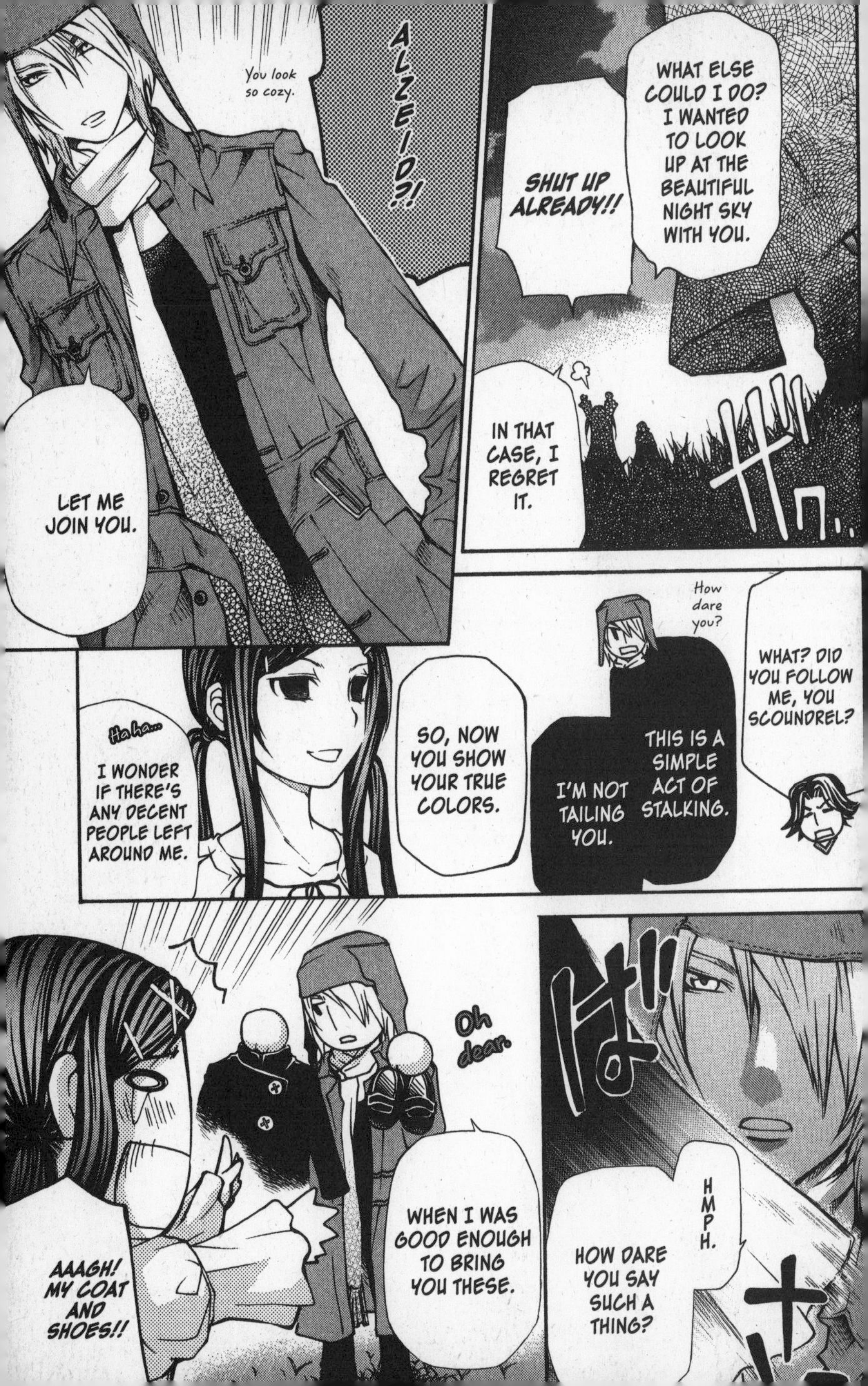
WHAT ELSE COULD I DO? I WANTED TO LOOK UP AT THE BEAUTIFUL NIGHT SKY WITH YOU.
SHUT UP ALREADY!!
IN THAT CASE, I REGRET IT.
ALZEID?!
You look so cozy.
LET ME JOIN YOU.
WHAT? DID YOU FOLLOW ME, YOU SCOUNDREL?
How dare you?
I'M NOT TAILING YOU.
THIS IS A SIMPLE ACT OF STALKING.
SO, NOW YOU SHOW YOUR TRUE COLORS.
Ha ha...
I WONDER IF THERE'S ANY DECENT PEOPLE LEFT AROUND ME.
HMPH.
HOW DARE YOU SAY SUCH A THING?
Oh dear.
WHEN I WAS GOOD ENOUGH TO BRING YOU THESE.
AAAGH! MY COAT AND SHOES!!

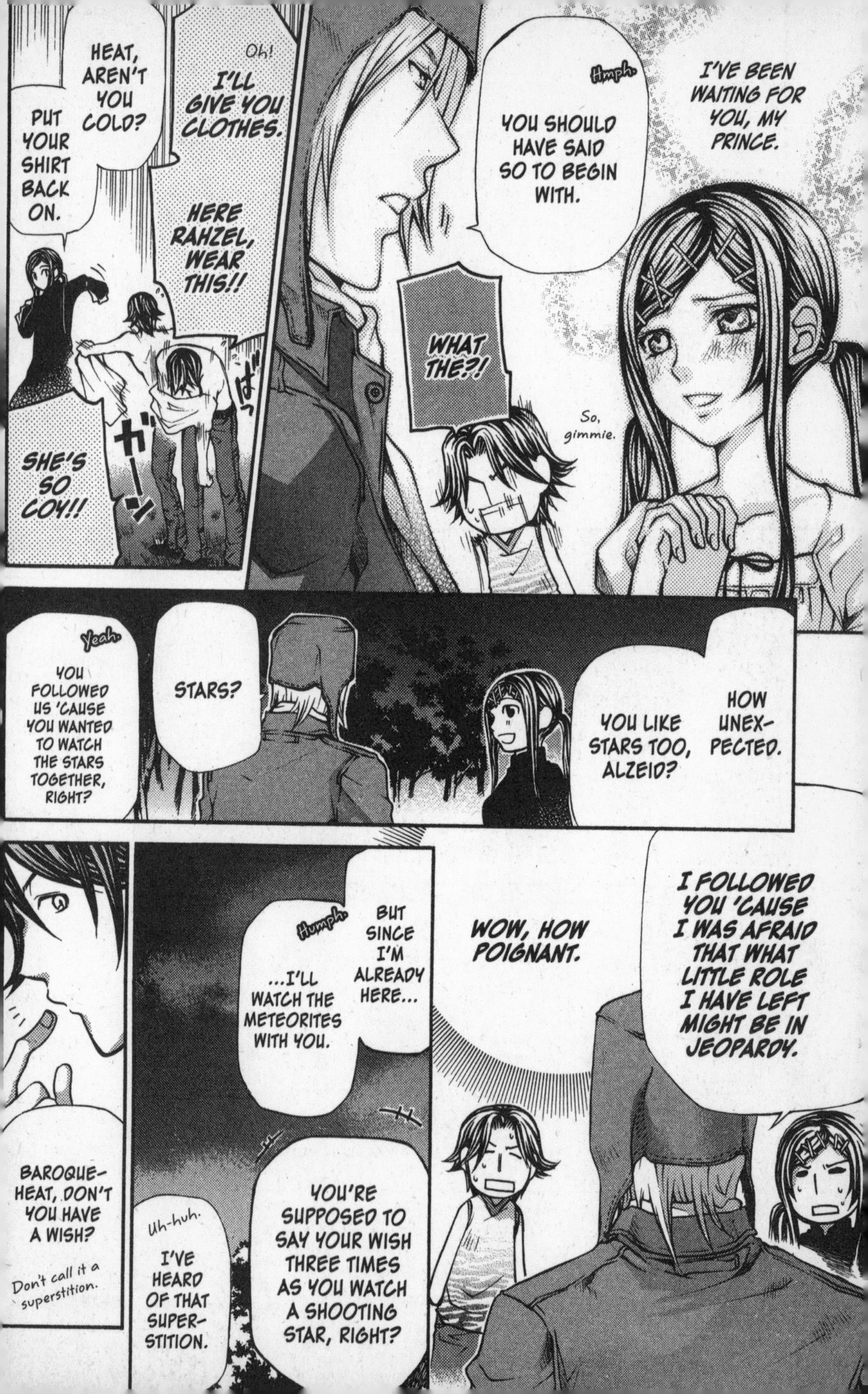
I'VE BEEN WAITING FOR YOU, MY PRINCE.
Hmph.
YOU SHOULD HAVE SAID SO TO BEGIN WITH.
So, gimmie.
WHAT THE?!
Oh!
I'LL GIVE YOU CLOTHES.
HEAT, AREN'T YOU COLD?
PUT YOUR SHIRT BACK ON.
HERE RAHZEL, WEAR THIS!!
ばっ
ガーン
SHE'S SO COY!!
HOW UNEX-PECTED.
YOU LIKE STARS TOO, ALZEID?
STARS?
Yeah.
YOU FOLLOWED US 'CAUSE YOU WANTED TO WATCH THE STARS TOGETHER, RIGHT?
I FOLLOWED YOU 'CAUSE I WAS AFRAID THAT WHAT LITTLE ROLE I HAVE LEFT MIGHT BE IN JEOPARDY.
WOW, HOW POIGNANT.
BUT SINCE I'M ALREADY HERE...
Humph.
...I'LL WATCH THE METEORITES WITH YOU.
YOU'RE SUPPOSED TO SAY YOUR WISH THREE TIMES AS YOU WATCH A SHOOTING STAR, RIGHT?
Uh-huh.
I'VE HEARD OF THAT SUPER-STITION.
BAROQUE-HEAT, DON'T YOU HAVE A WISH?
Don't call it a superstition.

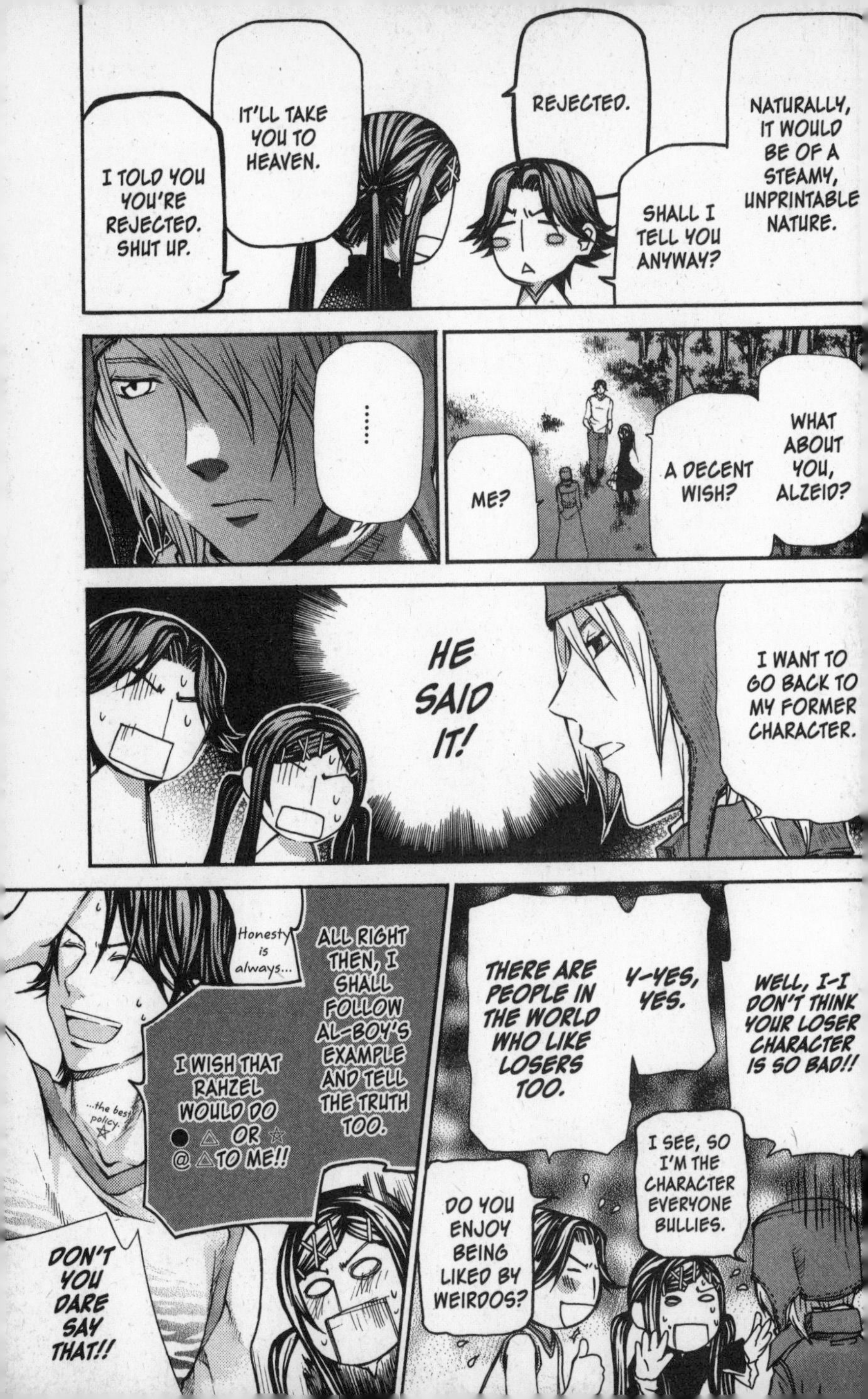
NATURALLY, IT WOULD BE OF A STEAMY, UNPRINTABLE NATURE.
SHALL I TELL YOU ANYWAY?
REJECTED.
IT'LL TAKE YOU TO HEAVEN.
I TOLD YOU YOU'RE REJECTED. SHUT UP.
WHAT ABOUT YOU, ALZEID?
A DECENT WISH?
ME?
......
I WANT TO GO BACK TO MY FORMER CHARACTER.
HE SAID IT!
WELL, I-I DON'T THINK YOUR LOSER CHARACTER IS SO BAD!!
Y-YES, YES.
THERE ARE PEOPLE IN THE WORLD WHO LIKE LOSERS TOO.
I SEE, SO I'M THE CHARACTER EVERYONE BULLIES.
DO YOU ENJOY BEING LIKED BY WEIRDOS?
ALL RIGHT THEN, I SHALL FOLLOW AL-BOY'S EXAMPLE AND TELL THE TRUTH TOO.
Honesty is always...
I WISH THAT RAHZEL WOULD DO ● △ OR ☆ @ △ TO ME!!
...the best policy. ☆
DON'T YOU DARE SAY THAT!!

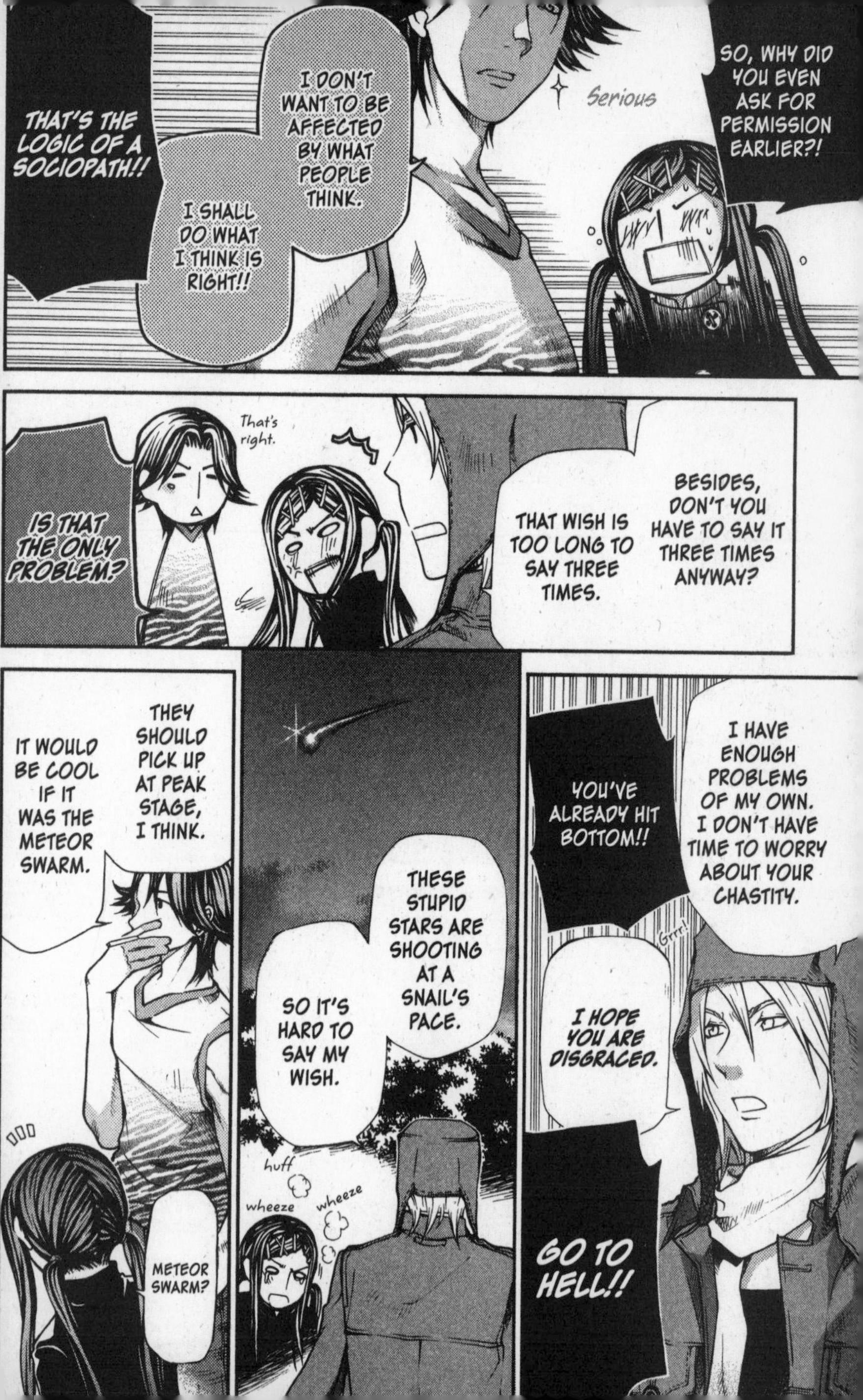
SO, WHY DID YOU EVEN ASK FOR PERMISSION EARLIER?!
Serious
I DON'T WANT TO BE AFFECTED BY WHAT PEOPLE THINK.
I SHALL DO WHAT I THINK IS RIGHT!!
THAT'S THE LOGIC OF A SOCIOPATH!!
BESIDES, DON'T YOU HAVE TO SAY IT THREE TIMES ANYWAY?
THAT WISH IS TOO LONG TO SAY THREE TIMES.
That's right.
IS THAT THE ONLY PROBLEM?
I HAVE ENOUGH PROBLEMS OF MY OWN. I DON'T HAVE TIME TO WORRY ABOUT YOUR CHASTITY.
YOU'VE ALREADY HIT BOTTOM!!
Grrr!
I HOPE YOU ARE DISGRACED.
GO TO HELL!!
THESE STUPID STARS ARE SHOOTING AT A SNAIL'S PACE.
SO IT'S HARD TO SAY MY WISH.
huff
wheeze
wheeze
THEY SHOULD PICK UP AT PEAK STAGE, I THINK.
IT WOULD BE COOL IF IT WAS THE METEOR SWARM.
METEOR SWARM?

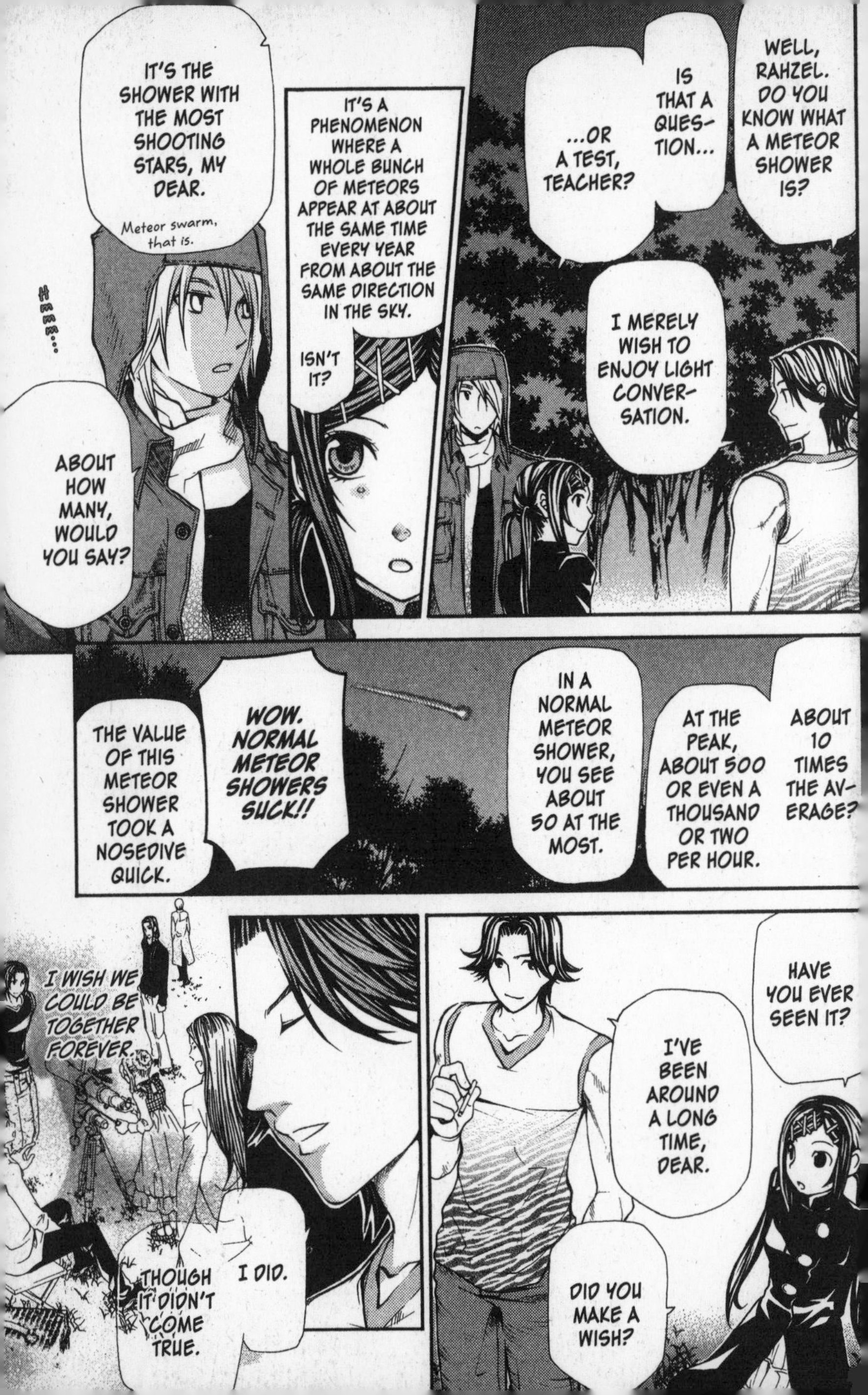
WELL, RAHZEL. DO YOU KNOW WHAT A METEOR SHOWER IS?
IS THAT A QUESTION...
...OR A TEST, TEACHER?
I MERELY WISH TO ENJOY LIGHT CONVERSATION.
IT'S A PHENOMENON WHERE A WHOLE BUNCH OF METEORS APPEAR AT ABOUT THE SAME TIME EVERY YEAR FROM ABOUT THE SAME DIRECTION IN THE SKY.
ISN'T IT?
IT'S THE SHOWER WITH THE MOST SHOOTING STARS, MY DEAR.
Meteor swarm, that is.
Hmmm...
ABOUT HOW MANY, WOULD YOU SAY?
ABOUT 10 TIMES THE AVERAGE?
AT THE PEAK, ABOUT 500 OR EVEN A THOUSAND OR TWO PER HOUR.
IN A NORMAL METEOR SHOWER, YOU SEE ABOUT 50 AT THE MOST.
WOW. NORMAL METEOR SHOWERS SUCK!!
THE VALUE OF THIS METEOR SHOWER TOOK A NOSEDIVE QUICK.
HAVE YOU EVER SEEN IT?
I'VE BEEN AROUND A LONG TIME, DEAR.
DID YOU MAKE A WISH?
I DID.
THOUGH IT DIDN'T COME TRUE.
I WISH WE COULD BE TOGETHER FOREVER.

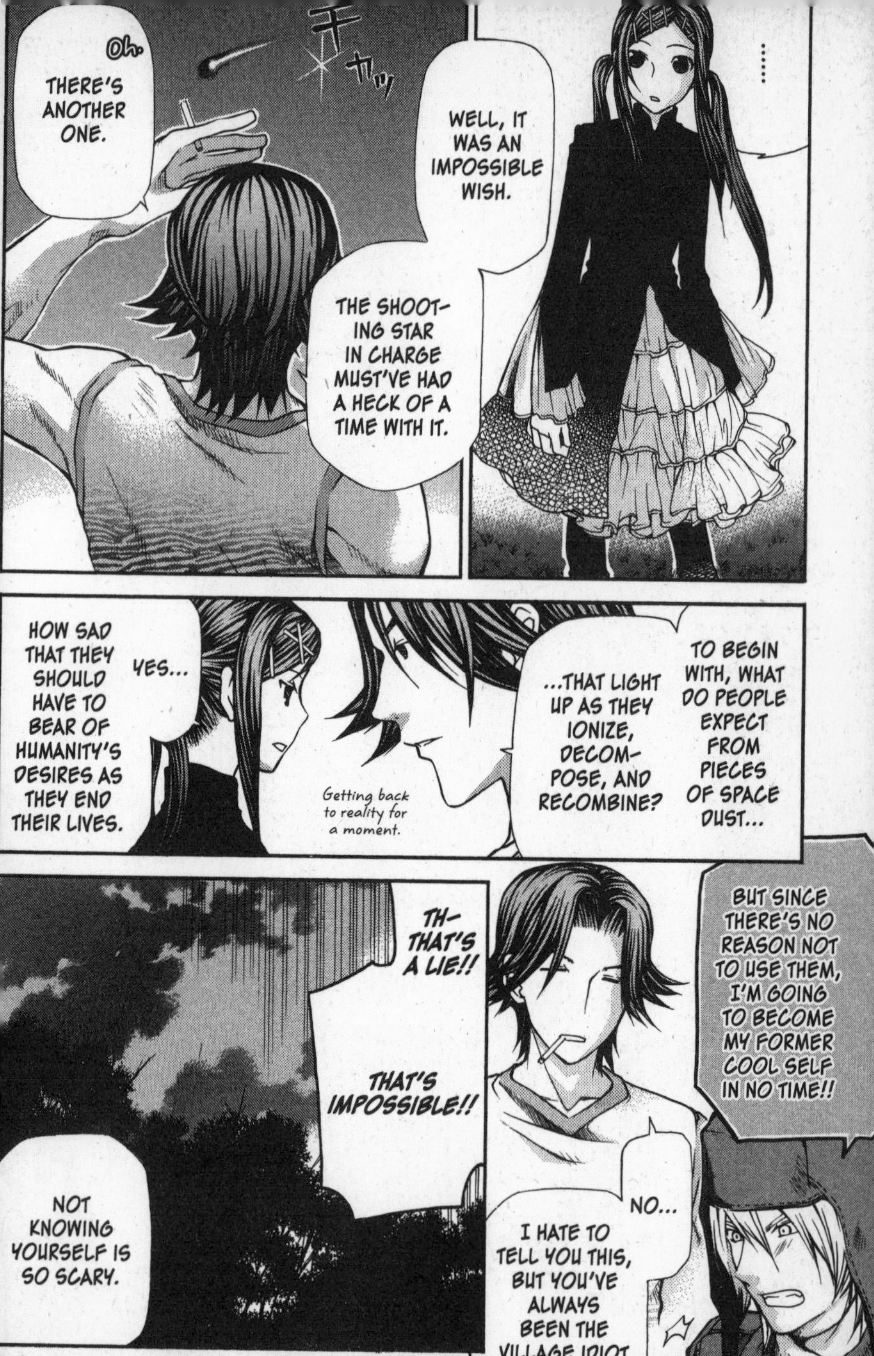
......
WELL, IT WAS AN IMPOSSIBLE WISH.
THE SHOOTING STAR IN CHARGE MUST'VE HAD A HECK OF A TIME WITH IT.
Oh.
THERE'S ANOTHER ONE.
TO BEGIN WITH, WHAT DO PEOPLE EXPECT FROM PIECES OF SPACE DUST...
...THAT LIGHT UP AS THEY IONIZE, DECOMPOSE, AND RECOMBINE?
Getting back to reality for a moment.
YES...
HOW SAD THAT THEY SHOULD HAVE TO BEAR OF HUMANITY'S DESIRES AS THEY END THEIR LIVES.
BUT SINCE THERE'S NO REASON NOT TO USE THEM, I'M GOING TO BECOME MY FORMER COOL SELF IN NO TIME!!
NO...
I HATE TO TELL YOU THIS, BUT YOU'VE ALWAYS BEEN THE VILLAGE IDIOT CHARACTER.
TH- THAT'S A LIE!!
THAT'S IMPOSSIBLE!!
NOT KNOWING YOURSELF IS SO SCARY.

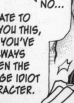

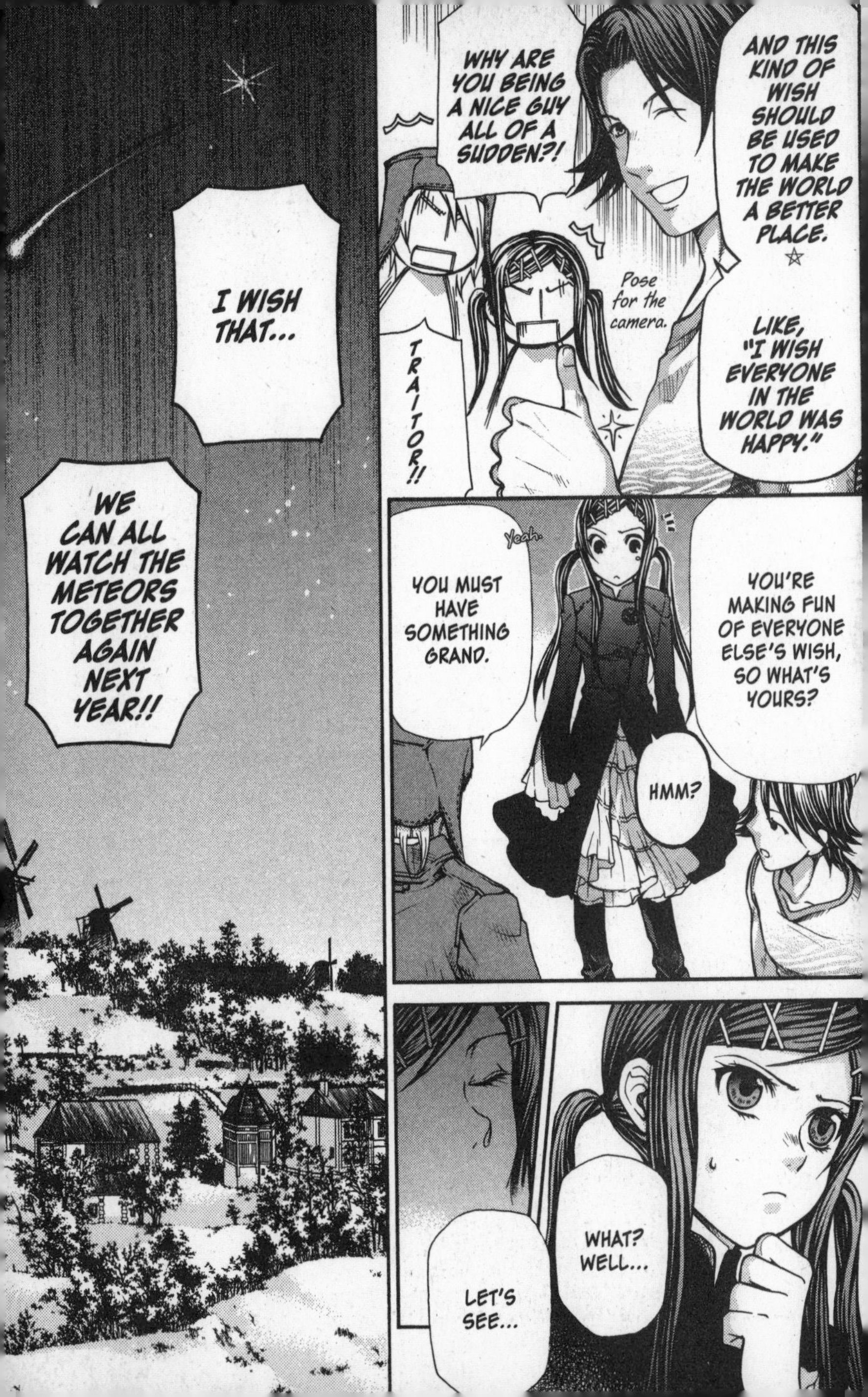
AND THIS KIND OF WISH SHOULD BE USED TO MAKE THE WORLD A BETTER PLACE. ☆
WHY ARE YOU BEING A NICE GUY ALL OF A SUDDEN?!
LIKE, "I WISH EVERYONE IN THE WORLD WAS HAPPY."
Pose for the camera.
TRAITOR!!
YOU'RE MAKING FUN OF EVERYONE ELSE'S WISH, SO WHAT'S YOURS?
Yeah.
YOU MUST HAVE SOMETHING GRAND.
HMM?
WHAT? WELL...
LET'S SEE...
I WISH THAT...
WE CAN ALL WATCH THE METEORS TOGETHER AGAIN NEXT YEAR!!

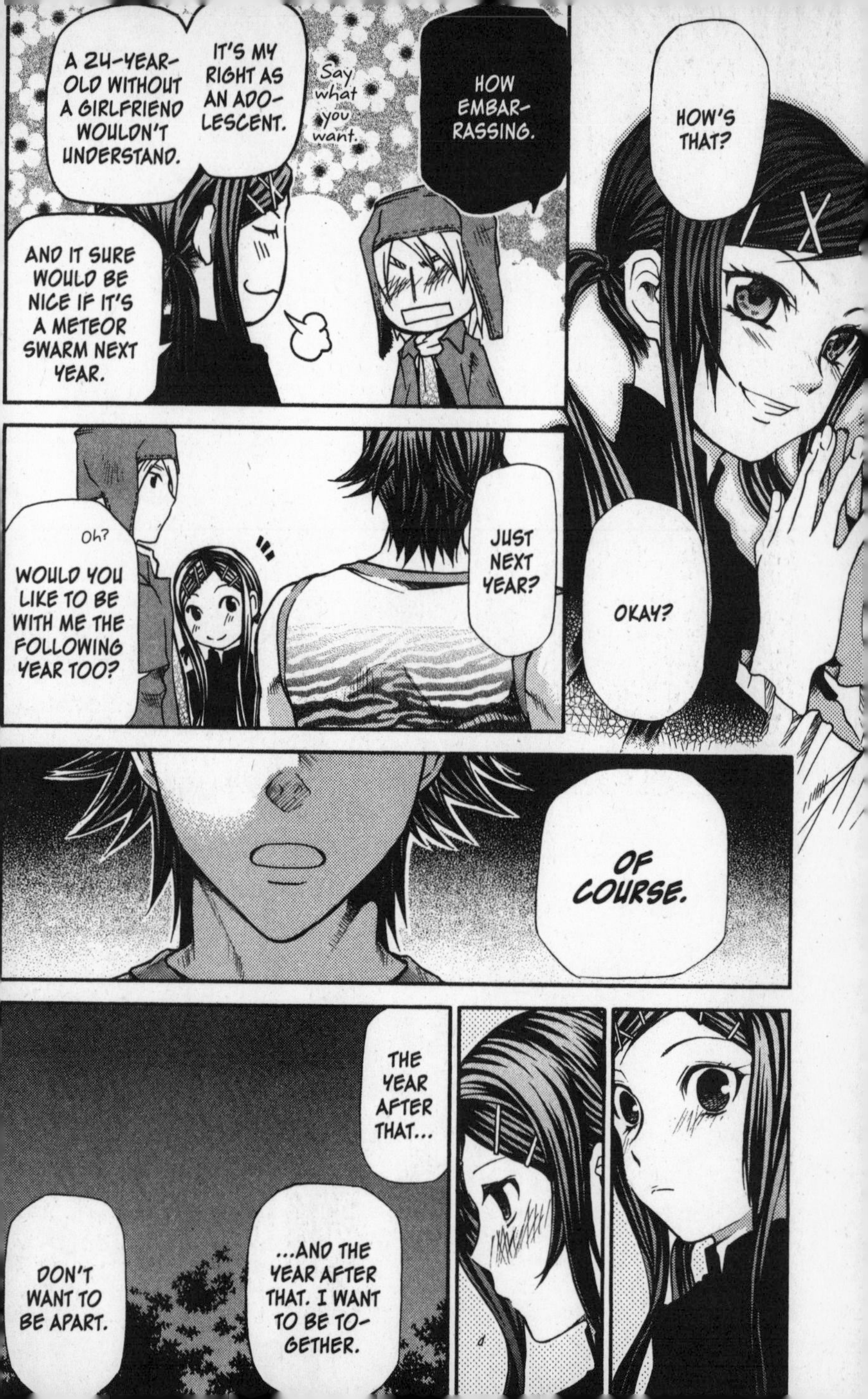
HOW'S THAT?
OKAY?
HOW EMBARRASSING.
Say what you want.
IT'S MY RIGHT AS AN ADOLESCENT.
A 24-YEAR-OLD WITHOUT A GIRLFRIEND WOULDN'T UNDERSTAND.
AND IT SURE WOULD BE NICE IF IT'S A METEOR SWARM NEXT YEAR.
JUST NEXT YEAR?
Oh?
WOULD YOU LIKE TO BE WITH ME THE FOLLOWING YEAR TOO?
OF COURSE.
THE YEAR AFTER THAT...
...AND THE YEAR AFTER THAT. I WANT TO BE TOGETHER.
DON'T WANT TO BE APART.

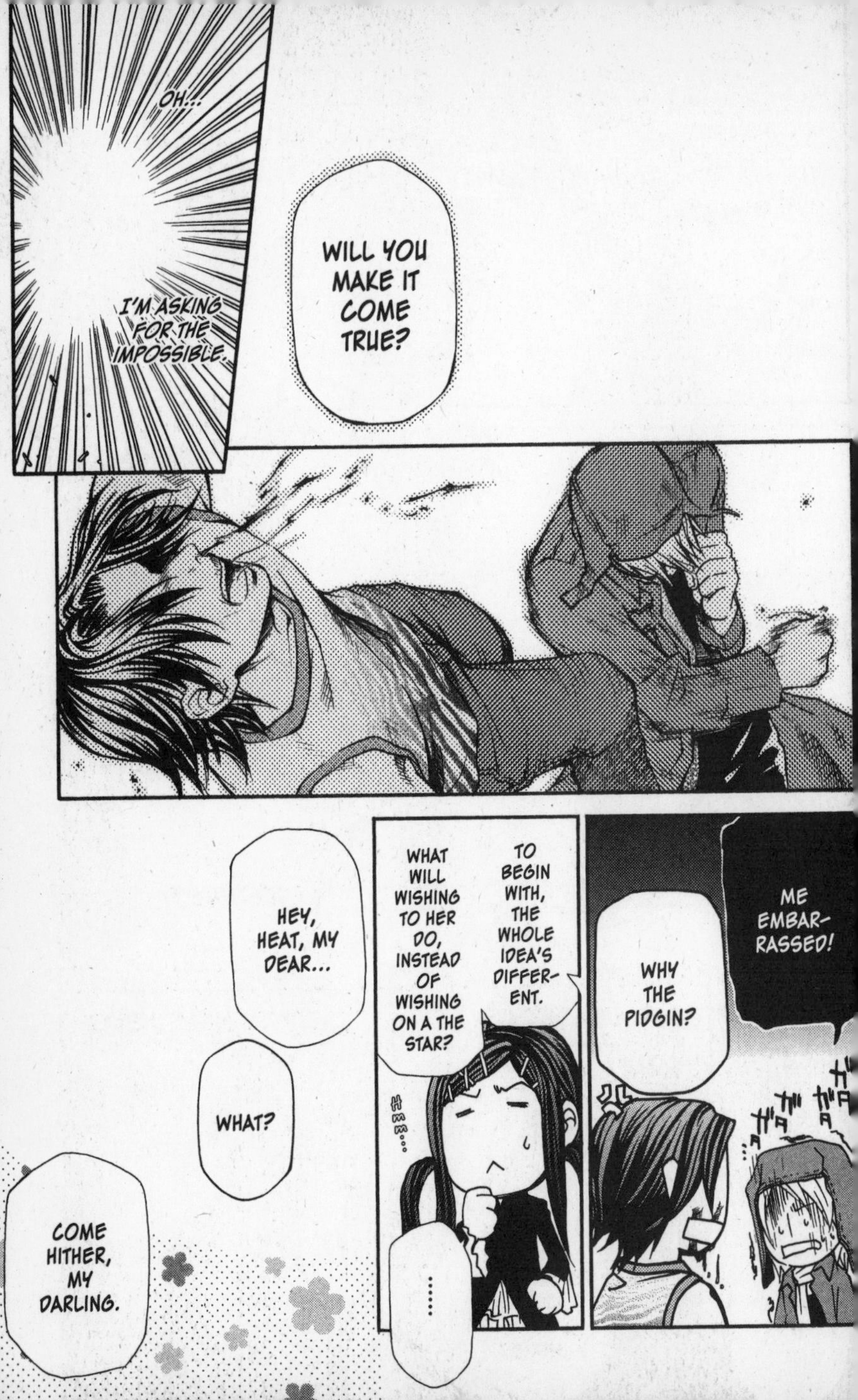
WILL YOU MAKE IT COME TRUE?
OH...
I'M ASKING FOR THE IMPOSSIBLE.
ME EMBARRASSED!
WHY THE PIDGIN?
TO BEGIN WITH, THE WHOLE IDEA'S DIFFERENT.
WHAT WILL WISHING TO HER DO, INSTEAD OF WISHING ON A THE STAR?
Hmm...
......
HEY, HEAT, MY DEAR...
WHAT?
COME HITHER, MY DARLING.

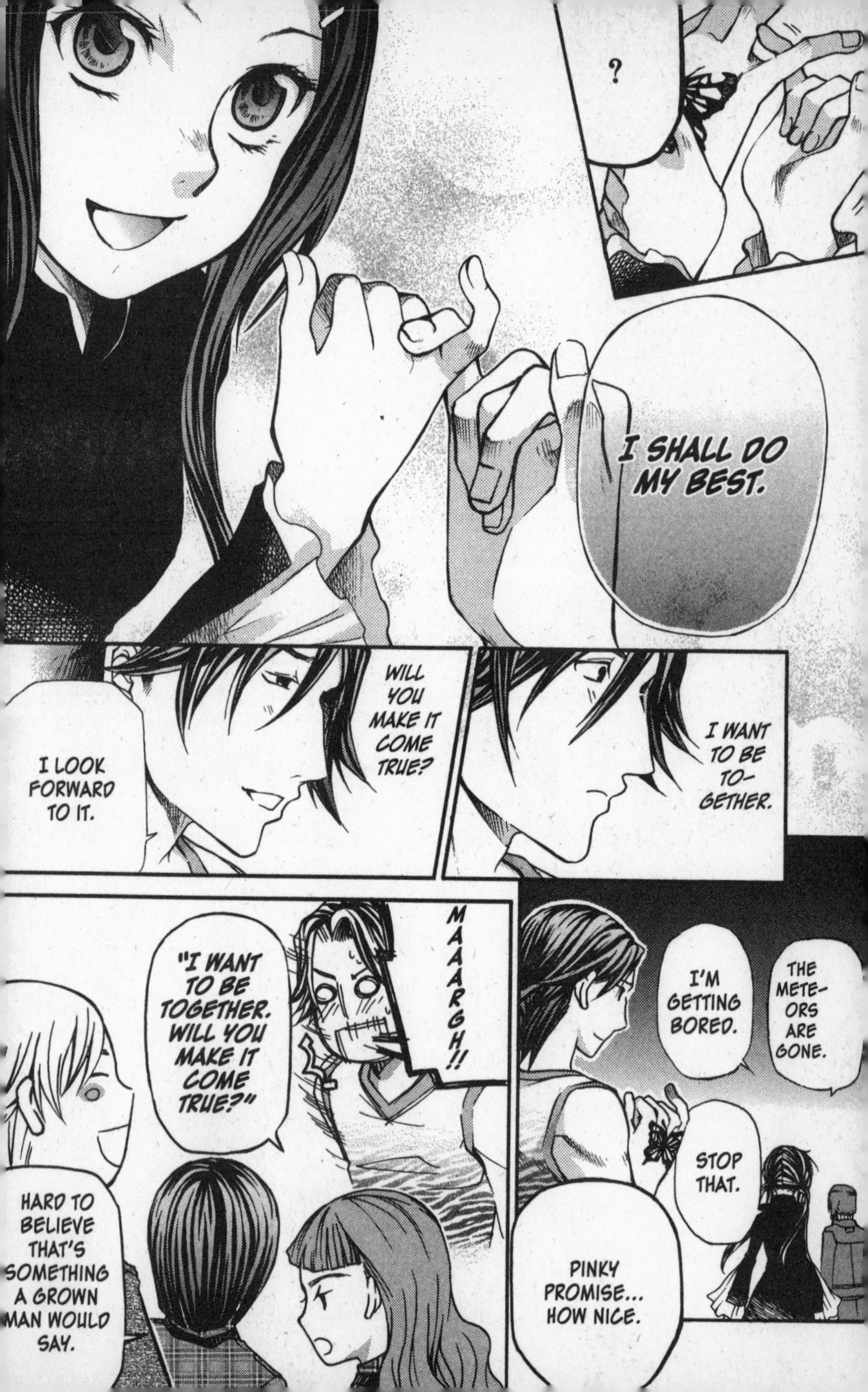
?
I SHALL DO MY BEST.
I WANT TO BE TO-GETHER.
WILL YOU MAKE IT COME TRUE?
I LOOK FORWARD TO IT.
THE METE-ORS ARE GONE.
I'M GETTING BORED.
STOP THAT.
PINKY PROMISE... HOW NICE.
MAAAARGH!!
"I WANT TO BE TOGETHER. WILL YOU MAKE IT COME TRUE?"
HARD TO BELIEVE THAT'S SOMETHING A GROWN MAN WOULD SAY.

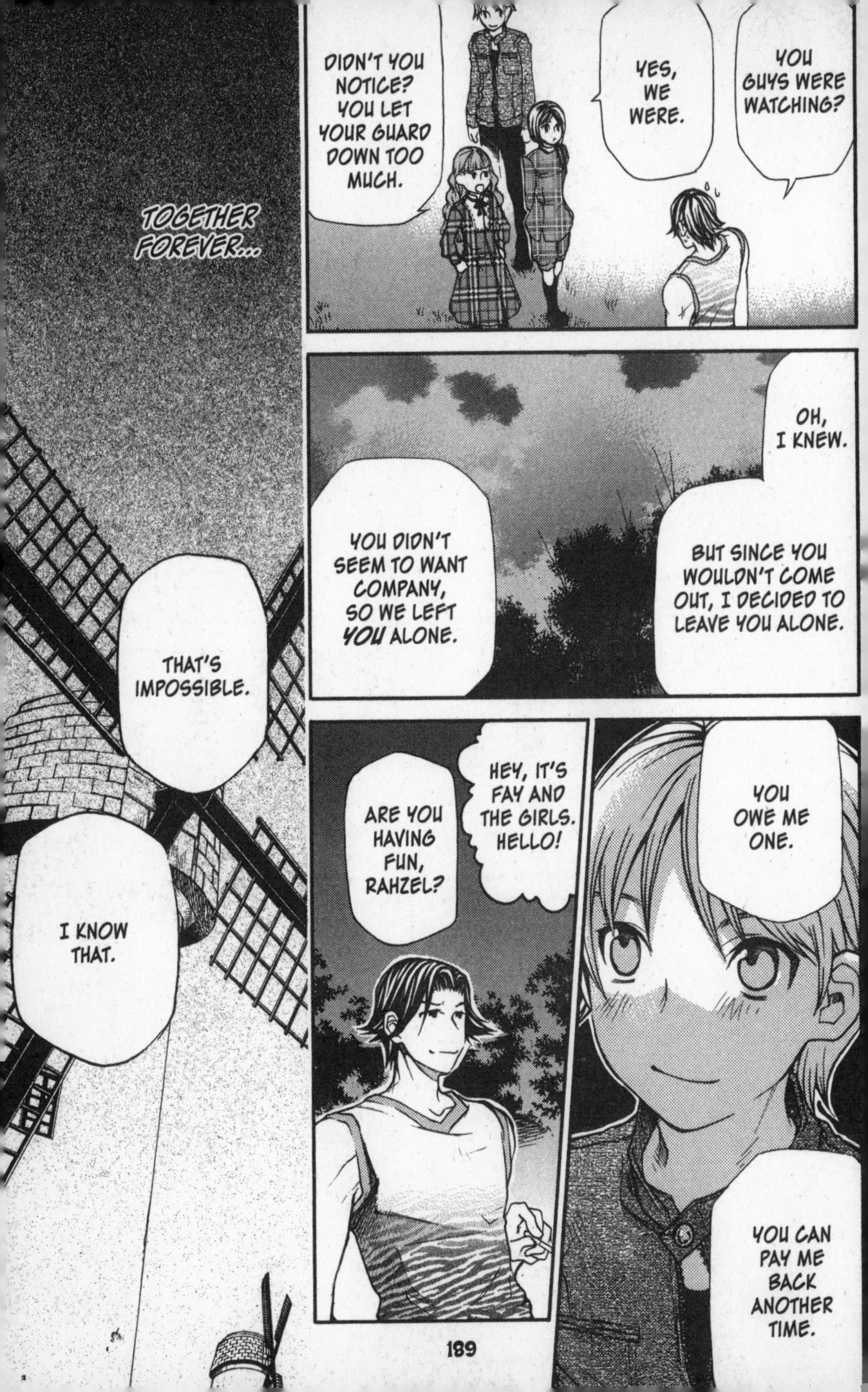
YOU GUYS WERE WATCHING?
YES, WE WERE.
DIDN'T YOU NOTICE? YOU LET YOUR GUARD DOWN TOO MUCH.
OH, I KNEW.
BUT SINCE YOU WOULDN'T COME OUT, I DECIDED TO LEAVE YOU ALONE.
YOU DIDN'T SEEM TO WANT COMPANY, SO WE LEFT *YOU* ALONE.
YOU OWE ME ONE.
YOU CAN PAY ME BACK ANOTHER TIME.
HEY, IT'S FAY AND THE GIRLS. HELLO!
ARE YOU HAVING FUN, RAHZEL?
TOGETHER FOREVER...
THAT'S IMPOSSIBLE.
I KNOW THAT.

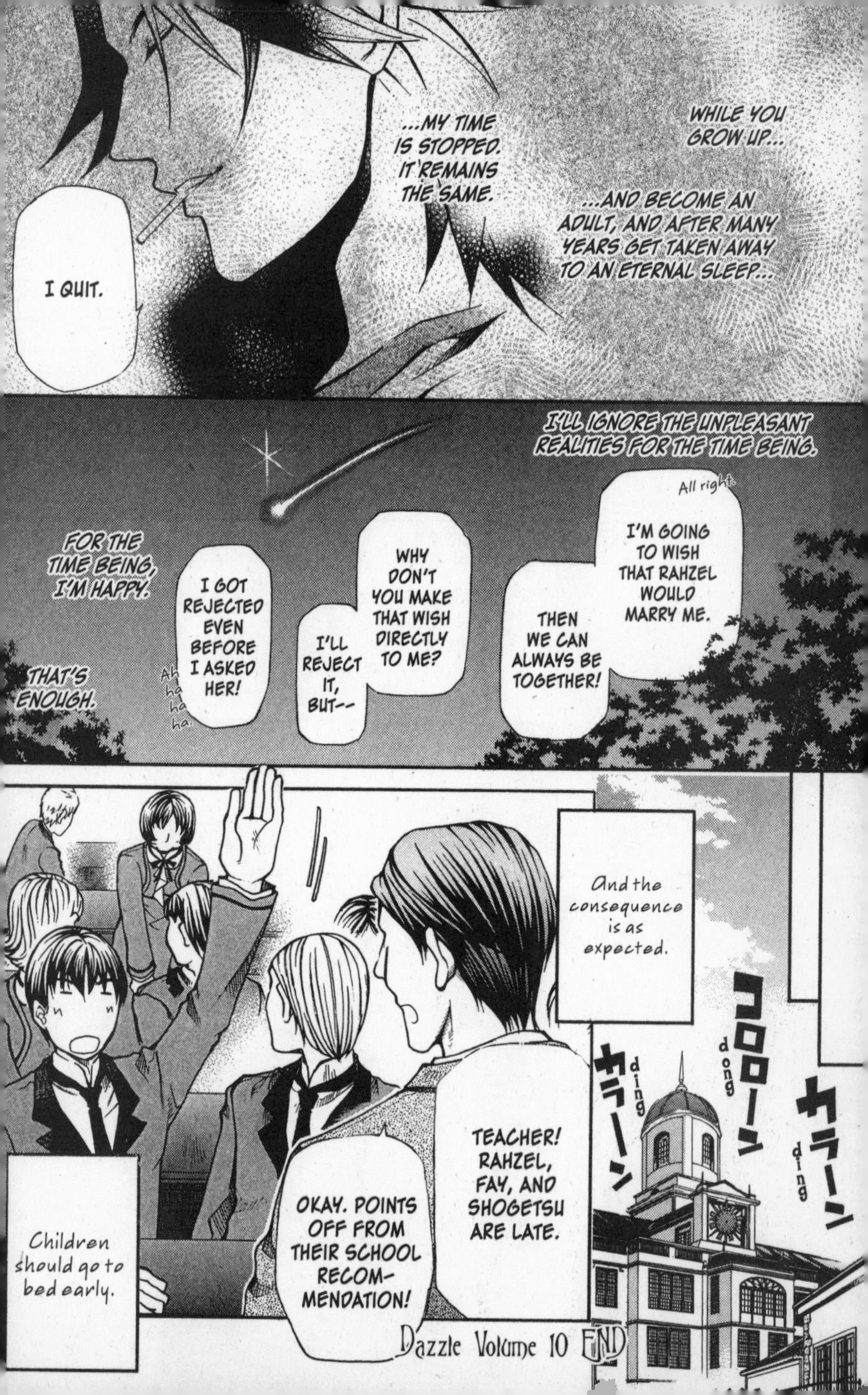
WHILE YOU GROW UP...
...AND BECOME AN ADULT, AND AFTER MANY YEARS GET TAKEN AWAY TO AN ETERNAL SLEEP...
...MY TIME IS STOPPED. IT REMAINS THE SAME.
I QUIT.
I'LL IGNORE THE UNPLEASANT REALITIES FOR THE TIME BEING.
All right.
I'M GOING TO WISH THAT RAHZEL WOULD MARRY ME.
THEN WE CAN ALWAYS BE TOGETHER!
WHY DON'T YOU MAKE THAT WISH DIRECTLY TO ME?
I'LL REJECT IT, BUT--
I GOT REJECTED EVEN BEFORE I ASKED HER!
Ah ha ha ha ha.
FOR THE TIME BEING, I'M HAPPY.
THAT'S ENOUGH.
カラーン ding
コロローン dong
カラーン ding
And the consequence is as expected.
TEACHER! RAHZEL, FAY, AND SHOGETSU ARE LATE.
OKAY. POINTS OFF FROM THEIR SCHOOL RECOM-MENDATION!
Children should go to bed early.
Dazzle Volume 10 END

Dazzle Volume 10 Postscript

So we're into the double digits! This time I have a ton of manuscripts that need to be retouched. About thirty pages or so. No, I'm not going to think about it too much. I'm not going to blame myself. I'm not going to fixate on reality.

Intermission: So Will You Please Hold My Hand Tonight?
Since it ran in the magazine, I've rewritten the entire story.
The fact that I finished the manuscript on the subway train is a very dark spot in my history--I mean a great memory for me.

Chapter 69: The Ordinary Everyday
I like the design of the uniform. it's easy to draw. I should have used it in a series I do for that other magazine (Problematic remark).

Chapter 70: The Destroyer Cometh
To do research for this chapter, I asked a bunch of people around me, "what happened the moment you fell in love?" There was one answer that really made my heart skip: "He made me a delicious meal!" It's brilliant, but doesn't help this story at all. It's as exciting as meeting a very eligible bachelor. it's a story about how men with high-level housekeeping skills are attractive.

Chapter 71: "A Fake of A Fake"
I'm really no good at action scenes.

Chapter 72: Yet Another Sideshow
The welder--you can't really use the pencil the way I drew it. You have to take the lead out of the casing, but since that was too hard to show, I left the pencil as it was. Kids! What you see in manga is full of lies!

Chapter 73: Moonlight! Shine upon This Miserable Child
I'd rather be a "number one" than an "only one." An "only one" is no match for another "only one" that's superior to it! Ranking is important!

Chapter 74: Somebody's Truth
Second wrote a diary. What an industrious person he is.

Chapter 75: The Sun Won't Rise
"Are nipples okay?!" That was the first thing out of my mouth when Mr. Editor-in-chief called. ".........Nipples are okay, but I don't know about innards...."

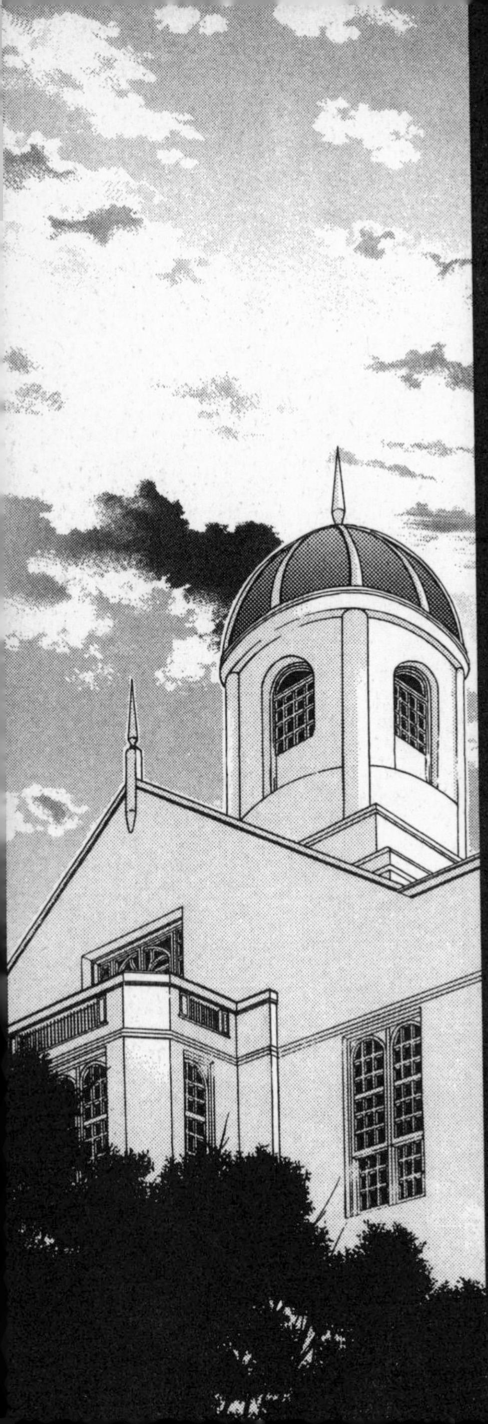

"Okay, I'm gonna do the best I can! I'll look at a map of the body and stuff and really make an effort! I'm no good at grotesque stuff, but I'll go at it!"

"Don't you just want to use mosaics and leave it at that? Why don't you?"

"I'm gonna do it!"

"Well, I'm not really looking for a huge effort in that department."

That's the kind of exchange that took place...or not.

By the way, I'm also drawing a manga about a very tough boy in girl's clothing, so I couldn't help but feel a little uncomfortable about Fay's reaction this time. This guy's really weird. There's no reason to be embarrassed about putting on a skirt and wearing some kitten ears, you weirdo!

...Oh, dear. My sensibilities are getting a little frayed. I long for the pure and innocent child I was back then. To be precise, when I was a prefertilized egg. Super pure through and through.

Intermission: The Stars Sparkle on an Endless Night

Baroqueheat's spin out on an endless starry night. He hardly had any lines in this volu--No, never mind.

Alzeid continues his loser streak. The next volume will be incredible. He'll stoop even lower! Stay tuned!

Oh, and Rahzel is okay. She's isn't dead. (That's not a spoiler or anything.)

遠藤海成

Minari Endoh

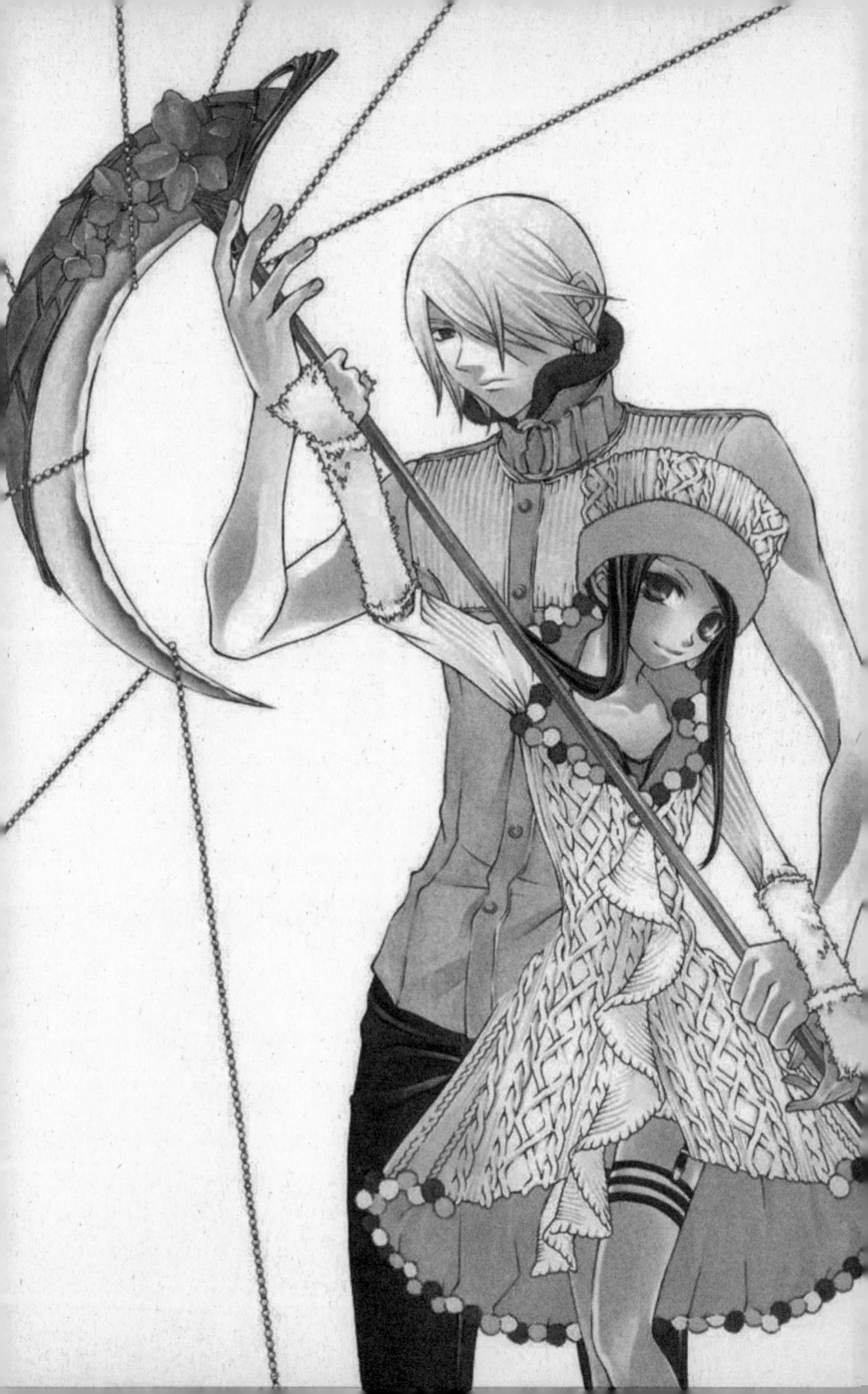

In the next
Dazzle!

Alzeid's older brother warned Baroqueheat to protect Rahzel, and Baroqueheat asked Fay to keep an eye on her, but Kiara was able to get Rahzel alone and fulfill his earlier promise that the next time they met, they'd be enemies. When Alzeid stumbles upon the gory aftermath of Rahzel's sadistic torture at Kiara's hands, can he do anything to save her life?

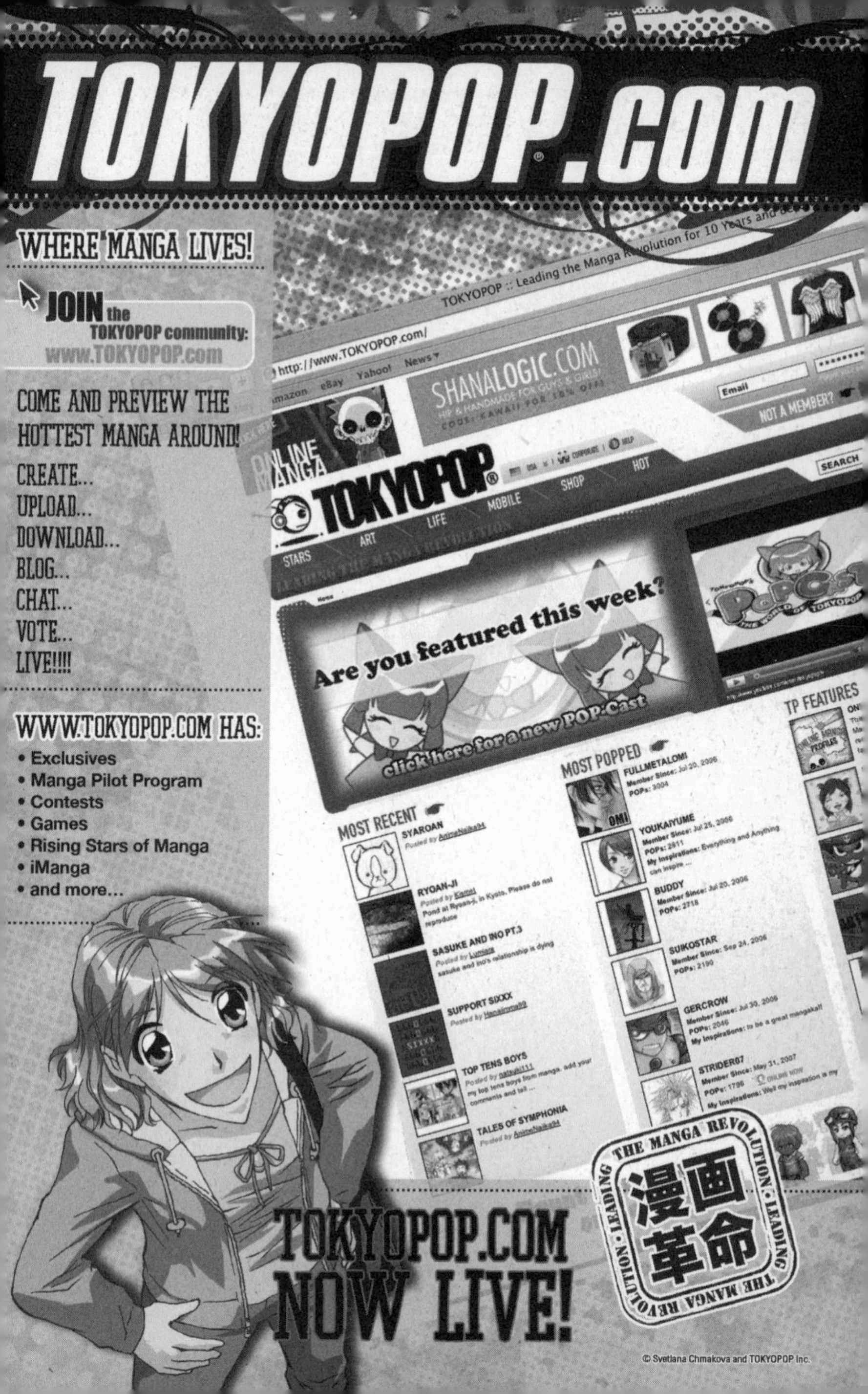
TOKYOPOP.com
WHERE MANGA LIVES!
JOIN the TOKYOPOP community: www.TOKYOPOP.com
COME AND PREVIEW THE HOTTEST MANGA AROUND!
CREATE...
UPLOAD...
DOWNLOAD...
BLOG...
CHAT...
VOTE...
LIVE!!!!
WWW.TOKYOPOP.COM HAS:
• Exclusives
• Manga Pilot Program
• Contests
• Games
• Rising Stars of Manga
• iManga
• and more...
TOKYOPOP :: Leading the Manga Revolution for 10 Years and Beyond
http://www.TOKYOPOP.com/
SHANALOGIC.COM
TOKYOPOP
STARS
ART
LIFE
MOBILE
SHOP
HOT
SEARCH
Are you featured this week?
click here for a new POP-Cast
MOST RECENT
MOST POPPED
TP FEATURES
THE MANGA REVOLUTION · LEADING
漫画革命
TOKYOPOP.COM NOW LIVE!
© Svetlana Chmakova and TOKYOPOP Inc.

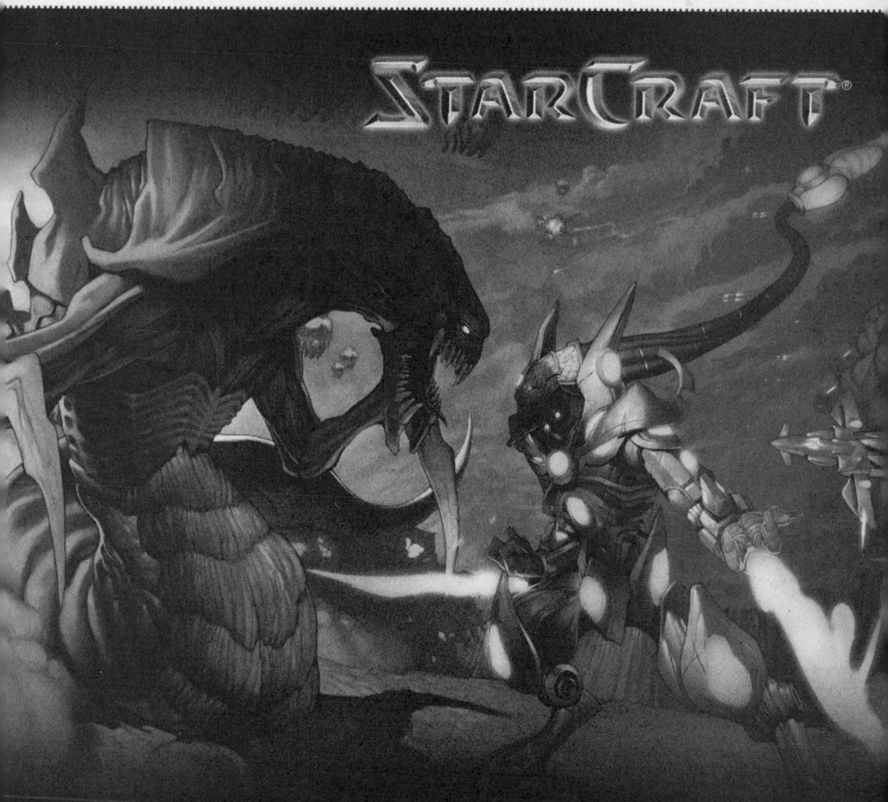
StarCraft®

AVAILABLE IN BOOKSTORES AUGUST 2008...AND BEYOND!

StarCraft: Frontline *Volume 1*

Check out www.TOKYOPOP.com/STARCRAFT
for exclusive news, updates and free downloadable art.

Art by: UDON with Saejin Oh

T TEEN AGE 13+

BLIZZARD ENTERTAINMENT

BUY IT WHEREVER BOOKS ARE SOLD

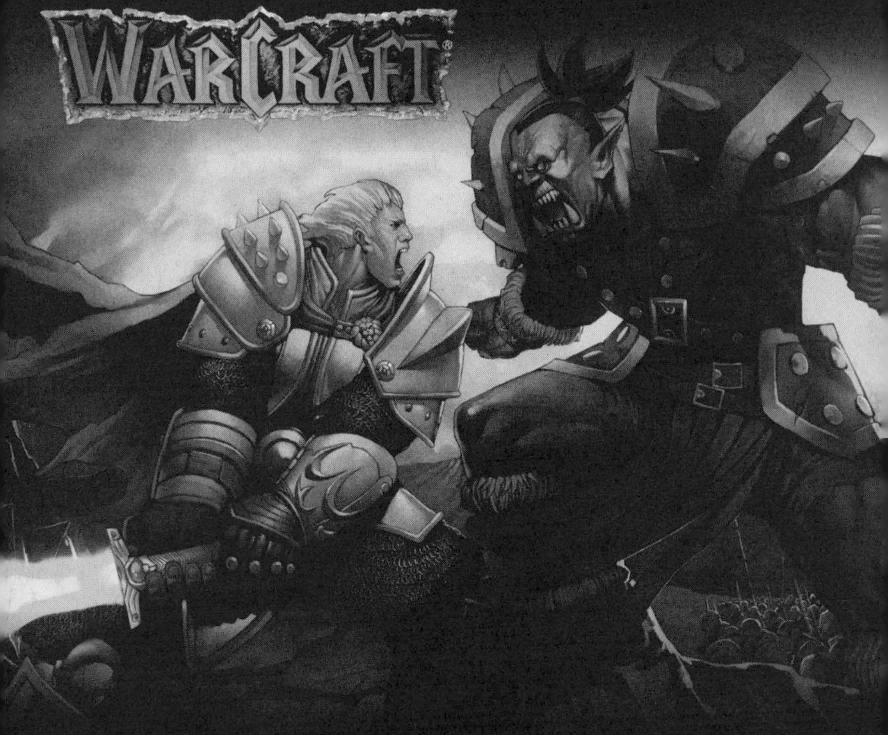
WARCRAFT®

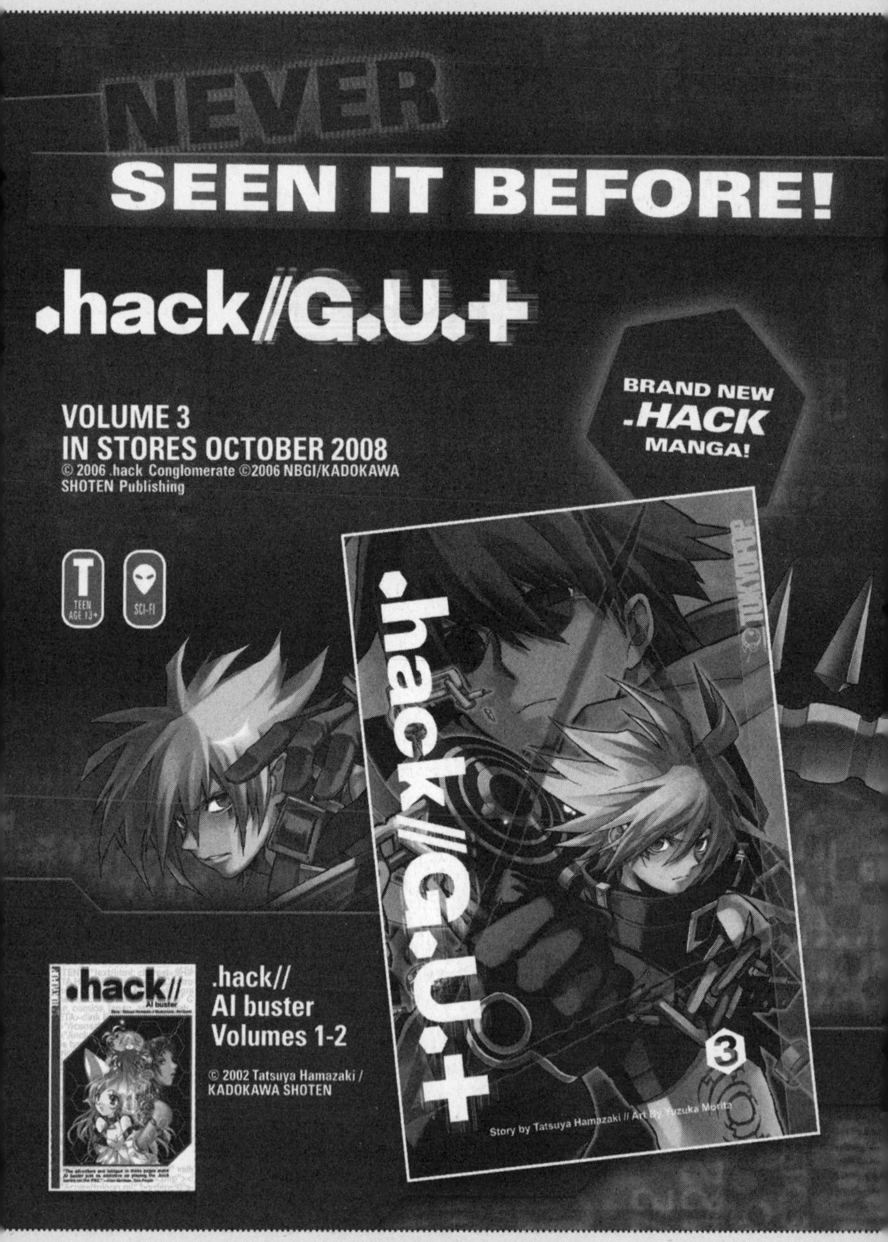

NEVER
SEEN IT BEFORE!
.hack//G.U.+
BRAND NEW
.HACK
MANGA!
VOLUME 3
IN STORES OCTOBER 2008
© 2006 .hack Conglomerate ©2006 NBGI/KADOKAWA SHOTEN Publishing
T
TEEN AGE 13+
SCI-FI
.hack//G.U.+
3
Story by Tatsuya Hamazaki // Art By Yuzuka Morita
.hack//
AI buster
.hack//
AI buster
Volumes 1-2
© 2002 Tatsuya Hamazaki / KADOKAWA SHOTEN

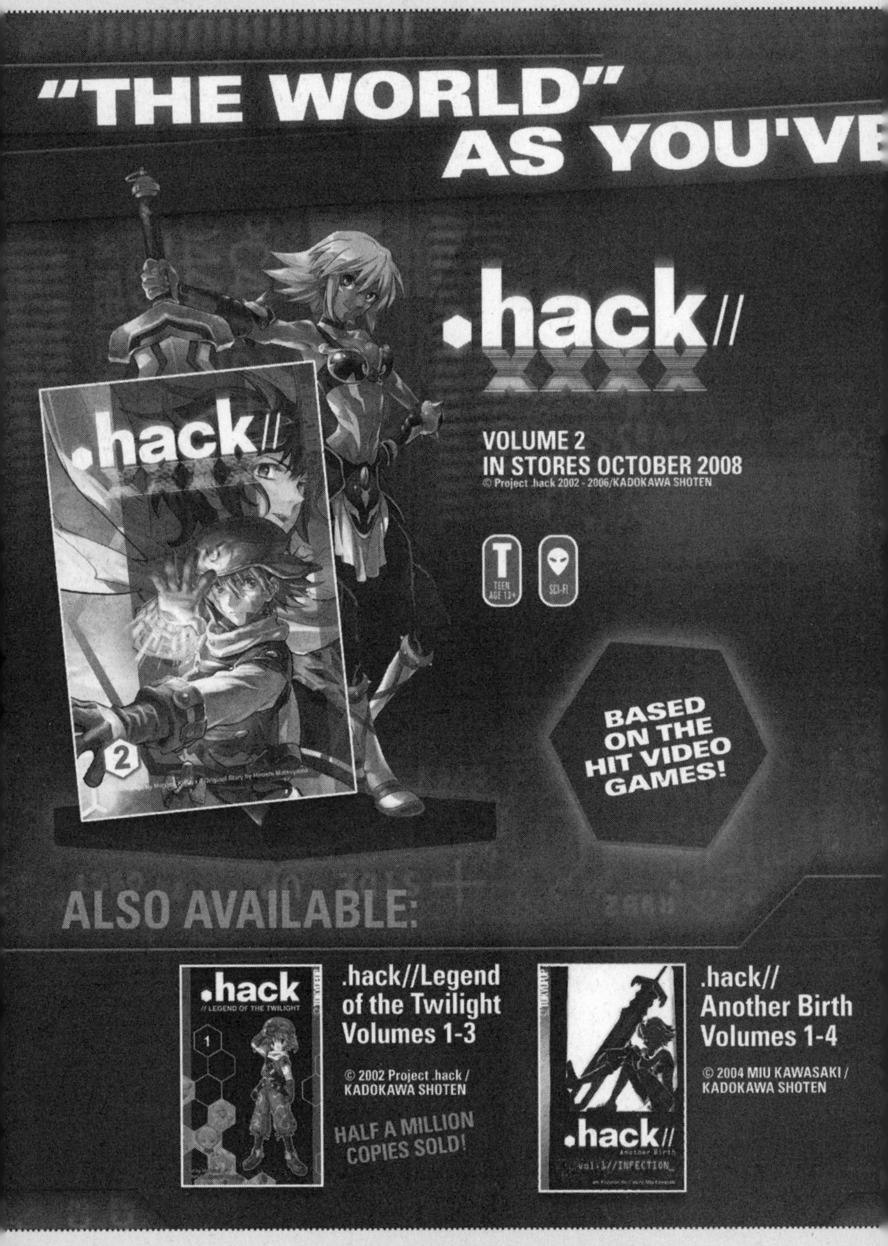
"THE WORLD" AS YOU'VE
.hack//XXXX
VOLUME 2
IN STORES OCTOBER 2008
© Project .hack 2002 - 2006/KADOKAWA SHOTEN
T TEEN AGE 13+
SCI-FI
BASED ON THE HIT VIDEO GAMES!
ALSO AVAILABLE:
.hack//Legend of the Twilight Volumes 1-3
© 2002 Project .hack / KADOKAWA SHOTEN
HALF A MILLION COPIES SOLD!
.hack// Another Birth Volumes 1-4
© 2004 MIU KAWASAKI / KADOKAWA SHOTEN

FOR MORE INFORMATION VISIT:

INCLUDES A PREVIEW OF FRUITS BASKET VOL. 22 (MARCH 2009)

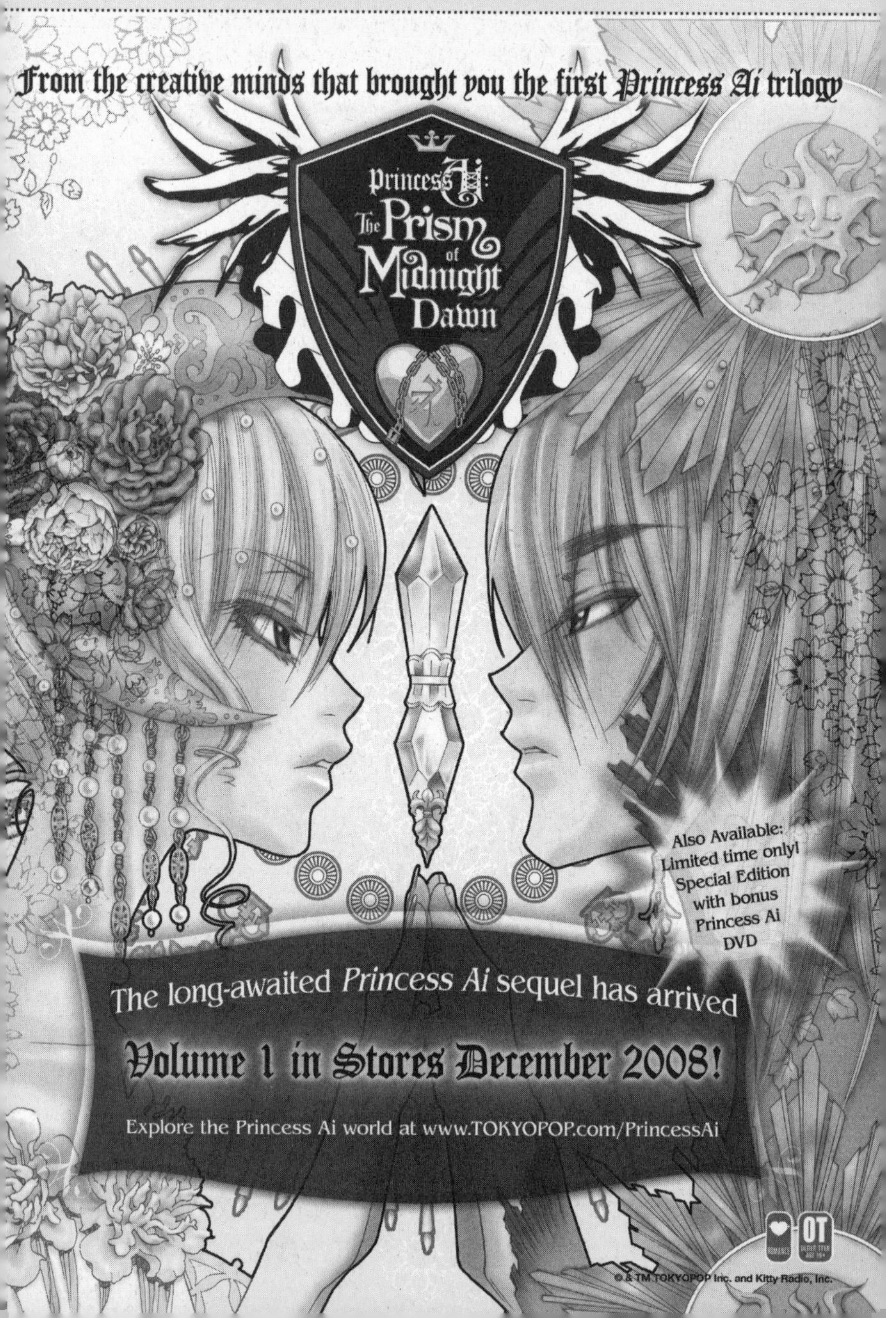
From the creative minds that brought you the first Princess Ai trilogy
Princess Ai: The Prism of Midnight Dawn
Also Available: Limited time only! Special Edition with bonus Princess Ai DVD
The long-awaited Princess Ai sequel has arrived
Volume 1 in Stores December 2008!
Explore the Princess Ai world at www.TOKYOPOP.com/PrincessAi
© & TM TOKYOPOP Inc. and Kitty Radio, Inc.

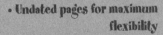

STOP!

This is the back of the book.
You wouldn't want to spoil a great ending!

This book is printed "manga-style," in the authentic Japanese right-to-left format. Since none of the artwork has been flipped or altered, readers get to experience the story just as the creator intended. You've been asking for it, so TOKYOPOP® delivered: authentic, hot-off-the-press, and far more fun!

DIRECTIONS

If this is your first time reading manga-style, here's a quick guide to help you understand how it works.

It's easy... just start in the top right panel and follow the numbers. Have fun, and look for more 100% authentic manga from TOKYOPOP®!